# I
# SAW
# YOU

## CHERANN WRIGHT

*For my daughters, who remind me every day that strength comes in many forms.*

# AUTHOR'S NOTE

I never intended to write fiction. But after my accident, nothing in my life made sense—not the bruises I couldn't explain, not the strangers who acted like they knew me, not even the man who claimed to love me.

My doctors said it was trauma. Anxiety. Possibly a stress response. I often wonder if it was something else.

The story you're about to read came from somewhere deep inside me. A place I didn't know existed. A tale that manifested once I finally stopped trying to remember the truth and started letting it remember me.

I don't know if this is how it really happened. Maybe it's all in my head. Sometimes I wonder if it would be better if I kept it that way. But now that I've put it all down on the page, something inside me has stopped screaming.

But sometimes, I still hear someone whispering to me when I turn out the lights.

So here it is...my first novel. A thriller shaped by the pieces in my life I may or may not have lived. Read it however you like.

As entertainment.
As fiction.
Or as something closer to a confession.
—*Paige Thomas*

# 1

P aige

The blackouts come without warning. When I wake, they greet me like an old friend with bad intentions.

Lately, it's become a troubling routine. I find traces of decisions I don't recall making, and whatever logic I must have used vanished with the memory. All that's left is the sinking feeling that I'm not in complete control.

I've always loved mornings, usually waking up eager to start the day. But lately, I wake feeling exhausted, and I'm not sure why. My memories of yesterday feel like a finished puzzle with the center missing, and this isn't the first time it's happened.

The gaps started after my car accident six months ago—a hit-and-run that left me with a fractured pelvis, back contusions, a concussion, and two broken fingers. I haven't worn my wedding band since. While my injuries have mostly healed, the blackouts remain.

I haven't told anyone, not even Michael, my husband. It scares the hell out of me, so I know it would terrify him. He has enough on his plate with conferences, patients, and working toward his doctoral degree. As a first-year psychiatry resident, he's already obsessively protective, dissecting everything like he's pulling apart a clock, gear by gear. He'd want to pick apart my brain the same way. In a loving way, of course.

Lately, the gaps have been more frequent. Sometimes it's just a few hours I can't explain, but these recent episodes feel like falling into a black hole.

The injuries occasionally flare up, but it's the lapses in memory that are worsening. In the beginning, they felt like walking into a room and forgetting why I went in. Last week, I drove somewhere but came home with no idea where I'd been. When Michael was in London three weeks ago, I lost nearly twenty-four hours. This time, twelve hours are blank.

Since the accident, Michael has been like a mother hen on crack. He hovers, worries, and spoils me worse than an only child. He monitors what I eat, my sleep, and whether I take my medication. If I told him about the blackouts—and knowing him—he'd hire a live-in nurse.

This morning is worse. Not only is there another gap in my memory, but I feel like a beached whale—too heavy to move. I have no reason to be tired. Michael has been away at a conference, so I've spent most of my time relaxing, reading, and writing. Yet I'm completely drained, with the feeling of being hungover, even though I only remember drinking a small glass of wine last night. I even measured it—exactly five ounces. Since Michael and I are trying to get pregnant, I'm meticulous about what I consume, and so is he.

Murray gets up from his plush dog bed, stretches, then pads across the hardwood floor and stands next to me as I stare out the window. Unlike me, mornings aren't his thing. Today, it seems our moods are in sync.

The fog clouding my brain feels like it's unraveling my sanity. I turn and pick up one of Michael's shirts from the chaise lounge chair, press it to my face, and inhale the woodsy scent that lingers in the fabric—part cologne, part something that's unique to Michael. Normally, this would be soothing, but immediate nausea boils in my stomach, and I have to run to the bathroom to throw up.

The cold tile floor stings the tops of my bare feet as each retch comes faster, sharper than the last. The regurgitated contents of my stomach have a strong odor of cheap wine—not just the tiny amount I'd thought I'd drunk, but a lot. My forehead furrows as I look at the contents floating in the toilet, and it forces me to throw up again. Not wanting to smell or look at it anymore, I flush several times before I'm finished emptying my stomach. When it feels as though I have nothing left to extract, I shakily stand, lean over the sink, and splash my face with cold water.

I catch a glimpse of myself in the shiny faucet, which prompts me to look at my reflection in the mirror. Shock and confusion steal my expression. I look like a lemur—my mascara smudged, more like caked around my eyes, which only accentuates the bloodshot corners.

What the hell?

I don't even remember putting mascara on. I stare at myself as I shift my face from side to side. My normally straight blond hair is a mess, but it's obvious I'd taken the time to curl it.

I don't remember doing that either.

My stomach feels as though a kitchen mixer is inside it, churning the acid at high speed. Maybe this is what it's like to be pregnant.

I know that what I'm feeling is probably just another blackout episode—or at least, this seems to be the pattern the morning after I wake up with a lengthy lapse in my memory. Only this time, I feel worse.

I grab a pregnancy stick and pee on it, then sit down on the closed toilet seat and wait. Murray sits in front of me and taps his paw on my knee, demanding his usual morning rub. As I scratch him behind his ear, I wait as my head begins to pound. I rest my elbows on my knees and my forehead in my other hand. I don't remember ever feeling this bad after a night of partying in college. Thoughts race through my swimmy head as I try to remember something, anything, from last night. I can't be hungover. I didn't drink.

A single line. Negative.

I feel relieved. Michael and I have been trying for a couple of months. Before we stopped preventing pregnancy, I had a thorough physical to make sure everything was okay after my accident. I'm perfectly healthy in that department.

Michael thinks it's not happening because I'm stressing myself out over the fact that I haven't gotten pregnant yet, which isn't true. In fact, I've pretty much stopped thinking about it. Especially lately.

I'm jolted back from confusion and self-pity when my phone vibrates on the bedside table. I hurry toward it.

It's Michael.

I glance at the clock—10:05 a.m. I cough, clear my irritated throat, and prepare myself to answer as though I've been up for a while. I'm usually an early riser, so if I let him know I've just gotten out of bed, he'll immediately want to know what's wrong.

"Good morning, my love." I have to clear my throat again.

Michael's velvety voice soothes me instantly. "Good morning, sweetheart. Sorry I haven't called earlier. I had a Zoom call during our normal talk time, so I missed it."

I've always found his voice comforting—melodic in some ways. Not too deep, yet not feminine either. I think that's why his patients keep coming back. He has a Hugh Jackman kind of voice, only without the accent, and can soothe the nerves just by a sentence.

"It's okay. I've been pretty lazy this morning. Trying to do a little writing, but my brain is choosing to do otherwise."

He hesitates, and I fear I'm not hiding my current state of mind well enough.

"Don't stress yourself—the words will come. Are you all right? Your voice sounds a little..." he hesitates, "off."

There's something in his voice. Concern? Skepticism? Or maybe it's my own guilt altering my perception. It's impossible to hide anything from Michael sometimes. It's as if he has a direct pathway into my mind. It's frustrating. "Yes, I'm fine. I got my coffee a little too hot and had just taken a big gulp right before you called." I fake a cough.

"Have you had breakfast yet?"

I lie. "I had my usual strawberry toast and peanut butter."

"You're going to turn into a strawberry."

"That wouldn't be a bad thing. They're cute, sweet, and juicy," I say in a forced playful tone.

"So are you," Michael says as his voice deepens into the sexy timbre he uses only with me. "I can't wait to sample you when I get home."

I feel myself blush. He still has the ability to do that, even after two years of marriage.

"Sorry, sweetheart. I wish I could talk longer, but I need to get ready for a meeting and then prepare for my presentation later. I'll call you on my travels, and we can continue talking about what I'd like to sample of you when I get home."

My heart quickens, and I let out a giggle. "Of course. Good luck today."

"I love you."

"I love you too."

He hangs up, and I flop onto the edge of the bed, clinging to his last words. *I love you.* I never get tired of hearing them—especially now. People say it out of habit, trimming it to *love you* or *love ya,* like the *I* doesn't matter. But it does. Michael and I never skip it. We don't cut corners—not when it comes to our relationship, even with something as simple as one little word. Sometimes, the smallest things matter most.

I force myself downstairs, holding onto the banister as I descend for support—Murray moving next to me as if to offer his own support. Each step down the slick wooden staircase seems to penetrate my nerves with every creak and pop. I try to avoid the areas of the steps that I know will make noise. It's hard to avoid them all. At the moment, the beautiful winding staircase isn't my favorite thing about the house anymore.

Michael and I fell in love with this place the second we walked through the door behind the realtor: the two-story vaulted ceilings of the kitchen and living room, the wall of windows from ceiling to floor giving a perfect view of the ocean. We knew it was way out of our price range, but we found a way to mortgage it anyway. It's why he does these trips and conferences. We need the extra money.

My writing career is like a yo-yo. Some days I sell an above-average number of books, and others I may go days with zero sales. I have two books that made best-seller lists, and then I have a couple that seem to be as unpopular as those are popular. That's how it is in this business. The public decides whether you're successful or not.

I've focused my career on nonfiction—self-help material. I tell people how to manifest the things they deserve, or steps to developing healthy habits. These are the sort of ideas I've always sought out for myself. It's also what sells. However, writing fiction has always been a dream of mine, but for some reason, it feels far more difficult than nonfiction. Ideas pop into my head all the time— themes that center around the mind playing tricks, or blurred lines between memory and reality. I told stories to everyone as a kid. I could imagine creating worlds, characters, and escaping from my present. But I fear I don't have a story inside me that's exciting or suspenseful enough to tell. Still, I've heard a lot of authors say it's mostly a head thing—doubt creeping in. It's a common thing among writers. But despite the doubt, I'm going to pitch an idea at my agent and hope that she likes it.

I fix my usual strawberry toast with coffee and step through the sliding glass door into the salty sea air. The cloudy sky blurs the line between ocean and horizon as the sound of the waves begins to calm my nerves. The breeze is stronger today, laced with the sting of early fall. I set down my breakfast and tighten my robe, turning into the chill to breathe it in.

My mind continues to loop with doubt about Michael and me having a baby. I didn't tell him about the negative pregnancy test this morning because I feared he might hear the relief in my voice. Lately, I can't seem to locate the detached segments of my life, and I'm starting to wonder if I want this at all anymore.

As I ponder, a thought occurs to me, and I immediately feel guilty for thinking it.

I could secretly go back to taking birth control.

I've never been dishonest with Michael, especially when it comes to something this serious. But I keep thinking: it's the right thing to do. At least until I find out what is going on with me. If I were to get pregnant, and something were to happen during one of these blackout moments, I could never forgive myself—neither would Michael.

Maybe I can find out why I'm having these lapses.

I stare at the waves as they swell like an undulating mirror reflecting the intensity of my emotions—massive and unpredictable. In the distance, as the sky turns darker, my train of thought is now a pendulum of repetitive scenarios. If I do this, I risk jeopardizing the trust that Michael and I have between us if he ever finds out. I'm not sure he could ever forgive me for such a deception. But I have to find out why I'm forgetting things and waking up feeling like this.

I pick up my phone and try to distract myself from my raging thoughts. I open my author email account and scan through membership payment reminders and fiction writing workshops that might be available in my area. As I'm scrolling, my phone gives a quick vibration, and a notification of a new email appears at the top of the screen. The bold headline reads: I SAW YOU

I set down my coffee and open it. The body beneath the bold headline reads: I know what you did last night. I look at the sender's email address, and it makes my skin crawl: *dirtylittlesecrets.*

This prompts me to frantically search my emails more thoroughly, but I don't find any more. I'm not sure how long I sit and stare at my phone, but fear has set up residence near the center of my thoughts, overpowering everything.

I blankly stare at the ocean, the warmth of the coffee cup against my palms. The waves seem to build, each one bigger, faster, until they begin to aggressively pound the shore. Receiving an email like this only confirms what my mind is trying to convince me to do. With each thunderous crash, the sound translates to words inside my head—as if they're screaming...*this is your only choice. This is your only choice.*

I have to see a doctor.

I can't tell Michael.

I return my half-eaten breakfast to the kitchen, my anxiety threatening to paralyze my ability to function. I realize I haven't taken my anxiety medication, so I take it and pace the floor, giving it time to do its job.

Anxiety is something I've always dealt with, and oftentimes I can manage it with medications or, better yet, with a more holistic approach, but lately even those aren't helping.

The doctor prescribed Anzilyte, a second medication to be taken as needed after my accident, but I hate the side effects. It helps with calming but causes drowsiness and some stomach discomfort. With my current physical state, I decide against it.

I call my doctor's office to see if they can fit me in. I've had the same gynecologist since I was thirteen years old. My mother, being the tough-love woman she is, dragged me to see him and forced me to start taking birth control as an early teen. Her reason for doing so was because she didn't want me to end up like her—pregnant with a child she didn't want—meaning me.

*Trust me, I'm doing you a favor. There's nothing worse than getting pregnant. Especially by someone you wish you'd never met.* That was probably the nicest thing she ever did for me.

———

"Hello, Paige," Dr. Banter says as he enters the examination room. He pushes his glasses higher on his nose, then shakes my hand. "What brings you to see me?"

I hadn't exactly thought about what I was going to tell the doctor, so my words catch in my throat, and I stutter as I start to speak. "I—I—um, I've...we've decided that we want to hold off after all on trying for a baby, and I'd like to begin taking birth control again."

Dr. Banter plops down on the wheeled stool, the wheels protesting as he moves to lean back against the wall. "Well, now, lots of women struggle to get pregnant. It's only been a couple of months. You sure you aren't letting that fact discourage you? Sometimes it just takes a while."

I shift on the examination table, the crinkling of the paper beneath me loud in the otherwise quiet room. "No, it's just that Michael is very busy, and honestly, I haven't felt like myself lately. We just think it would be better to wait a couple of years until he's finished with his degree. And, after the accident, I—"

"Explain what you mean by haven't felt like yourself lately," he interrupts.

I feel another stutter hiding beneath my words as I'm about to speak, so I take a deep breath and clear my throat. "I don't know—tired a lot, brain fog, some fatigue."

He tilts his head to the side, and I can see through his thinning gray hair. He looks at me with concern as he asks, "You getting enough rest, eating right?"

"Oh yes. It just seems as though things are fuzzy sometimes, like I'm forgetting things or something. It's hard to explain."

"You sure you aren't already pregnant?" he chuckles. "Those are the sort of things you'll encounter."

A thin, forced laugh escapes me. "I actually took a test this morning. It was negative."

"Well now, there are lots of things that can cause this. Let's draw some blood and check to see that everything is in the normal range —you know, iron, A, D, and K...things like that.

Sometimes it can be something as simple as that."

I nod.

"We'll have to do a pregnancy test as well, just to make sure. You don't want to start taking birth control if you actually are pregnant."

I nod and give a half-hearted smile this time.

"Sit tight, and I'll have Mary come in and take some blood. We'll check everything. You should get the results for most of it before you leave today, and the rest will be on your patient portal later this afternoon." Dr. Banter shakes my hand again and gives me one of his warm smiles. "It's good to see you."

I sit in the cold examination room for what seems like hours after the nurse finishes drawing my blood and wait for the doctor to return. I move from wringing my hands like a doctor preparing for surgery to picking at the cuticles around my fingernails. The measured tap of the clock above the door begins to sound more like a ticking bomb when the door finally swings open.

"Well, Paige," Dr. Banter says as he closes the door behind him, his tone careful but edged with concern. "Your pregnancy test came back negative, but I have some concerns." He crosses the room and leans against the counter. "This may seem like a silly question to you, but have you been taking any kind of hormone replacements?"

"Hormone replacement? No. Why?"

"Your hormone levels are peaked as though you are pregnant, only not quite that high."

"But I'm not pregnant?"

"No, but your hormones are at a level as though you're either pregnant or are already taking birth control."

I feel the shift in my facial expression as I frown and try to guide it back to neutral.

Confusion kidnaps it anyway. "Is there any other reason my hormones could be elevated?"

"No. I mean, there are foods that contain similar hormones, but you would have to eat half your body weight for it to really show up on a blood test. What your levels are showing could only be caused by pregnancy—though it isn't that high—or birth control."

I do my best to disguise my voice with an unconcerned tone as I try to keep my mind from spiraling out of control. "I have been eating crazy healthy lately—flaxseed, soybeans, berries, things like that. Maybe I'm overdoing it?"

The doctor's expression wavers briefly before settling into a look of mild reassurance. "I'm sure it's nothing to be concerned about. Make sure you're eating a well-rounded diet. Let's wait until the rest of your blood tests come back, and we'll go from there. This office will call you if there is anything out of range. Change up your diet a bit, and we'll plan for another blood test in a couple of weeks."

I inhale hard and hop down from the examination table as my breath escapes. Eager to get away from the doctor, I head toward the exit door before he has a chance to say anything else as I blurt, "Thank you, Dr. Banter."

I frantically leave the doctor's office without stopping at the checkout window. My mind is spinning like a tilt-a-whirl, whipping from one thought to another. I know that I'm not taking hormone replacement, and the doctor said I'm not pregnant, so that just leaves one option. Birth control. That might explain the not being able to get pregnant. But lots of couples have to try for a while before it happens. But I also know that I'm not taking a pill every day either.

For some reason, my mind spins in another direction, and out of nowhere, I think of my mother. She was a woman who did everything she could to keep from being pregnant. Up until now, all I wanted to do was get pregnant.

Even as my mind searches for a possible explanation, somewhere in the back of it a voice whispers one question.

What's really happening during these blackouts?

# 2

## Michael

These conferences are often as monotonous as a treadmill—boring, repetitive, and taking me nowhere.

The low hum of indistinct chatter fills the air, and the weight of the lanyard around my neck feels heavier than it should. It's usually caused by having to make small talk and interact with intellectual strangers who often make me feel inadequate. Sometimes it's intentional, and other times it's truly because they are some of the top scholarly people in the world of psychology. They're so smart, they don't know how to have a meaningless conversation to pass the time. The nerdy man next to me adjusts his oversized glasses and mumbles something about neurotransmitters and the psychotic mind. His one monotone voice could lull God himself to sleep.

I tune him out, wipe a bead of sweat from my forehead, and begin to practice one of the meditative breathing techniques I use with my patients. I hear the announcement of my name as I stand behind a curtain just slightly offstage.

"Please give a warm welcome to psychiatry resident and trauma researcher, Michael Thomas."

I keep my eyes closed for a second or two longer as my heart thrums in my chest. The applause begins, then I shove my glasses high on my nose, smooth down my tie, and take one last deep inhale as I step into the blinding spotlights. It seems as though there are a thousand of them, even though there are only three.

This is the part that isn't tiresome. In fact, it's the only part where I feel as though I am making a difference, even though it makes my heart pound and my emotions raw. This is the fourth time I've given this lecture, and yet I still catch myself stumbling at the beginning.

Talking about the death of my mother never gets any easier. I've memorized the speech, but as I say the words aloud, my emotions battle with my vocal cords and threaten to shut them down.

"Good evening." I clear my throat, breathe in deeply, and start again.

"Glad you could join me. Tonight, I'm here to talk with you about my research on trauma—particularly acute trauma and the effects on the mental and physical body."

My gaze sweeps the front row, meeting a few curious eyes, but the intensity of their attention drives me to look past them. I fixate on one of the bright beams of light instead, letting its discomfort anchor me.

"I would like for you to take a moment and look at the person sitting on your left." I pause, giving the audience ample time to do it. "Now look at the person on your right." I pause again. "Do you think you could tell if either one of these people has suffered a traumatic experience in their lifetime, just by looking at them?"

The audience remains quiet, but the first two rows— which is the only part of the audience I can actually see—shake their heads.

I step out from behind the podium and say, as I wave my hand down the front of my body, "Based on my appearance, do you think I've suffered a traumatic experience in my lifetime?" Again, heads shake no.

"No—we can't. But one in three of us have experienced some form of severe trauma at some point in our lives. Maybe the person on your right witnessed a fatal car accident and someone died. Perhaps the person on your left was in the fatal car accident, losing a loved one." I pause again and look over the crowd, then continue. "I, myself, am one of those three."

I step back behind the podium and grip the edges tightly as I fix my eyes onto the center beam of light that pierces downward on the stage—the heat radiates across my face, and the intensity of the light stings my eyeballs. I use its discomfort to drown out the visions that my mind conjures as I recall the memories and expose old wounds to complete strangers.

"When I was thirteen years old, I came home from school one fall day to find my single mother partially submerged in a bathtub full of water. Her skin was tinted blue, her lips were purple, and her eyes were unseeing and hollow. Somewhere in the back of my mind, I knew she was dead, but on the surface of my mind, there was a hope that she was just cold—that she had been in the bathtub too long. My instinct was to grab anything and cover her naked body because I was worried about her being embarrassed that her son had just seen her naked. In that moment, fight and flight waged a war with one another in my brain. And in that moment, my brain chose flight. It saw that moment as a threat that I needed to escape from, not confront. I stayed in flight mode and escaped it for years—avoided it. I built a wall so thick and strong around the memory that I'd ensure it would never hurt me again. But one day, that wall crumbled."

I shift my gaze down to the podium as I speak the last few words and choke down the knot that forms in my throat. Talking about it feels like salt on a raw wound, and although it gets a fraction easier every time I do one of these seminars, it will never be a story I can tell without it feeling as though someone is cutting open my chest.

As I move my presentation into the terminology of the psychological brain, I relax. I feel more in my element—I'm safe hiding
behind the fancy words that make it seem less personal. Like it's
someone else's story. I've gotten good at that. In fact, it's a skill I use
in all aspects of my life. I've learned that the more I shift the pain of
that memory toward helping others, the less it hurts me.

I'm not sure I've actually come to terms with the death of my
mother in the same way that I help my patients deal with similar
trauma. Many of us can easily tell others how to cope with such a
tragedy, but we often fail to do it ourselves. The saying "do as I say,
not as I do" applies to me in this situation. We each find our own
way of dealing with the stressors or traumas of our past. Many shift
it into other forms of coping skills, often not the best.

We are all addicts in one form or another. Some drink, some
gamble, while others take on different forms of addiction. There are
too many to list. I suppose I'm no different. What others might see as
an addiction, I see as a necessity. I don't do it just to feed my own
need, but to protect others.

Being a respected therapist, I'm often looked at as a saint, free of
bad habits and flaws. But I'm a far cry from being perfect. I don't
claim to be a good man; people just label me as one. So, I have to act
the part. I'm human, and there isn't another human on the planet
who is the perfect saint. Even Mother Teresa had her flaws—she just
knew how to hide them. Everyone, living or dead, has some sort of
nasty secret or secrets hidden away. And a secret is much like a
splinter beneath the skin. At first, it may seem small and unseen, but
eventually, it'll fester and ooze.

Even though I have my flaws, there is one thing that I do very
well—that's love my wife. I would take a bullet for her if need be. But
sometimes I'm not perfect in that either.

I get through the rest of my lecture still mentally intact and with
a standing applause. It always ends with handshakes and a *congratu-
lations on such a wonderful presentation.*

I endure it as long as I can, then stomp my way through the rest of the unwanted pleasantries and head straight to the airport. I'd rather fly all night than hang out with some of these quack head doctors any longer. My plan is to get in a long nap on the plane and go home to swoon my wife.

The ticket line in the airport is much shorter at night than during morning flights. There are only three people in line, and the woman directly in front of me provides me with a distraction by the array of patterns plastering the surface of her loose-fitting dress.

Planes tend to make me nervous, so I always find something to focus on. It's not just the idea of being thousands of feet in the air, but the cramped, claustrophobic space has a tendency to stress my respiratory system—not to mention my nervous system.

I fix my eyes on the back of the woman's dress, splattered with shapes that remind me of cells. I trace the outline of one shape, which leads my gaze to another, and then another. Inside each multicolored figure, I can make out the semblance of cell organelles, although they're all situated in an unorganized pattern. The chaotic arrangement is having the opposite effect on me, and I feel an over-whelming urge to reach out and organize them. But I'm certain that if I put my hands anywhere on her dress, I would find one of hers landing across my face. Reluctantly, I divert my gaze to the pattern of the tile floor instead, following the grout lines around each tile directly at my feet.

"Sir? Sir? May I help you?"

When the woman's voice finally registers, I smile and move to the counter and follow the same routine I've done so many times, then make my way onto the plane. I plop my ass into the cramped seat next to the small round window and stare out at the long wing. I've made it a habit of counting the large screws, if visible, that line its edgings and determining if there are any missing. On one side of the wing, each is lined up in a perfect straight line, spaced evenly apart.

The screws on the opposite side are spaced progressively closer together as the wing tapers to a smaller size. I trace each round head around the wing over and over until the plane starts to move, then I remove my glasses and drape them over my knee. I shove my earbuds deep into my ears, turn on noise-canceling mode, close my eyes, and attempt to relax to the rhythm of Nordic folk music. Once the plane smooths out, I snooze lightly until it's time to land. I don't open my eyes until the wheels touch the ground, jolting me back to reality.

I climb into the back of the Uber driver's car and catch myself before giving the driver the wrong address. Not tonight. Tonight, I just want to be home.

"Take me to Harbor View Drive," I say, rubbing a hand down my face.

The driver nods, and I lean my head against the window, watching the blurred airport lights as they rush past. My pulse slows, the tension in my shoulders eases.

I just need to see Paige.

# 3

## Paige

I tap my tea mug down on the kitchen table. I'm not pregnant, even with rising hormone levels, but apparently my body wants to behave as if I am. With the uncertainty of everything that's going on with my mind and body lately, I'm one hundred percent sure I don't want a child right now. Not the same way my mother never wanted children, just not right now.

My mother didn't want me, but then again, having her as a mother wasn't ideal either. She and I never functioned well together; we were the true definition of dysfunctional. Most of the time, she was a bigger shit than a truckload of manure, and she could crush dreams faster than telling a kid that Santa Claus has been canceled.

There were times when I felt it was blatantly obvious that my mother didn't want me—even before I was born. Often, during one of her drunken binges, she would admit just how much she didn't.

She would jovially tell me stories of all the ways she tried to get rid of me while she was pregnant.

The earliest confession I can recall is a story about how she punched herself in the stomach over and over, so hard she left bruises. When that didn't work, she used the end of a five-pound dumbbell. Apparently this happened not long after she found out she was pregnant with me.

On another drunken occasion, she swayingly stood like a car-lot balloon man, a cigarette bouncing between her lips as she demonstrated riding a bicycle around and around in circles, all while slamming her crotch down on the bicycle seat. She proceeded to laugh as she said, *I should've patented that one as a birth control because it was days before I could stand for my clit to be touched.*

What seemed to be her fondest memory was how she douched with a full bottle of cheap whiskey. She'd laugh and say, *you know how whiskey burns going down? Try shooting it up your puss.*

To this day, I cringe at the sight or smell of whiskey.

I'm sure these memories grew bigger and more distorted in my mind over time. That's the thing about memories, they're often like reflections in a rippling pond—at one time seemingly clear, they morph with time, bending under the weight of emotions, perceptions, and what we wish had been true, or what we wish hadn't been true.

Later on, my mother tamed just a little and said that if we were going to be stuck with one another, we might as well make the best of it. There were times when she could be fun, and during my teen years she treated me more like a buddy than a daughter. It wasn't what I needed, but it's what I got.

I would never, ever go to the extremes my mother did to prevent having a baby, but at the moment I know I don't want to get pregnant. Dr. Banter's revelation about my hormone levels continues to baffle me and trying to figure it out is the equivalent of walking into a crowded room blindfolded while trying to figure out which person in the room is the oldest. It's impossible.

I return home and note that I still have a couple of hours to pull myself together before Michael gets home, so I draw a full bath, adding the light scent of calming lavender. I strip down naked, letting my clothes fall onto the cool tile floor and observe my reflection in the full-length mirror. It's an image that I judge with cruel loathing every time, and somehow with the hope that it will be more pleasing to me than the last time I saw it. But each time I do, my opinion remains like most women do in our society—never good enough. I hate it, but with Michael's help, I've learned to shut out those voices that want to hurt me.

As summer fades rapidly, taking my sun-kissed skin with it, my bikini lines are barely visible now. I sigh, dreading the cool weather, and turn to check my back in the mirror. My gaze catches on a discolored mark on my left shoulder—a spot I've scratched absent-mindedly, assuming it was a mosquito bite. Leaning closer, my frown deepens as I reach over my shoulder, struggling to touch it. My fingers graze the edge of something slender and needle-like beneath the skin, just over an inch long. A wave of revelation washes over me.

I know exactly what this is.

Women get this implanted under the skin of their arm to prevent pregnancy. Birth control. But why is mine on my shoulder? Why do I have it at all? And—when?

It's a little tender, which means it must be recent. But I can't remember a doctor's visit. No office. No needle. No consent. If I would have had this done at Dr. Banter's office, surely he would have pointed it out.

My breath catches as another question arises: Did someone do this to me?

The fear of these lapses in memory suddenly intensifies and now I'm frantic to know what is happening to me. I retrace my steps over the last couple of weeks, specifically focusing on my time with Michael. How could he have not seen it? He's been so busy lately and I recall having sex with him once in between his last trip and this one. It was missionary and in the dark, so I'm sure he hasn't seen me naked lately.

I debate on skipping the bath and just go straight to bed. Sleep has always been my go-to when I become too stressed or overwhelmed. But now that I'm waking up with lapses in time and memory, I don't want to sleep for fear of what I might wake up to. Besides, if I'm in bed when Michael gets home, he'll want to have me examined. I look at my shoulder once more—an examination is out of the question.

I have to hide this from Michael until I can get it removed. Then I'll switch to taking a pill.

At the moment, I'm questioning every aspect of my life. I feel as though some unreliable narrator is retelling my story, and it's completely unrecognizable. As though it isn't my life anymore, but that of a stranger and I'm stuck in the first part of someone else's narrative with no idea of the direction the story is going.

With my mind out of control, I submerge myself deep into the oval tub of water until it covers the tops of my shoulders. I lay back, resting my head on the bath pillow and close my eyes as I begin to practice the diaphragmatic breathing Michael taught me. I rest one hand on my naked stomach and the other on my bare chest and count slowly with each breath, willing my muscles and brain to relax. After a few breaths, it begins to work and I sink down heavier, yet I become weightless in the water. Sleep overcomes me.

I watch the woman as she presses her face closer to the mirror, pulls down her eyelid, and paints a thin black line along its edge, then repeats on the other eye. She brushes on thick mascara which plumps her eyelashes into appearing thicker and longer. Next, she lines her lips with a red pencil and fills them in with bright red lipstick followed by pressing her lips together several times as they make a plopping sound. She backs up and takes in her full image as I do the same. For a moment, I wonder why I'm here, in this woman's bathroom, watching her prepare to go out. I glance around me and realize, it's my bathroom.

I turn my attention back to the familiar-looking woman who is dressed as if she's heading to a rock concert, or a street corner. Black leather miniskirt, cropped tank top, and strappy stilettos. She grips handfuls of her curly blond hair and plumps a few times, then turns and leaves the bathroom. I fall in behind her watching her hips sway as she confidently walks in extremely high heels. Her walk, body, and confidence makes me envious of her.

She moves along the landing toward the stairs and grips the handrail as she descends. The wall of windows is pitch-black, indicating that it is well after dark. The chime of a grandfather clock strikes twelve times and I pause on the stairs—confused.

I don't own a grandfather clock.

When I look back toward the foot of the stairs, the woman is gone. I sprint downward and search the living room and kitchen, then the spare bedrooms and bathrooms. There is no trace of her. I begin to second-guess whether I had seen her in the first place. I'm feeling almost frantic when I return to the center living area and my attention goes back to the large windows. I know it was dark just a few minutes ago. I heard a clock strike twelve, but I remember that I don't have that kind of clock.

Now, the sun is peeking just over the ocean—it's morning. What happened over the past few hours?

I suddenly feel as though I've been run over by a truck. My head pounds and I feel nauseous, which shifts to an urge to throw up. I run back to the closest bathroom and hurl into the toilet as the feeling of déjà vu plagues me. I've been here before—just this morning.

I have to pull myself together before Michael gets home.

I begin to hold my breath in an attempt to ward off throwing up again. As I try to determine how or why I ended up in the downstairs bathroom, I make my way back to the stairs and climb. Each step feels like an impossible feat, as if my legs refuse to work. When I finally reach the top, my eyes seem to glitch as if the landing in front of me were some old home movie, morphing into something else. Then everything around me becomes dark.

*Where am I?* The question floats in my mind as I recognize the cool water surrounding me. Not just around me, but I'm in over my head and I can't take in a breath or I'll drown. I realize I've been under for too long and I'm desperate to inhale. I try to raise up and get my face above the surface of the water, but my body is limp—void of strength or the ability to move.

I can't breathe—I'm drowning.

"Paige!"

A muffled cry sounds from somewhere in the distance. It comes louder.

"Paige!"

Someone grabs my arm and I begin to punch and kick. I take in a breath of air as my eyes fly open and quickly realize I've just punched Michael.

"Oh my god! Are you all right?" I practically choke on my words as I lean over the bathtub to find Michael sprawled on the floor cupping his nose, his glasses thrown to the floor beside him. I search to see if he's bleeding, but he doesn't appear to be. I cough and cover my mouth. "Oh my god—I'm so sorry."

Michael waves his other hand and speaks through the one cupping his face. "It's my fault. I panicked." Murray huddles in close and nudges him with his nose followed by a low whine.

"No. It's definitely my fault. I was having some weird dream. I guess I fell asleep."

He pulls his hand away from his face—I assume he's checking for blood as well. His eyes are watery, but there's no blood. He picks up his glasses and examines them before he puts them back on and pats Murray on the head. "I'm alright, boy."

I suddenly remember my shoulder and shift my body so that he isn't able to see my back.

Michael moves onto his knees and props his forearms on the side of the claw-foot tub. "I'm sorry I frightened you. I don't know why I panicked. You didn't seem to be breathing and—." Michael seems to choke on his words and clears his throat.

"I'm so sorry, Michael. I didn't mean to scare you."

"It's alright." He brushes my chin with an index finger. "Let's start over." Michael leans in and gives me a gentle kiss. "How has your day been, sweetheart?"

I swallow and fake as much enthusiasm as I can. "It's been great. I'm still in relaxed mode, I guess."

"Well, there's nothing wrong with that. So, what's on your agenda between now and when I return home?"

I ponder for a moment with a long exhale. It's more like debating with myself as I try to decide if it's something I'm actually going to do. "I'm thinking about going to see Darlene."

Michael raises an eyebrow. "Your mother? What brought this on?"

I try to sound a little more eager about the idea. "I haven't been in a while and I can use the excuse of you getting home from a trip to make it a short visit. Get in and out quickly."

"Ah, I see. I'm proud of you, honey. I know you usually dread your visits with your mother." Michael takes on a more serious face. "Are you sure you're alright?"

"Yes...I'm fine. I promise."

"Make sure you take your anxiety meds before you go. That is, if you're feeling anxious about it—or about driving that far."

"I've been taking as I need. I'm good."

"The doctor said it works better if you take it regularly. And the combination of driving and going to see your mother is a pretty big step for you."

"You're probably right." I smile. "That's a double for stress."

Michael stands to check his appearance in the mirror and my gaze locks on his ass.

He turns around and catches me. "Were you looking at my ass?"

"Me? No." I tease and shift my face into an innocent expression.

Michael squats down beside the tub once more. "I hope your visit with your mother is a good one." He sticks his hand down into my bath and swishes it around. "Good God. How long have you been in here?"

"I guess my nap lasted longer than I intended."

"I was going to suggest that I crawl in and join you a bit before I leave, but I think I'll wait and get you naked later." He laughs.

I try to mask my relief with a mischievous smile. "You promise?"

He cocks one side of his mouth and winks. "I wanted to come in and see you first before I go to the hospital. I have a couple of patients to see today, then I'll be back later and make good on my promise."

"Can't wait," I say and bounce my eyebrows. "Did you get some sleep?"

"A little on the plane. What do you say, when I get back, we curl up and take a power nap, then we'll decide on our second dinner."

"Second dinner?"

"You'll be my first." Michael kisses me on the tip of my nose, stands, and backs out of the bathroom, keeping his eyes locked on me before he turns and heads toward the stairs.

I plop back into the cold water and exhale. My thoughts scurry back onto the same hamster wheel they've ridden all day, and the endless round and round has gotten me nowhere. The one thing I do know for sure: I'll have to be clever and figure out how to keep my shoulder hidden from Michael later tonight. Tomorrow, he has to leave for another trip, and while he's gone, I'll get it removed.

# 4

# D arlene

**Twenty-five years ago**

*I'm not a bad person; I'm just misunderstood.* That's what my father used to say.

I down the shot of whiskey and as soon as it hits my stomach, I realize that I've allowed myself to drink one shot over my limit per hour. I step outside the bar, hoping the fresh air will keep the buzz from hitting too hard.

My father also liked a good cold brew just the same as I do. He also liked his whiskey. I suppose that's when he was misunderstood, which often ended up in a bar fight. He could be cruel, but never to me. He was like fire—capable of burning everything in his path, yet he could be warm and provide light to those who understood him—

mainly me. I often wonder what life would've been like if he'd raised me. But life short-changed me when he died and left me with only my mother—who didn't seem to want me after that. I guess that's why I've grown into the hard-hearted person I am.

Now that I'm away from the bar's blaring music, my ears feel like they've been stuffed with cotton. I take one last drag from my cigarette, drop it onto the sidewalk, and stomp it out. The man of choice this evening follows me outside. He's managed to match my energy in dances and drinks all evening. We've locked eyes before, but tonight is the first time he's given me his attention, and he's been stuck to me like a horn dog since. He has this bad boy appeal, which is always trouble, but that seems to be what I attract. Let's face it, bad boys are more fun and never come with strings attached.

"Come on, baby—let's ditch this place and go back to mine," he says as he crowds in closer to me.

"Who said I was going home with you?" I ask, even though I know I will.

"You know you want to." Now dangerously close, he stands in front of me and braces his hands against the wall on each side of my head. I lean my back against the rough brick of the building with both hands tucked in behind me as I stick my cleavage forward, teasing him. He slips a hand behind my lower back, pulling my hips against his as he leans in, his tongue brushing lightly across my lips before he pulls back, his face just an inch away.

"I can take you places you've never been before, baby."

I laugh in his face. "Try a new line. I've heard that one."

He grins and lightly taps my lips with his and speaks in a deep, sexy tone. "Okay then.

Come with me, give me five minutes, and you'll be begging to have my baby."

The words that come from his mouth cause a knee-jerk reaction which sends mine directly to his groin, forcing him to double over. I shove him aside. "Not the way to get into my pants, dumb ass."

He moans, his upper body hunched over while holding his balls as he speaks through a growl. "You fucking bitch."

"That's right. Don't forget it." I turn and walk back to the door of the Thirsty Lobster, sling it open, and disappear back into the chaos. I stomp through the crowded room to the bar as I look at my watch and note the time, then I pull out the piece of paper in my pocket. I motion for the bartender who comes over to me, hands me his pen, then says, "Time for another drink?"

"Yep." He's gotten used to my routine. I write down the time and then make my seventh tally mark alongside the others I've made throughout the night.

"You keep a journal of how many drinks you have?" the man says from two stools down.

"Yep—got to drive home. I've never gotten a DUI before and don't intend to now."

"Clever." He looks down at the empty stool between us and I shoot him a sideways glance.

"If you're thinking about scooting over here to say some bullshit line about how you're so good in bed and that I'll want to have your baby, I'm going to warn you, it'll only get you kicked in the balls."

"Noted." He gives me a partial smile, revealing a dimple on his right cheek.

I glance at him again and lock eyes with his—I immediately know he's trouble. But he also seems different than the last five guys that have hit on me. He has a slight innocent charm in his dimpled smile.

I fold the piece of paper and shove it back into my jeans pocket, then I grip the whiskey and Coke and turn on my stool toward the stranger. "You dance?"

"Nope. I'm just a people watcher."

"Oh—you're one of those."

"One of those?" He cocks an eyebrow and gives me a sideways glance.

"A creeper."

"You saying you don't people watch?"

"Not really. Too busy having fun." I raise my glass toward him then take a sip.

"You should try it. It's pretty entertaining. Especially if you go to Walmart to do it."

He turns his face straight ahead and takes a slow sip of whiskey. I don't typically tell anyone my name, especially right away, but there's something about this man that makes me want to. "I'm Darlene," I say and stick my hand out to offer him a handshake.

He smiles without looking my way and I can see his dimple again. He eases his glass down onto the bar and it takes him a second to respond, then he turns to take my hand as he says,

"Nice to meet you, Darlene." He doesn't say anything else, just turns back to his drink. I wait for more of a response, but he doesn't give one.

I squint my eyes at him then turn back to my own drink, feeling slightly irritated. I think to myself that I'm not going to beg for his attention, so I turn to get up with the intention of moving elsewhere when he finally speaks again.

"Ever go to Walmart?"

His question throws me off guard and I stutter. "What?"

"It's a simple question—you ever go to Walmart?"

"Occasionally when I need something, but not for pleasure."

"Then let's go."

"What?"

"You ask that a lot."

"That's because this whole conversation is confusing."

"No it's not. It's simple. I'm asking you to go to Walmart and people watch with me. We don't even have to go in. We can just watch the people of Walmart come and go."

"This is a first."

"What?"

"See. This conversation is confusing. I was saying, this is the first time I've had someone use this line to get into my pants."

"Who says I am?"

"Isn't that what a bar is for?"

"I suppose." He turns his body to face me fully for the first time and I take in his broad shoulders and tanned skin. His dark hair falls down over one eye and he runs his fingers through it, slicking it back into a feathered look. It's the first time I notice his gorgeous green eyes, which seem to pierce through me, and for the first time ever, my heart flutters in my chest.

There's no doubt that this man is trouble with a capital T.

"I'm not saying I won't ever try to get into your pants, but I think you need to live a little first."

"By...people...watching?" I ask the question in disbelief. This is the strangest encounter I've ever had, and for some reason I find it more thrilling than any other.

He nods and shows me the dimple on his left cheek this time.

"Okay. I suppose if you were a serial killer, you can't kill me in the Walmart parking lot. Hell, why not?"

He stands from his tall chair, his body not changing much in height—in fact, he grows well over six feet tall. He waves a hand for me to walk in front of him and as we're making our way toward the front, another tall man bumps into him, spilling his drink, some splattering in our direction.

"Watch it, asshole." His voice takes on a completely different tone as he shoves the drunk man with both hands, almost causing him to fall. He stares at him for a moment as the man with the drink backs away. When he turns back toward me, the look in his eyes is almost scary and I start to second-guess going with him.

He flashes his dimpled smile, which shifts them back to the sexy green eyes from before, and I forget all about it.

# 5

# Michael

The moment I climb into the front seat of my car, I twist my fingers around the steering wheel in an attempt to reduce the intensity of my anxiety. Every now and then, old wounds break open and ooze emotions that catch me off guard. Seeing my wife seemingly lifeless and submerged in a bathtub catapulted me down a dark memory lane where I often choose not to travel. But sometimes my mind takes me there unexpectedly.

That's the thing about memories—pleasant or unpleasant, they choose when to visit. But oftentimes, it's the not-so-pleasant memories that show up like an unwanted guest only to ruin a happy moment.

I take a few minutes to practice what I preach to my patients and acknowledge that the feelings are real. The idea is to observe them without letting them take over. Give them ample time to exist, then allow them to pass quickly without letting them influence the course of my day.

Pretending they don't exist only buries them and gives them the power to unearth later, at inopportune times. I was able to hold it together in front of Paige, but now I must deal with what is going on inside me. Seeing her in the same position as my mother when she died conjured raw emotions that threaten my ability to function.

I breathe through the visions and attempt to perform the five-sense method I teach to my patients. As I roll down the window, I look for five things I can see, four things I can touch, three I can hear, two to smell, and lastly, one that I can taste. My focus lands on the lines of a window shutter and my eyes trace them one by one, back and forth, until they begin to run together. The only problem with this calming technique is that I have a tendency to get lost in the first part of this method and lose myself in patterns, which can deter me down a different obsessive path.

Once I'm calm and my shoulders have relaxed, I head toward the hospital.

I soak in the ocean's breeze as I drive from our gated community. Bar Harbor is one of the most famous beach destinations on the East Coast—especially during the summer. This particular neighborhood is one of the most sought-after places on the island. If a piece of property goes up for sale, it's snatched up before it ever hits cyber world. Paige and I were lucky when a fellow colleague of mine took another job on the West Coast and gave us the first crack at his house. The realtor didn't even have a chance to show it to anyone else. We fell in love.

After my mother's death, I found out that she had opened a custodial IRA account just after I was born. She contributed small amounts into it over my thirteen years with her, and by the time I reached twenty-five—which is the way she had it set up—it had just over a hundred thousand dollars in it. Laura found out about it during our adoption proceedings but kept it a secret until just before I turned that age. She continued to add to it as well. It was enough for a down payment, which allowed Paige and me to purchase our house.

There are times when I have to pinch myself just to believe that my life actually belongs to me. A beautiful wife, a gorgeous home, and a job that allows me to feel a sense of worth. It took me years to feel worthy of it. Now, my life is perfect—or at least it was up until a few months ago. It's still somewhat perfect, but others may not see me as such if they knew about certain parts of it.

Over the last month, I've had to make decisions that were hard but I felt were necessary. For everyone's sake. Laura doesn't agree. I'm sure Paige wouldn't either. There's only one other person I trust in this world besides my wife—Laura.

The night of my mother's death, Laura was one of the police officers who responded to the 911 call. She had newly graduated from the academy and I don't think she had been on the job for very long. When she walked into my childhood home that day, she found me huddled over the bathtub trying to cover my dead mother's naked body with blankets and towels. The look on her face matched mine when she found someone she once loved dead in a bathtub.

My mother was no stranger to the police officers in our small town. She had been picked up for a DUI on one occasion, and on another, for possession of a narcotic not prescribed to her. Laura knew her before she got into drugs, and at one time, she and my mother were best friends. They truly loved and looked after each other. She used to say that my mother was one of the prettiest women in town—chocolate eyes, high cheekbones, and thick, dark hair. Laura referred to her often as Pocahontas's twin. But years of excessive partying, booze, and drugs robbed her of all the things that made her pretty.

I inherited all of those same traits except height. My mother was petite and I managed to far surpass six feet, and in my late teens Laura referred to me as the clone of Wind In His Hair. I learned later she was referring to some old movie with a tall, dark, and handsome Indian. And she was obsessed with old Harlequin romance novels.

When I was seven, Laura stopped coming around because she couldn't stand to watch my mother abuse herself anymore. A couple of years later, she was accepted into the police academy, and I never saw her again until that awful day.

The night of my mother's death, I went home with Laura. She contacted a lawyer friend, went through the proper proceedings, and adopted me. The strings and connections she formed being a part of law enforcement took away the wait and pain of the process. She raised me through the rest of my teenage years, pushed me through college, and has been there for me ever since.

My mother was fifteen when I was born, and Laura was a year younger than her, making her an even younger parent than my mother was. But she never complained about having to do it. She took on the role as if she were born to. She's still great at it.

The rituals I use for calming stress carry me through my drive to the hospital. I arrive and find my reserved parking space, then use my badge to enter a door marked *Staff Only* and shuffle down the stairs to the basement. Attached to the hospital is a clinic that operates independently but remains connected for referrals and inpatient care. Our offices are where we see private patients.

The assistant, Trish, converted the space little by little using a Feng Shui touch. The whole space flows in a functional and pleasing manner. Her office is in the center and off to each side are mine and Jack's. I can see she's made some new additions—a wooden decorative plate on the outside of each office. Mine reads *Michael Thomas, DO Candidate* since I'm completing my first year of residency, and Jack's reads *Dr. D. J. Eirkson, Doctor of Osteopathic Medicine.*

Jack became *Doctor* Eirkson a couple of years ago and now mentors me as I'm completing my own doctoral status. I couldn't do it without him, and I don't think either one of us could function without Trish.

When you step into our three-room office, the lighting is dim and warm. Around Trish's desk are miniature lights that give the space a warm appeal, while a bamboo chandelier reflects light patterns around the room as if they're fireflies dancing on the walls. The space flows in a pleasing pattern which I find soothing the moment I walk in.

When you enter my office, the lighting is also warm and inviting with two matching chandeliers that provide the same delightful patterns around the walls. I sometimes get lost in them and have to pull my eyes away.

Along the opposite wall is a cream-colored chaise sofa, and across from that are two matching wingback chairs with a plush matching rug in the center. It looks soft enough to sleep on. The walls are painted a deep forest green, and on the left side of the room is what Trish calls a living wall. It's elegantly covered from floor to ceiling in lush green vines with a horizontal fountain along its base. The sound has the ability to truly send one's mind into nature. It's wonderful for teaching my patients meditative focus.

"Good morning, Michael." Trish looks at her watch. "I mean good afternoon. How was your trip?" Trish sits behind her desk with her usual faded cardigan wrapped around her. She's always cold and keeps a tiny heater under her desk for those times when her internal thermostat is really broken. *Her words, not mine.*

"Great. Long, but good." I exhale loudly.

"How's Paige doing? I haven't spoken to her in a while."

"Paige? She's good. Successfully procrastinating on her new novel."

Trish laughs. "That means it'll be a good one. Procrastination is just perfection waiting to be born."

I smile. "I'll need to write that down and relay that to her. She struggles sometimes, but she always gets it done." I glance back into my office and let out a long exhale. "I guess I'd better go see some patients."

"I'm sure Vincent is patiently waiting for you." She props her chin onto her clasped hands while giving me a mischievous smile.

"Vince? Patient? Ha."

"I dare you to call him Vince and see just how patient he is,"

Trish teases as she brushes a strand of her salt-and-pepper hair over her ear.

"Nope." I shake my head in exaggeration. "I value my life. I made that mistake once and it's one I'll never make again."

My first session with Vincent was one for the record books. I was very fresh into my job, so it was recommended that two orderlies accompany me into my first session with him. They said it was for precaution until they saw how he would react to me. In fact, they insisted I not be alone with him. I remember my knees shaking as I walked into the room.

After I pulled myself together, I entered a tiny, windowless room to see a blindfolded man lying back on his bed. I sat in an uncomfortable chair across from Vincent's bed and said, "Hello, Vince, very nice to—"

He leapt from the bed like a wild animal, and before I could react, the two orderlies were pulling him off me. When it was over, they both laughed hysterically, then casually explained they'd stuck around because I'd referred to him as Vince. They wanted to see how Vincent would react to hearing the name he despises. They knew exactly what was coming.

I haven't had any issues with Vincent since then.

The hospital staff wasn't the only one who got a good laugh out of my first visit with Vincent—Jack did too. He never warned me, even though I inherited the patient from him. His caseload is astronomical, which is how I ended up in this position. When I applied for residency, I knew Jack was one of the best in the field, and I'm lucky to have landed here. He's the kind of mentor anyone would wish for —and now, an even better friend. I honestly don't know what I'd do without him.

"Any messages?" I ask Trish.

She gives me a smirk. "When have I not left them on your desk?"

I grin.

Trish is the kind of assistant that is always positive, but in a negative sort of way. She comes off as pushy, nosy, and somewhat aggressive but always has the best intentions. She knows how to get things done and won't allow anyone around her to slack in their duties either. She knows everything that goes on around here, and if she doesn't know it, she always finds out. Keeping a secret from her takes skill, which is why Jack and I often meet after she's gone home for the night.

"Did I miss anything while I was gone?" I ask.

"Only that some of us worked while others napped on their couch," Trish says as she leans over, sending her words toward Jack's open office door.

"Ha. Funny. I didn't know we'd hired a comedian for an assistant." Jack appears in the doorway of his office and leans against the frame as he crosses his arms in front of his muscled chest.

"Always knew you were a slacker." I look at Jack with a crooked grin.

The office behind him reflects the same atmosphere as my own except his furniture and walls are the opposite. Green couch and rug with cream-colored walls. When seeing patients, his lighting is adjusted to a dimmer setting to counteract the light walls. When he isn't seeing patients, he adjusts it to a setting known as the pearly gates of heaven. That's what Trish calls it. It's bright and blinding.

"Takes a slacker to know a slacker." Jack grins. "How'd the presentations go?"

"Great. The usual interesting people—smart, boring, and insufferable."

"Sounds like you met some of your doppelgängers." Jack chuckles.

I flip him off.

"Children," Trish scolds in a teasing manner. "Solve your sibling squabbles elsewhere. I have work to do." She adjusts the unruly strand of hair once more, this time tucking it into her usual up-do style. After she turns to look at her computer, I flip him off with both hands and give him a fake smirk.

I turn toward my office.

"Oh, Michael. Let Paige know that I finally had the chance to read her latest book. The one about self-discovery and inner peace."

I stop and turn back to him. "Oh yeah. What'd you think?"

"She's very talented."

"I'm sure she'd love to hear that. Be sure to tell her during her next visit, in case I forget."

"I will...whenever she comes back to see me."

"She's been really busy. But she'll be back."

Jack gives me a smile and a nod—the kind that feels more like it's coming from a friend than a therapist or colleague. He's been a godsend since Paige's accident. Actually, even before that. She'd been seeing Jack for several months as her therapist before the car wreck. Seasonal depression has always been a struggle for her, often sending her into a slump, but she's never been afraid of therapy. In fact, she encourages it in her books. That's how I ended up here. I guess I have Paige to thank for this internship—she talked about me in therapy, and I suppose Jack liked what he heard. Told her to have me give him a call. And now, here I am.

Paige's anxiety has only worsened since the car accident, and Jack stepped up even more without hesitation, offering to help when we were barely keeping up with the medical bills. He's gone out of his way for us more times than I can count. But that's just the kind of person he is.

I enter my office and check my desk for messages. Trish has introduced a new scent. I sniff a few times and determine that it's sandalwood—woodsy yet sweet. I'm sure it has something to do with grounding and calming. I don't question Trish's choices; she's very good at choosing comforting additions to our space.

After I finish checking my messages—which I decide can wait for now—I grab the file with the notepad I use exclusively for Vincent. Sessions with him always generate pages of notes to reflect on after-ward. Jack handed Vincent off to me because he felt the two of them just weren't making the kind of progress Vincent needed. Sometimes it's like that—just as a teacher and student might not mesh well, a doctor and patient might not either. Jack thought that because I'm not quite a doctor yet, Vincent might feel less intimidated or judged. He did warn me, though: Vincent has a tendency to read people's minds—or at least, he thinks he can.

There is always one thing that stands out during my sessions with Vincent—the last statement he says to me before I leave the room. They often contain some sort of quote by a famous psychologist or thinker and for some reason always resonate with me for days after. I always write them down at the bottom of the page and sometimes in all caps. After our sessions, I look them up and make a note of the person that said it and write that down as well.

I grip a chunk of the pages and flip through them, letting several pages fall, pausing and reading at random.

*When we're no longer able to change a situation, we are challenged to change ourselves.* Viktor Frankl.

I flip through a few more.

*When an inner situation is not made conscious, it appears outside as fate.* Carl Jung.

The last page I land on, I really hadn't paid much attention to. It was our last session before my trip, which I had written in all caps. This fact makes me pause and ponder.

*THE MORE WE TRY TO STOP OURSELVES FROM INDULGING IN A PARTICULAR HABIT, THE MORE WE BECOME OBSESSED WITH IT.*

I take a moment to look up the owner of this quote and write it down. Also Carl Jung. Vincent must like reading about this particular psychiatrist.

I often wonder if these quotes are meant for me or if they're personal to him in some way. It's hard to tell with Vincent.

I climb the stairs to the third floor and enter the tiny hospital room one minute after our set time. Vincent's six-foot frame lies on the twin bed dressed as he always does—hospital scrubs, long-sleeved shirt underneath, thick white socks, and a blindfold over his eyes. He turns his blindfolded face toward me. "You're fifty-eight seconds late, Michael."

"I know...I'm sorry, Vincent. Other duties call."

I hate being even two seconds late for our sessions—I feel as though I might be cursed in some way because of it.

I insisted in the beginning that Vincent call me Mr. Thomas, but his reply was, "When you become an actual doctor, then I'll call you Dr. Thomas, but until then, you're no different than me, so we'll stay on a first-name basis."

After our first encounter, I didn't push it.

Vincent's story is a long and complicated one. I've been seeing him for more than a year and I have yet to dig into many parts of his past or childhood. My sessions with him have taught me more than any school or training. It has challenged my patience more than once, but it has also taught me how to have it.

Vincent has been in and out of hospitals most of his life—in more than out. According to his records, a hospital is what he's called home since he was a boy. When he seems to be doing better and has proven he can handle the outside world, he's released on a structured program. He lives in group housing, has his own room, and makes money working through freelance platforms or creative-services marketplaces—mainly as a beta reader. It's something he can even continue doing from the hospital.

But despite having these things—space, purpose, a little freedom —the outside world always becomes too much. And he ends up back here.

It's my goal to help him...and make it stick next time.

Our sessions mostly consist of Vincent describing his dreams, which could be strewn together, organized, and written into a best-selling psychological thriller. The most twisted kind. The sort of fiction novel Paige talks about writing.

Today we've discussed one of his most recent dreams, followed by working through how it might relate to the childhood trauma he endured for the first seven years of his life. The details of it are so horrific, it's the reason why he wears a blindfold most of the time. He feels safer in the dark.

The only place he doesn't wear one is when he is alone in this tiny room. The only light he is exposed to is the tiny reading light, which he can control and is only on whenever he chooses.

I've often wondered how he learned to read in the first place, but I haven't asked the question yet.

Today's session is coming to a close when Vincent sits up to face me blindly and says, "I had a dream about you last night, Michael."

I catch myself leaning away from him.

"About me? Would you like to tell me about it?"

Vincent pauses as he turns his face down toward the floor. It remains in this position for a long pause as if he's thinking, and my nerves go from sizzling to feeling like two hot wires making contact. He raises it toward me again and it's as if he's looking at me through the blindfold.

"I'm pretty sure it will scare you."

"How so?" I ask.

He leans closer to me as he props his elbows on his knees. "Well, I don't know about scare you—but you won't believe me."

"Try me."

His voice deepens, taking on a more serious, possibly sinister tone. "Someone is going to hurt you."

My voice abandons me for a moment and I have to chase it down. "You mean you dreamed that someone wishes to hurt me?"

"That isn't what I said. I said, someone is going to hurt you. That is—unless you fix your problem."

"Problem?" Now it just seems Vincent is speaking nonsense.

"You're not listening. I try to help you all of the time, Michael, but I don't think you listen to me. I mean, actually listen to what I tell you."

"I always listen to you, Vincent."

"You don't. Not really. I mean really listen. But I do hear you writing down the quotes I leave you with—so—that's a start."

"You're right—I do."

"So let me leave you with this one." Vincent lies back on the narrow bed, his blindfolded face toward the ceiling as he quotes, "People will do anything, no matter how absurd, to avoid facing their own souls. That includes keeping secrets from those they claim to love."

I ponder for a moment and realize that I actually recognize this quote. "Another one by Carl Jung. So how does this quote have anything to do with someone wanting to hurt me?"

"Again—not wanting—going."

"I don't understand, Vincent."

He turns his face toward me again. He sits there for a moment unnervingly quiet, then leans forward and pulls down his blindfold. The dim reading light casts a faint streak across his face, revealing his eyes for the first time. They look empty.

"You'll do anything to keep from facing the truth, but secrets will ooze like festering wounds, Michael, and eventually, they'll burst open. They can't be contained. You have one dark secret, but others have more. Sometimes it's not just our secrets we have to worry about."

He pulls his blindfold back in place, then flips himself around to lie on his left side, turning his back to me. "I'm tired. I'm going to rest now."

I attempt to speak again, but I know Vincent—I'm not going to get anything else out of him today.

# 6

## Paige

The guilt I'm feeling won't go away, and now that it's been turned on, there isn't an off switch.

I hate lying to Michael. Keeping these blackouts from him isn't just a little white lie—it's a boldfaced deception. He knows me too well, and he'll soon pick up on the fact that I seem to be losing my mind—literally.

I've never been a good liar—that was always my mother's expertise. But it's a skill I'm going to have to practice. Who better to teach me than the master?

I rarely ever see her and only pop in to visit occasionally. I show up unannounced because if I call ahead of time, she won't answer when she sees it's me. She says it's not because she doesn't want to talk to me, she just hates talking on a phone. Her theory is: *If you want to talk to me, then come and see me. Otherwise, don't waste my time.*

She's one of those people that grew up in the head of a hollow and never left. She still has the old-fashioned landline equipped with caller ID, but I'm not sure why she has a phone, because not only does she never answer my calls, she rarely answers it for anyone. I pay for her to have a cell phone, but she rarely charges it. I suppose it's useless out in her corner of the world anyway. She'll occasionally turn it on if she leaves the hollow for booze or cigarettes.

When I was a teenager, the few friends that were brave enough to come around always made the same comment: *How did someone like you come from something like her?* I wonder the same thing myself sometimes. We're nothing alike, yet in many ways we are. It's not something I like to admit.

I go to visit my mother mostly because I feel I'm supposed to—not out of love, and definitely not out of respect. In my opinion, respect is a two-way street—she never had it and, as far as I'm concerned, never earned it. I mostly go to see her because Michael seems to think I'll regret it one day if I don't. I don't argue his point because I know losing his mother the way he did is a trauma he'll probably never come to terms with. It's a circumstance he can't change or fix, but as far as my mother goes, I get to pick and choose how and when I see her. He often points out that it's a luxury he doesn't have.

Aside from all that, I've learned there are just certain things that drive us to do something even when we can't explain why our brain tells us to do it. It's instilled in us as children and, as our brains are developing, it somehow molds out a spot—or wrinkle—in our minds. I'm not sure why, but there is a tiny spot in my brain that says I should check in on Darlene even if she was a shitty parent.

My mother's mother was even worse at parenting than mine, and regardless of how much Darlene despised her, she dragged me and herself to see her anyway. Darlene's theory was: *Sometimes life hands you shit, and sometimes you've got to eat it whether you want to or not—but you don't have to like it.* She liked going to see her own mother just as much as I like going to see mine. I guess that's why she never complains about how little I come around.

Today I'm taking it a step further—not only am I going to eat shit and visit her, I'm going to ask her for advice. Darlene is the type of person who won't sugarcoat anything. She'll shoot it to you straight and won't even bat an eye even if she makes you bleed.

I finish getting dressed, and as I'm putting on my shoes, an email notification pings on my phone. Since the last ominous email, I've switched on notifications for this account. I sit down on the foot of the bed to check it, adrenaline forcing my heart to flail against my chest.

*I Saw You*

I look to see the sender's email address again—*dirtylitlesecrets.*

I open it, and this time there is a short text along with a rather large file. I read the text first:

*Three may keep a secret, if two of them are dead. –Benjamin Franklin.*

I hear the swishing of blood in my ears, driven by the relentless pounding of my heart. With a shaky hand, I click the thumbnail. The screen fills with a silent video and the camera is focused on the outside of an orange brick building. At first, I don't recognize it, but I look closer at the sign across the front of the building—Frederick Staten, OBGYN. It's a women's clinic, but not my regular doctor.

I stare at the video trying to figure out what I'm supposed to be seeing, then I recognize my car pulling into a handicapped space in front of the clinic. My eyebrows furrow deeper, to the point it begins to make my skin tingle as I stare at the phone screen.

I would never park in a handicapped spot.

I watch as I get out of my car from the passenger seat. Someone else is driving, but they don't get out of the car. I zoom in using my thumb and index finger to get a better view of the car, but I can't even make out an image of someone else in the vehicle. I use my fingers to move the screen around and look at myself as I'm walking toward the building.

I don't recognize the clothes I'm wearing. In fact, I'm wearing something I would only wear if Michael and I were going out on a Saturday night. Why would I be wearing a black strapless dress in what appears to be the early morning and in the cool air?

I turn back around to look toward the car before I enter the building. The tops of my breasts, shoulders, and arms are on full display.

As I disappear into the clinic, the video goes blank for a split second. It reappears and I'm looking at the front of the clinic again. This time I see myself walking out. When I walk around the side of the car and turn so that my backside is visible, I see a bandage on the back of my left shoulder. I know right away what it's for.

I watch until I see my car back out and pull away, then the screen goes dark.

I don't realize that I'm shaking all over until I try to click back to the email.

"Who the hell sent me this? Why send me this?" I catch myself saying aloud. I feel a tremor course through me as I try to speculate who it could be.

Michael? Why would he?

Better yet—who was driving the car?

I remain frozen in place and stare at the phone as if it might somehow reveal something different than what I'd just watched. As if sensing my unease, Murray gets up from his bed and waddles to me, then drops his head onto my lap and looks up at me.

Now I'm sure I'm doing the right thing by going to see my mother. Maybe she can help me figure it out.

Darlene's no stranger to blacking out, even though her episodes were always self-inflicted. The weird thing about her is that at some point she was always able to recall what she did later. She said that was because she set herself up so that she could at least bring to mind people and places. She didn't like not knowing. Her goal was to get sloshed, slightly lose control, but only so far.

I've never paid much attention to her stories, especially those about her drunken excursions, but now, I want to know more. The next time I have a blackout, I want to use the skills Darlene used—

those where she's able to remember, or at least have an idea of what happens while she's in one of her drunken blackouts.

I step out the front door of my house and notice that the weather must have changed its mind about storming, because now the sun is on full display. I climb behind the wheel of our used Range Rover and feel a sense of nervousness at going to see my mother, but also at the idea of driving. Driving since my accident still lands me in a front-row seat for panic mode, but at the moment, I'm feeling surprisingly calm.

My mother only lives a few miles outside of town near the entrance of Acadia Park. Distance-wise, it isn't that far, but the mountainous, winding roads make it seem like a long trip. Then there's the hollow where she lives, which requires a four-wheel drive for passage. Darlene lives at the end of it, and her only neighbors include rough terrains, mountains, and an assortment of friendly and not-so-friendly wildlife. I don't worry about her when it comes to these aspects, though—she's a lot meaner than a five-hundred-pound bear.

The hollow resembles an ATV trail—dirt, jagged rocks, and muddy holes—and its entrance isn't marked with a road sign. I roll down my window and take in the smell of trees and moss, much different from the salty air I've just left behind. That's the amazing thing about this part of the world—you get the best of both.

Each side of the road is equipped with views of rusted-out cars and trucks, all surrounded by tall grass and puny trees. Driving down this trail is like traveling back in time to a place that most people don't even know exists. A type of scene you might see on a documentary about the poverty-stricken mountains of northeast Maine.

You know you're getting close to my mother's place when you spot the rusted green Chevy with a tree growing through the truck bed. Just past it, there's a tripwire made of fishing line stretched low to the ground, running all the way to her trailer. At the end of the line, several old tin cans are tied together and will clank loudly when a vehicle runs over it. It's been there for as long as I can remember.

Darlene says she hung it to make sure she'd always know when someone was coming.

In fact, she has all kinds of homemade contraptions scattered around her property for safety. Most are designed to alert her to trespassers, while others are meant to trap—or even kill—unwanted intruders. According to her, they work on both animals and humans, if necessary. When I became a teenager, she showed me where all of them were and taught me how to trip and reset them. Several times a year, until I moved out, she'd take me back to each one, walking me through the lessons again and again.

I pass the first one, continuing to bounce through and around giant holes which are hard to miss, then the sight of my childhood home comes into view. As if on cue, my joy for life takes its plunge into descent. Seeing my old home place has always done this to me. Maybe it's because it wasn't the happiest of homes. How could it be when you have a mother who often behaved as though she didn't want you? Now that I've grown up and moved away, she seems to like me more now than she did back then—at least, that's how I sometimes feel.

My eyes land on the single-wide trailer with a makeshift shed built around it. The metal roof is built wide enough to provide a covered porch down one side. The trailer is a combination of rusted white walls and holes that have been patched with expanding foam. It's so old that the windows crank out instead of the kind that raise up and down.

Behind it is a shed that is in better shape than the trailer she lives in. It's where she makes her living. Through the teachings of her grandfather and her own experimenting and discoveries, my mother makes herbal and medicinal teas and sells them to local shops. She has quite the clientele, and tourists eat it up.

Despite her wild nightlife at times, she always managed to get up early in the morning and stomp through the woods to collect mints, wildflowers, and the roots of various plant life which grows naturally in the forest. She always said the key was to harvest early because that's when the oils in the plants are the strongest. I never had much interest in learning about all of it. I just wanted to get out of this lonely hollow as soon as I could.

The second announcement of my arrival comes from the droopy-faced bloodhound that has always been the pet of choice for this woman. I think he makes the fifth, maybe sixth bloodhound she's owned. His name is Ginger. So were all of the other hounds before him—male or female. She said she refers to her dogs just like she does her men—that way she never says the wrong name. Every dog's name is Ginger, just as every boyfriend she's ever had is referred to as Sugar, regardless of their name. She's had so many, I lost count by the time I was ten. It only makes sense to nickname them all the same.

I slam the door on my Rover and pause as I look around the property. Nothing has changed other than a few fallen trees. I rotate my head and my body to locate the cluster of trees that still makes me ponder its existence even now. I follow them with my gaze to look upward and spot it twenty-five or more feet above me. There it is, a large log, around the same length as it is high above me, shaped like an outstretched serpent. It looks as if God himself picked up a tree trunk, rotated it into a horizontal position, and stacked it on top of several trees as though it were a Jenga block. Cryptozoologists who roam the mountains of Acadia Park searching for Bigfoot claim that it was he who put it there. That's the legends of these mountains. Bigfoot is a common occurrence, or so some believe.

Darlene steps through the open front door of the trailer onto the rickety porch with a bottle of beer in one hand and a cigarette in the other. She's wearing a loose-fitting tank top, her braless breasts sagging slightly toward her pot belly. On her feet she wears a pair of gray, tattered house shoes that look as though she may have used them for hiking shoes.

She looks at me—no smile, no hello—and sits down in the old wicker chair as she sticks the cigarette between her lips and leaves it there. A beam of sunlight peeks through the trees and shines across her, highlighting her dark, leathery skin and streaked, dishwater hair. In the last couple of years, her face has aged drastically.

"Hi, Mom," I say without really trying for enthusiasm. Excitement between the two of us doesn't exist, and we never waste our time faking it.

"What do you want?" Her voice seems to deepen each time I visit as well. Her words and tone sound even less enthusiastic than mine. Not hateful, just Darlene.

"I had a little time to kill before Michael returns from his trip and thought I'd drop by."

"Nice of you to make time for me." The cigarette dances in front of her face as she says the words with as much sincerity as she's capable of.

"What've you been up to?"

She raises her bottle toward me then takes a drink. "What I do best."

I cock one side of my mouth and nod in agreement. She's right about that.

"You going to sit down?" she points to the other wicker chair that has a hole in the seat but has been patched with a criss-crossed pattern of gray duct tape. "It'll hold you. Duct tape can fix anything —except for a man. But it can come in handy." She cackles then coughs. "That is, unless you're afraid of ruining those bright, white pants of yours."

I didn't really think it through when I picked out my clothing, or my shoes. A person needs rugged clothes and hiking shoes to roam around here—not that I plan to. I sit down on the edge of the seat and drop my hands into my lap.

"I'd invite you inside, but I know how much you hate cigarette smoke."

"Out here is fine," I say as I look around the small yard that rarely needs mowing because it even more rarely experiences sunlight. The most sun it sees is during the middle of the day when the sun is high in the sky. Soon it will be gone as it passes over the mountains behind us.

In the distance I hear the chattering sounds of a squirrel. They perform a series of barks as if to warn its friends that danger may be close by. I search for what might be making it nervous. During the day I'm not as nervous about a wild animal sneaking up, but as a child, I rarely ever went outside after dark.

"You still haven't said what you want." Darlene sucks on the cigarette, then pulls it away from her mouth as she sticks out her bottom lip and blows the smoke above her. The breeze blows it in my direction and despite holding my breath, I get a taste of it anyway.

"I need to ask your advice about something."

Darlene gets choked on the next puff of her cigarette and says through her coughs, "You're asking me for advice? Miss, I know it all."

"Ha, very funny." I give Darlene a smirk then say, "I'm being serious. I have a problem and I don't know how to handle it."

"Okay—what's up?" She sits up straighter in her seat and I detect a slight smile threatening to show underneath her permanent scowl.

"I've been having some—" I hesitate. "Sort of blackouts."

"Well...drinking too much will do that to ya." She raises her bottle of beer high, then presses it to her lips.

"But it's happening when I haven't drank at all—or very little."

"Well, now, I hope you're not dumb enough to shoot yourself up with some stupid shit."

One thing I could never accuse my mother of doing is drugs. Her addictions were always alcohol and cigarettes, and only those. She only drank coffee because it was always equipped with a shot of whiskey. "No. I'm only taking anxiety medication. I've never used drugs in my life."

"That a girl." Darlene interrupts, then lights another cigarette from the one that's burned itself down to a nub.

"I'm just waking up with hours of my life missing. There are times of the day, or night, I can't account for." I proceed to tell

Darlene about the last few episodes. "I want to know if there is a way for me to recall what is happening during these blackouts."

"What are you asking me for?"

"Well—" I pause for a second. "You always seem to remember everything—even when you were, uh," I pause again, "shitfaced."

She laughs. "Well, I don't necessarily remember, but I make sure I have an idea. I just got into a habit of making myself a note. When you have a mother who takes you to a stranger's house, forgets you were there and leaves you behind, you learn to figure out how to find your own way home. After a couple of times of being stranded, cold, and alone, I started making a note of where I was every time my mother dragged me somewhere. I don't write down details, just cue words. And—" she raises her arm. "You don't think I wear this Fitbit Fucker to track my health—do ya?"

My eyebrows squeeze together as I look at the black band around her arm.

"I might wear it to track my steps, but not for my health. It lets me know if I've roamed around very much. If I hang around here, I don't rack up much of a step count. I keep up with it when I leave home. I jot down where I'm going, who I'm going with, and no matter how shit-faced I get, I still jot down the time I get home. I write down everything...whether I'm fucked up or sober. As far as the water-drinking counter on this thing, I track my booze. Not fucking water. I like a good buzz, but I always make it back home."

My mother could write a playbook on the skills of a functioning alcoholic. She must have a liver made of steel. She pauses to gulp down a drink of her beer, takes a deep drag from her cigarette, then smashes it into a bucket of wood ash next to her chair and continues.

"When you wake up a few times, bloody, bruised, and not sure if you've killed someone or if you fucked someone to death, you learn to keep track." She laughs at herself. "I may be exaggerating a bit, but you get the idea. What I mean is, keep up with where you've been, who you've been with, and the time. Time is always important. Never lose complete control of time."

I catch my shocked expression and blink it away. I remember my mother coming home at night after I had spent most of it curled up in my bed, alone, terrified of the horrifying creatures that lived outside the thin walls of my bedroom. She always made it home, even if it was just before sunrise.

"That's my problem…I can't account for my time lately. I woke up this morning feeling hungover, even though I don't remember drinking."

Darlene gives me a skeptical frown. "Then I guess you better start writing down every time you shit, piss, and fuck."

I choke back a chuckle and a cough, sounding as if I've taken a toke of Darlene's cigarette. "I haven't told Michael that I'm having these episodes. It'll be hard to keep a record without him finding it or thinking that I've lost my mind."

She laughs again. "Sounds like you already have."

I don't think I've ever gotten this much enthusiasm or response from my mother, ever.

"Make it simple. Make everything simple. I'm sure that fancy phone of yours has everything you need to keep track of your movements. Hell, take selfies."

"I hate taking selfies."

Ginger finally finishes his sniff inspection of me and lays his bony body down across my feet, smelling like the typical bloodhound. I reach down and scrub his slick skull, then stroke his droopy ear. It's velvety soft and the act digs up a memory of me sneaking a childhood Ginger into our trailer at night when Darlene was out.

"I do record a lot of things in my notes app. There's also tracking apps. I suppose I could use those."

Darlene scoffs. "I've never used that shit. Just good old-fashioned pen and paper works just fine. But if you've got a nosy husband then do what you have to."

"He's not—" I begin to say in an attempt to defend him, but my mother's not the biggest fan of Michael. She thinks he's the goody-two-shoes type and has never really trusted him. Then again, she doesn't trust anyone who wears a tie. "I get it. Write everything down," I say. I decide against telling her about the strange email. I'm sure the shock of me telling her this much is enough for now.

"Despite what you young people think...we old fuckers aren't idiots, and no matter how many brain cells we've killed, we're still smarter than you Gen Q, X, Z...whatever the fuck you call yourselves."

I huff and start to say more, but I look at my mom and take in the deep wrinkles on her face—a roadmap of jagged lines. I could never begin to understand or contemplate where they've taken her in life. I suppose they're deep for a reason. My mother could be a walking survival guide and could easily tell someone how to make a trip to hell and back and still come out on the other side pissing shit and vinegar. She's tough, and if I were thrown into a survive-or-die situation, I'd want her by my side, regardless of my shitty childhood.

That's Darlene—the opposite of sugar and spice—she's snips, snails, and serpent's tails.

It's why I've decided to trust her, and only her, with my problem.

# 7

D arlene

**Twenty-five years ago**

Christian. He's the bad boy from the bar that took me to Walmart to people watch. I can't seem to stop thinking about him.

Since that night, we've seen each other almost daily—I can't get enough of him. The one thing I know for sure is being with him is like holding a lit match—I'm bound to be burned if I hold on too long, but I can't bring myself to let go.

I've never actually dated a man before. I play with them until the new wears off, then I toss them like a burned-out toy. Today marks the end of two whole months seeing Christian, and I can't get enough. There's something about him that's intense—dangerous. Every time he touches me it feels as though electricity courses through my body. When we're in public together, he places his hands on me as though I'm the most precious thing he's ever owned —it's as if he presents me in a way to show me off—like I belong to him—and for the first time in my life, I don't mind being owned.

This is why part of me wants to run before I go up in flames.

But I can't help it, I'm mad about him.

My insides scream that he's too good to be true, but yet, I can't stop playing with fire. He's even convinced me to go with him to get matching tattoos. I don't even know what my tattoo is going to be yet—he has me so lust-struck that I don't care. I just agreed.

Life has always taught me that people should be kept at a distance. It's easier that way. But there's something about Christian that breaks down my defenses, or at least weakens them. If he told me to leap, I'd be halfway in the air before he even finished the sentence.

"You ready for this, Dar?" he asks as I round the corner to meet him in front of the tattoo shop.

"Hey baby. You thought I would chicken out, didn't you?"

"You'll never catch me calling you chicken." He cocks his mouth upward in a crooked smile, and I'm sure I see the devil in his pretty little dimple, but I don't care.

Christian has a wicked tattoo on the inside of his forearm: a skeleton key with a chain that wraps in a swirling pattern around his arm. He's convinced me to get one that will go well with his, but he won't tell me what it is yet. He says it's a surprise.

After a quick, hard kiss, he places his hand on my low back and guides me through the door into the dimly lit parlor. The front area of the store has tattoo art covering the walls, which are illuminated with black lights. To the right is a separate room equipped with two comfy-looking, adjustable chairs and brighter lighting.

In the corner behind a tall counter sits a tattooed, middle-aged man with long hair pulled back into a ponytail. He stands and leans into his arms on the counter. "Hey, Christian."

"You ready for her, Dave?"

"Sure. Evie's got us all set up." Dave's eyes are a bright blue and seem to glow from the purplish light around the room. The black lights also make his teeth look incredibly white.

"You already had this planned?" I ask.

"I'm a planner. Got to do this right," Christian says.

"So now can you tell me what I'm getting?"

"You'll see."

"Look, I like you and all, but just so you know, I don't want any man's name tattooed on my body."

"Come on baby. You wouldn't want my name on your body?" Christian grabs me and dramatically rubs his hands over my back. "You've allowed every other part of me all over your body, and you love it." He teases.

"I mean it. No names."

"I'm not getting my name tattooed on your body. Trust me— you'll like what you're getting."

I give him a hesitant look and he gives me the dimpled smile that I can't resist. "Nothing stupid?"

"No. I think it's sweet. Ask Evie. What do you think, Evie? It's very sweet, right?"

The tattooed woman who appears to be around the same age as Dave steps into the doorway of the artist's room. "We do this tattoo for lots of people, not just couples."

This answer satisfies me, so Evie directs me into the bright room.

She instructs me to lie back in the reclining chair, and I rest my arm on the armrest. She drops onto a stool beside me, and Christian does the same on a matching one on my other side.

"No peeking," he says as he uses a hand to gently tilt my face toward him, away from my arm.

"You ready?" Evie asks.

Christian nods for me.

"Just relax—this'll take a while," she says as she lays a cool piece of paper down across my arm.

The first initial prick of the needle feels uncomfortable but surprises me by not hurting nearly as much as I anticipated. But after about twenty minutes, the intensity increases as the needle seems to pound the same spot over and over. Evie must sense my growing discomfort. "This spot requires a lot of detail, so it will probably be the worst part."

"I'm great." It hurts, but I'm not about to let on.

After about an hour or so, Evie says, "Almost done."

Relief floods over me as I think I must be getting close. Another thirty minutes goes by and she's still pounding away—at least that's what it feels like. I don't ask how much longer, but I'm dying to.

She finally taps my hand to let me know she's finished, and I exhale a sigh of relief. "Make sure you stand slowly. You might be pretty dizzy at first."

I look to Christian, who is smiling. "How'd you like getting your first tattoo?"

I fake an enthusiastic tone. "Piece of cake."

"You can look now." He grins, and I see the devil again.

I lift my arm to examine it to find a bold, heart-shaped lock entwined with a long, slender chain. Two roses, their stems intricately detailed with leaves and sharp thorns, crisscross in front of the lock. Toward the base of the lock is an oddly shaped keyhole, one that seems designed to match the key on his tattoo.

At first, my heart flutters at the thought, but then something about it unsettles me—especially when he leans in close, his breath warm against my ear. In a hushed tone, he murmurs, "You can't get away now. You're mine."

# 8

## Michael

"How was your visit with your mother?" I step in behind Paige as I wrap my arms around her waist, kiss her neck, and look over her shoulder to see what's simmering on the stove.

"Oh, you know Darlene—sugar, spice, and everything not so nice." She presses her head back into my chest, then bumps me lightly with her hips. "How does Alfredo sound for dinner?"

"I thought you were going to be my first dinner?" I squeeze her harder and pull her body in tighter against me.

She feels just as home should.

"Sorry, but I'm starving, so I guess you'll just have to save me for a nightcap." She turns and wraps both arms around my neck and presses her body against mine.

"Even better." I give her a soft kiss and squeeze her one more time. "What would you like to drink?" I ask as I release her and turn to the fridge. "Sparkling water? Lemonade?"

"Sparkling water's fine." Paige turns back to the stove where the pot of water splatters, making a sizzling sound. "How was your visit back at the hospital? I'm assuming you had to see Vincent."

A chuckle escapes me. "Vincent is always Vincent. Never dull. He did something unusual, though. He pulled down his blindfold and allowed me to see his eyes."

"Oh?"

"They were slightly unnerving." For a split second I almost tell her about his revelation—someone is going to hurt me. I'm not sure it'll make for a good topic of conversation. Nails on a chalkboard couldn't unnerve me as much as his warning has, and the idea of talking about it is even more unsettling. In fact, his revelation has played like an annoying song in my head all day, and just like an annoying song, it's set itself on repeat. I know the best way to stop it is to talk about it, but I don't want to raise any concern for Paige. I'll save that conversation for Jack.

In the past, I've told her a great deal about Vincent, probably more than I should. But even therapists have to blow off steam, talk about their day. I've told her what I know about his childhood, without going into great detail. I've also told her about his quotes he leaves me with sometimes. She loves hearing about him—says he would make a great character in a book. Although, she also knows anything I tell her can't be repeated.

I decide to shift our conversation back to her. "How was your drive? Do the meds seem to be helping with your anxiety about driving?"

"I was okay. I think I'm getting more comfortable with it every time I make myself do it. You'll be proud of me—this time I actually did it without taking any extra medication."

I feel my eyebrows furrow slightly but straighten them before I turn back around. I focus on the polka dots of her shirt, letting my eyes jump from dot to dot to distract myself from sounding irritated. "You really shouldn't neglect taking them if you need them."

The room falls silent for a moment, except for the hum of the fridge and the sizzling on the stove.

"I don't. I did fine with just my anxiety medicine. I want to slowly wean myself off of any kind of meds if I can. You know how I am—holistic approach for me all the way, and the sooner I can get back to that, the better."

I detect a slight defensiveness to her tone, so I move in behind her to run a hand down her arm and rotate her around to face me. "I know you think you'll be fine, but I just feel safer when you follow the doctor's advice. You remember just a little while back, right? Laura had to drive you home because you froze. I can't stop thinking about what could've happened if she hadn't been there. With me leaving for another conference tomorrow, I would just feel better if you follow what's recommended. I even double-checked with Jack— he said all of it's fine even if you get pregnant."

"I'm fine, I promise." She wraps her arms around my waist this time and looks up at me. I smell the strawberry scent of her chapstick. "I have to run a few errands tomorrow and my agent is coming to town to discuss my potential fiction novel. So, if you're worried that much, I promise I'll take everything prescribed. Besides, my apprehension of meeting my agent is much worse than my fear of driving."

"Thank you." I tap the tip of my nose against hers and say, "And just so you know, your novel isn't just potential. It's going to happen and it's going to be a bestseller."

She smiles up at me then stands on her tiptoes and kisses me briefly with soft lips. "I'm glad you have enough confidence in me for the both of us."

I give her a deeper kiss, then look down at her. "You know we could just skip dinner and go straight to bed."

She releases me and shoves me jokingly. "I think I'm going to make you wait."

I slouch over and slump my shoulder in pretend disappointment. She smiles at me and winks with both eyes. Two things Paige can't do—wink with one eye, or raise just one eyebrow. It's as if each side of her face doesn't want to do something without the other. It's cute when she attempts to make either one happen.

After dinner, the two of us sit outside together in a blanket on the extra-large lounge chair. The sound of the ocean's waves are light in contrast to the noisy evening insects. The clouds from earlier have moved on, revealing a clear, darkening sky. Another hint that fall is creeping in.

The rest of our evening is spent in light conversation, but I sense a distractedness in her behavior. Then again, I'm not so sure if it isn't my own distractions that seem to be drawing an invisible wall between us.

"I know I asked you this earlier, but I can't help but wonder if something is bothering you. Did your visit with your mother stress you out?"

"No, not at all. In fact, she was actually pleasant to be around."

"Really? That's surprising."

"Well, maybe pleasant isn't quite the word, but she actually asked me to come back for a visit."

"Whoa. Is she feeling okay?"

"Seems to be. She's just as big a smart-ass as ever," Paige says through a slight laugh.

"Good. Maybe aging is good for her." I smile and kiss the top of her head, then slide down deeper into the chair, pulling her in closer.

I realize I'm probably just being paranoid, deflecting my own behavior by focusing on Paige's. People do that sometimes—project their guilt onto someone else, even when there's nothing to feel guilty about. It's a way to avoid looking too closely at their own flaws.

Am I doing that now? The thought unsettles me, so I shove it aside and remind myself to focus on the moment instead.

Later, we're lying in bed, naked in a spooned position. Our love-making tonight seemed more distant, unlike the usual sex we have when I return home from a trip. I'm not sure if it was me or her that made it more routine, but it was out of character for us. Typically, it's hungrier after I've been gone.

Tonight, Paige insisted on switching sides of the bed, saying she wanted to mix things up a bit. It feels a bit odd lying on my left side. I didn't question it. God knows I will do anything she asks of me. Even though my actions lately may not be ideal for maintaining a healthy marriage, this is truly the one place where I feel safe and completely satisfied.

I know I've been distracted, but she seems to be somewhere else entirely. I've noticed it more often lately. I don't bring it up because I don't want to draw attention to myself. At the risk of sounding repetitive, I decide against asking her again if she's okay—there's no point in both of us losing sleep. My internal monologue feels like a broken record, and I force myself to silence it. Pulling Paige closer, I try to win the battle against sleeplessness.

———

This morning, the same uneasiness consumes me as I take a detour before heading to the hospital. There's something I need to find out.

I park in front of the painted brick apartment building and punch the number 6-1-2-6 into the keypad that allows entrance through the heavy glass door. The code matches the last four digits of a phone number—one that I shouldn't know or use, but it's part of a life that I can't seem to fix or change. It's another life that, for now, I have to keep a secret.

I climb the stairs to the third floor and scan the hall from left to right before I enter the studio apartment. The space has an open floor plan and the only interior walls are those that surround the bathroom. Four wooden posts are spaced in a square pattern for support about the room, and the exterior walls are a faded red brick. I assume it's the color the exterior of the building used to be before it was painted white. The back wall of the apartment is lined with windows from floor to ceiling, and in the center is a disheveled bed which is bathed in morning light. It doesn't appear to have been slept in recently, but the covers are in the same disarray as the last time I lay in it.

I tour the room and search for signs of someone being here recently and find a half-empty bottle of whiskey and three shot glasses on the kitchen bar. I'm completely certain they weren't there the last time I was here. A perplexed expression mixed with a frown seizes my face as I look around more. I step into the bathroom and it looks as though it has been used heavily, with makeup residue on the sink and miscellaneous items in the trash can.

Just as I feared, someone's definitely been here.

Not sure how to feel about that, and knowing there isn't anything I can do about it now, I return to my car. Just as I open the car door, a familiar voice barks my name behind me.

"Michael!"

I take in an exaggerated breath and turn to look at the marked car and meet the appraising eyes of the cop sitting in the front seat.

"What's up, Laura?" I attempt to mask my voice with enthusiasm.

"I'm going to be nice since I know you're just getting home from a work trip by not saying you're playing with fire."

I roll my eyes like a bratty teen. "You just can't help yourself, can you?" I walk toward the driver's side door, lean down, and prop my forearms on the open window.

"What can I say, it's my job."

"As a cop or as my fill-in mother?"

"Both." Laura smiles. "Get in—I'll take you to get some breakfast."

I let out a deep sigh. I climb into the cramped space of the police cruiser next to her mounted laptop and an assortment of coiling cords and buttons. The police radio lets out a static sound, then a man's deep voice blares over the speaker.

Dispatch, this is Unit 24. We have a 10-51, 11-42 needed at the intersection of Maple and 5th. One male, approximately 50 years old, unconscious but breathing. Requesting EMS.

Laura reaches over and turns a knob, quieting the man. "How was your trip?"

"Oh, the usual. Good, bad, and the uglies."

Laura lets out an understanding chuckle. "I have a joke for you. Would you like to hear it?"

I give her a tilted sideways look. "Do I have a choice?"

"What did the elephant say to the shrink?"

I return a playful huff. "Okay, I'll bite."

"Sometimes, even if I stand in the middle of the room, no one acknowledges me."

"Ha. Is this your attempt at therapy?"

"No, but one day you're going to have to acknowledge the elephant in the room. That your double life can't last forever without ending in disaster."

"Laura, you know I can't fix it, change it, or avoid it. It's something I have to do."

"Look, I know you have your reasons, and the shrink in you feels this is necessary in order for you to cope with everything in your life, but I worry that it's all going to blow up in your face."

"It won't. I promise, and when I find an answer, I'll find a way to fix it."

"Contrary to what you've convinced yourself to believe, you can't fix everything."

I inhale deeply. "Just please tell me that you won't stop helping me for now?"

She huffs. "You know I'm always here."

I let out a long exhale and stare out the tinted window at the swelling, stormy sky. "I know."

It's my intent to say more but my words get stuck inside my mind. Words that I truly believe.

But I have to do this. I need to do this.

Laura drops me off to get my car, and I steal one last glance at the building before slipping behind the wheel. The uneasiness lingers as I drive to the hospital, a heavy presence I can't shake. To distract myself, I check in on a few patients before my upcoming trip— anything to keep my mind occupied. I hate having these trips so close together. Especially now.

Of course, Vincent is one of the patients I plan to visit. Not because he's scheduled, but because I need to ease my mind.

This isn't unusual. I'm often on call if Vincent asks for me. So once in a while, I like to make him feel as though I need him—which at the moment, I do. There are times when I visit patients outside of their appointment time to make them feel as though they truly are a priority of mine. I tend to gain just as much from it as they do. It's similar to being a teacher. Often the teacher becomes the student and the student becomes the teacher. And like the teacher, I learn things about myself in the process.

But I suppose today, I do need Vincent more than he needs me. Our last session has turned my life into a game of Trivial Pursuit. My head is so full of questions, and the biggest one in particular is all about me having an enemy, so to speak.

I dart into my office to grab the notepad that always accompanies me when I see him. I can't help but wonder if the quotes he ends our sessions with carry a hidden message. They feel less like words of wisdom and more like pieces of a puzzle he's challenging me to solve. I intend to quiz him about them—that is, if he's receptive to me today. Some days, surprise visits don't sit very well with him and I have to wait until our appointment. Then there are days when he's happy to see me. Well, as happy as Vincent is capable of being.

I enter our hole-in-the-wall office and Trish is already there, sitting under the soft glow of her self-made sanctuary, writing something on a giant desk calendar. Without looking up, she says, "I didn't expect to see you today. I'm pretty sure you don't have any patients scheduled."

"I know, but you know me. I thought I'd check in on a couple. Vincent didn't seem himself yesterday." I lie. It's me that isn't myself.

"Vincent? Two days in a row? He'll either be flattered or irate." She laughs and continues to copy things from her computer onto the old-fashioned calendar. I'm not sure I've ever seen her use something that I thought was a thing of the past.

"What's with the dinosaur calendar?" I ask.

She finally looks up at me with a quirky look on her face. "Between your trips and sporadic visits to patients, Jack's enormous patient load, and the constant questions of where you've been and where you're going, I can't keep up. So, I'm resorting to writing everything down the old-fashioned way. This way, if one of you asks me a question about who you saw and when, all I have to do is look down at this without having to click this and close that. You two come and go so much, I get whiplash."

I nod as I press my lips into an agreeing frown. "Got it." When it comes to Trish, I don't ask a lot of questions. She has a system and messing with it could force this entire practice to crumble.

"You know you could just tell us to look it up ourselves."

"You better not touch anything on my desk." Her tone is jovial but I know she's serious.

I raise both hands in surrender and take a step back. "Yes, boss." I walk backward toward my office and wink at her with one eye.

After I've taken care of some patients' notes, I stuff them into my messenger bag, then head toward the psychiatric section of the hospital. I speak with some of the personnel that works on Vincent's floor to gauge his mood for today to determine if it's a good day to pop in on him. I'm assured he's no less charming than usual, so I tap on his door lightly as I open it.

I don't even make it all the way into his dark room before he says, "I had a feeling you might be back today."

His words immediately send me into regret mode—I wish I hadn't come.

I have to allow my eyes to adjust to the darkened room where the only light is a small reading lamp clipped to the headboard of his bed. Vincent is seated with legs in a v position, knees toward the ceiling, back leaned against the wall. As my eyes begin to adjust I find the one chair in the room, then search his blindfolded face as I try to say with fake confidence, "And what made you think I'd be back?"

"I suppose if you'd told me that someone was going to harm me, I would want to know more. I'm sure you do."

I traipse on the side of caution with my words and tone. "I don't usually believe in dreams, so although it did make me curious, I haven't given it much thought." I lie again. I seem to be doing that a lot lately.

"Who said it was a dream?"

"I'm pretty sure you did." I emphasize the word but immediately get my tone in check to hide my growing frustration and try to appear unenthused.

"I said I had a dream about you, but I didn't say that was what my dream was about. I specifically remember telling you that it would scare you—so I decided to tell you something else instead."

"You were worried it would scare me more than someone is going to hurt me?" I do air quotes around my words as if I were an actor in a teen film, and as if Vincent can see me.

Vincent turns his face away from me as he leans his head back against the wall again. "I'm just not ready to tell you that part yet."

"Don't you think that's a little unfair?"

"Michael, you're soon to be a doctor. You know that life isn't a test you can study for—so therefore it's going to be unfair. It has no other choice."

Frustration bubbles and I push it down. "Then why don't you tell me about your dream. I don't think you would have brought it up if you didn't want to tell me about it."

"I could tell you, but again, you're a psychologist, not an oneirocritic. Even if I told you I don't think you could interpret it."

"Try me. It's not that I want to interpret it, but maybe we could figure out why you might have had the dream in the first place."

"Don't say I didn't warn you."

"I'm sure it will be fine, Vincent. I'm a big boy," I say the words through a deep, frustrating exhale.

Vincent takes in a sharp breath then pauses before he speaks, and something about it makes me regret pushing him to tell me.

"I dreamed I was leaning against a tree. It was dark, as all of my dreams are, and I could hear you crying."

An involuntary swallow rises in my throat.

"It took me a moment to realize where I was. I stood in a cemetery, and the only person I could see was you, sitting alone in a chair beside an open coffin. I walked up behind you to look into the coffin. There was a woman inside, but she looked more like a porcelain doll than a corpse—blond hair, pale, and beautiful. I assumed she was your wife. I touched your shoulder, but you didn't feel it. You had no idea I was there."

He pauses, and I try to steady my thoughts to keep them from spiraling into something unreasonable.

"I walked around you, closer to the coffin. As I took in the rest of her body, she no longer resembled a porcelain doll. She morphed into something straight out of Burton's animated world. Her body was dressed in a tattered corset with the laces clipped and torn. Her legs were wrapped in shredded fishnet stockings, partly hidden by knee-high boots, their crevices caked with mud."

I open my mouth to interrupt, but the words catch somewhere between my vocal cords and my lips, refusing to form. I don't know what to make of his ramblings and at the moment, it's probably better not to play into them.

"I looked back at your wife's face, and the innocence was gone. Her lips were painted crimson, but the color was smeared, as if a hand had dragged across them, streaking like blood down her cheek. Her eyelids were shadowed in black, inked with the permanent stain of a secret life she didn't want anyone to see. But do you know what stood out the most?"

I shake my head even though Vincent isn't aware through his blindfold.

"It was the lock on the inside of her forearm."

"Lock?"

"Yes. I understood it to be out of place. As though she had been marked in some way."

My forehead shifts deep into a frown and I feel my glasses shift away from my face. I attempt to brush off the recount of his dream he's claiming to have had. One that at this point seems a little farfetched, given he has never met my wife. "That's some dream, Vincent."

"How well do you know your wife, Michael?"

His question sparks a slight irritation. "I suppose as good as most husbands know their wives. I'd like to think maybe even a little better."

"Then you know about your wife's double life?"

I stare at Vincent, speechless, while his question sinks in. I do my best to keep my voice steady without responding unprofessionally, but the edge in my tone comes through anyway.

"That's not something you say to a man about his wife, Vincent. Especially to a man who is only here to help you."

"I think I've told you enough for one day, Michael. You're not ready to listen—not yet. But I will tell you this, every choice you make can behave like a knife. Some cut the things that bind us, others can cut even deeper—and when they do, the wound can be deadly. It isn't just yours—it's everyone's. That's the thing about deceptive choices and the consequences that come from them... they're rarely yours alone."

# 9

## Vanessa

I'm not sure how these fuck-fest arrangements started, but they give me a high like none other.

Having an affair is the most addictive drug one can experience. It's the kind of high that lasts for days and the hangover leaves me with erotic memories that only make me want more. It's the act of sneaking around that sends my mind into an anticipation so strong that parts of me ache. A need that can only be fixed by tangling myself up with this forbidden lover—my drug of choice at the moment.

When our liaisons began, he was an uptight, robotic monogamist. He didn't know how to let go and embrace his dark side. It didn't take him long to learn that raw, physical attraction can bandage emotional scars and fulfill needs he didn't know he had.

When he's with me, he lets his animalistic urges free—and I let him release them on me. He gets what he needs, and so do I.

I don't like a yes ma'am kind of man. I like them rough—dominating. That mostly pertains to when we're in bed, or wherever we decide to fuck.

He wasn't like that the first time I laid him. He was gentle, as though he might break me. I shoved him off—called him a pussy. I told him I wasn't a porcelain doll and if he didn't know how to fuck me—go home.

When he got the green light to do whatever he wanted, he gave himself permission to be free and now he sends us both on a regular high that takes days for me to come down from.

The problem with our arrangement is that he always goes home to his wife. Mind you, I don't want to be tied down, but the more I have of him, the more I need him to get high. The worst part is coming down, because when I do, I crash...hard. It sometimes sends me into a sort of madness—makes me want to chase him. I contemplate finding his wife and often daydream on how to get her out of the picture. Make him all mine.

I brought up the subject of his wife in one of our conversations—but only once—I haven't done it again.

The topic of my wife is off limits. As the words leave his lips, his eyes darken and his voice shifts to a tone as though the devil himself can come out of him. It's the first time I've seen this side of him. It's clear that when it comes to her, he plays the role of protector—like he's her savior. I don't get it.

I'm sure she's beautiful. A beautiful man like him wouldn't have anything less. I imagine that I'm the opposite of her. I may be beautiful in my own way but I'm also wilder—freer. I must be, because why else would a man like him seek someone like me out.

I must have been fucked up when he did, because I'm not sure how it all got started, I only remember giving him the night of his life.

He came back for seconds, so what does that say? What I do

know more than anything, is that he had me hooked quicker than any drug I've ever experimented with.

Today, I get to take him in again—and hopefully again and again.

I sit at the bar of The Thirsty Lobster and after taking a shot of liquid courage, I dial his number and immediately hang up.

This lover and I have a system we've worked out when I decide I want fuck him. With a cell phone he provides, I call his and let it ring only once, then hang up. He has my number stored in his phone as Potential Spam. Everyone ignores those calls, so it's easy to disregard it and no one suspects a thing.

The way he responds in return is by using an app called Text Hide. It's an app that uses a password-protected decoy. The app looks like a game and functions like a game. It appears to the outside person as an app for play which uses a password to save your progress. No one wants to start over on a game, so no one would question having a password to get into it. By using this app, we can send each other texts and it stays hidden inside this decoy.

Once he responds, we begin our sexting marathon, and finish it off when we meet. By the time we're able to place hands on one another, we're on fire.

Now that the fun has started, I down one more shot and head toward paradise.

As soon as I enter his apartment today, I find the outfit he's laid out for me on the bed—our primary meeting place. We've used this spot forwards, backwards, and upside down—or at least that's all of the positions he likes to put me in. He can't get enough of my legs thrown over his shoulders, or my feet behind my head. Yoga has its perks.

I pick up the lacy, white thongs and bra, followed by the pleated school-girl skirt. For the last tiny article of clothing, I hook my index finger underneath the silky fabric and hold it in the air as I smile—one of his ties. This last piece tells me he wants it rough tonight. It shifts my smile into a pleasing grin as I contemplate the fun that is about to unfold.

Once I've dressed in the naughty-girl attire, and have loosely situated the tie around my neck, I slip back into my own high-heels and cross the large open room to a small kitchenette. The only thing separating this space from the rest of the apartment is the tavern-style counter that has tall, bar-style chairs along the front. I pull the bottle of whiskey from my bag and pour myself a shot, then sit at the personal bar to wait.

After I pour a shot of whiskey for sipping, a slight click turns my attention to the door. I lean back and prop my legs, stacking one on top of the other, onto the bar. He steps through the door and slings his bag and keys onto the floor, slips out of his shiny, black shoes and proceeds to undress as he walks toward me.

Neither of us say a word.

I squeeze my thighs together in anticipation as his bare chest and broad shoulders are unveiled. Every curve of his muscles are highlighted in the late morning light. God I'm glad this man works out.

He makes his way across the room, wraps a hand around one of my ankles and lifts my leg from the bar. With the other hand, he removes his glasses and slings them onto the counter. He spreads my legs apart, then moves his hips in between them, pressing his hips into mine. I feel his already hardened penis against me as he leans in and gives me a hungry kiss. I slide my other leg from the counter and wrap both around him and squeeze him in as I press my hips harder into his. He lifts his face from mine, then grabs the tie around my neck and tugs on it. Like an obedient dog, I stand and let him lead me toward the bed.

He gives me a gentle shove, forcing me to fall backward onto the crumpled sheets, and he kneels down, hooking his knees underneath each of my spread legs. We crawl like two four-legged animals, one on top of the other, toward the headboard of the bed. He slips the tie over my head and moves it down over my wrists, tightens it, then ties the silk fabric around the bedpost. He stands, leaving me spread diagonally on the bed, and stares down at me with wanting hunger in his eyes.

For more than two hours I let him have anything he wants from any direction he wants. He falls over, exhausted, as I feel the aftereffects from head to toe. The skin of my ass and throat are on fire from intervals of choking, slapping, and biting. I know that I'll be sore tomorrow, but I don't care.

I'll never come down from this one.

I don't want it to end.

I feel as though I could let this man use me forever and I know now, he is the drug I would die for. Or, the one I would kill for.

# 10

P aige

Michael leaves early this morning, but not before kissing me softly on the cheek just before he slips out. Today is another where I no longer resemble a happy, morning person. It's mostly because of my looping train of thoughts.

As I stare out my bedroom window across what is usually a breathtaking view, the hues of gray in the sky bleed together like watercolor on a damp canvas, threatening to shape the course of my day. The sun doesn't seem to rise this morning as the dark clouds block it out. It could very easily portray the downward spiral that seems to be happening in my current state of mind, but I'm determined not to allow the dark mood outside to affect the direction of my internal train of thoughts.

I often feel like this when Michael leaves on one of his trips. It's even stronger now because the unknown seems determined to invade my life far too much lately.

I skip coffee and go straight to showering and getting dressed to meet with my agent. I decide to keep my dress casual—jeans, sweater, and booties with heels. I'm determined to focus my thoughts on the positive—writing my first fiction novel—so I start rehearsing the rough pitch I want to run by my agent.

I've found that writing something and talking about it are two entirely different beasts. I struggle with the talking about it far more than the safe space of writing about it. With my breakfast toast in hand, I look at myself in the foyer mirror and practice what I'm going to say a couple more times.

"A woman begins losing time and waking to strange clues in her apartment—messages, bruises, objects she doesn't recognize..."

I stop and press my palm against my forehead as I search my creative brain for the rest.

"—and must confront the terrifying possibility that either someone is manipulating her... or she's doing it to herself."

I say it flatly. Then again, with more intensity. Then softer, like a secret.

"A woman begins losing time..."

I already hate it.

Not the idea. Just how I sound saying it. Like I'm trying too hard to make it make sense. To make me make sense.

"Or she's doing it to herself," I repeat, under my breath.

I force myself to stop spiraling, to quit second-guessing every thought—just move forward. I wolf down my peanut butter on toast and take my anxiety meds—non-negotiable this morning. Before stepping outside, I grab the little pocket journal I bought to start tracking my every move. I've decided to take Darlene's advice.

I look at my watch and note the time and write beside it, *left the house*. I intend on noting everywhere I go today and what time I get there. The notepad is smaller than my phone and even thinner, so I can easily hide it in my pocket if I want to.

I dart out the door with all the things I need for my meeting and leave the house resolved to keeping my focus set on the intentions of the day. A few errands, my meeting, some writing, and then home.

I park my car in the diagonal parking space in front of the West-side Café. When I swing the door open, a mixture of pleasing smells wafts over me as I enter, which is only shortly after they open. As I'm being seated, I immediately smell their famous clam chowder soup from the booth next to me. My meeting isn't until eleven-thirty, but I wanted to arrive early to prepare myself a little more by rehearsing my pitch in my head in the same environment where I'll do it for real.

I glance around the mostly empty café which hasn't yet begun filling up with the usual lunch crowd. I picked this spot because it's busy enough with distractions and décor, but quiet at the same time. Perfect for redirecting my focus if I feel my nerves taking over.

I hear someone say my name and I look up to see the dark-haired, petite woman and wave to grab her attention.

"Never mind, I see her," she says as she walks toward me. She slides into the booth across from me. "Hello dear, how are you?"

"Hi, Grace. I'm good. How are you?"

"Oh, you know. Buried in mounds of manuscripts from dreaming writers."

"I'm sure."

"I'm so excited to hear some more of your ideas for the new book. I know you sent some of these thoughts in the email, but I'd like to hear more. Besides, it's a good way for us to catch up." Grace removes her red suit jacket and pulls at the black, silky collar of her blouse, revealing a small hint of cleavage. She's probably in her mid to late thirties but looks just as young as I. As far as I know, she's single with no children. She doesn't strike me as the type that would want to settle in one place with one person for very long. She rubs her hands together. "So—your first fiction novel. How exciting."

The waitress comes by the table to bring us a glass of ice water and to take our order. We inform her that we only want coffee at the moment.

"So, tell me—what are your thoughts about this book?"

"It's not fully formed yet," I say, swirling my coffee nervously, "but I keep coming back to this woman—she's... losing time. Waking up with markings or bruises, strange objects in her apartment, maybe strange messages. She's scared she's losing her mind, but wonders what if it's something else? Something darker? Maybe she's being manipulated. Or maybe she's doing it to herself. I don't know." I pause, then force a smile. "I guess I'm still trying to figure out the best direction to go with the story."

I keep talking, letting the ideas spill out—plot points, flashes of scenes, the shape of the main character as she forms in my mind.

Grace leans forward, interest piqued. "So it's a psychological thriller? Unreliable narrator kind of thing?"

"Exactly." I nod. "But instead of just playing with what's real and what's imagined, I want to explore that terrifying moment when even you don't trust your own mind."

Grace takes a sip of coffee, then sets it back down. "I love it. I say go for it." Grace's phone pings with a text message, so she picks it up to read. "Sorry, I have to respond to this."

I lift the cup to my lips and savor the aroma feeling my nerves settle a little, yet still unsettled at how real it all sounds. As I sip my coffee, my eyes scan the café. The room has filled with more patrons scattered about the tables and booths. For some reason, I get a sudden feeling of unease. It's subtle at first, just a faint prickle, but I get the feeling that I'm being watched. I scan the room a little slower this time and try to pass it off as nothing more than lingering worries.

I occupy myself with looking up at the painted, wooden canoe that hangs upside down over the bar area and the hanging plants placed pleasingly around the room.

It does nothing. I still feel as though I'm being watched.

I allow my gaze to shift, flicking my eyes from one face to another trying to find the source of what's making me feel uncomfortable. In the far corner of the room I lock eyes with a man who looks out the window quickly when our eyes meet. I watch him a moment longer and look back down at my coffee as I bring it to my lips, blow on it, and try to convince myself I'm being paranoid.

I sense his eyes on me again, and I shoot mine upward. He looks away again.

There's something about his eyes—they're almost familiar, yet I don't think I've ever seen him before in my life. He keeps looking at me as if he knows me.

But why do I feel as though I've looked into those eyes before? Or eyes very similar to them. Something about them sends a chill down my spine and for some reason I want to run from the restaurant.

I'm being silly, I know.

"I think your ideas are great, Paige. I say get to work on a synopsis, or a rough outline, and email it to me as soon as you can."

Grace's words snap me back into focus.

"Um—yeah." I say, and my own words sound far off for a second.

"Are you alright?"

I realize that I'm gripping the coffee cup so hard the tips of my fingers are turning white. I take a quick breath and exhale, attempting to shake it off. "Yes, sorry. I'm just running through my list of things I have to do today." I breathe in deep again and set my cup down. "So, you think I have a good start?"

"Yes, you have a good solid foundation for your story."

I fake a smile and briefly look to the man again. He stands from his chair and pulls his wallet from his back pocket and throws some money onto the table. He turns his head toward me one last time, not quite looking at me, his stance tall, chest out. He's handsome, in a bad-boy sort of way.

I'm not sure if he sensed me looking at him or if he intended to look back at me as he shoves his wallet back into his pocket. I think I have my answer when he looks me straight in the eye. An involuntary shudder courses through me and for a split second I think I see one side of his mouth cock upward, revealing a deep dimple on his right cheek, before he turns and leaves the restaurant.

I feel myself begin to shake as I look back to Grace, not really seeing her.

She doesn't seem to notice. She's rambling on about something she needs to do back at the office. The rest of her words barely seem to register.

"I—." My words don't want to form as I look back to where the man was standing, still stuck on the last look in his eyes. I clear my throat as I slowly turn my head back to Grace and attempt to speak again. "Thank you."

"I think you'd better get started," Grace says as she looks back down at her busy phone.

I'm still shaken even as I try to shake it off. But one question keeps looping through my mind—

*why did he act like he knew me?*

# 11

M ichael

Panic, as a result of Vincent's words, hits me like a sudden drop in an elevator, my stomach threatening to lurch, and at the moment I feel as if there's no way to stop the fall. No matter how hard I try, I'm not able to distract myself from his last question—*how well do you know your wife?*

It manages to steal my thoughts, which land perfectly on an endless loop...again. According to him, I may die, and Paige has a double life.

He's never met Paige. Why would he dream about her, and how would he have the slightest idea of what she looks like? He doesn't know her and he can only be assuming. He's just trying to get into my head. But through our conversation, he was able to describe Paige perfectly. Her body lying in a coffin. Dead.

He said something about a lock on her arm. That doesn't make sense either. None of this does. Maybe he meant locket. Or maybe lock is a metaphor for something else—something's locked away, or something that can't be seen or reached.

Why am I listening to a patient in a psych ward? There's no scientific explanation behind this, just Vincent's ramblings. But his last words are hard to shake. *Paige has a double life.* As the words cross my mind, I hear how absurd they sound. I'm not going to let him get inside my head.

I literally shake my head in an attempt to stop thinking about it.

Maybe it's my own guilt leading me to this conclusion.

Vincent's final thought wasn't from some famous thinker, it was his. A warning. But what does Vincent know? He sits in a psych ward, alone, and in the dark.

I step outside the hospital into the crisp, cool air as the sun attempts to smile down on everything—unlike myself. I approach a familiar face from the hospital, but my ability to smile back at the moment has been blocked out by the dark cloud of Vincent's dream, so I just nod and keep walking toward my car.

As I cross the hospital parking lot, I attempt to call Paige, feeling the need to hear her voice. Maybe she can distract me by telling me about her meeting with her agent.

She doesn't answer.

I look at my watch and realize she may still be in the meeting. Since the attempt at a distraction fails, my mind immediately goes back to the mental maze it's been trapped in all morning.

I pause at my car and prop my forearms on top of it and stare off into the distance, not really seeing anything in front of me. Maybe I'm just reading too much into all of this.

Paige and I have a somewhat long and touchy history. She was actually my first. She took my virginity and my heart, then disappeared. She wasn't ready to settle down.

I didn't see her again for four years. During my senior year at college, she floated back into my life—carefree, fun, and everything in between. She was all the things I was looking for. I admired the way she took a shitty childhood and turned herself into a walking, self-help guide, handling life with calm and ease. It seems she has always been the calm to my storm. The secure life everyone wants.

Even though we've both found the life that everyone seeks, we aren't short of flaws, secrets, and imperfections. I suppose this is true for many couples, and I'm not so naive to think that anyone is immune to bad habits or bad decisions.

I'm no exception. I often feel like a wandering pet—always searching for something. Not out of curiosity or because I think the grass is greener on the other side, but because I need to feel less invisible. Noticed, validated—important. I know that most of these unsettling urges have to do with my troubling childhood, but I feel as if I should be doing even more than I already am to give back to the world. As though I'm racing against the clock of my own life.

I suppose it's why I've chosen to do the one thing that could rip my marriage apart.

Just as the thought crosses my mind, it's as if my demon finds me in the ring of my cell phone. One ring, then it abruptly silences. An eyebrow raises in slight confusion at its timing. I know who it is and hearing from her this time of day is unusual.

Displayed on the screen is *Potential Spam*.

My heart rate skips into overdrive with a rush of adrenaline.

Then a separate notification appears.

It's my gaming app of choice. I look around me to make sure there isn't anyone I know nearby before I check it. Anyone who uses it knows that it really isn't for a game and I'm like a teenage boy logging on to check it.

I tap the fake app and a pop-up message prompts me to enter a password. When I do, a rectangle-shaped box appears and inside it are the words: *secret626 has sent you a message*.

I tap it.

*I want to fuck you!*

A shiver of excitement courses through me, followed by an immediate shift to my train of thought. The timing is a perfect distraction, yet not ideal either—but is it ever ideal for something like this? In many ways it's just what I need, but it also means I have to shift my schedule around to make it happen. When this woman calls, I can't let her down. When I text back, our sexting begins.

Then I aim to please.

I begin immediately shifting my schedule and book a later flight.

Another message appears.

*First, I want you to fuck my mouth.*

At the next stoplight I check the app to read her next message, already feeling an erection starting in the anticipation of opening it. Then I respond while watching for the light to turn green again.

*Then I'll fuck you forward and backward.*

With each text, my need grows, making the never-ending stoplights grueling.

*I want you to cum all over me.*

I make the last turn and park in front of the apartment building.

*I'm going to. Two minutes.*

Regardless of the excitement I feel, I still hesitate right before I enter the apartment building and question whether I'm doing the right thing or not. Despite the physical enjoyment I get from my visits here, I'm here because this woman needs me just as much as I need her. She just doesn't know it. I think it's why I don't let my hesitation turn me away.

I punch in the code to enter and take the stairs to the top floor apartment—it's never locked unless the two of us are inside.

When I step through the door, my eyes land immediately on the dark side of paradise sitting on a barstool chair. Her legs are propped on the counter and my tie is loosely knotted around her neck, ready for me to lead her into a world that takes me away from mine and her away from hers.

This woman is the embodiment of the eighth deadly sin. She surpasses all of the things that make sin...a sin. I can't resist her, nor have I been able to fix her—I just know that I have to save her. In turn, she's saving me.

I tie her wrists inside the loop of my tie and secure it around the bedpost, then stand and stare down at her as my body responds to its full potential at what I'm about to do.

I grab both her ankles and guide her to roll onto her stomach, then force her legs wider with my knees as I crawl on top of her. I fist a handful of hair and tilt her head backwards and begin a parade of kissing and biting her neck, then move down the back of her body repeating it over and over.

For the next two hours, I worship her, torture her, and fuck her just as she begs for, then fall over, exhausted beside her.

The tie around her wrists has long been removed, and she lies on her side next to me, breathing just as hard as I am.

Once my breathing has calmed and I'm coming down from it all, I glance at my watch. Vanessa raises her head from the mattress and rests it in her hand as she props her elbow onto the bed.

"Let me guess—you're going to fuck me and run."

I smile at her. "I still have a few minutes before I have to go."

"A dick and a bit is all I ever get. You know, despite the fact that I'm pretty much a cold-hearted bitch, I do still have feelings."

"Since when?"

"Ouch."

"I'm joking." I sense a sudden insecure side to Vanessa that I've never seen before. She always comes off with this rough exterior but today I see something different in her eyes. "What's wrong?"

She rolls away from me, then hops from the bed and walks across the room naked, then disappears into the bathroom. After a couple minutes she parades naked to the bar where our evening first began. She picks up her shot of whiskey, then turns around and leans back against the counter, propping one elbow on it while taking a drink with the other hand. "Maybe I'm getting tired of being nothing more than a fuck for you."

"Since when?"

She ignores the question. "I almost followed you the other day."

"When?"

"Don't freak out, I didn't. But, I'd like to see where you live—what your wife looks like. It'd be nice to know why you rush out of here all the time."

"You know that I'm married, Vanessa. So leave it alone."

"So it is her you rush off to?"

"I've told you before—the discussion of my wife is off limits."

"Why? I haven't even heard you say her name. Why is it such a secret?"

"That's none of your business." I stand from the bed and begin to gather my clothes strewn across the floor.

"I guess she's too precious for me to know anything about her?"

I glance at my watch again then turn to look at her. "You and I fuck. We have a blast doing it. I've never told you that it's going to be anything more than that. Now, if you'd like to tell me all about yourself, I'm all ears. I'll listen all day to anything you want to tell me."

She downs the rest of her whiskey, then turns to pour another shot. I drop my clothes into a pile on the floor and immediately march over to take the bottle from her hand. "You've had enough of this."

Shock takes over her expression then anger steals it as her eyes narrow. "You're not my fucking father." She attempts to grab the bottle from my hand and I hold it high over her head.

Still naked, she jumps to grab it and I find it amusing as my eyes move down just in time to see her bare breasts bounce. I can't help but grin and say, "Do it again."

She punches me fairly hard in the stomach and it forces a cough through a laugh. The whole situation begins to lighten the mood and as I'm still holding the bottle over my head I wrap the other arm around her mid-back and pull her naked body against me. I press her back against the counter as I set the bottle down and mesh my fingers through her hair. I grip a fistful and pull her back over the bar top, then bring my mouth close to hers but stop just short of our lips touching. Our breathing merges, slowly increasing in pace and intensity.

"You want to fuck me again?" she asks.

One side of my mouth lifts into a devious grin.

"Tell me your wife's name and I'll let you fuck me as much as you want."

It immediately rattles me, so I release her and occupy myself by grabbing the bottle of whiskey and placing it high above her reach onto the top row of cabinets. I feel her narrowed stare as I finish picking up my clothes and say, "How about instead, you tell me more about yourself? You haven't exactly been an open book, you know."

Regardless of the fact that I'm fucking this woman and enjoying every second of it, I'm still here to help her.

"I'm a good lay. The way I see it, that's all you seem to care about. That, and your wife, apparently. She's too precious to even say her name to your mistress."

I get the feeling she's trying to get under my skin. It's working so I proceed to get dressed and attempt to turn the conversation back to her again. "Are there skeletons hidden in your closet that you don't want me to find?"

"I think you're the one with skeletons and as far as I can tell, I'm one of them."

Her words sting, but they're true.

I decide not to comment, which I know will either piss her off or force the whole subject to drop for now. I'm not going to get through to her today.

She huffs and thankfully she drops it. "So when will I see you again?"

I walk back to her and reach out to brush a hand across her cheek. She leans her face away to prevent my touch, then looks me in the eye. God knows I can't resist this woman. "You know that all you have to do is message me and I'll be here."

Her silent stare stabs me in the gut. I know that's what she intends.

"I'll see you soon, I promise."

"Why? Because you feel sorry for me? Don't. I don't need anyone."

"Yes, you do. Whether you want to admit it or not, you do need me."

Her eyes narrow, but even as they try not to show that I'm right, I can still see disappointment and a lost look in them.

As I step out the door, I'm torn between telling her the truth and staying the course that I know I have to take—for everyone's sake.

# 12

D arlene

**Twenty-five years ago**

"So this is how it is? You catch me working then make a beeline to the bar without me?" a voice says next to me.

I turn to see Christian standing there, and the first initial look in his eye isn't a look I've seen before. What I thought looked like irritation doesn't last long as it fades into his pretty dimpled smile.

"Don't be jealous because you had to work and I get to sit here and have a beer." I tease as I turn to hug him.

He hugs me back, then plucks at my crop top which shows off a tiny peek of my belly button. "Coming in here dressed like this is enough to make any man jealous." His eyes quickly scan the room before looking back at me, his eyebrows raised but still smiling. His tone is teasing, but I sense a slight sincerity to his voice.

I move my arms up to wrap them around his neck and press my body to his. "Don't tell me that my handsome green-eyed man is a little jealous?" I tease some more, enjoying the idea of him caring enough about me that he doesn't want anyone else looking at me. Something about it makes me feel special.

"Well, there isn't a man in here that wouldn't want to take you into his bed, or woman for that matter." He presses his body back against mine and rocks us gently from side to side as if we're slow dancing. "But in all seriousness, I really don't like you coming here without me."

Something about his jealousy is flattering. I don't know why, but I love it and hate it all at the same time. Maybe it's because it's the first time anyone has ever shown they care about me this deeply before. It matches everything else about him—sexy dangerous. I eat it up even though I know I should probably run.

I pull my upper body back a little to take in his whole face.

"Seriously? I've been coming here a lot longer than we've been together."

"I'm not a man who likes to share." He gives me a quick peck on the lips. "I want to be the only one who sees that sexy stomach of yours." He squeezes me tighter. "But I guess you better flaunt it while you can because once we have a house full of kids that'll all change."

I lift my eyebrows. "Kids? I'm never having kids."

He freezes for a moment and frowns. "What?"

"What? You mean you want kids?"

"Well yeah. I want a whole house full," he says, releases me, and grabs my hand. "Come on. I think it's time for you to meet someone."

"What? Who?"

"Just come. I'll show you." He laughs, then takes my hand and leads me to his truck. I climb into the passenger seat and ask, "Got any beer in here?"

"You know I do." He reaches into the small backseat and opens a cooler strapped in behind me, then drops the silver can onto my lap, forcing a gasp as the cold aluminum hits my bare legs.

"You asshole."

"Don't forget it." He cocks his mouth to the side, showing a deep dimple, and I can't help but smile back.

I open the beer and take a large gulp, then place it in the cup holder between us. The stereo speakers boom bass from his souped-up sound system and I recognize the opening guitar riff of the Aerosmith song, prompting me to turn up the radio. As we're heading away from town, I take out a hand-sized notepad and pen from my purse to note that this is the fourth beer of the evening, then ask, "Where are we going?"

He looks at me and grins, then says, "You'll see."

"I mean it. I like to know where I'm going."

"I want it to be a surprise."

"Then just give me the address. You don't have to say where it is exactly. I like to write down where I'm going and who I'm with."

"What's with this obsession of writing everything down?"

"It's a habit. I don't question your weird quirks."

"That's because I don't have any." He looks at me and winks.

"Oh, but you do. Lots of them."

"Name one."

"You keep your fingernails longer on your left hand than you do your right, like some cocaine addict."

"Maybe I am."

I give him a questioning look. "I can tolerate booze—drugs are out of the question."

"I don't. Well, maybe occasionally, but I play the guitar and I like the precision of using my nails to pick a song. Plus, they come in handy for other things, as you should know." He bounces his eyebrows as he reaches over and scratches his nails slowly from the tip of my shoulder down my arm.

I shiver. "Address?"

"Okay, we're going to seventeen Sea Sid Lane. Happy now."

I nod and write it down.

"Why the secrecy?"

"I figured if I told you before now, you'd have run like hell."

"Now I'm scared." I say it in a teasing tone, but I get a sudden feeling of apprehension.

He turns his souped-up Dodge Ram down a one-lane road barely wide enough to fit his truck. On either side, dense thickets of brush and trees crowd the road, and with the headlights cutting through the overgrowth, it feels like we're driving through a tunnel. Along the way I look for houses nestled among the trees, but aside from the two at the road's entrance, there aren't any. There's not a single address or road sign in sight, as if this road were never meant to exist.

We reach an opening, and a two-story wooden-sided house comes into view. There are only a couple of windows where light is visible, but the rest of the house is pitch black. The full moon illuminates everything around it, giving it an almost creepy vibe.

"Do you live here?"

"Home sweet home."

"I wondered when you were going to grow some balls and show me where you lived. I was beginning to think maybe you were homeless."

The headlight beams bounce off the trees on either side of the house as a gust of wind blows through, sending leaves through the air in a chaotic pattern. Wind chimes resound from the dark porch but not in a serene or inviting way—they clang in a hollow, creepy melody and something suddenly stirs in my gut.

"I figured it's about time I told you everything." He twists his body in his seat to face me then says, "Hell, you can't get away from me now—I hold the key to your freedom." He taps his arm where the tattooed key is and gives me a sadistic grin.

My face involuntarily frowns as I stare at him, my words coming out slowly. "What's going on?"

A movement catches my attention and I turn to see the front door of the house open. A small boy runs outside. Christian removes the key from the ignition and gets out of the truck, slamming the door behind him. I watch as he walks around the vehicle and places a hand on the boy's head, then ruffles his hair as he says something, but I can't quite make out what he says. He turns to look at me then waves for me to get out of the truck.

I'm speechless and paralyzed. *He has a kid?* The words go through my head disbelievingly as I finally bring myself to open the door and step from the vehicle. I sidle along the side of the truck toward them, feeling as though I've left my voice behind.

"Darlene, this is my boy, Donovan."

I stare at the boy, wide-eyed, and open my mouth to speak but my words come out barely more than a whisper. "Hi."

"Hi," he says and gives a shy wave, looking up at me only briefly.

"You get your chores done?"

The boy answers without looking up at his father. "Yes."

"Good. Go on in. We'll be there in a minute."

I stare after the boy, baffled, and even my mind doesn't know what to say other than to repeat itself.

*He has a kid.*

# 13

## Vanessa

Why does it feel as though my heart has left its normal spot in my chest as if it will never return until I see him again? I've never felt this stupid need for anyone before, and I despise it.

He walks out the door and I immediately crumble onto the bed. At first, the feelings that course through me could be compared to a cocaine addict being told they'll never snort another line again. Immediate panic courses through my veins and quickly shifts to insecurity mixed with the beginnings of rage. Each emotion starts to burn inside me like a wildfire threatening to destroy all of my self-control not to follow him.

The silence of the room becomes deafening, and it only makes the battle that's beginning in my head louder. A battle of *should I or shouldn't I follow him.*

The battle is won when the question is answered... *I shall.*

I slam my legs into my low-rise skinny jeans and hop as I hurriedly pull them over my hips, then pull and tug them into place as they hug my curves from hips to ankles. With my black lace bra fastened in place, I cover it with an equally black, fishnet crop-top that I left here on a previous occasion. Lastly, I slip into a pair of black stiletto heels. I dart into the bathroom to quickly check my face in the mirror, tidy up my smeared makeup, and jerk a brush through my bedhead hair. After I've shoved my things into my bag, I pause and look at the disheveled bed once more and feel an ache in my stomach at the thought of leaving it already.

All I want to do is stay in it—with him.

I hesitate a moment longer, then say aloud, "Fuck it. I'm going."

After carefully descending the stairs, I step outside and feel a bit disoriented as the bright afternoon sun blinds me. I prefer nighttime and the life that goes with it. Nightlife has a way of making me feel alive.

My heels tap the concrete sidewalk as I head toward the parking lot, which is located around the side of the building. I get a sudden feeling that I'm being watched or followed when I spot movement to my left. I turn my head slightly to look, then look straight ahead again when I see the cop car creeping alongside me.

"Do you need some help?" the policewoman asks from the open passenger window.

I frown, then turn my head all the way to the left to see that the cop is indeed a woman. I tilt my head up slightly as if to show confidence—or maybe it's defiance—and say, "Do I look like someone who needs help?"

"You seem a little lost." The cop turns her head to look around. "You're a little out of place for this part of town, or this time of day."

I feel my eyebrows squeeze together as I stare at her. A cool breeze washes over me, stinging my bare stomach while it penetrates the holes of my top. I feel my nipples respond, so I hook my arms across my chest, lean into one leg with my hip stuck out to the side, and attempt to position my body in a stance that screams annoyance. "The last I checked, walking down a sidewalk isn't a crime, and I can be wherever I want to be, whenever I want to be."

"There's no need for an attitude. I'm just doing my job."

"Harassing people for just walking down the sidewalk?" As the words leave my mouth with sarcasm, it occurs to me that I've encountered this cop before. Of course, I was drunk—really drunk—so I don't remember much about that night. I'm pretty sure she didn't arrest me because I didn't wake up in jail. But I *do* remember being in the back seat of her patrol car.

"This attitude of yours is what got you into trouble before."

She remembers me as well.

"I'm just heading to my car—that's all." There's something about this cop that annoys me. I do remember that she wasn't so nice that night she picked me up outside a bar. I think that's just how it is with cops—they target you once you've been put on their radar. Now that I think about it, I've seen her several times. Maybe this is her part of town to patrol. But there's something about her I don't like.

"So where're you headed?"

"I don't think that's any of your business."

"Work? The store? A street corner? Being dressed like that in the daytime either means you're taking the walk of shame, or heading somewhere to make some money."

Her words immediately light a fire under me. "Some of us have the body to wear whatever we want whenever we decide to wear it."

The cop turns her head to stare forward, her wrist draped over the steering wheel as she chews on her jaw for a second. Her profile shows a neat bun pinned tightly against the back of her head, then she turns her judging stare back toward me. Another puff of wind blows a brunette strand of hair that has escaped from her military-style bun. She brushes it away as she raises an eyebrow. "I suppose. Do you live here or just visiting?"

"Again, I don't think that's any of your business."

"Oh, but it is. Especially in this area. I've had a report of a distur-bance in this complex, so it's up to me to figure out who's causing it."

"I assure you, it isn't me." I tilt my head to the side, giving the cop my best version of a bratty teen bored with this conversation.

"Well, I have to check out all of the people coming and going from this building closely. Let me pull my car into that spot up there," she points, "then we can talk."

I start to open my mouth, but it does me no good. She's already pulling forward, then parallel parking into a spot. I haven't done anything wrong, but something about being questioned by a cop—whether it's being pulled over for speeding, or in this situation—makes the wrong kind of adrenaline mess with my cardiovascular system, and as she approaches me, my respiratory system insists on being a bitch as well.

I attempt to dress my mental self back into the confident woman that I'm actually dressed as before I speak. "Is this going to take long? Because I'm in a hurry."

The cop walks with confidence toward me as she presses and tucks at all of the gear strapped around her waist. It all squeaks like shiny new shoes with each step.

"Can I see your license and registration?"

I try to hide my *what the fuck do you want to see that for* expression. I glance down at her name badge and say, "Well, Officer Laura Walker, if I'm not in my car, why do you need to see that?" I'm sure my tone spews attitude.

"It's just procedure. At least a license?" she asks as politely as I've ever heard an officer speak. Something about it makes me skeptical.

I narrow my eyes at her in frustration but try to contain it. If I don't cooperate with her, I'm stuck here longer.

I dig into my bag and shuffle through makeup paraphernalia, worn black stockings, and, just like the Prince song, a pocket full of horses—Trojan, and some of them used. But I can't find a license or even a wallet to hold them.

"Is something wrong?" the officer asks.

I hesitate. "I seem to have misplaced my wallet."

"Maybe it's in there." She points toward the apartment complex and raises her eyebrows. "That is where you just came from—right?"

For some unknown reason, I don't want to tell her that. Maybe it's because I don't want to have to explain that I was in one of those apartments with a married man. There's something about a cop's demeanor that makes me believe they're born with a moral compass and would never do anything immoral, like cheat on a spouse or tell a little white lie. I don't know why I care, but there's something about this woman that switches on my own moral compass—not that I've ever had one.

"Well, if you can't find your wallet, then I guess I'll just have to settle for you telling me where you're headed."

"Again, I don't see how that's any of your business. But, I'm heading to see a friend."

"And where is that?"

I'm becoming agitated so I answer through a huff. "Harbor Ridge Road. Now, if you'll excuse me, I have to go."

The officer holds her hands up as if she's been told to put them up and steps aside. "Sorry if I've held you up. Have a good rest of your day."

I stomp down the sidewalk, annoyed with the officer, and decide to hit a bar for a drink instead. I'm too frustrated now to follow Michael and decide that getting into some mischief to spite him would be better. *If I can't have his full attention, I'll just go find it somewhere else.*

# 14

# Darlene

**Twenty-five years ago**

I wait for the kid to disappear back into the house before I attempt to speak, not quite sure if my vocal cords will cooperate. My words manage to form barely above a whisper. "Don't you think this is a detail that should have come up at some point? Like maybe on our first date."

"Then you would have never climbed into my truck that night to go people watching with me. You were the one who told me that you kicked a man in the balls that same night we met when he said something about a baby."

He steps in close to me and slides his hands along my sides and around to my low back, pulling me against him. I lean my upper body back away from him to look him in the eye, feeling somehow... betrayed.

"But you have a kid and it never occurred to you that maybe you should tell me?" I ask again. "You purposefully hid this from me."

He sways our bodies from side to side as he presses his hips to mine, performing his loving move as if we're dancing. His attempt at affectionately smoothing things over forces a smile that I'm not quite ready to give yet. I don't know if I'm upset or just shocked. I think a little of both.

"Look, I know I should have told you."

"Yes... you should. How would you feel if I had a kid and didn't tell you?"

"You're right. I'm sorry. I just felt like I needed to wait until the time was right."

I look past his shoulder at the trees behind him as I attempt to identify what I'm feeling.

"I tell you what—just hang out here for a bit until you're ready to come in and really meet him. I understand if you need a minute to process it." His tone shifts deeper and a bit snappier. "But you have to understand, he is my kid. There's nothing I can do about that, and you're just going to have to accept it."

He disappears into the house and I lean back against the truck, wrap my arms around myself, and take a moment to understand how I feel about all of this. I'm not sure I'm ready to play house just yet. Knowing he has a kid changes this relationship entirely. Part of me wonders how he kept it a secret this long. We've spent so much time together. How could he not have let it slip? Why didn't he? Have I made him think that he couldn't? Did he think I might run off if I found out? I don't hate kids that bad, but I've definitely made it clear that I don't want kids anytime soon.

Part of me wants to run like hell, but the other part of me sort of understands his reservation about telling me. I've made it clear that I don't want kids. But it seems there are only two choices here—accept it and hold on to the best thing that's ever happened to me. Or, don't and lose Christian completely.

I don't want that to happen, but part of me is still upset that he would deliberately deceive me.

I'm not sure how long I stand in the same spot internally arguing with myself, but it's long enough that my hands have turned to ice and my toes are beginning to ache. My internal monologue consists of trying to figure out what bothers me more—the fact that he has a kid or the fact that he didn't tell me about it. Either way, I need to make a move. If I stand out here too long, he's going to think I'm completely against it. I don't want to mess up what we have.

I finally succumb to a *fuck it* mentality and decide there could be no harm to going inside just to see what life is like behind the closed doors of Christian's life. It's a kid, not a disease. Although, for myself, getting pregnant with one might be a different story. I'm not committing to that by accepting this, and as long as he doesn't insist on having kids with me right now, then everything will be fine.

"I can handle this," I say aloud and drag my feet toward the house.

With a light tap on the door, I don't wait for anyone to answer. I just ease it open and speak softly as I enter. "Hello?"

I step directly into a dark living room, small and lightly furnished. A worn-out brown couch sits on the opposite wall and a matching recliner adjacent to it. It's even more worn out than the couch, tilted slightly, the seat bottom sagging in the middle. As my eyes wander over the walls of the room, I notice sporadic patches of drywall mud or white paint scattered across the surface. They seem as though they were hastily applied to cover some underlying flaw, yet the patches themselves are imperfect. Instead of hiding the imperfections, they draw attention to it.

I hear dishes clanging from the lit room to the left of the couch, and I assume it's the kitchen. To the left of that is a set of dark, wooden stairs with twin railings that line both sides and steep steps that disappear into the ceiling. On the other side of the stairs is a small dining room, the table small with only four chairs. The walls are bare but have more of the strange splotches of paint. The furnishings around the house are minimal and worn. It looks and feels like a bachelor pad, but it's spotless. With a kid living here, I would expect to see toys scattered. As far as decor, it's obvious there hasn't been a woman's touch here in a long time.

With hesitance at first, I take a deep breath and cross the room toward the open doorway, and just as I'm halfway, a movement in my peripheral forces me to freeze. At the base of the stairs, and just on the other side, crouches a boy staring at me in what I could only describe as wide-eyed wonder. His eyes are familiar, but young and innocent, yet I see fear in them. Almost a pleading expression.

He appears to be around seven or eight years old, I'm not sure. I haven't made it a habit of observing children. His face is smudged with dirt, and the hand wrapped around a spindle of the stair railing reveals long fingernails, dark and caked with grime beneath. I remain frozen, transfixed on him when a deep voice startles me so badly that it feels as though my heart might leap from my chest.

"I see you decided not to run."

I open my mouth to speak as I turn to look back at the boy.

He's gone.

Donovan steps from around the doorway of the kitchen to stand beside his father. I turn to look again, but I still don't see the other green-eyed child. I'm now wondering if I had seen him in the first place.

Between the sudden spike in my heart rate and the mysterious boy, I stutter before I can speak clearly.

"Uh, yeah." I look at Christian then back toward the stairs. "I guess I've had time to swallow it."

He takes a couple of steps toward me and says in a partially teasing manner, "You've never had trouble swallowing before."

His dirty innuendo conjures a slight chuckle, but I only manage to give a half smile. I look at the little boy standing next to him and ask, "How old is he?"

Christian frowns at first, then says, "Donovan? Oh, he's eight."

"You let him stay home by himself?"

"He's a tough boy. He can handle it."

I hesitate. "So, he's your only kid?"

"Yeah, why?"

I glance back at the stairs again. "You don't have another kid," I say the words in a half-question, half-statement.

"As far as I know. Unless some skank from the past shows up on my door claiming I knocked her up."

I'm not sure what kind of face I pull because Christian frowns at me.

"What's that face about?"

*If you don't have another kid, then you have a ghost,* I almost say, then change my mind. I glance at the boy standing next to him and realize that it would probably scare him. I have no idea how to behave around kids. "Nothing." I shake my head and erase the look on my face.

"There's some mac-n-cheese if you're hungry."

"I think I'd better get home, I have to be at the factory at seven in the morning."

"I guess you're shit out of luck tonight. I got to get Donovan in the bed for school tomorrow."

"Christian, I don't have extra clothes, a toothbrush—nothing."

"Sleep naked."

"I can't miss work."

"I'll take you early enough in the morning to get to work."

He turns and disappears back into the kitchen, leaving me standing in the middle of the room with a kid who just stares up at me with a sheepish look on his face.

"Donovan. Get in here and clean up your mess." Christian calls, and the boy immediately turns and runs back into the kitchen as well.

I stand still trying to understand what just happened, but it's as if Christian has made his mind up and he's not going to take me home. I feel speechless and slightly upset. To the point I have a strong urge to turn and stomp out—walk all the way back to town. But I know I'm not going to do that either.

I decide to make the best of it and enjoy the rest of the night.

# 15

Vanessa

What is it about being told you can't do something that makes you shift into a bratty teen, determined to do it anyway?

We're all like that. I don't care who you are; there will always be that young rebel inside us until the day we die. Even old folks, who may no longer be able to act on it physically, mentally return to those rebellious years—especially when a younger person tries to tell them they can't do something. I'm sure I'll become one of those cantankerous old women who dares anyone to tell me I can't do something —I'll do it or die trying.

Michael behaved as if I were some underaged junkie by taking the whiskey from me. More or less treated me as if I were a child, then abandoned me.

Then there was the cop who seems to keep showing up wherever

I am. The one who treated **me** like a hooker. I may love sex, but I don't sell it. I'm fine with giving it away for free. Why wouldn't you when it's so damn good?

I swing the door open at The Thirsty Lobster and enjoy the sound of my heels tapping the hardwood floor as I make my way to the bar. It draws just the right amount of attention from the men in the room.

"You're back," says the tattooed bartender. "Same?"

"Yep." I hop up onto the tall tavern chair and rest my forearms on the counter.

He sits a shot glass in front of me and fills it to the rim. I down it, then tap the glass down in his direction—who hasn't yet put the bottle away—as if he's expecting me to want another. He pours it, then moves on down the bar to talk to a group of women who had his attention before I came in.

I look around the bar hoping to see the green-eyed devil I've drank with before in this same tavern. He's sexy, fun, and the perfect revenge to get back at Michael for running back to his needy little wife.

I don't see him at first, but then I spot his intense stare locked in my direction from a table in the corner of the room. He cocks one side of his mouth into a wicked smirk and I do the same.

Revenge never looked so hot.

He raises his shot glass at me; I follow, and we both down it together. I tap the glass down onto the bar, then slowly and seductively walk toward him, pause to stand with my hip jutted to one side, my hand resting on it. Something about the whole encounter makes me feel confident and sexy. He doesn't say a word, just motions to the chair across from him.

I don't sit—instead I ask, "What's a girl have to do to have some fun around here?"

"If it's fun you want, I think I can deliver." He leans back in a casual way, one arm resting on the table, the other forearm hooked over the back of his chair. His eyes stare deep into mine and I know I see the devil himself in them, and it gives me goosebumps.

"Well first, we need to get out of this dark little corner. Let's go sit at the bar. It's where all the fun is at."

We both turn to look in that direction, seeing only one bar stool open—the one I just came from. Along the rest of the counter, people are gathered in pods conversing, laughing, and drinking.

He motions his hand as he says, "Lead the way."

I give him a sly grin, and as I turn, I see his eyes slide down my body and land on my ass. I give him a show by swaying my hips slightly more as I walk. He wants me.

I prop myself up onto the stool while he comes to squeeze in next to me, his hip pressed hard against mine. Something about it gives me a thrill, like I'm doing something that's forbidden, even though I'm not. It occurs to me that Michael doesn't own me, nor does he want a long-term arrangement with me, but I'm certain he wouldn't like this.

The bartender makes his way toward us and only glances at the stranger next to me for a moment before looking back at me to ask, "What's your poison this time?"

"Anything with whiskey, and mix it strong."

The bartender looks at Mr. Green-Eyes next to me and gives him an upward nod. "You?"

"I'll have what this sexy thing is having." He cocks one eyebrow as he looks at me.

The bartender walks down to one end of the bar to make our drinks, and Green-Eyes turns to me to say, "Be right back." He strides around clusters of people gathered around the bar to the other end where the bartender is fixing our drinks, then leans over and says something to him. The bartender looks at him slightly puzzled, then nods. When he's finished, the man behind the bar sets the drinks in front of him, takes payment, then turns to tend to another customer.

As he carries our drinks back toward me, his gaze lingers, and in his eyes I see danger wrapped in an allure that no woman could resist. I've picked the perfect revenge.

He continues to buy me drinks, each time picking something different for me to try. All of them contain dark liquor, yet I can't quite hit the level of buzz I want to hit. At least not enough to make me forget about Michael.

As his name crosses my mind, a twinge of anger flickers to life, but I push it aside, swiveling on my bar stool to look the devil in the eye, my leg brushing against the outside of his thigh. He reaches down and pushes my other leg to the side, then scoots in close between them. He scans my neck, chest, and shoulders with his gaze and says, "Truth or dare?"

I arch my eyebrows and grin. "Dare. Truth requires too much thinking or talking."

"Why can't I see any tattoos on that pretty little body of yours? Are they hidden?"

"Why, you want to check me?"

"A girl like you is bound to have one or two."

"Actually I don't."

"Are you scared of needles?"

"Hell no. I'm not afraid of anything."

"Then here's your dare."

A devious grin stretches across my face.

"Just how daring are you? I say we go get one. There's a shop just two blocks from here."

I stare at him but don't answer right away.

"I thought you weren't scared."

"I'm not." I toy with the idea for a moment, and as a wicked thought occurs to me, I bite my bottom lip to hold back the devious smile. Michael would hate it.

I know this because I mentioned doing it once as we were lying in bed, naked, and he immediately rolled to his side and shot the idea down. His words were, *you shouldn't be marring your body that way.*

In that moment, it was flattering that he thought enough about me to even care, and now I see it as the ultimate payback. It'll be the first thing he sees the next time he gets me naked, and maybe he'll think twice about walking out on me so quickly after he fucks me.

# 16

## Michael

As I pore over my choices of late, it feels like a mechanical metronome is ticking back and forth, each beat dragging my mind to the same place over and over—into a pile of problems with no solutions.

Isn't that supposed to be my job? Helping people solve problems? How can I do that when I can't even rectify my own?

I continue my ritual of counting the screws on the plane's wing and all the patterns I can find in my fellow flyers' clothing. It has done very little to ease the tick, tick, tick chaos of my mind. My thoughts are so loud, I barely acknowledge the high-pitched roar of the plane taking off.

Now that the plane is in the air, I know a nap or rest of any kind is impossible, so I pull out my laptop and phone in an attempt to focus my mind elsewhere.

I open my emails and weed out those that I have no desire to answer and focus on those that are a priority. As I click the down-arrow button, I focus my eyes on each bold subject line until one vivid headline catches my eye.

I Saw You.

I frown, then click it, seeing one single sentence:

*Three may keep a secret, if two of them are dead.*

I sit forward in my cramped airplane seat as a gasp escapes me. The disgruntled-looking woman sitting in the aisle seat to my right shoots me a sharp look. I think she's still pissed because she didn't get a window seat.

I let my next exhale ease out slowly as I sit back.

Something about the video clip below the quote unnerves me even more, and I reach into my carry-on bag for my AirPods. After putting them in place, I set them on noise-cancelling mode and dim my computer screen down slightly, then click the thumbnail.

The video opens onto a wide shot of an apartment building. The one that requires a code to enter. My heart stops for a moment, then becomes erratic.

I watch as the image of myself pauses at the entrance to punch in the code, then I see myself disappear into the building.

I realize I'm holding my breath and release a quick exhale.

The video glitches, goes black, and then the front view of the building opens again, only this time the lighting outside is different —switching from bright sunshine to a gray atmosphere—much like my dwindling frame of mind. I watch with anticipation and disquiet when I see a woman exit the door of the building.

It's Vanessa.

I look to the woman in the seat next to me and she's oblivious as her head leans back against the seat, mouth slightly open, and a drop of spittle seeming to form at the side of her lips.

I turn my focus back to my computer screen and follow Vanessa as she walks down the sidewalk only a few feet, then the video goes black again.

As though I'm on autopilot, I watch it again and again trying to make sense, or as I always do, analyze what I'm seeing.

Who sent this? Why? My analysis begins with a mental list of potential people who might've sent it.

Paige? Does she know?

Laura? No. Why would she? I suppose she could've done it as another means of trying to warn me that I'm playing with fire. She would just flat tell me rather than taking the time to set up a fake email address.

When my mind finally descends from its circus ride of thoughts, I stare at the email sender's address:

*dirtylittlesecrets*

Someone knows about Vanessa, and they want me to know that they know. I stare out the small window of the plane at the darkening sky, then fixate on the wing, looking for any patterns. They're hard to find with little light. What I can see of this particular wing is that it has hundreds of visible screws for me to focus on. I focus on the ones I'm able to see, but even as I'm doing it, my mind is racing toward unwanted destinations—it wanders on an unguided path back to the *what ifs*. Distraction isn't working. I glare at my watch.

I have to get off this plane.

And do what?

I need to pace, but that's not an option.

After three more grueling hours, the plane finally touches down in Ontario and for the first time, I don't even notice the anxious habits that come with it. I'm too distressed about everything else.

I instruct the Lyft driver to take me straight to the hotel, despite having not eaten all day. My appetite left when the disturbing email arrived.

I enter my room and toss my things on the bed, then flop down on my back beside them. I wonder if I could just disappear, right here. Move to Canada and start a new life.

Fuck no. I couldn't do that to Paige. Not having her in my life would be a thousand times worse than losing your only security blanket or a favorite childhood toy.

My phone pings, alerting me of an email.

Since receiving the disturbing one earlier, I'd decided to turn on email notifications. I hate being prompted by work stuff, especially when I'm outside of work hours, so up to this point, I've always kept them turned off. Since the disturbing video that arrived via my work mail, I now find myself tied to it—not by choice, rather from fear.

Without raising my head from the bed, I grip my phone and lift it above my face. The mail icon along with a preview of the message is lit near the bottom of my phone.

*I Saw You.*

As if on cue, my heart responds by punching my chest.

I sit up, then swipe to the right and it opens. Another brief message and below is a video thumbnail.

*A lie can travel halfway around the world while the truth is still putting on its shoes. – Mark Twain*

I feel a shudder travel up the course of my spine and I hesitate at clicking on the video. When courage finds its way to me, I push forward and tap the screen.

It's very similar to the previous one, only this one is from earlier today, and it's me exiting the apartment building again. I walk out of sight and around the building to my car. The video continues with little movement in the frame. I wait, and I wait some more, and all I see is the stupid front of the building. Finally, movement appears center screen and I see Vanessa exit. She walks down the sidewalk and a car pulls alongside her, and I recognize it right away.

It's Laura's patrol car.

I watch as she parks the car into a spot and turn my focus back to Vanessa, who looks distraught.

Laura approaches.

They converse with one another, but I can't read their lips. Laura looks like the professional cop, and Vanessa looks agitated. Then the screen goes black.

I flick my thumb upward, scrolling farther down the email attempting to understand more, and then I see one last sentence from the sender:

*Once truth's shoes are tied... he will find you.*

Panic mixed with the urge to flee back home consumes me, but I force myself to stay put—to sit with what I've just watched. I try to piece together what it all means.

I practice what I preach by shifting my sharp, ragged breaths to a slower, more controlled pace.

Someone is watching me. Are they trying to scare me? Or warn me?

A sickening chill courses through me, sending my gut into a spiral as I grab my phone and scroll through recent calls. I find Laura's number and hit dial. She picks up on the third ring.

"Hey, Michael. I know you're wondering, but everything's okay."

I swallow hard, forcing the words out. "Laura, I think someone is stalking me."

There's a beat of silence. "What do you mean?"

I hesitate and scan my hotel room as if I might catch a shadow shifting in the corner. "I got two emails today. Both with videos of me leaving the apartment building. One was taken last week. The other today." I exhale, trying to keep my voice steady. "Someone is watching my every move—Vanessa's too."

"Why would someone be watching you?"

"I don't know." My grip tightens around the phone. "But someone wants me to know that they know about the apartment. About Vanessa."

Laura is silent for a moment. A long, thoughtful pause that sends unease through me.

"Any idea who it might be? Or why?"

"No." The word feels hollow, like I'm trying to convince myself as much as her. "But whoever it is, I think they're trying to scare me."

Laura exhales, and her voice drops to a more serious tone. "That doesn't make sense. Why would anyone else care? Have you told anyone about Vanessa?"

"No."

"Forward me the emails. I'll take a look, see if I can trace where they're coming from."

"Thanks."

I run a hand through my hair, exhaling slowly, but the unease doesn't let up.

Then Laura says what I already know is coming—what I've been trying to push off.

"Michael, I think it's time to fix this. Or at least tell Paige what's going on."

I clench my jaw, staring at nothing. Her words settle over me like a weight **too** heavy to carry.

"I know."

I don't know if I say it out loud or if she hears the hesitation in my breath, but before I can speak, she does.

"You have to tell her before someone else does. Or before something bad happens."

# 17

D arlene

**Twenty-five years ago**

I plant myself down on the worn-out couch, and soon after, Donovan creeps quietly into the room without me noticing. When I turn my head, he's standing right next to me. I jump and slap a hand to my chest.

"Want to see my room?" he asks.

I stare at him, wide-eyed and speechless, attempting to catch my breath. I'm not sure if I've ever had a conversation with a child before.

"Uh."

He grabs my hand and begins to tug. "Come on. It's upstairs."

I stand clumsily. "Okay," I say, shocked. "I guess I am."

We climb the steep steps, and I can't help but steal another glance toward the dining room, searching for the strange boy. If he's a ghost, it seems he's too afraid to show himself again.

The boy's room is bare with the exception of a twin bed, chest of drawers, and a child-sized desk. It isn't what I'd picture a typical boy's room to look like. It's spotless. Even the floor. The bed is neatly made and the items on top of the desk are stacked and organized.

"Want to see some of my artwork?"

"Um, sure."

He drags me over to his desk, and I feel like a turd in a punch bowl. Just being alone in a room with a kid makes me feel strangely out of place. Even as a kid I was always a loner. I never played with other children, nor did I want to.

He hands me pieces of sketch paper one by one, each showcasing a different technique. Some are painted, others rendered in colored pencil or charcoal. A few seem to depict their house or the surrounding landscape—not that I'd recognize them. It was too dark when I arrived. Others seem to be self-portraits, though I can't be sure. Then he points to a set of sketches and explains that they're of him and his dad. The detail in each piece is surprisingly intricate.

In a whisper, he asks, "Can I show you my secret art?"

I feel myself frown at him.

"You can't tell anyone, especially my dad."

I stare at the boy and can only nod.

"You have to promise." His voice shifts into an even lighter whisper, edged with a frantic tone.

I nod my head. "I promise." He stares at me as if unsure, so I imitate something I've seen on television. I hold out my pinky finger and say, "I pinky swear."

He grins and hooks his little finger around mine, and we shake our hands together. Something about it gives me a funny feeling.

He opens the bottom drawer on his desk and removes a couple of worn notebooks, their covers tattered and stained. Beneath them, he carefully lifts out a false bottom, revealing a hidden compartment.

Next, he retrieves a few more pieces of sketch paper and hands them to me.

Each sketch contains not just one boy, as in the others, but two. Though slightly different in each drawing, the figures are eerily similar. I flip through the pages one by one, and when I reach the last two, a chill runs down my spine and I feel the hair on my arms rise.

Both pieces are done in a mix of charcoal and crayon, their details revealing the time and care he poured into them.

The first illustration depicts a door drawn in heavy, dark tones at the center of the page, with the surrounding space shaded in muted gray. The doorknob features a large, exaggerated keyhole, and within it, an eye stares back—a single, almost cat-like eye. The drawing is very detailed.

The second drawing is split in half, with a door at its center. The perspective shifts on each side of the page: the left depicts the outdoors, while the right reveals a dark, cramped interior, as if the outside wall has been removed to offer a glimpse inside.

The right side of the page features a shakily drawn rectangle resembling a shed or shack, its edges heavily scribbled in thick, dark lines. The door is shaded with heavy black strokes, the doorknob visible on both sides. On the left side of the door, the outdoors is depicted with rough, sketched trees and jagged patches of grass. A portion of a large house is sloppily drawn at the far-left edge of the page, only part of its structure visible.

Outside the shed, a stick-figure boy stands with arms reaching toward the door. His head, a wobbly oval, bears simple dots for eyes and a straight line for a mouth. Inside the shed, another boy is crouched low with his knees drawn tightly to his chest. His wide, uneven eyes are two black circles, and a single jagged line marks the door's keyhole, where he peers out into the light.

I flick my eyes from the drawing to Donovan then back again as I ask, "Who's the boy in the shack?"

Donovan drops his head. "I can't tell you."

"Why?"

"He told me not to."

"Who—?"

"Donovan!" Christian yells from downstairs just before his feet hit the steps. He begins to stomp up them.

Donovan yanks the drawings from my hand and quickly stuffs them back into the drawer, then shoves the false bottom into place. He drops the notebooks in as well and closes the drawer quietly. Before he speaks, he holds his index finger over his lips, then calls back, "I'm in my room."

Christian appears in the door and asks, "What are you two doing up here?"

"I'm showing her my room."

For a second, I'm speechless, which seems to be a recurring event this evening. I clear my throat. "He was showing me some of his art." I hold up the drawings that aren't forbidden.

"Glad to see you two are getting to know each other."

I fake a smile. "Yeah. We are."

Christian looks at his son, his eyes narrowing slightly. "You forgot to wipe off the kitchen table. You're not finished until that's done."

Donovan drops his head and immediately leaves the room.

"He's definitely obedient," I say.

"If you're going to live in this house, you better be."

# 18

Vanessa

Truth or dare—a game I can never resist. Of course, I'm the type of person who'll never pick truth as my choice. Most of us would rather not face it. A dare is much more fun.

What good is living life if you don't approach it like a river after a storm—wild, surging, and impossible to contain? This is how I prefer to live my life.

Mr. Green Eyes asked me if I was willing to play the game and of course I said yes. The dare was to get a tattoo. But not just to get one, but allow him to pick the one I get. His exact words were, "Just how daring are you?"

Of course, I'm not the type to show weakness outwardly, so I accepted his dare. His challenge was that he get to choose the design and I can't see it until after it's finished. The only thing I'm allowed to have a say-so in is that names and words are forbidden. He agrees.

He decides that it will be on the inside of my forearm, which is perfectly fine. It can be hidden with a sleeve if I decide I don't like it.

Rob, the tattoo artist, thought it was one of the best dares he had ever heard in a game of truth or dare. So naturally, I couldn't be a chicken shit.

I sit through more than an hour of what feels like a miniature jackhammer chiseling away at my skin, often feeling as if the needle hits bone. I don't show my discomfort; I just lay back with my eyes closed, smile mischievously, and focus on this being the perfect plan for getting under Michael's skin.

Rob pushes away from me on his mobile stool and says, "You're all done, sweetie."

I rise to a sitting position and look down at the fresh ink as it glistens under the light.

It's a crude, heart-shaped lock etched with jagged lines that has the appearance of being tangled in a haphazard chain. At the bottom of the lock is a poorly aligned keyhole, slightly off-center and distortedly placed. The tattoo has an amateurish quality to it—rough and unpolished, as though it were sketched by a child rather than inked by a professional.

I frown slightly at it, not quite sure what to think about it. It isn't what I pictured. I just assumed this sexy man would choose something a little spicier for me.

Michael will hate it, I'm sure, but the fact that it's a tattoo—he might find it seductive, alluring even. He'll know I've been pissed with him, but he'll enjoy fucking me while he looks at it. I'm sure it will give him that feeling of having a piece of strange, as men like to boast about. Isn't that what they do? Why do men dream about having a strange piece of ass when they have a good thing right in front of them? If their partner gets a new hair color or tattoo on their ass, they'll turn them backwards to fuck them so that they can imagine they're with someone new. I've come to the conclusion that all men are bastards in that way.

But for some reason, I'm obsessed with this bastard. I'm not sure why. Even as I plot different ideas to get back at him, I still want to be with him—all of the time. Which means the only way to get him out of my system is to sleep with someone else. Then maybe he won't have such a hold on me.

"What do you think?" Mr. Green Eyes asks, holding up his phone to take a picture.

I tilt my chin, resting my fingers just beneath it, my forearm angled outward. Then I purse my lips, blowing an airy, Marilyn Monroe–style kiss as the camera clicks.

"It's wicked—just the way I like things." I loop my arms around his shoulders, leaning in until our lips are almost touching. A teasing smile curls across my face. "How about we find a nice, big bed where you can admire this piece of artwork in its entirety?"

He flashes me a sexy smile, his voice lowering to a deep whisper. His green eyes lock onto mine. I watch them shift, and they become cold and unyielding, and it sends a chill down my spine. "I've already accomplished what I came here for."

I hold my breath as my face freezes into a confused expression. I frown. "Is this you turning down a good lay?"

His devilish grin widens. "I didn't come here to fuck you—I came here to brand you."

He gives me a quick peck on the tip of my nose, then backs out of my arms as he takes a few steps back toward the door. His eyes never leave mine and the smirk on his face deepens. "Consider this the beginning."

I stand frozen, speechless, as I try to understand what just happened. I sense Rob staring at me, so I laugh nonchalantly and say, "That guy. He's such a bastard sometimes." Then I give him a wink. "What do I owe you for the tattoo?"

"He already took care of it."

I nod and attempt to sound jovial. "At least he's good for something." Rob looks at me with a blank expression. I'm not sure if he knows something I don't, or if he's just clueless, period. He looks like he's burned a few brain cells in his days.

I step outside and the wind slices through my fishnet sweater. The breeze feels soothing on my irritated skin.

I walk the two blocks back to the tavern, all the while looking over my shoulder for Mr. Green Eyes. His words plague me as I try to figure out what the meaning could be behind them. Brand me? And, consider this the beginning.

Typically this type of encounter would excite me, but something about it almost seems...dangerous. But not the sexy kind of danger. I plop down at the bar and the same guy that served me earlier looks around as he walks toward me. "Where's your friend?" he asks.

I shrug my shoulders. "Who cares?" I say, trying to make myself believe it as well.

"That fresh?" He points to my arm.

"Yep. What do you think?"

"Wicked." I catch a hint of a frown before he shifts it to a sheepish smile.

His comment makes me feel slightly better, and I'm hopeful Michael will hate it and love it at the same time. The thought sends me back to my earlier frame of mind—angry with Michael and missing him all at the same time.

"Drink?"

"Give me a double shot this time." My earlier buzz is long gone, and before my head spins out of control with negative thoughts, I want to get it back.

Several shots of whiskey and a few hours later, I find myself at the far end of the room, surrounded by strangers all here for a good time—I'm determined to have one. I show off my tattoo as I brag about the stranger who dared me to get it and boast about how I'm not afraid of anything. I prove it further by laying back on the bar, offering belly shots to the strange men I've only met this evening.

A blue-eyed cowboy leans over me, grazing his tongue across my stomach as he licks the salt, sending a thrill through my alcohol-hazed mind. The crowd cheers him on as he grabs the shot glass perched on my belly button with his lips, tilts his head back, and downs it, never using his hands.

A woman's face suddenly appears closely over mine, interrupting the rowdy energy of the room. "Don't you think you've had enough fun for one night?" she says, her voice cutting through the noise.

Annoyed, I narrow my eyes, trying to place her. There's something familiar about her, but my brain is swimming in tequila and adrenaline. I squint harder and then I realize who she is—the cop from earlier. Except now, she's dressed in civilian clothes.

I grope for balance, holding my hand up toward one of the guys at the bar. He grabs it and swiftly yanks me into a sitting position. The room tilts wildly, and I reach out, grasping at the air as if it'll stop the spinning. "Whoa," I mutter.

"Yep. Just what I thought," she says, crossing her arms. "I think it's time for you to go home."

"Aw, come on," a bearded guy groans. "We just started having fun."

"Well, I think she's had enough fun for one night. Besides, it's closing time."

I glare at her, trying to muster some semblance of authority. "I don't think this is legal. You can't just come in here out of uniform and threaten me."

"I'm not threatening you." Her tone is calm but firm. "But I do think you need some air. Trust me—you don't realize how drunk you are until the night air hits you."

"I'm not drunk."

"Then it won't hurt to step outside with me, will it?"

"Why are you following me?"

"I'm not. I just happened to stop in for a beer and saw you here. Thought I'd be a Good Samaritan and help you get home."

"Since when do cops help people get home?"

"I'm not a cop right now—just someone being nice. Besides," she adds, glancing at the men leaning on the bar, "I don't think you want any of these drunks driving you."

She gestures with a wave of her finger at the group, who collectively groan in protest. "Come on," she says, her voice softer now. "Just walk outside with me."

The spinning grows worse, and I finally give in. She steadies me as I climb down from the bar, my feet unsteady on the sticky floor. Together, we make our way toward the door.

The door swings open, and the night air slams into me like a giant punch—cold and cruel. The spinning intensifies and my ears feel as though they're stuffed with cotton. My stomach lurches violently and I barely make it to the edge of the sidewalk, past the outdoor seating area, before I double over. My stomach churns harder than a blender, and I lose whatever's left of my fun onto the pavement.

"Come on, let's go."

My brain glitches, like a skipped frame in an old film, and the next thing I know, I'm sitting in the front seat of a car. My cheek is pressed against the cool glass of the window, the vibration of the engine humming. There's another glitch, and now my arm is draped around someone's shoulder as I'm half carried, half guided along a manicured sidewalk.

My ears begin to tune in to my surroundings and I hear the rhythmic sound of waves crashing against the shore.

"Where are you taking me?" My voice is scratchy and strained, as though I've smoked a pack of cigarettes.

"Somewhere to rest," the woman replies, her tone distant.

When my mind tunes in again, I'm being dragged—no, guided— across an elegant foyer. The air smells faintly of polished wood and something floral, like a candle or air freshener. I tilt my wobbly head from side to side, trying to make sense of my surroundings—an open kitchen, dining, and living area with large windows that let in the faint glow of moonlight.

"Whose house is this?" I manage to ask, my voice slurred and uneven.

She hesitates. "A friend's," she says finally. "It's close by, so I thought I'd bring you here."

The warmth of the room wraps around me, but it only makes my stomach return to its churning, which causes my head to spin faster. I clutch at my middle. "I think I need to throw up."

"That's why we're headed to the deck. I think you need a little more fresh air."

She leans down with me, guiding me carefully as she settles me onto a cushioned chaise lounge. The cool night air brushes against my skin, grounding me for a moment. She steps back, her hands finally releasing me.

"I'll get you a blanket."

# 19

## Paige

I wake up shivering, not knowing where I am or how I got here. I can't seem to open my eyes, and my body feels as if it weighs a thousand pounds.

The first thing that comes to my mind are the piercing green eyes staring into mine, his face close—breath hot on my lips. My back is pressed into a wall as his hips press hard against mine. Grinding. I respond by spreading my legs so that I can feel his hardness better.

I bolt upright.

What the hell?

My head immediately behaves like a Carnaval ride, prompting my hand to instinctively grab it as if to steady it, while I lean on my other hand for support. The sound of the ocean penetrates my ears, and I'm finally able to make out where I am. Our back deck overlooking the ocean is pitch black as I attempt to look around. There's no way I can stand just yet. I'm too dizzy.

More like, I'm too drunk.

What just went through my head? Was that a dream?

I can't hold myself up anymore either, so I flop back onto the chaise lounge and notice the blanket draped over my legs for the first time. In an attempt to reduce my shivering, I pull it up around me.

I close my eyes and picture the green ones staring into mine again. I think of the man from the restaurant. Did he have such an impression on me that I'm dreaming about him?

The vision I just had was so vivid—more like real. As if it's a memory instead of a dream.

It can't be.

I squeeze my eyes shut as I try to remember how I got here. I'm forced to open them again because otherwise it makes the world around me spin way too fast, threatening to make me wretch.

I'm waking up like this way too often lately. Especially when I don't even remember having fun getting into this state.

The last thing I remember is sitting in the café discussing my book with my agent. Then the man with the intense eyes and watching him leave. I seem to remember feeling slightly dizzy toward the end of the meeting, but I assumed it was only because of my reaction to the disturbing man. But as I now try to recall more, I can't even remember getting up to leave the café. From that point on everything becomes fuzzy. I don't even remember getting into my car or driving away.

I force myself to sit up again, slowly. Only then do I realize I'm wearing my thick bathrobe, and as I spread the top open to see what I'm wearing underneath, I realize the only thing I have on is my underwear. This forces me to attempt to stand up slowly and make my way through the patio door. Murray jumps from the couch and lazily stretches, then wobbles to me. The only light is the lamp above the stove and the light at the top of the stairs. I scoot myself slowly in search of any sign of my movements before I apparently passed out on the deck.

Nothing looks out of place on the first floor. I lean heavily on the stair rail as I practically crawl up the steps and into my bedroom, where I spot my clothes draped across the top of the hamper. My first thought when I see my jeans is my tiny pocket journal. I sway as I pick them up and proceed to shove my hands into the pockets.

First, I find a matchbook with *The Thirsty Lobster Irish Tavern* on it. I frown. This explains my current lush state. I have no recollection whatsoever of going.

Next, I find my pocket journal and then plop my ass onto the bed, my vision slightly blurred as I try to read it.

*9:30 – leaving the house*

*9:52 – at the post office mailing signed copies of books*

*10:02 – bank*

*10:20 – Bayside Landing Mall to buy a birthday gift for Laura*

As I read through the list, I remember stopping and completing each errand. I perused three different shops inside the mall.

*11:05 – Westside Café*

*12:15 – going to The Thirsty Lobster. I deserve it.*

What? Why can't I remember writing this down? And what on earth possessed me to go to a tavern in the middle of the day?

This is the last entry in the journal. I note the time and then look at the clock on the bedside table for the current time: two-thirty in the morning.

I'm silently scolding my past self for getting into the situation, but I have no idea who my past self was or what she did for the last fourteen hours.

I don't remember anything. Where I went. What I did. Or who I talked to. I don't even remember talking to Michael.

God, he must be worried sick.

Or maybe I *did* talk to him. Something about that scares me even more.

I feel a stinging itch on the inside of my forearm and slide the sleeve of my robe up to scratch and inspect it. I wince and immediately stop when I see what's causing it.

I gasp and look closer.

A fresh tattoo—red, irritated, and covered in a shiny substance.

It's of a rough, heart-shaped lock inked with uneven lines, tangled in a simple chain that loops messily around it. At the base of the lock is an awkwardly drawn keyhole that sits slightly off-center. The tattoo doesn't even look professional—it looks homemade, almost as if a child might have drawn it.

Shock feeds my physical discomfort, and I feel literally nauseous at the sight of seeing the tattoo that I don't remember getting.

In the past, I've debated on getting a tattoo but always chickened out. I remember searching for tattoo designs and saw some similar to this one, but far more feminine and much more attractive.

If I remember correctly, my mother has one very similar, but hers looks professional and definitely prettier. It's so puzzling that I would choose this particular tattoo, since I have no desire to follow in her footsteps, much less have matching tattoos with her. But here I am, seemingly following in her path step for step.

Every part of this is mind-blowing—an unsolvable puzzle. I'd be better at trying to read a book in a different language and attempt to understand it, as opposed to figuring out what is going on with me.

The pounding of my heart becomes too noticeable, and I'm not sure if it's from too much alcohol or if it's because I feel as though I'm spiraling out of control and can't stop it. I'm so confused and scared—I don't know what to do.

I open the medicine cabinet, dump four ibuprofen in my hand, and down some water, then grab the small bathroom garbage can and fall over into bed, hugging it to my chest.

I can't do anything right now, but I'm going to see Darlene first thing this morning. She's the only person who can—or will—help me figure this out.

# 20

## Michael

I fake an illness, cancel my conference, and catch the next flight home.

Within just a few hours of checking into a hotel, I'm back on another plane. At this point, being in this claustrophobic space isn't my discomfort anymore. It's everything else going on in my life.

I hate being deceptive, but I'm not going to tell anyone other than Laura and Jack that I'm back yet. I've decided to stay with Laura for a couple of days to try to get my head on straight and figure out what exactly is going on with my wife—and even worse, why someone is sending me disturbing emails about my whereabouts.

I think walking down a busy street blindfolded would be easier, but I know it's something I have to do.

After very little sleep on the plane, I park outside the hospital before 7:00 a.m. I'd phoned Jack to let him know I'd canceled my conference and to see if he would meet me at the office before Trish comes in. This is not something I want to talk about in front of her, plus I don't want her to know that I'm back yet. I'm not sure I want to tell Jack everything. But at the moment, he may be the only person who can help guide me in the right direction.

"What's up, squirt?" Jack asks from behind his desk as I enter his office.

I drag one of the comfy patient chairs noisily toward his desk and plop down as a loud exhale escapes me.

"That bad, huh?"

He's called me *squirt* from day one because he said I had the face of a ten-year-old boy. I don't see it, but in the beginning my patients asked me if I was old enough to even be a shrink.

I widen my eyes and nod my head.

Jack's about two years older than I am and a couple of inches taller. He has a thicker build and is very much the ladies' man. But I think he's the type of guy who could enjoy the company of a male just as well—definitely open to both at the same time and easily attracts the attention of all. He's good at everything: sports, martial arts, and his competitive nature drives him to win at everything. I don't even try to compete with him—in anything.

On my drive to the hospital, I debated how much I should tell him about Paige, Vanessa, and the whole situation. Jack sees Paige a couple of times a month—routine check-ins, really—so it's not like he's privy to the day-to-day changes I've been seeing. And I guess part of me wants to keep it that way. Not because I don't trust him, but because once I say it out loud, it becomes real. Besides, Jack's already doing us a huge favor just by seeing her at all. I don't want to burden him with my paranoia.

In the end, I decided to frame it as if it were a case involving one of my patients. I'm not entirely sure why—maybe because I don't want to believe it myself, or perhaps because I feel the need to protect Paige's reputation. She's not exactly acting like the esteemed, idolized author the world sees. And if no one else is noticing, why should I draw attention to it? But what's terrifying—someone *is*. They're watching. Now I need to push faster, harder, and find out what's causing her behavior.

Over time, Jack has given me more and more responsibilities and trusted me with my professionalism to take on more patients without always consulting with him. If I pitch this to him as a patient of mine, he shouldn't suspect I'm talking about Paige.

After I've finished explaining Paige's gradual changes in behavior and her extreme personality shifts, Jack sits back in his flexible desk chair and clasps his hands behind his head. All he says at first is, "Huh?"

Jack remains silent for a moment as he rocks back and forth. He leans forward slightly, his expression neutral but his eyes narrowing just enough to convey thoughtful interest.

"Sounds like your patient's partner is either under a lot of stress or maybe—I don't know—hiding something. People do weird things when they're not coping well. Could be unresolved trauma, a hidden addiction—maybe they're just acting out for attention."

He tilts his head, giving me an unreadable grin. "You're working your way toward being an independent psychiatrist. Use those researching skills of yours. I have all the confidence you can figure it out. If this was a sudden onset, there's probably a trigger some- where. Meds? Stress? Something external? People don't just flip a switch like that for no reason."

Jack reclines again, crossing one ankle over his knee. "You got this, squirt. I'm here to mentor you—not give you the answers. But if you need to bounce more ideas off me, I'm here. I don't bite—unless you ask." He smirks, then smiles his charming Jack smile. "I'll do some digging and see if I can come up with anything."

"Thanks, Jack."

"Shifting gears now—how's our patient Vincent doing?"

I let out an amusing yet nervous laugh. "Never a dull moment. He has a bad habit of zinging Carl Jung quotes at me."

"Oh yes. He likes to do that."

"You were right about his claims to read a person's mind. Sometimes the things he says are borderline unnerving."

"How so?"

I try to speak as if it's no big deal, but I want to see if there's any need for concern. "Nothing in particular. Just some of the things he says—dreams he tells me about. He claims he even dreamed about Paige."

Jack's face furrows. "Paige?"

"Yeah. He dreamed of her lying in a coffin. Gave a pretty accurate description of her. He talked about her as if he knows her—or things about her. I found it pretty unsettling."

Jack waves a hand. "Oh, don't worry about it. I warned you—he has a tendency to get inside your head if you let him. I think that's what he wants to do. Patients can pick up on comments, cues that we might not even realize we say in our sessions. A person like Vincent grabs onto something you've said and then runs with it. Just try to keep it professional and keep working toward helping him get out of this hospital and out into the real world."

I think about my sessions with Vincent lately—none of them have been about him, and if Jack knew, he wouldn't say it was professional. They've all been about *me*. I have to get better at steering my sessions with Vincent and making them specifically about him.

"Thanks, Jack." Feeling slightly better and confident I can handle myself with Vincent professionally, I leave the office before it's time for Trish to arrive. I don't want to have to explain why I'm here and not in Canada.

I decide to go see Vincent despite Jack's warning about letting him get inside my head. I have every intention of not allowing that to happen. I'm not sure why, but it's almost as if something is pulling me to go see him, and my feet automatically respond by taking me toward the psychiatric wing of the hospital.

I slip quietly into Vincent's room, but the man clearly has a sixth sense. It's obvious he knew I was coming. It's unnerving.

Relaxed on his bed, he sits with his forearms resting on his knees, gripping a plastic cup of orange juice in his hands. His dark hair is a mess and, in the dim light, what I can see of his face—aside from the blindfold—is that his lips are curled upward. Not quite a smile, but more like a smirk. I find it disconcerting, but it doesn't scare me away.

"I think I need to start charging you for these visits, Michael."

"Hello, Vincent." My voice comes out shaky, so I swallow and try to clear my throat without making a sound.

"You're nervous."

"Nervous?" I force myself to ask the question with confidence.

"I know these things. I knew it before you walked into the building. I knew it even as you sat on the plane just before it landed." Vincent pauses, his smirk growing slightly more. "You hate plane rides."

I feel my brow descend into a frown. I'm pretty sure I haven't told him about getting on a plane nor my loathing of it. "Don't most people?"

"You're worse than most. You think that if you focus obsessively on patterns, it'll fix your fear. But you can't fix fear, Michael."

His words are weighted down with nothing more than the truth, and I'm thoroughly confused. I avoid responding directly. "I'm not sure I agree with that. I have patients who face their fears all the time."

"Facing your fear and fixing it are two very different things. Fear is like a shadow—it's always there, and just like shadows, fear hides in the dark. You might think that if you turn on the light to face it, it will fix it, but just like our shadows, it clings to the edges of you—it will shift, bend, and morph into more—if you let it. For most people, and more often than not, it morphs into a monster. I see trepidation morphing inside you now."

I open my mouth to speak and at first nothing happens. I take a hard swallow and try again.

"You're wondering how I can see you?" Vincent asks.

I nod.

"If you're nodding, Michael, I can't see you."

Frustration boils and I clear my throat. "Yes."

"I can't *see* you like you're seeing me, but I can see you better than you can see yourself."

I don't attempt to speak this time. I just wait for Vincent to continue.

"I've lived in the dark pretty much since I was born. I was forced to, and now I choose to. What people don't understand is that there's a whole other world in the dark, and it's much brighter than the illuminated world you live in. By living in the dark, my senses were forced to become something else. Over time, they became more. Every sound, every scent, every tiny vibration has become a map. Whispers can be screams. Thoughts are messages. I, myself, am like a human sonar. I can emit sounds and wait for them to bounce back to me, or I can take on a more passive role and simply listen for echoes in things that are already around me."

Vincent pauses as though he's thinking.

"If I had to compare it to something, it's like the way bats navigate—for them, and for myself, each shift in the air tells me where things are, who's near, what's moving—what's happening. Even inside someone else's head. It's why I rarely remove the blindfold. To do that is equivalent to you wearing a blindfold and trying to maneuver around this hospital."

He takes another pause and adjusts the one covering the majority of his face.

"What I endured as a child only created a fearless shadow of myself. It altered my mind to do things others can't do. Trauma has a way of teaching you things you'd rather not know, but it also teaches you things you would never know otherwise. It just so happens that my mind and my senses can move me outside of this room—this hospital—whenever I choose to. Contrary to what it appears to everyone else, I'm not trapped here. I have a full life sitting right here."

Vincent's words sound as though I'm learning about a character in an upcoming horror film. As far-fetched as it sounds, I know there's a lot of truth to it. I'm not sure if I should fear it or allow Vincent to help me embrace it. Something tells me it's not going to matter what I want.

"You came to ask me something, Michael."

I start to run through the list of quotes Vincent has spouted out to me in the past. At this point, I have them all memorized. They haunt me.

"I can't get one of your quotes out of my head."

"Just one?"

I stutter. "For now—this one in particular. You said, *the more we try to stop ourselves from indulging in a particular habit, the more we become obsessed with it.*"

"Michael. You're the shrink. Surely you know what that means? It's just like a heavier person trying to diet. The more they try to force it to happen, the more they become obsessed with food."

"What does it have to do with me?"

"Your obsession with fixing people is an indulgence that isn't going to fix you."

I frown, and even though he can't physically see me, he notices. This isn't what I expected to hear. I'm not sure what I *did* expect.

"You're doing what you always do. You've become obsessed with something and you can't let it go. It makes you walk through your life with a blindfold on. Only this blindfold isn't beneficial to you—it can cripple you."

I rub the palms of my hands across my thighs and fix my focus on the patterns the single light makes on the floor. The debate going on inside my head behaves like two storms colliding. Do I ask him to continue, or do I cut him off and leave? He doesn't wait for my debate to be solved; he proceeds anyway.

"I don't think you really came to ask about just this particular quote. You came to find out much more than that."

"I-uh—" I stutter again. "And what would that be?"

"This moral dilemma you've found yourself in. Specifically, this desire to fix the woman you love, but also the need to fulfill your psychological curiosity. The conundrum of wanting to study this phenomenon objectively and your ethical obligation to care for your wife."

I search for any patterns in the room to focus on, but this dark, suffocating space makes it difficult to breathe. How does Vincent stand to live like this, day after day? I would go insane. My train of thought scurries in chaotic patterns and I can't seem to find my way to a rational response. I can only manage to start the question.

"How do you—?" My voice trails off and I can't finish.

"You've allowed yourself to become fascinated by her transformation and, for a few indulgent moments, lost sight of this goal to help her. You're human. When insecurity rules our life, we look for the opposite."

Vincent leans forward, and the dim reading light casts a streak of light across his face. He slides the blindfold down to rest beneath his chin and looks at me with hollow eyes. I freeze and stare into them.

"*He who has a why to live can bear almost any how.* Do you know who said this one?"

I shake my head as though I'm a child being asked to do something they don't want to do.

"Friedrich Nietzsche. He was a philosopher who believed life might endlessly repeat in a cycle. He lived his life through thought experiments. The concepts he used were to challenge people to think about the weight of their choices. He wanted you to imagine having to live life exactly as it is now—with every joy and every sorrow, every event and every choice—over and over again, for eternity. Could you live with that?"

"I'm not sure I would want to. Why would anyone want to?"

"Would you like to know what I believe?"

I hesitate, unable to give him a response.

"I believe that you have fooled yourself into thinking you can solve anything—fix anyone. You need to prove something to the world. By doing this, you are blind. You see too much, but don't see at all. I believe that you're making both kinds of choices—right and wrong. What you have to figure out is which one will save you and this woman without it ending in tragedy. Sometimes wrong choices are the right ones. And the opposite is true—right choices are often the wrong ones."

Vincent pulls his blindfold back onto his face, then stretches out on his small bed.

I stare at him, dumbfounded and speechless as I try to contain my frustration. His riddles are driving me insane.

We both sit in silence for a moment, but my mind isn't quiet. In fact, it screams a thousand questions, but I can't bring myself to ask any of them. Vincent finally speaks one last time.

"I'll leave you with this, Michael, and I want you to think about it before you make the wrong choices or trust the wrong people. *The pendulum of the mind oscillates between sense and nonsense, not between right and wrong.*"

Vincent rolls over, giving me a dark view of his backside, and I know our conversation is done for today.

# 21

D arlene

**Twenty-five years ago**

A noise downstairs snaps me awake, and my body tenses beneath the weight of Christian's arm.

I hold my breath, straining to hear past the steady hum of the box fan at the foot of the bed. It isn't hot, but Christian insists on the sound—says it helps him sleep. I think it has the opposite effect on me; it takes me forever to fall asleep.

The noise comes again. A faint shuffle. I lift my head slightly, eyes flicking to the cracked bedroom door. The hallway is empty, but unease slides down my spine. Christian must sense my movement because his arm tightens around me.

Another noise. Farther away this time—definitely downstairs.

I think about the little boy I saw crouched by the stairs earlier, and curiosity wins over caution. Carefully, I ease Christian's arm off me and slide to the edge of the bed. He exhales softly, shifts onto his back, but doesn't wake.

I move on light steps, avoiding the floorboard I noticed earlier, but the door betrays me, groaning as I ease it open. I wince as Christian stirs again, then stills.

The stairs creak beneath my weight, each step loud in the silence. As I reach the bottom, my gaze sweeps the dining room on one side, the living room on the other. Then Donovan suddenly pops around the railing. For a split second, I swear my soul leaves my body. My hand flies to my chest, trying to calm my racing heart.

"What are you doing down here?"

My gaze flicks toward the dining room. The table is bathed in pale moonlight, and the air feels strange. Still, like it's holding its breath. Something shifts in the farthest corner—a shadow, a flicker of movement. Then a faint click—like the latch of a door.

Donovan presses a finger to his lips and shakes his head—no.

A chill waves across the surface of my arms. "Is someone else down here?"

Again, he shakes his head.

"Donovan, what were you doing down here?"

His cool fingers wrap around mine, and his grip feels firm, almost desperate. "We have to go."

Before I can respond, he tugs me toward the stairs. His voice is barely above a whisper. "Don't wake him up."

A sharp whisper from the darkness halts us both.

"What the hell is going on?"

Donovan's grip tightens, trembling now.

Christian's voice drifts from the top of the stairs, thick with irritation. "What are you two doing? Donovan, why are you out of bed?"

I feel the boy shrink beside me.

I hesitate for only a second before covering for him. "I got turned around trying to find the bathroom. Donovan heard me and just wanted to check on me."

Christian's skepticism is immediate. "Why the hell would you come downstairs? There's one right down the hall."

He stomps down the steps, eyes flicking between us, his face wearing a sleepy frown.

I catch my stutter before it escapes. "I was half-asleep. I never stay away from home."

Christian's gaze shifts to Donovan, and the boy seems to fold in on himself.

The weight of discomfort feels unnecessarily heavy. I hook my arm around Donovan's small shoulders, pulling him in. "He was being a perfect little gentleman. Since he came to my rescue, the least I can do is walk him back to bed."

Without waiting for Christian's response, I steer Donovan up the stairs. As we reach the top, I glance back. "You coming?"

Christian frowns, his attention shifting toward the bottom of the staircase. "I'll be there in a minute."

I hesitate, but Donovan tugs on me again, his tiny hand insistent.

I follow, but not before I see Christian disappear around the side of the stairs—into the dining room.

What is it about that room?

The question lingers as I follow Donovan into his tidy bedroom. As I tuck him under the covers, his voice is barely a whisper. "Don't make him mad."

A small frown pulls at my brows. "Who?"

"Dad."

I wave dismissively. "Ah, I'm not worried about him."

His eyes flick away. "You haven't seen him angry."

There's a beat of silence, then he says, barely audible, "When he gets really mad, he breaks things. Like doors. Walls. One time... he broke a person."

A slow, icy feeling trickles through me, and the room seems to grow colder. I stare at Donovan, but he won't look at me. The way he tugs the blankets higher, the way he curls in on himself, makes my stomach twist into a knot.

Then, forcing a weak smile, he adds, "I was just joking."

But I see it. The way his fingers pick at the fabric, his voice just a little too timid.

Something tells me he isn't joking.

# 22

Paige

The faint sound of my cell phone in the distance cuts through the fog of my hangover, dragging me from the heavy darkness of sleep—or what I'd imagine a coma would feel like. At first I have no idea where I am, but the pounding of my head and the cotton in my mouth remind me.

I become aware of daylight flooding through the bedroom windows and realize it must be Michael calling. I sit up slowly, trying to determine where the ringing is coming from. My phone isn't on the bedside table where I usually charge it at night. I realize it's coming from somewhere around the clothes hamper across the room.

I attempt to stand and realize there's no way I can rush anywhere to do anything at the moment. I'll just have to call him back—tell him I was in the shower. I collapse back onto the bed, trying to piece together the seemingly shattered remains of myself that barely exist in this moment.

First, I need to come up with an excuse for not calling him last night—that is, if I didn't talk to him. I hope I didn't talk to him.

If I did, I'll let him lead the conversation and answer everything as vaguely as I can.

I ease my way over to the laundry hamper and pick up my jeans from yesterday, then find my phone lying on the hamper lid. When I tap the screen to check it, I see that, sure enough, it's Michael.

I can't talk to him right now.

For the first time, I realize the only clothing I see from yesterday is my pants. I lift the lid to look for the fall sweater I wore, but it isn't there. I search the rest of the room and bathroom. I feel panic threaten to rise, and I breathe deeply to ward it off.

I check the time, and it's only a few minutes after eight o'clock. This eases me slightly because if Michael thought anything were wrong, he would have called me before now—at least, I hope. I check to see if I talked to him last night or if I had any missed calls from him.

There are none.

Relief floods me. I attempt to mitigate my misery by leaning heavily on the stair railing as I descend, Murray at my side as if ready to catch me if I fall. I open the back door to let him out into the fenced backyard while I make some coffee. As I wait for it to brew, I sip on a vitamin water and wash down a couple of Tylenol—the rapid-release kind. I follow that by eating an apple in an attempt to replenish my glucose levels and remove the shakes.

Even though it might be a lost cause, I search through contacts on my phone and find Darlene. I don't know who else to turn to at this point.

She picks up only after the third ring, and shock robs me of my voice for a moment.

"Well, two times in a week. Shit must be getting real." Her voice sounds more hoarse over the phone. I'm sure it's due to the early morning hour and the obscene amount of cigarettes she's smoked in her lifetime. "I don't know whether to feel honored or scared."

"Hey, Mom."

"Look, I'm flattered and all, but you know the rule if you want to talk to me."

"I know. I just wanted to give you a heads up that I was going to stop by."

"Since when? What's wrong with you?"

Any other person that might hear her tone in the question might lose their nerve to even answer it. I know my mother; it's actually filled with concern, even for her.

I actually have to choke back a sob. I've not let my mother see me cry since I was in middle school. Back then, she would tell me to dry it up and quit being such a pussy. It was usually followed with, *I'll give you a reason to cry if you don't.*

"I just need someone to talk to, that's all."

"Then I guess you better drive your ass over here then." She doesn't say another word, and she doesn't even give me a chance to —she hangs up the phone.

I spend very little effort getting ready—a little water on my face, hair thrown into a messy ponytail, and I half-heartedly brush my teeth. In less than an hour, I'm passing the old green truck with the tree growing through the truck bed.

Ginger's lazy *woo-woo-woo* has a mournful yet determined tone while her tail wags as if to say she's only pretending to be vicious. Darlene steps onto the rickety porch with a blanket wrapped around her and a cigarette in her mouth. The fall air has a cool bite to it as smoke pours from the stovepipe that sticks above the roof of the trailer. The smell of wood burning puffs from the potbelly stove inside.

She takes one more puff from her cigarette and crams it into the same bucket of wood ash, then turns and walks back through the door without saying a word. I follow behind her, and the smells of my childhood wash over me—cigarettes, burning wood, and Pine-

Sol. It doesn't give me the warm fuzzy feeling some might get when visiting home, but today, I'm not feeling anxious about it either. I suppose it's because I actually wanted to be here.

The warm stove sits in the same corner it's always been in, and I sit in one of the chairs next to it—across from the one Darlene always sits in. Her chair is worn more than this one. I remember huddling in this spot in the mornings when I was a child, waiting for the stove to warm the rest of the house after the damper had been closed all night.

"Coffee?"

"Sure."

"Just looking at ya, you look like you could use it black and strong." Darlene steps around the wall out of sight into the small kitchen and returns with two cups in her hand. I scan my eyes down the old robe she wears that now has holes in it and is faded, leaving only a faint print of flowers splattered on the material. It's the only one I remember as a child, and she still insists on wearing it even though I've bought her several for Christmas in the past.

"Do I look that bad?"

"You look like you've been rode hard and put up wet."

It's ironic. This is the exact phrase that I've heard people whisper about my mother from time to time. Anyone who knows her knows that she's wild and likes to party. It's strange, because I'm not the partier. I don't think I ever have been.

"Okay, spill it. What happened?"

"That's just it—I have no idea. I woke up on my deck at two o'clock this morning, and I don't remember how I got there. I can't account for more than fourteen hours of my time yesterday, except for the fact that I apparently went to The Thirsty Lobster."

"Like mother like daughter," Darlene mumbles, then says louder, "I told you to write everything down."

"I did for a while, then I suddenly stopped. The last thing I remember writing down was before I went into this café to meet with my agent. The last thing I wrote down was that I was going to the bar, but I don't recall writing it down. It's almost as if a switch flipped at some point while sitting in the café. Everything goes black from around noon yesterday until two this morning."

"Well, it's definitely clear by looking at you—you're hungover from the hard stuff. Not some fancy wine."

"I know, but I don't even like whiskey. I've never liked it. And from the god-awful taste in my mouth this morning, I had a lot of it."

Darlene stands and cranks open a window behind her chair, then lights a cigarette. This is something new for her. Growing up, I smoked as many cigarettes as she did.

"Well, spill it. There must be more than you just getting plastered for you to come and see me twice in one week."

I take a deep breath and stare at the floor for a moment, then decide to show her instead of saying it. I pull the sleeve of my sweat-shirt up to reveal the fresh tattoo. Darlene squints her eyes halfway closed and leans forward in her chair to take a closer look. Her eyes shift from squinting to a full frown, then shift to a look I can't quite discern.

Shock? Horror?

She smooths it out quickly, clears her throat, then says, "Is this your first one?"

"Yes, but I don't remember getting it. Apparently I got it last night."

"Why this one? It looks like a kid drew it. Not trying to be mean and all, but it looks like shit."

"I don't know."

"Was this planned?"

"I've thought about getting one before, but I always chickened out. This is similar to the one you have, right?"

Darlene sticks her cigarette between her lips, then pulls up her own sleeve. "Yeah, but mine looks a hell of a lot better." The cigarette bounces as she speaks, and she holds one eye partially closed to avoid smoke filling it.

Her tattoo is of a heart-shaped lock, and coiling through the lock itself is a long, slender chain. The front of the lock is detailed with two long, stemmed roses in an X pattern. The difference in her tattoo and mine is that hers appears to be more professional and innocent.

She pulls her sleeve back down, takes a puff of her cigarette, and hesitates before she speaks again. "When I got my tattoo, I wasn't alone. Like a dumbass, I let some idiot fucker talk me into it. He already had a key tattoo, and he wanted me to get the lock. His lying ass said, *I'll hold your heart forever*—" Darlene says in a mocking tone —"or some bullshit line like that. Or maybe it was he would own me forever. Whatever. Men are idiots, and women are stupid because we believe the lying fuckers."

I'm shocked by her story. She's rarely ever talked about the men of her past, let alone one that she cared enough about to get a tattoo for.

"What happened to him?"

"He's history now, so it doesn't matter."

I press my lips together and nod my head and wonder if I should ask more. She'll sometimes talk about a certain boyfriend here and there, but has never mentioned anyone serious enough to get a tattoo with.

Darlene takes a long drag and blows the smoke toward the open window, and for a moment, there's a far-off look in her eyes. I catch a glint of anger or maybe even hatred in them before she shifts her gaze back to me, then asks, "What else do you remember before everything goes dark?"

"I remember a strange man in the café. I'm not sure if I was being paranoid, but there was something about the way he looked at me— like he knew me, or hated me, or something. It was unnerving."

"Had you seen him before?"

"I don't think so, but I'm not sure. I think there was something about him that was familiar, but again, I can't remember anything after sitting in the café."

She sticks her cigarette in her mouth, sucks on it, then speaks, letting the smoke escape through her words. "Well, you know for sure that you went to The Thirsty Lobster?"

I nod. "I found a matchbook from there in my pocket."

"I think you need to start there. Maybe you talked to someone. Or you could ask the bartender if he remembers you. Unless you're somehow covering your tracks during one of these blackouts— which I doubt you are—there's a trail of where you went and who you were with. Find out if you left the bar with anyone."

I open my mouth to defend myself and think about stressing the fact that I would never cheat on Michael, but she's only saying the words aloud that I couldn't allow my own internal monologue to speak.

I fear this has gone way beyond just innocent blackouts. I'm terrified to know the truth.

# 23

D arlene

**Twenty-five years ago**

Stubbornness is a virtue. At least, it is in my world.

After spending the rest of the night lying next to Christian, drifting in and out of sleep, the piercing buzz of the alarm clock drills into my skull, waking me from the brief stretch of true rest I'd just managed to find.

The restless night was all due to the little boy's words, which still echo in my mind—just as they did through most of the night. Not just one thing he said, but several: *I can't tell you. Don't make him mad. He broke a person.*

Their relentless replay through the dark hours has me wondering if there's some mystery he and Christian are hiding in this house—or if it's simply the ramblings of a little boy's imagination.

Christian drops me off at my car at five o'clock in the morning, two hours before my shift. I barely have enough time to speed home, let Ginger out, change, and rush to the factory.

By the time my shift ends, exhaustion clings to me like a second skin. I trudge toward my truck, already thinking about my bed, when I spot Christian. He's leaning against my driver's side door, arms crossed, one leg kicked over the other.

That easy, dimpled smile flickers across his face, and I smile back automatically. Even though everything seems normal, I still can't shake the nagging feeling I've had since meeting Donovan—that maybe I don't know Christian as much as I thought I did. Based on what his son said, there's another side to him that I haven't seen.

*You never know what goes on behind closed doors,* my mother used to say when I was a kid about our neighbors down the street. She was right because I remember one night the police arrested the preacher father for abusing a kid in his church. Right after that, his daughter came forward as well with the same accusation.

My mother also used to say, *if you don't want to know what's under a rock, don't turn it over.* Those words were about my father when he would be out late at the bars and she had a feeling he was up to no good. She was probably right. But who could blame him with a mother like mine? My father liked to have a good time, and she never knew the whole story because she never turned over the rock to see what was under it. She just went on playing the victim, and her reward was other people's sympathy and attention.

I've had a nagging gut feeling all day that there's something under a rock that Christian is hiding. I don't know why, but I have. I've never ignored gut feelings and they are almost always right. But at the same time, I have a tendency to allow insecurity to plant doubt in something that's too good to be true. I've always struggled to believe I deserve such good things in life.

I've also found during the course of my life that picking up a rock to see what's underneath only reveals what's been hidden there all along—usually something rotting and vile. We avoid looking, not because we don't suspect the truth, but because we're afraid of what it will cost us. And I *am* afraid. Because Christian is the first person who has ever made me feel warm. The first person I've ever truly loved. And my fear is if I turn over the rock, I might lose him.

Having a mother like mine—cold, cruel, relentless—taught me to question everything. To see the lies people tell themselves just to keep love alive. But Christian is the first person to make me want to believe in love. The way he puts a hand on my back when we're in public like I'm a prized possession. The way he holds me in his arms and won't let go when I try to pull away, long enough to make sure I pay attention to it. The way he looks at me even when I'm rambling, as if what I have to say really matters. All of this terrifies me. Because I let him crack something open in me that has never been opened before.

If I allow my paranoia and insecurity to turn over the rock of trust, I risk driving a wedge or, worse, planting a seed of doubt in the very foundation of our relationship. But truth be told, this feeling actually started before what Donovan said—it started the day I got the tattoo, but I've fought it off as another attempt of my ego ruling my life's decisions.

"What are you doing here?" I ask.

Christian reaches for my hands, taking both in his. "Thought you might like to grab a drink after a long day."

I shake my head. "Honestly? I just want to go home, curl up with Ginger, and rest." With all the inner chatter going on in my head, I just want to be alone.

His smile falters. "What? Since when?"

"Since now. I was gone all day yesterday, last night, and today. My poor dog has only been let out once since yesterday evening. I have to go home."

His grip tightens slightly. "Go home, then meet me at The Thirsty Lobster after."

I give him a sheepish smile. "If I go home, I'm staying."

A breeze rolls in from the harbor, carrying the faint scent of salt and his cologne. He studies me, then exhales through his nose. "Way to shoot a man down."

I frown. "I'm sorry. I'm just tired."

"You're punishing me because I didn't tell you about my boy." His voice is calm, but there's something beneath it—something edgy.

"Punishing? No."

"I guess you're going to be one of those women. Pouts... treats me like shit for a while just to get back at me."

I blink, thrown. "What are you talking about?"

"If anyone should be upset it's me. Going to a bar without me. Half dressed. But I didn't. I kept my cool. But now you're going to treat me like shit because I didn't tell you about Donovan right away."

"What? No. I just want to go home, that's all." This whole conversation ignites frustration, even a hint of anger, because it makes no sense.

"Or maybe this is all about me having a kid in the first place?"

"This has nothing to do with that," I snap. "I'm just tired. That's it." I force my voice to slow, to stay measured.

He studies me for a long moment—then drops my hand abruptly, turns, and slaps the back of his hand onto my passenger window.

I grab his arm. "Wait—"

He yanks his arm free. "Go home and pout then. Call me when you're over your mad spell."

I stare after him, my breath caught in my chest. I don't say anything for fear it will only make this whole thing worse. Whatever this is. The debate that has been festering inside me—the one about whether or not to turn over the rock—is over. Christian just gave me a peek under it—I don't like it.

# 24

P aige

I pull into a parking spot across the street from The Thirsty Lobster and stare at the entrance in an attempt to conjure a memory that doesn't exist. At least, not in my conscious mind.

Despite the chill in the air there are a handful of brave customers sitting on the streetside benches just outside the tavern. The bar doesn't appear to be busy, so I find the courage to leave the safety of my car and approach the front door.

I hesitate at the entrance, but my heart is doing anything but, pounding against my chest as though it were trying to escape—much like I'm finding myself wanting to do.

"Don't be such a pussy." I hear the words echo in my head in Darlene's voice. I know that's what she would say if she were standing next to me.

I swing the door open with an air of false confidence and step toward the bar. The atmosphere inside is warm and inviting, the walls lined with dark wood paneling and adorned with model ships, fishing nets, and nostalgic framed photos of Bar Harbor. Simple wooden tables and chairs are scattered across the space, their occupants engaged in quiet conversation. I make my way toward the long, polished bar, trying to ignore the unease churning in my stomach—a feeling only heightened by the mingling scents of fried seafood and the tang of draft beer.

The bearded bartender, seemingly in his mid-thirties and wearing tattoos as sleeves, looks up from wiping the counter. I internally hope he's the same one that worked yesterday, not that I would know or remember.

"What can I get for you, dear?" His deep, gruff voice is thick with a southern accent—odd for this part of the world. It's the kind that one couldn't forget, yet I fear that I have. I feel my words threatening to fall over one another, so I stop it by pausing to sit in one of the tall chairs before I speak.

"This is going to sound like a crazy question, but—" The threat hits me again and this time I clear my throat. "Do you remember me?"

He stares at me for a moment, a slight frown on his face, then his eyebrows raise as a smile forms. "Yeah." He chuckles. "You look a little different than you did yesterday."

"So I was here yesterday?"

His frown returns and then his chuckle, which has shifted to a less confident one. "You don't remember?"

"Um—no." This time it's my turn to force a laugh, but it's more like a tense giggle. "I'm afraid I don't."

"Well, you definitely had a good time."

It's not the words I want to hear, but then again, I'm not sure what it is I do want to hear. "How long was I here?"

"You pretty much closed the place down."

Nausea returns, an unwanted guest that insists on visiting me far too much lately. "And what time was that?"

"We close at eleven through the week."

"Any idea of what time I came in?"

"You came in around noon, maybe noon-thirty. You ordered a shot of whiskey, texted on your phone for a bit, then you left. You came back a couple of hours later."

"Was I with anyone? Talk to anyone?"

"You talked to all kinds of people. You were definitely the life of the party here last night."

I feel my frown continuing to grow deeper, so I force my face to relax and attempt to appear less alarmed at everything he's telling me. "Do you have any idea of how I got home?"

The bartender strolls to the far end of the bar where a bald man takes a seat on the last stool. Without a word, he fills a tall glass with beer and places it in front of him, nods his head at him, then walks back toward me.

"I'm not sure how you got home, but a dark-haired woman, maybe close to my age, came in and got you."

My frown returns as I disappear into my thoughts for a moment. Thoughts that are only a bombardment of unanswerable questions. I finally choose one to ask aloud. "Do you know who she was?"

"Nope, but I don't think you were happy to see her. Someone said that they thought she was a cop, off duty. Not sure. Pretty sure I've seen her before, but I can't remember. She convinced you to go outside with her, then I never saw you again after that."

The only person I know with dark hair that would even remotely come to find me would be Laura. But why? How? She would have to know that I was here.

Bile moves up into my throat as I try to speculate her reasoning for showing up here. This unsolvable puzzle continues to become more complicated. I might as well be chasing smoke through a hurricane.

I'm not sure what kind of face I'm wearing because the bartender says, "If it's any consolation, you really didn't drink that much until later in the night. At least, as far as I could tell. Not enough to make you forget being here."

His words really don't make me feel any better—they only make the situation seem even more dire. "Was there anyone else that I interacted with—I mean, more than others?"

He pauses as if to think for a moment. "You got hit on a lot, of course. But there was this one gentleman you hung out with quite a bit."

"Did I call him by name?"

"Mr. Green Eyes. I think." A raspy laugh escapes him. "I've seen you talking to him before, but never heard you call him by name."

I shake my head.

This whole conversation only manages to send my mind into another stage of confusion—a critical one. I stare down at my shaking hands resting on the bar. I'm not sure if it's from alcohol use or the threat of a panic attack.

The bartender disappears through a swinging door at the end of the counter and emerges with a box that has Jameson Irish Whiskey plastered on the side. He plops it down onto the bar and I feel my stomach do a somersault.

I pick my phone up from the wooden surface and turn on my bar chair to leave. I want to know more, but at the same time all I want to do is run. The bartender's scratchy voice stops me.

"The reason I'm able to remember you not drinking very much is because that guy asked me to weaken your drinks. I found it kind of odd—most men ask me to fix 'em strong hoping to get lucky."

I stop, my body half-sitting, half-standing, one foot unsteady on the floor.

"The two of you disappeared together for a couple of hours, then you came back alone."

I pore over his last revelation feeling like a lost sailor in a fog with no idea of what lies in front of me, or behind me. Fear surrounds me like a straitjacket and I feel as though I'm suffocating with no hope of being set free. It isn't just my mind that has become a stranger to me these days, but I feel like a stranger in my own skin as well. I'm doing things I would never do and behaving in ways I never thought I would.

"Could you describe him to me? This man I left with?"

"About my height." The bartender holds his hand up next to his head to demonstrate and if I had to guess he's at least six feet tall, maybe more. "Dark hair and green eyes, I think. I'm not for sure—I didn't find myself staring into them." He chortles. "He had sort of a chiseled chin, fair skin—handsome."

His description of this man isn't conjuring a face from my memory. Nothing. At least, no one I care to remember. I sift through the old boyfriend files of my memory and I know for certain I wouldn't be hanging out with any of them—not that there are many.

The bartender's final recollection feels as if it could be the final blow that could paralyze me.

"I think what made him stand out to me the most was his arrogance. He leaned over the bar and sort of whispered, *you see that girl?* He pointed to you then said, *I bet you a hundred bucks I can convince her to do anything I want.* I just assumed he was drunk and blowing off at the mouth. If I'm being honest, I thought he was"—the bartender pauses—"a bit of an arrogant asshole. Being a bartender puts me right up there in the same ranks as a kindergarten teacher—drunks and children reveal everything."

This actually prompts a small laugh from me.

"But this guy, there was something about him."

I continue to peruse the aisles of my mind trying to locate the slightest image of the man he's talking about, but it's as if my brain has discontinued the memory altogether.

"I'm pretty sure he's also the one that convinced you to get that fresh tattoo you were sporting yesterday," he says as he nods his head in my direction.

My hand instinctively goes to my arm and all I can do is stare blankly at the bartender.

"If I'm being even more honest, I don't think a pretty lady like yourself should be running around with the likes of him. If you ask me, he's trouble—and not just the kind you find in a bar."

# 25

M ichael

My conversation with Vincent has me feeling as though I'm a ship going under—I feel like I'm literally drowning. I can't make heads or tails of my own thoughts or his quandaries.

He rambled yet another quote by Carl Jung: *The pendulum of the mind oscillates between sense and nonsense, not between right and wrong.*

The more I run the idea over in my mind, the more I'm slowly grasping what it is he's trying to make me understand. But I still don't know what to do about it.

The human mind isn't always confined to black-and-white. It can swing between sense or nonsense—clarity or absurdity. I think he's trying to make me understand that believing I can fix everything is absurd. I need to realize that weakness isn't the end of the world. Often, the end result of being weak is becoming stronger. You just have to shift your mindset and be honest with yourself. Then you have to realize what your weaknesses are and embrace them.

I slip down the back stairs of the hospital, keeping my head low and hoping to avoid anyone familiar. This isn't the set of stairs I usually travel, so it's unlikely that I will.

I push open the heavy metal door, which drags loudly, and step outside the back of the hospital. As I hurry around the corner, I slam into Trish, sending her cup of coffee flying through the air and almost succeed in knocking her down as well.

"Michael!"

"I'm so sorry, Trish." I bend down to pick up her empty cup.

"I thought you were in Canada."

I have to ransack my brain quickly for a lie—I hadn't prepared one. "Um, I wasn't feeling the best, so I canceled and thought I would use this opportunity to study for my Psychopharmacology exam. I wanted to come in and grab some notes before I head to the university."

Not entirely a lie. I do have plans to go to school today to get some studying in—but also to do some research of my own.

I'm so distracted conjuring a half-truth that it doesn't occur to me she's doing the same thing until she tries to explain herself. "Uh, I'm late coming in this morning and didn't want anyone to notice, so I guess great minds think alike."

"Oh." I chuckle softly. "My lips are sealed." I slide my index finger and thumb across my lips as though I'm zipping them shut, then say, "You didn't see me."

"Same. I hope you feel better soon." She smiles as she slips through the loud hospital door, and I rush off to my car.

I phone Laura to let her know where I'm going and to see if she's found out anything about the email.

She hasn't. Just as I imagined, emails are hard to track—especially since it's so easy to create one.

After an hour-long drive to the University of Maine, I make the lengthy trek from commuter parking to the library. I pass through the massive columns, around the central circulation desk, and the young university student behind it barely looks up from her phone. I smile, nod, then make my way to the second floor to find a quiet table nestled among towering rows of books, providing a more secluded place to focus.

The space smells of aged paper and ink, a scent I usually find strangely comforting—but not today. Today, I can't seem to relax, even in this familiar haven. As I pull books from the shelves to study for the PEP exam—a task that's taken a backseat lately—my brain threatens to misbehave by throwing distractions. The effort to focus seems impossible, and I struggle to even begin.

In an attempt to quiet my chattering mind, I shove my AirPods into my ears and blare classical music. The swell of violins and the crash of piano keys wash over me, drowning out the relentless noise of my thoughts. I crack open the thick textbook titled *Clinical Psychopharmacology for Psychologists*. This is the section of the exam I've been told is the most grueling—the one most people fail. According to Jack, it's the hardest portion of the test. But the test isn't the only reason I've chosen this topic to focus on.

Surrounded by stacks of medical and psychological volumes and annotations, I turn to my well-worn study guide detailing the pharmacological treatment of anxiety disorders. My decision to focus on this area is driven by my need to help Paige. I prefer to think of it like the old saying: feeding two birds with one crumb.

Maybe there's an answer to what's been happening to her somewhere in these books. During my search for sleep last night, I found myself reflecting on life with Paige since the accident. She began showing odd behavior a few months back, but nothing alarming. Mostly forgetfulness, then a gradual change in her demeanor. Not often, just the occasional snap or response that was out of character for her. Thinking back to those arduous days of physical therapy, the first episode happened then. I didn't pay much attention to it at the time—I assumed the pain, stress, and pressure to return to normal were taking their toll on her, bringing out a side of her I'd never seen before. I just assumed that the car accident had more of an impact on her than even she cared to admit.

Paige has always struggled with anxiety, and she despises the idea of taking medication. She would love nothing more than to discontinue taking it altogether. I understand her reasons why, but anxiety isn't always curable—only manageable. After the accident it became extremely worse. She began to have nightmares, which can be a common occurrence after such a traumatic experience. I convinced her to see a therapist—one that I think highly of—and he prescribed her an additional anxiety medication to take as needed.

I decide to focus on the medications she's currently taking as well as those she was taking before the accident. I want to see if there's any possible connection. I pore over information on SSRIs, benzodiazepines, and other anxiolytics, delving deeper into their mechanisms, indications, and side effects.

As a psychiatrist, I understand the complexities of dissociative states, but the earlier episodes with Paige—and then the appearance of Vanessa—I've always felt that none of it could be occurring organically. Or, I just want to believe that this isn't an illness that's here to stay. After my first encounter with Vanessa, I began taking notes on Paige's behaviors, trying to note anything that may have been out of the ordinary beforehand.

I flag every reference to the medications Paige is currently taking, tracking their interactions and side effects. Everything I've found indicates there shouldn't be a problem with what she's taking.

I sit back, pondering, and a question nags at me—could other medications, when taken together, cause symptoms like Paige's? Curiosity continues to drive my search as I cross-reference two anxiety medications I came across earlier, and a chilling pattern emerges. Individually, each drug seems harmless, but when combined, they could trigger the very symptoms Paige is experiencing—memory lapses, emotional instability, and even dissociative episodes. What I find is a disturbing truth: this combination could create the perfect storm of dangerous chemistry.

I yank off my glasses and toss them among the pile of books and papers to rub my face. According to Paige's medicine bottles, these aren't the medications she is prescribed—but based on her behavior, it's exactly what she is taking.

# 26

P aige

Fear has a way of creeping into the cracks of your mind you didn't even know were there.

After my conversation with the bartender, I'm struggling with how I'm going to mend the frayed edges of my life, much less function like it's a normal day. I feel as if I'm spiraling out of control—like a violent wave in the ocean ready to be consumed by another. In my case, consumed by another blackout that could have me doing something irreversible—worse than getting a tattoo.

I climb into the front seat of my car, the smell of this morning's coffee clinging to the interior, feeling as if I have nowhere to go. I have a strong desire to hide from everyone. If I had to have a meaningful conversation with anyone right now, I doubt I could piece the right words together to form a coherent sentence.

I could just go home, but even it feels foreign. Yesterday I left there as myself but returned last night apparently behaving as though I were someone else—getting tattoos, partying, and passing out on my own deck.

Thank God Michael wasn't home.

But if he were, would it have even happened?

The question strikes me, sending my mind into more questions. Why does this only seem to happen when Michael isn't around? Or has it—and he's just not telling me?

If he is clueless to the changes in my behavior, it's only a matter of time until he notices.

I'm jarred from my playground of thoughts when an email notification pings on my phone. My heart lurches when I see the three bold little words—I SAW YOU.

My hands immediately begin to shake and I almost drop the phone. The email opens with the same message I received last time, except now there are additional words:

*Three can keep a secret, if two of them are dead. One will soon die.*

My breath comes faster, sharp and shallow, as I read the words over and over. My whole body tightens even more than it already is, and I instinctively glance out the car windows at the buildings and sidewalks around me. The world outside is moving forward peacefully, calm and oblivious, while the storm inside my head rages out of control.

This time, there are several thumbnails indicating the email contains a number of photos to download. With a shaky thumb, I tap the first one.

The picture opens to a white brick building, two to three stories tall. Something about its plainness is unsettling. Nothing about it is familiar, so I close it and click the next thumbnail. It's another shot of the same building—only this time, I'm standing in front of it. Or maybe I'm walking away from it. Either way, something about the sight of myself in the photo makes me sick to my stomach.

I zoom in, my index finger trembling as I move the photo around. I take in my outfit—a see-through black top with a visible black bra underneath and jeans. I recognize the jeans but not the top. The makeup on my face is thick, foreign, like a mask I don't remember putting on. I feel as though I'm standing outside myself, looking at pictures of a life I didn't even know existed.

I close the photo and open another. It's the same building, but this time I'm entering it. The lighting in each photo is different, as though they were taken at various times of the day. My stomach twists as I zoom in on the building, searching for an address—1325 Vesper Avenue.

I glance back at the email and then at the photos again, my chest tightening further. The address is unfamiliar as well.

Where is this place? What was I doing there?

Without thinking, I open my maps app and type in the address. The search pin drops almost immediately, and the location is close— too close. My breath catches and holds as if it's afraid to let go. The building is only a few blocks away, in the opposite direction of where I came. This is a part of town I rarely visit, but in the past two days, it seems I've spent a lot of time here.

Unsure of what I'm going to do once I get there, I start the car and drive a few blocks to find the building. My palms are clammy against the wheel, and I can feel the low hum of the engine reverberating in my chest. I find the building, then find the parking lot just off to the side. I park and unsteadily get out of the car.

The cracked pavement crunches under my feet as I round the corner and stand in front of the building. A faint chill in the air brushes against my skin, carrying the scent of rain on concrete. The sign above the entrance reads: Vesper Apartments.

A slight hint of déjà vu washes over me, and I shiver despite myself. Something about standing here feels hauntingly familiar, as if a ghost of me has been here before.

I step onto the front stoop and pull at the door, only to find that it requires a code to enter. My stomach knots tighter. I have no idea what it is.

Apparently, I did yesterday.

With a sense of being lost, I give up on trying to enter the building. I wouldn't even know what apartment to look for even if I did get in.

I linger a while longer and realize that rain is pelting the concrete and the top of my head. I finally give up on figuring it out and return to my car. All I've managed to do at this point is drive myself closer to the edge of crazy.

I drive back in the direction I came from and spot a small shop nestled between an antique store and a used bookstore—a tattoo parlor. I hit the brakes rather abruptly and stop in the middle of the street. The car behind me honks, holding down their horn a second or two longer than customary. I ease my car over to the sidewalk and put it in park.

Given that I'd spent most of my day at The Thirsty Lobster yesterday and apparently visited an apartment building only a few blocks away, the chances of this being the tattoo shop where I got my tattoo seems pretty high.

I dart from my car and through the shop's door to avoid the rain, which is coming down much harder now. The small space looks and smells as much like a barber shop as it does a tattoo studio. In fact, on one side of the room is a black barber-style chair with a tattooed, burly man seated in it looking at his phone. On the other side of the room is a larger chair with a reclining seat. The business appears to offer both services.

The man looks up at me and raises his eyebrows. "Well, if it isn't Truth or Dare."

I squeeze my eyebrows together and lose my words before I can get them out. I swallow and try again. "I guess you recognize me?"

He frowns. "Why wouldn't I?"

I'd hurried into the shop before even thinking about what I was going to say. I feel like a puzzle piece shoved into the wrong space—awkward and out of place. I push myself to respond.

"I'm afraid I don't remember much about my visit here yesterday. I think I'd had a little too much to drink."

"Ah." He nods upward, his thick beard shifting stiffly away from his chest.

I hesitate but force myself to ask the question I'm not sure I want to know. "Did I come here with anyone?"

He lifts his eyebrows, but his tone stays neutral. "You really were drunk." He pauses, stroking his long beard, squeezing it into a point each time. "Yeah, you were with some guy. Apparently the two of you were playing a game of truth or dare. You waited outside while he reminded me of the tattoo you would be—"

I interrupt. "Reminded?"

"Yeah, he actually came in a few days ago and had me design the tattoo."

I'm struggling to form words. "A few days ago?"

"Yeah. He had an idea of what he wanted and had me draw it up."

I replay his words again, only this time in my head—*came in a few days ago.*

"Did I come in with him when he asked you to design it?"

"No. He was alone."

"Do you know his name?"

He scratches his head. "You really don't remember being here?"

I shake my head.

"I'm not quite sure what the ethics are on me giving out that information."

I take a deep breath, feeling as though I'm barely holding myself together. He must sense it because his dry demeanor softens a little.

"He didn't give me a last name, only his first." He pauses, still debating whether to do what is professionally acceptable or morally appropriate in this moment.

"He said his name was Christian."

# 27

# D arlene

**Twenty-five years ago**

It's been four days since I've talked to Christian, and the silence is deafening. I guess the virtue of stubbornness plagues us both.

I keep telling myself I miss him, that's why I feel like this—hollow, restless, on edge. But there's something else, something heavier pressing down on me, a weight I can't shake.

My period is over a week late.

The thought sends my head spiraling.

I've been staring at the pregnancy kit for fifteen minutes as though it's a challenge I can't accept—which is nothing more than pissing on the stick. My bladder aches from holding my morning pee, but I'm not ready to face the consequences if the answer is yes. But deep down, I know the result will be the same, whether I do it now or later.

With a deep breath, I finally suck it up and do it.

My tiny trailer bathroom feels suffocating as I wait for a single line or two. The ticking clock down the hall seems so loud it's almost more than I can bear. The results begin to show in just over five minutes, and my entire respiratory system seems to shut down as soon as I see it.

Two lines.

I plop down on the side of the bathtub and stare at it in disbelief. I don't know why I'm surprised—there've been a few times in the heat of the moment Christian didn't pull out fast enough before getting off. I have no one to blame but myself for allowing it to happen. Although, he has a way of coercing me into doing anything in the heat of any moment.

Minutes go by as I continue to sit on the cold, hard bathtub. I look down at the pregnancy stick again as if the results would have magically changed. If anything, the two lines seem darker, mocking me.

The plastic feels suddenly hot, and I toss it into the wastebasket as though it scalded me. I get up and start pacing the trailer's narrow floors, my bare feet making soft thuds against the worn linoleum. The tiny space feels even smaller as I move from one end to the other.

I start to think about Donavon. He didn't seem like a bad boy. In fact, he seemed like a sweet kid. Maybe being a mom wouldn't be so bad. I walk and talk to myself in an attempt to make this all okay in my head. Christian will probably be ecstatic. Won't he?

I pace some more.

Of course he will. He said he wanted a whole house full.

I grab the landline before I can change my mind and dial his number.

He picks up after the second ring.

"Hello?"

His voice nearly makes me hang up. But I clear my throat and force my words out.

"Hi."

Silence.

"How are you?" I ask.

A long pause. "Better than I was a few minutes ago."

The tension in my chest loosens slightly. Relief, warm and unsteady, spills through me.

"Can I come over?" I say. "I need to tell you something. And I don't want to do it over the phone."

Another pause.

Then: "Is this you coming to break up with me? Because if it is, just do it now."

His voice is sharp. Mean. But there's something underneath it—something raw.

"God, no. I just... I need to talk to you."

He exhales, slow. "Okay. Come on, then."

"I'll be there in thirty."

The drive to his house feels longer than I remember, every mile stretching like it'll never end. I turn off the main highway onto the one-lane road, which looks different in the daylight—less eerie but no less isolated. The road is nothing more than a narrow strip of cracked asphalt framed by towering trees. Sunlight filters through the canopy, scattering golden patches onto the windshield and dashboard. The branches arch overhead, dense, feeling as though they could close in and trap me. The forest on either side seems to stretch endlessly, with no sign of houses or even a path leading into the woods.

Then the tunnel begins to break apart as the road widens, and Christian's house comes into view. It doesn't look quite as foreboding as it does at night. Its weathered yellow paint peels in long strips, but the sunlight softens its worn edges. The wraparound porch sags, yet it's still charming.

Christian steps onto the porch, shirtless in checked pajama

pants, his feet bare against the weathered boards. His half-cocked smile makes my stomach flutter, but I can't quite read it. Part of him looks happy to see me, but the other half... not so much.

My heart pounds as I force a smile and walk into his arms. Relief washes over me when his hug feels warm, genuine.

Maybe I've been a fool all along.

He leads me into the house, and the smell of bacon and paint wafts over me. On the TV there's some strange cartoon with a talking yellow sponge—the voice of the character is annoying. I look around for Donavon but don't see him.

"Where's Donavon?"

Christian stops, picks up the remote, and pushes a button to silence the TV. "He's being punished."

I frown. For some reason, I look toward the now-lit dining room. The furniture is covered in drop cloths, as well as the floor, and the walls appear to have a fresh coat of paint, the patched places in the drywall now gone.

I follow Christian through the living room where the walls still bear patchy spots, and step into the surprisingly large kitchen—a place I didn't visit the last time I was here. It appears to be a work in progress, as though the updates have been stretched over a long period of time. The countertops are a mismatched combination—one side gleams with new granite while the other holds faded laminate, curling slightly at the edges. The cabinets are half-painted, their lower doors still bearing scratches and stains from years of use. The floor is a mix of exposed subfloor and freshly laid tiles, the air a mixture of bacon grease and sawdust. Despite the disarray, the space holds potential, as if it could one day become polished and welcoming.

"You hungry?"

"I ate." I lie.

I notice his hands then—splattered with paint.

"Been painting?"

"Yeah. Figured it was time to cover up the ugly holes in the wall."

"Holes? How'd they get there?"

He turns, eyebrow raised. "Better the wall than someone's head."

The words land like a fist, and I almost flinch. My mouth goes dry as my gaze drops to the table, then to the mismatched coffee cups as he sets one in front of me.

"So," Christian says, sitting across from me, voice smooth but firm. "What did you want to tell me?"

I trace a finger along the rim of my cup, my throat threatening to close up. Christian leans in slightly, dropping his chin, forcing me to meet his eyes.

"That bad?"

I draw in a deep breath, trying to steady myself. Then, finally, I whisper: "I'm pregnant."

He sits up straighter as I try to read his expression. It's unreadable.

"Really?"

I nod.

"I assume, since you're telling me, it's mine?"

A flare of anger sparks, and before I can catch myself, I snap. "Who the fuck else would it be?"

His hands lift, palms up. "Whoa. Don't get all pissed off. I'm just asking. We haven't exactly been Romeo and Juliet lately."

I press my lips together, swallowing the burn in my throat. "Christian, there hasn't been anyone else. Not in a long time. It's insulting you'd even ask that."

He exhales sharply, glancing at his coffee. "So... how do you feel about this?"

My fingers tighten around my cup. "I don't know. I feel better about it than I thought I would."

His grip slides over my hand. "Really?"

I nod, but my voice wavers. "But it scares the hell out of me."

Christian doesn't smile. "Nothing to it," he says, but his tone is unreadable.

I study his face. "How do you feel about it?"

He gives the question a long, heavy pause.

"I guess it's alright," he says finally. "I just think I need a minute to process it."

Something in me bristles. "A minute's not going to change anything. We're already in it."

Christian stands. Steps to the doorway.

"Hey, Donovan. Get your ass in here."

I flinch. "Christian, what—"

A door creaks, and I hear small footsteps shuffle toward the kitchen. Donavon appears, his little chest bare and his pajama pants hanging loosely on his skinny body. But my eyes land on his forearm where there's a dark drawing made from a marker or dark ink. He moves his hand up to scratch his head, and I can't quite tell what the drawing is.

Christian drops into his chair, taking a slow sip of coffee.

"Go on," he says. "Tell him the news."

I blink several times, then direct my shocked gaze at the boy. I stutter, unable to get the words out.

"What she's trying to say," Christian interjects, as Donavon moves cautiously into the room, "is that I knocked her up. You're going to have yourself a baby brother." He pauses, glances at me briefly, and adds with a shrug, "Or sister."

The boy scratches his head, giving me a better look at the ink on his arm. It resembles a drawing of a small padlock with a chain sketched to look as if it's wispily hanging from the lock. At first glance, it seems like something out of a gumball machine—a temporary tattoo meant to fade in days—but the closer I look, the more real it appears. Something about it makes my insides quiver.

Surely Christian wouldn't tattoo a child. Even as the words cross my mind, I internally scold myself for thinking something so irrational.

Christian drains the rest of his coffee in one long sip, sets the cup down, and stretches, twisting his bare chest from side to side. "See? I'm happy about it. I think we should tell the world." He says the words, but I don't hear the enthusiasm I'd hoped for. "I need to go piss and put on some clothes. You two can talk about names or whatever until I get back."

He stands and gives the boy an odd, stern look before saying, "You learn your lesson, boy?"

Donavon nods, dropping his gaze to the floor.

"Good." Christian steps toward me, his presence pressing in as he leans close, his lips just inches from mine.

"Spare the rod, spoil the child," he murmurs.

Straightening, he adds casually as he walks away, "Can't use a rod these days, but you can put their ass in a dark closet for a while —it works just as well. You'll see."

I stare after him, beyond stunned, my mind struggling to make sense of what I'd just heard. My eyes shift to Donavon. He steps toward me hesitantly, glancing over his shoulder before he speaks.

"Don't worry. I won't let Daddy do to your kid what he does to the other one."

His words send a shiver through me.

I frown, tilting my head. "What do you mean, Donavon? Who?"

He presses a small finger to his lips, then looks over his shoulder again. The movement is quick, instinctual—like he's making sure Christian hasn't returned—then he grabs my hand. His grip is small but firm as he tugs at me to stand. Silently, he leads me to a door, which I assume leads to the backyard. The top half features a panel of glass, partially obscured by loosely draped curtains. Donavon pulls one curtain aside and points.

I hesitate before stepping closer, pulling the curtain back further. "What am I looking at?"

"He's in there."

My eyes land on a rickety shack. It's nestled beneath a canopy of trees, crooked, uneven, as if they're trying to swallow it. The wood is warped and discolored, streaked with dark patches and peeling paint. The rusted door at the center has a chain and padlock.

I've seen it before.

It's eerily similar to the crude drawing Donavon showed me the
first time I came here.

My voice is barely a whisper now. "He who?"

Donavon looks up at me with wide, sad eyes.

"The one I'm not supposed to tell you about," he murmurs. "The
one Daddy says doesn't count."

# 28

M ichael

Accidents aren't always accidental; sometimes, they're deliberate decisions dressed as chance.

My eyes pop open, and for a moment, the Avatar poster above me throws me off as I struggle to figure out where I am. I roll over, spotting the giant NASA tapestry of an astronaut holding the moon in his hands, and realize I'm lying in my adolescent bed at Laura's. I guess I'd fallen asleep with the lamp on.

I stare at the tapestry, sending my eyes in circles around and around the moon. Then I get lost in light and dark patterns that make up the craters of the moon, following one line, then the next. I force myself to squeeze my eyes shut and break myself away from it.

I'd debated on staying in the apartment where I usually meet Vanessa, but I decided to stay with Laura instead. I knew my mind would only show me reruns of the physical encounters I've had there with the alter ego of my wife. Right now, I need to focus on fixing her and then try to figure out who is terrorizing me.

The apartment came about as a result of the first encounter with Vanessa. It had been Laura who'd first spotted her at the bar downtown, a couple of months before Paige's blackouts became impossible to ignore. Laura called me after she had approached Paige—or Vanessa—and cautiously talked to her.

Paige didn't even recognize her.

"I saw her coming out of a bar, dressed like she was headed to a street corner," Laura had said. "But Michael... it wasn't Paige."

That was the first scary encounter.

The next time, I was only a couple of towns away and Laura, on patrol, spotted her again at the same bar. She called me and this time I showed up and approached her myself.

She didn't have the slightest clue who I was either. The way she came on to me was unlike anything I'd ever experienced. She was bold and unapologetic—it was both thrilling and terrifying.

That same night, I took her to a hotel, and the ride was unlike any other in the time Paige and I have been together. She was a completely opposite version of the woman I married.

The next day, I gave Laura the G-rated version of the encounter. She insisted that I "get ahead of this" before Paige found herself in a situation she couldn't come back from. And that's how I ended up with the apartment.

With Laura's help, I've been able to maintain safety in this double life of Paige's, up until now.

I throw back the worn gray comforter and sit on the edge of the bed, rub my face, and recall the words from the dream I've just woken from. What I remember the most is another quote by Vincent: "Accidents aren't always accidental; sometimes, they're deliberate decisions dressed as chance."

I search for the rest of the dream. I'd dreamed that Vincent was sitting in the corner of my sectional sofa in my home, feet propped on my coffee table, with his blindfold pulled down below his chin.

His eyes looked just as they did the other day—black with only a hint of color around them.

I reach for my phone and type the words he'd said to me into Google, hoping to see if it's a quote from someone or just the ramblings of my subconscious.

I don't find anything that matches. This means that my subconscious is trying to warn me of something, or scold me.

I spend a little longer searching for the rest of the dream but finally give up. The rest of my senses catch up with my brain as the smell of bacon seeps into the room, mixed with undertones of coffee. I kick off the worn-out comforter, throw on a t-shirt, and make my way down the narrow hallway to the kitchen.

Laura is already dressed in full uniform, minus the loaded belt and gun she usually straps on just before leaving the house.

"Well, look who's alive."

"I guess I needed the sleep. I feel like I died."

I grab a mug from the dish drainer and pour myself a full cup of coffee, the rich aroma doing little to mask the unease that seems to have taken up permanent residence in my stomach. I slide out a chair —the one I always sit in at the small kitchen table—and take a seat. It protests with its usual pops and cracks.

"Any updates on the email address?" I glance up at her, trying to read the expression in her profile. She stands at the stove, the glow of morning light tracing the sharp angles of her face.

She hesitates, her lips pressing into a thin line before she speaks. "Not much. Dirtylittlesecrets.com is a dead end so far. The domain's been scrubbed clean—no registered owner, no real trace of who's behind it. Whoever set it up knew exactly what they were doing."

The room falls quiet except for the sizzle of the bacon. I sip my coffee, the bitterness matching the pit growing in my stomach. "So, no leads?"

She exhales sharply, turning to face me. "No, not yet. But this isn't over. We'll find them. Whoever sent those emails has, or will, make a mistake somewhere—they always do."

I nod, trying to let her confidence reassure me, but the words "I Saw You" replay in my mind like a looping nightmare. "What if they don't make a mistake?" I murmur, almost to myself.

She tilts her head, her gaze assured. "They will."

I give her a hesitant smile, wishing my confidence matched hers. Laura has always worn confidence like a tailored suit from the finest store, and it usually spills over to me. But not today.

Today, I feel as though I'm fumbling in the dark for answers that don't exist.

Laura stares at me, and I can see a debate going on inside her.

"What?"

She takes a deep breath. "Paige got a tattoo."

"What? Where?"

"It's on the inside of her forearm. I saw it when I helped her put her robe on. It's definitely odd and out of character for her. It was homely-looking, like a child did it—it looked like a padlock with a chain attached to it. Not what I would picture Paige picking out. She's going to be pretty freaked out when she wakes up and sees it. But Michael—" she pauses—"if she didn't know anything about the blackouts before, she will now."

Reality slams into me as though I've been walking in the dark and didn't see it coming—but I should have. She and I both remain silent for a moment, seemingly lost in our own train of thought. Mine is chaotic and taking me in a million different directions. As if she senses my spiraling, she asks,

"So what is your next move?"

"I'm going to go find a friend of mine from school—he's a pharmaceutical major. He's only been in the program for a year, but I want to see if he has a way of figuring out what's in Paige's medicine."

"You thinking it's the meds that might be causing her shift in behavior?"

"Has to be. At least, I hope."

"Well, it would explain a lot. Either way, I think you need to talk to her before Vanessa does something really stupid. Worse than getting a tattoo. You've been lucky to catch her in time, and so have I, but something tells me these emails are connected. I think you're on the right track by looking into her meds. Maybe whoever is sending the emails has found a way to tamper with them."

I stare into my coffee.

"I really think you should let me file an actual report."

I debate it for a long moment. "Not yet. If this leads to a dead end, then yes, we will go that route. I just don't want to risk the chance of this getting into the media and ruining her reputation, or worse."

———

I tap on Jacob's apartment door, knowing it's much earlier than he usually stirs, but there's a greater chance of catching him home at this hour. He answers the door after a few repetitive knocks, hair twisted in all directions, eyes squinting at the invasive light of the hallway.

"Michael?"

"Hey, Jacob. Sorry to wake you so early."

"Uh, it's okay. Come on in," he says, stepping aside. He's shirtless, dressed in blue flannel pajama bottoms. His posture is relaxed, but his expression is curious.

"I need a favor," I say, stepping into his cramped apartment. The place smells like leftover takeout and dirty socks. "Actually, I need to talk to you about Paige."

Jacob frowns. "Paige? What's up?"

"That's what I'm trying to figure out." I explain Paige's erratic behavior, the appearance of Vanessa, and even touch a little on the emails. When I mention the possibility of her medication being tampered with, Jacob's eyebrows shoot up. "So I guess you know what the favor is that I'm asking for."

"You think someone is messing with her meds? That's fucked up, Michael."

"I know," I say. "But you're in the program. You've got access to the tools, the knowledge. I just need to know if there's something in them that shouldn't be."

Jacob hesitates as he rubs the back of his neck. "I'm just a year into this, Michael. I'm no expert. But... there is a basic analysis kit I've been using in labs. And there's this app we can use to check pharmaceutical compositions—get a basic idea of what is in the pills. I'm not sure how accurate it will be, but it could tell you if it's what is supposed to be in them or if someone has possibly swapped them out."

"Will you do it?"

"Sure. But I don't think I want anyone catching me doing it. We'll have to go much later tonight. Can you meet me outside Lappin Hall around ten?"

———

On the campus sidewalks, only a handful of students linger. Sporadic lights shine from a few windows in the educational buildings, glowing faintly against the dark. Jacob and I enter the hall devoted primarily to science classrooms and labs. The usual buzz of daytime activity has been replaced by the occasional hum of a vending machine and the faint whir of the heating system. Jacob leads the way to the lab, his keycard dangling from his neck as he fumbles with the scanner by the door. A soft beep sounds, and the lock clicks open.

"Welcome to my playground," he says, gesturing to the setup.

He pulls out a small metal case from under a workstation, setting it on the shiny counter. Inside, he explains that it's a chemical analysis kit, complete with vials, droppers, and other contraptions. He handles it with the care of someone who has spent countless hours learning its mechanics and uses.

"Alright, let's see one of those pills," he says, pulling on a pair of gloves.

I fish the bag of prescriptions from my jacket pocket, giving it a light shake, forcing a faint rattle of pills. Luckily, I had picked up Paige's prescriptions the other day on my way to the hospital.

"This'll take a minute," he says.

First, he grinds a small fragment of the pill into a fine powder and mixes it with a few drops of something in a clear vial. The liquid fizzes faintly and turns to a pale green. He connects a spectrometer to his cell phone and explains that he has an app that can give us a complete breakdown of the primary ingredients in the sample.

"The app cross-references known pharmaceuticals with their chemical signatures. We can see if any of the ingredients you researched is in these pills."

We wait. Then wait some more.

Jacob's phone pings with an unfamiliar sound, and he immediately begins scrolling with his finger. As the results populate on the screen, he leans in, squinting as he skims through a list of chemical compounds. His expression makes a sudden shift—his eyes widen, and his eyebrows shoot up.

"What is it?" I ask, my heart suddenly making itself known.

"This isn't right," he says, tilting the screen toward me. "The main ingredients check out—anxiety meds, just like you said. But there's something else here." He taps on the name of a compound I struggle to pronounce.

"Neurocortexin?"

"This doesn't belong. It's not listed in any of the standard formulations."

"What does it do?"

"It's a neural amplifier," Jacob says, his voice low. "I think it's only in the experimental stages right now. I don't know for sure. It's meant to heighten certain brain responses, but the side effects can be... unpredictable. Especially if mixed with what she's already taking."

"Unpredictable how?" My voice rises and I catch it and lower it back to just above a whisper.

He gives me a grim look. "Mood swings, loss of control, erratic behavior. As you said, based on your research, if mixed with what she's already taking, it's chemically dangerous."

I stare at the screen, my pulse now thudding in my ears.

I have to go home and talk to Paige... now.

# 29

D arlene

**Twenty-five years ago**

Christian's footsteps pound on the stairs, and Donavon drags me away from the back door toward the table, then instructs me to sit. "Please don't tell him I told you. Don't say anything or he'll put me back in the closet."

*He's in there... no one's supposed to know.*

The words are still flying around in my head as if they're trying to find a rational place to land. Is this just the wild imagination of a child? Why would he make up a story so morbid?

Christian strides into the room, his gaze landing on my face, and whatever expression I'm wearing, it's not one he expects.

"It doesn't look like you two are discussing names. What's going on?" His tone is sharp, accusatory.

Donavon stiffens, his eyes growing round with what I read as fear. I act fast and pull him close, wrapping an arm around him as if we're simply sharing a joke. "That's exactly what we're doing. Donavon here came up with some off-the-wall name, and I was giving him my best horrified face." I exaggerate the expression, widening my eyes and twisting my mouth into something ridiculous.

Christian doesn't look convinced. "Really? What was it?"

My brain scrambles for a believable answer. Then I remember the irritating cartoon I heard earlier. "Squidwork."

Donavon hesitates, then catches on. "Not Squidwork—Squidward."

I force a laugh and shake him playfully. "See? I can't even say it."

Christian studies us for another moment before heading to the coffeepot. He pours himself a cup, then leans against the counter, watching us over the rim as he sips. Donavon takes a step back, pretending to pick something off the floor—though I don't think there's anything there. Christian finally speaks.

"I've been thinking about it. I like the idea of another little Christian running around."

"Or Christina," I counter, keeping my tone light.

"I guess I'd accept it if it were a girl." He smirks. His words sound playful, but there's something unsettling in the way he says them, like he's already staking his claim on a future that isn't certain.

He sets his coffee down, reaches for my hand, and pulls me to stand. His palm presses against my stomach. "This is going to get all fat and sexy."

I let out a short laugh, but unease boils in my stomach. "Sexy? Since when is a fat stomach sexy?"

Christian grins, wrapping his arms around me. "I love pregnant women. That's when they look their best. And just wait—you'll have orgasms like you've never had before."

My face burns as my eyes dart to Donavon. The little boy is staring at us, his expression unreadable.

"Christian," I scold.

He dismisses my concern with a wave. "Oh, he doesn't know what I'm talking about." Then he leans around me and orders, "Go play, boy. The adults need to talk."

Donavon hesitates, his gaze flicking to me for a split second. I give him a reassuring nod, and he scurries off. Seconds later, the sound of that grating cartoon laugh fills the house.

I exhale, turning back to my coffee, but my mind is still tangled with Donavon's hushed confession earlier. *He's in there... the one Daddy says doesn't count.*

I force myself to shake it off. "I've never asked before, but now I'm curious—what happened to Donavon's mother?"

Christian's expression darkens. His grip tightens on his cup. "She's dead. She died giving birth."

Something about the way he says it makes my skin prickle. *She died giving birth.*

Not *during* childbirth.

The phrasing feels deliberate. One implies she delivered the baby. The other suggests neither made it.

My thoughts circle back to Donavon's words.

"To Donavon?"

"I said I didn't want to talk about it." His eyes turn a darker shade of green, and I drop asking about her death.

I glance at the back door. Despite my instincts screaming at me to let it go, I push forward. "Were you two married?"

His gaze snaps to me, cold and hard. He waits a beat too long before answering. "Yes. For three years."

No elaboration. No emotion. Just a fact.

I open my mouth to ask another question, but he cuts me off. "I told you—I don't want to talk about it."

I swallow my curiosity. For now.

Christian stands, takes his cup to the sink, and rinses it. As he looks out the window, something outside makes him pause. He leans in, squinting, then his posture stiffens.

"Donavon. Get in here."

My stomach clenches as the boy appears in the doorway, his hands clasped in front of him like he's bracing for a blow.

"Did you leave the lock off the shed?"

Donavon's head shakes in tiny movements. "No, Dad. You did. Last night."

Christian's brows draw together. He studies the boy with an intensity that sucks the air out of the room. Then his expression shifts, softens—but not in a comforting way.

"Get out there and lock it."

Donavon doesn't hesitate. He rushes to the back door, pausing only for the briefest glance at me.

"Don't go in," Christian warns. "Just put the lock on it."

Before I can stop myself, I blurt, "Got some buried treasure hidden out there?"

Christian hesitates just for a second. But I catch it.

"Just a lot of thieves around here," he says finally.

I arch a brow. "Right. Because the neighbor ten miles down the road is a real threat."

His gaze sharpens, but he only gives me a condescending smirk. "It's not like you live in a populated area either. Besides, a man's gotta have his own cave. A place that's all his—no women and children allowed."

"Uh-huh."

My curiosity quadruples. Between Donavon's secret, the strange drawings he showed me, and now this locked shed—something is very, *very* off in this house.

Christian watches me closely. "There's a lot you don't know about me. Things you never will know. And some things you don't need to know." His voice is casual, but the warning is unmistakable.

A chill creeps over me.

Then, just as suddenly, his tone shifts. "I need to run over to a friend's house—he's having trouble with his furnace. What're you doing today?"

My head is still spinning, but I force a shrug. "The usual. Chores, maybe the library."

"Then grab a bag and come back here?"

I hesitate. "I don't want to leave Ginger overnight again."

His expression flickers. He doesn't like being told no. I learned that last time.

"Bring her with you."

"Really?"

"Yeah." He flashes a smile. "I'm sure Donavon would love it."

I nod, but my mind is already elsewhere—on the shed. On the locked door.

And on *the one who doesn't count.*

# 30

P aige

"Who the hell is Christian?" I say the words aloud as I climb into the Rover and slam the car door.

Stuffy heat pours from the vents, but it does nothing to shake the cold chill consuming my body—a chill that has nothing to do with the air outside.

I don't understand how I can feel completely alone in such a suffocating world, but at the moment I do. I could call Darlene again, but I'm sure she's sick of hearing from me at this point. I've talked to her more in the last few days than I have in our entire lives.

I've never been much of a drinker, but despite my current physical state, I could almost use some numbing medicine right now. Getting myself a drink could do two things—put a bandaid on my current hangover and shut up my racing thoughts.

But that wouldn't fix anything, only delay it.

The feeling that I have nowhere else to turn only sends me home feeling lost and alone. I suppose it's the one place I can disappear—but I can't hide from myself, or my thoughts.

They race straight to three definite outcomes. I have apparently hooked up with a man from a bar, gotten a tattoo, and partied like it's 1999. These revelations take me back to the café from the other day and then to my dream this morning—the green-eyed man appearing in both. Something tells me they're not coincidental. It's possible he's the one who was with me when I got a tattoo. He is invading my life for a reason, and he may have the answers that I need. But something about the thought terrifies me.

I drop my things on the kitchen counter, the clatter of my keys unnerving. I can't even remember the last time I ate, but the thought of food only churns my stomach, my tongue thick and bitter. Pushing the idea aside, I head straight for the shower, hoping the hot water will wash away more than just last night's decisions—whatever those were.

After allowing an obscene amount of water to pour over me, it does nothing to wash away the heaviness pressing on my chest. I step out of the shower and wrap myself in a towel. The steam clouds the mirror, but even without a clear reflection, I can feel the weight of my own gaze staring back at me. I can see the shaded outline of a tattoo I don't remember getting.

Something else feels... off. It's not just my exhaustion or the fog of my memory, it's a quiet, gnawing sense that the section of the puzzle I'm missing from yesterday should terrify me. That something, or someone dangerous, is out there—waiting.

I swaddle myself inside the terrycloth robe Michael bought me for Christmas last year and slide my feet into the soft, matching slippers. An empty effort at making myself feel more secure. I step to the door to the right side of the long counter of sinks and mirrors—to my closet; Michael's is on the opposite side. As I'm searching for something cozy to put on, it occurs to me that maybe there's a clue to my mystery life stashed in here. I don't know why it hadn't occurred to me before to search.

I slide my fingers, along with my eyes, across the racks of clothes on both sides of me, then begin to open lingerie drawers and scan my shoe racks. Nothing seems out of the ordinary—my usual clutter looks the same. I'm not sure why, but I decide to move over to Michael's closet and look there as well. Or maybe I just need to feel close to him right now.

When I step into his closet, I shove my face into the first article of clothing I come to and breathe in deep. The whole space smells like him, and for a moment, I feel content and safe. I allow myself to become lost in admiring some of my favorite shirts that I love to see on him. I open drawers and feel the fabric of silk ties, neatly folded T-shirts, and my favorite boxers.

I pull open a drawer near the back of the closet, low to the floor. My hands freeze just above the contents as they begin to shake, then my heart pounds against my chest. I feel instantly sick as bile rises and a tight feeling forms in my throat.

The items inside aren't the kind a man would house in his closet unless he were a cross-dresser, and Michael is not. The item on top is a black sweater made of fishnet material. Underneath are black high heels, a leather mini skirt, thigh-high stockings, and more apparel that one would wear to a bar or concert—or the kind that wouldn't be worn long at all.

The air around me thickens, and I can't take in a full breath. My mind spins, desperately trying to piece together an explanation that doesn't destroy everything I thought I knew about my marriage—my husband. A costume, maybe? But for what? He doesn't even attend Halloween parties.

I can feel my chest rising and falling, but it's as though I'm outside my body, watching a stranger live this moment. The woman in the closet looks like me, but she's unraveling. She's spiraling into questions she isn't ready to answer.

Maybe it isn't what it seems. Maybe there's an explanation. I don't want to acknowledge the darkest thoughts clawing at the edges of my mind—*my husband is cheating on me.*

I shudder at the words. They're foreign and unreal. Not my Michael—he wouldn't do that to me.

Wouldn't I have suspected it? Seen signs? There have been no lingering glances at his phone. Everything has been... normal.

*Or has it?*

The past few weeks replay in my mind like a reel with missing frames. At least, he's seemed normal, except for the mother-hen routine.

I frown as my thoughts snag on that. He's been unusually attentive, hovering over me with concern. Checking on me constantly, asking how I'm doing, if I need anything. At first, I thought it was sweet. But now... was that all a decoy? A way to keep me from noticing something else?

My stomach churns as another possibility slams into me.

*What if this isn't about another woman? What if this is about me?*

I stare down at the items in the drawer, my breath hitching. Could he have been hiding these for another reason? Could they be... mine? Could he have found them after one of my blackouts? Does he know something is happening to me?

That doesn't make sense, though. None of this makes sense. My blackouts don't explain the shoes. Or the stockings. Or why these clothes are hidden in his closet. Unless he's keeping them for a reason he hasn't told me.

One more thought occurs to me.

*What if he knows about my blackouts, and what if he is the one making them happen?*

I shake my head no and sink to my knees, the drawer still open in front of me, my thoughts unraveling so fast I can't catch any of them. My pulse pounds in my ears as I press my hands to my face, trying to breathe, trying to think. I remain frozen on the floor of Michael's closet until pins and needles creep into my legs. My hands won't stop shaking, and my breath staggers, each one faster and harder.

Words escape my lips barely above a whisper. "I can't take this anymore." On unsteady legs, I stumble to the medicine cabinet.

The bottle of Anzilyte sits inside—the anxiety meds prescribed to ward off panic attacks. I feel like I've waited too long. The symptoms are already overwhelming. The doctor said I could take two if needed. Right now, I *need* them.

I pop two pills into my mouth, fill the cup on the sink with water, and swallow hard. My eyes skim the label: *May cause drowsiness. Do not exceed six in twenty-four hours.* I'm pretty sure I've only had one—maybe two—in the last twenty-four hours. I'm not sure. But the way I feel right now, I almost decide on a third.

Instead, I move to my chaise reading chair in the corner of the bedroom and sink down onto the edge, rocking back and forth as I force myself to breathe slow—in through my nose, out through my mouth. Minutes pass, and it's not enough. Frustrated, I slip out of my slippers and curl into a fetal position, tucking my feet inside the robe. I clutch a throw pillow tightly against my chest as the pills finally begin to work.

They not only calm me, but I feel extremely relaxed and want nothing more now than to go to sleep and forget everything.

# 31

D arlene

**Now**

Being a mother was never planned, but fate decided that I should be. I never understood why.

When I got pregnant with Paige, it wasn't that I didn't want her, I just didn't want all the fear that comes along with being a mother. Because of my own childhood, I didn't believe I was capable of the kind of love a mother is supposed to have. Contrary to what people may believe, motherhood isn't always instinct and it doesn't always come naturally. I suppose genetics and horrible upbringings often collide to make a storm of mental problems in one's mind—I'm a perfect example of that. And colossal storms like myself are never gentle or forgiving.

But sometimes bad people are forced into good things whether they feel worthy of it or not.

It isn't the only reason I didn't want a child—I didn't want to raise a child alone.

After my father died, I grew up in a home with a tyrant mother who hated life and everyone in it, including me. At least, that's the kind of attention she gave me. I figured I was doomed to be the same kind of person, so I tried everything to prevent becoming a mother— literally. Except climbing into bed with a man. I was foolish enough to believe that sex was love. I was deprived of love so much as a child that I chased it in all the wrong places. And the places and people I picked to love me weren't even capable of loving themselves.

When you're forced to view life from the cheaper seats, the only perspective you gain is a tiny, far-off version of what life should have been. Or one that will never be.

It's okay though—it made a survivor out of me. Hardened my heart to loneliness and love. Neither one plagues me like it does the majority of the human race. How can I be lonely when my thoughts are my own version of a crowded room? And how can I miss love when I've never truly had it to miss?

As far as my love for Paige, I loved her the only way I knew how —tough. Tough love creates a tough person, and she'll survive long after I'm gone.

I push open the squeaky front door, the metal knob cool in my palm, and step outside. Grabbing wood from the stack against the trailer, I stoke the fire before my morning hike. Far off in the dark distance, an owl hoots, claiming its territory while squirrels chatter their own reclaiming of proximity. The damp, crisp air carries the smell of pine and decaying leaves, mingling with the faint smoke from the fire—a combination I've come to associate with home.

That's the life of these woods—each and every creature carves out its own space, including myself, and I've always respected that. As darkness descends and daylight takes its turn, I tiptoe through these woods with Ginger by my side. His sleek tan fur brushes against my leg as he pads along, his nose to the ground. He knows how to maneuver this forest just as quietly as I can.

Living out here alone, I've formed an understanding with the wildlife. I disturb only what is needed and nothing more. I may be rough around the edges and labeled as a cold-hearted human, but nature is the one thing I love and take care of. One should respect it, treat it as a treasured friend. Preserve it and take care of it for future generations.

I shift the revolver strapped to my belt slightly around to my back as I squat down to dig some burdock root. I've never had to use the gun for protection, but one should never traipse through these woods without one. Especially in the parts of the forest I like to travel. It's rarely visited by humans and it belongs solely to nature.

I've encountered bears on a few occasions. The earthy musk of their fur and the crack of branches under their massive weight always sends my heart racing, but as long as I don't panic and stay far away from cubs, they're just as spooked as they are fierce.

I use the small hand tool shaped like a miniature shovel to scoop some roots from the earth, leaving a few behind so that it can replenish itself. I pack it gently into one of three canvas bags strapped around me, careful not to mix or taint anything by mixing them together.

I don't have a degree or education as an herbalist—nature has been my classroom. One doesn't have to be a botanist to do what I do, but over the years, the local library has provided me with my own collection of well-worn, annotated herb guides. I've spent hours experimenting and observing plants in their natural environment, and my success has come from curiosity, patience, and respect for the land.

One of my favorites to gather is wild mint. I like to chew on a leaf while I work.

I spend the better part of the morning gathering roots, sweet-fern, and wild mint. Ginger's keen nose guides us around the side of the mountain, following his own marked paths that avoid the rough terrain near the entrance to the hollow. It's the usual route we take out of the woods. We always stop to check the mailbox, then stroll leisurely down the rugged road back to the trailer.

The mail I generally receive is the regular monthly utility bills, scheduled checks from local shops for my deliveries, and coupons. Personal mail, I've learned, is a thing of the past, which is why I frown when I see the envelope with a messily handwritten address on the front.

I walk and open it at the same time, but my steps falter to a stop when I unfold the letter and something falls to the ground. Something about it causes a surge of adrenaline which sends my heart into a race against itself. My eyes drop to the rectangular card on the ground, and I immediately recognize the familiar Kodak print across its white surface—the kind once stamped on the backs of photographs.

Before bending down to pick it up, I open the paper the rest of the way. The paper feels oddly heavy in my trembling fingers, and the bold, jagged handwriting seems to scream at me from the page: I SAW YOU.

Below that, written slightly smaller, is the phrase: *Three can keep a secret, if two of them are dead.*

Something tells me that my past has traveled through time to find me, and it isn't a history that I want to remember.

I bend down to pick up the photo, turning it over as I straighten back to standing. My shaking legs threaten to give out, so I lower myself onto the cold, damp earth. Ginger comes to my side, sniffs me briefly, then settles next to me.

The eyes of the devil stare back at me, framed by the empty smile of someone who I thought I'd left behind twenty-five years ago.

# 32

anessa

A strange warmth engulfs me.

Light peeks into the room from the large windows, and I get the sense of being in a dream. The plush surface beneath me is smooth, velvety. My eyes dart around the unfamiliar room as an unsettling realization sinks in—I have no idea where I am.

I bolt upright and grip the thick, cream-colored robe as I tug at it, trying to remember even putting it on. I don't even own anything such as this. I turn in circles, taking in the cozy bedroom, the soft bed, and, across from me, an armoire. There's a giant piece of art painted in multi-colors above the bed with words that proclaim this is the Best Place In The World.

A slight, stinging itch registers on my arm, and I remember being at the tavern, drinking, and getting a tattoo—the devilish green-eyed man.

Is this his house?

No... wait. I remember now—the cop who was out of uniform. She brought me here—to a friend's house, she said.

I spot the matching, girlie slippers and slide my feet into them before stepping to the window to take in the expensive ocean view. In order for someone to be able to see this kind of view from their bedroom window, they would have to either be rich or in debt up to their eyeballs.

A noise behind me makes me jerk around to find a black lab stretching lazily as he opens his mouth into a big yawn, a moan escaping like that of an old man. My eyes grow wide as I freeze in place and size him up. He doesn't appear to be alarmed that I'm here.

"Good dog," I say in a soothing tone. He pads up to me, sits down, then looks up as though he wants something. I ease my hand down toward him and his tail wags, then I look at the tag on his collar. "Hello—Murray. Aren't you a friendly boy. That's good—I'm glad," I say as I rub behind both ears. "Why don't you show me around?"

I wander through the spacious bedroom and bathroom, the dog at my side, then step out into the hallway, where the staircase landing offers a breathtaking view beyond. It's the same as the bedroom, just on a larger scale. The massive windows demonstrate just what a big world it is out there.

My slippered feet make a light swoosh sound as they scoot across the floor while I descend the stairs. The thought suddenly occurs to me that there might be someone else in the house. Someone I don't know.

Why would the cop bring me—a stranger—to someone else's house? The thought hits me as I reach the bottom of the stairs. My steps falter when I spot the large canvas above the fireplace. It stops me mid-step, and my gaze grows cloudy for a moment. I squint as I move closer, as though the act might somehow help me make sense of what I'm seeing.

I recognize Michael immediately—his dark hair and boyish smile are unmistakable. He's seated on the ground, his back resting against the trunk of a massive tree. One leg is stretched out in front of him; the other is bent, with his forearm draped casually over it. But it's the woman sitting in front of him, leaning into his chest, that forces me to stop walking—leaves me frozen in place. She's seated intimately against Michael, her legs stretched out in front of her—sexy, long—with one crossed over the other. Her smile is casual, subtle, and relaxed.

"It's... me?"

I say the words aloud, questioning my own eyes. She looks like me, but not quite. There's something off—buttoned up, a little more conservative. The woman in the picture wears a short black dress with a ruffled skirt, and at the end of her bare legs are red high heels —a striking detail against the earthy tones of the backdrop.

Neither of them is looking at the camera; it's their profiles that hold my attention, like a haunting glimpse into someone else's intimate life.

My thoughts scatter frantically, and I begin to follow suit, pacing as my panic grows. I start searching the rest of the house, desperate for answers.

Maybe Michael just has a type, I think, clinging to a shred of reason.

But even as the thought crosses my mind, my eyes catch on a tri-panel collage screen in the corner of the room. It resembles a Japanese shoji screen, and it's covered in rectangular grids, each one filled with photographs—wedding photographs.

I move closer, holding my breath as my heart pounds erratically. Several photos resemble the large one above the fireplace: profile shots of Michael and the woman. My stomach knots as I study the details. In the center of one panel is a close-up of the two of them— straight on.

Michael smiles at the camera, and the woman next to him...

She—**is**—me.

She has my eyes. My lips. Even the tiny scar above my left

eyebrow. She stares back at me as if to mock me. As if to say, *I'm the version of you he truly wants.*

For a moment, I feel like a ghost—a person standing outside my own body as though I'm having a near-death experience. Strange tears burn the corners of my eyes so aggressively, I brush them away with both hands.

"I've got to get out of here." My words are low but audible as I race back upstairs to search the strange bedroom for clothes. I internally scold myself for being an idiot. But I can't even explain to myself why.

I feel like an Etch A Sketch toy that's been shaken too hard—overly played with, leaving only faint leftover memories or ghost images of previous parts of my life. What I once thought were carefully drawn lines of my identity have blurred or vanished entirely. I suddenly have no idea who I am or where I came from.

I race through the bedroom into the spacious bathroom and see two doors, both ajar, on each side of a massive mirror. The reflection grabs my attention and forces me to pause. I look like the woman in the photo downstairs—like me, but the confident eyes I usually adorn, I no longer wear. This woman is now tainted by an image I can't get out of my head. An image of someone familiar, yet a stranger. I have to force myself to move.

I open the medicine cabinet and find several medicine bottles, all with the same name on the labels: Paige Thomas.

Now I know her name. The one he wouldn't tell me.

I rummage under the sink and even go through the contents in the small garbage can. At the bottom, I find a pregnancy test—it has a faint single line. I guess he and his little housewife are hoping for a baby. I pull the robe down and turn to look at my shoulder in the mirror and say aloud, "But I guess he didn't really want to have a baby after all."

I know this because he's the one that took me to get birth control. Early on in our sexcapades, he's the one that suggested it. We would be free for spontaneity whenever we liked. And he was right—sex is so much better without a condom. But now, I wonder what his true motive was.

I turn now to open the closet door on the right—definitely belongs to a female. The smell is familiar, yet I don't recognize the clothes. I yank on a pair of jeans from the coat hanger and slam my feet into them, then slide my fingers down the pile of neatly stacked sweaters and sweatshirts. I choose a black sweatshirt and after I position it in place, I realize it has patchwork letters sewn onto the front that state one should, **READ.**

*What a pussy.* The words snap through my mind, but I don't have time to change into something else. I want to get as far away from here as possible. I grab a pink cap from the top shelf and slap it onto my head, tucking my hair inside it, and lastly, I throw on a pair of sneakers.

As I'm sprinting down the stairs, a cell phone rings somewhere in the large open space. I follow the sound and find it on the counter space that separates the kitchen from the living room and dining area. I pick it up to find Michael's face plastered on the screen.

Immediate anger pulses through me.

*He's calling her,* I think, and look at the massive canvas over the fireplace. I press the button on the side to silence it, then again to end the call, erasing his face from my sight. My stomach twists itself into knots.

I toss the phone aside and my eyes land on the mom-looking purse sitting on the counter. Without hesitation, I dump the contents out and sift through the mess until I find the matching wallet. Inside, a few bills—just enough to matter—but the rest is empty.

My gaze flicks to what's left on the counter: a tiny blue book, some loose change, and a tube of strawberry chapstick. I flip through the book's pages, skimming notes scrawled in ink—times, locations. I don't know what they mean. Probably nothing. Probably some-thing. Either way, I shove it back into the purse with everything else —except the phone.

I yank open kitchen drawers, the contents clattering as I rifle through them, slamming each one shut in frustration. Then I see it in the last drawer. A driver's license. My own unsmiling face stares back at me as confusion holds me in place. My mind scrambles to make sense of everything, which is useless. Then, acting on instinct, I shove it back into the drawer.

I hook the purse over my shoulder and move fast toward the foyer. I peek out the front door and scan for a car—something, anything that will get me out of here. A Range Rover sits outside. I spot the key fob on the foyer table and snatch it up, press a button, and thankfully hear a quick beep. Relief rushes over me.

I have to get out of here.

# 33

## Michael

Jacob's test results are stuck on repeat, parading around in my chaotic thoughts. A neural amplifier—experimental, unpredictable—something that should have never been a part of Paige's medication.

I pull my phone from my pocket and call our office—the direct line to Jack. Now that I know more about what could possibly be causing Paige's personality shifts, I can better explain what I was trying to explain to him yesterday. I guess it's time to let him know that it isn't about a patient, but about my wife. If anyone can get to the bottom of it, he can.

I now wish I would have told him the full story yesterday—maybe he would have put me on this path sooner, rather than being a mentor and letting me figure it out for myself. I just felt the less anyone knew about Paige, the better. He picks up after three rings.

"Jack?" I barely wait for him to greet me. "You remember what we talked about yesterday?"

I go on to explain in detail what's been happening with Paige, minus my role in finding some pleasure in it.

Jack is silent for a long moment, too long, and I feel my impatience start to take over. "Jack?"

He doesn't seem to notice. "This could be a number of things. You said she was taking a benzodiazepine, right? Combine that with hormone shifts and a little trauma history, and boom—that could cause dissociation and memory distortion."

"But that wouldn't explain the neural amplifier I found in her medication."

"You said it's Neurocortexin?"

"Yeah."

"I'm not a hundred percent sure—I'll have to look it up, but Neurocortexin shouldn't even be available outside of controlled trials."

"That's what Jacob said."

"This could be serious, Michael. Why would someone want to mess with Paige's meds?"

"I don't know, but this is the only thing I can link all of this back to. I've made myself sick trying to figure out what has been going on with her. It has to be this."

"But who would want to do this to Paige?"

"I don't know. I can't understand why anyone would want to do this."

"At any rate, it would have to be someone in pharma manufacturing or distribution, maybe even in research—someone with deep enough access to slip something through unnoticed. Maybe, or maybe not—I don't want to jump to conclusions. Let me do a little digging. There's a lot of rumors around Neurocortexin. Maybe some off-label testing, but none of it verified, and it's out there. Whatever it is, it could be bigger than Paige, Michael. I think you've stumbled into something, and if that's the case, we need to be careful how we move forward."

Everything Jack is saying barely registers, but it all scares the hell out of me. I have to go home and explain all of this to Paige.

"What pharmacy did the pills come from?"

"Our local one, Bar Harbor Pharmacy."

"Who picked them up? You, or Paige?"

As I start to answer the question, I pause, wondering why this would matter. "Me. I always do on my way home from work."

The phone stays silent a beat longer than it should, then he finally says, "Get those pills to me, and in the meantime, I'll get her some more that we know will be safe. I'll also contact a friend of mine who works in pharmaceutical regulation who might be able to trace the origin."

"Yes. Thanks, Jack." I try to mask the despair in my voice, but Jack picks up on it anyway.

"We'll figure it out, Michael. Don't worry. Where's Paige now?"

"At home. I'm going to go talk with her now."

"Good. Like I said, get those pills to me. In the meantime, get rid of any you might have at home."

"I will."

The long walk back to my car seems endless. I debate on calling Paige right away, but this is something I have to talk to her about in person. At the least, I need to warn her about taking the extra anxiety meds.

I tap the name at the top of my favorites list in my phone and listen as it rings. She doesn't answer. Despite my current frantic state, I'm able to leave a calm message on voicemail.

"Hi, sweetheart. Listen, I've been doing some research this morning and based on what I've been reading, I think you should hold off on taking one of your medications. Don't take the Anzilyte this morning. At least, not until I can explain what I've found. I'll talk to you soon. I love you. Bye, baby."

I shove my phone into my pocket, then attempt to rehearse what

I'm going to say to Paige when I get home, but the words are lost to me. I should have talked to her before now.

Events from the past couple of months replay, and as I go over them, I realize there's no way to explain the delay in telling her without risking her distrust.

Was I playing the role of protector or was I partially indulging in a fantasy? I think the answer is both.

Lots of couples role-play, but when one is unaware they are participating in such a game, then they might not see it that way. Even though Vanessa is Paige, just a bolder version of her, enjoying this side of her may have gone too far on my part. But it was the only way I knew how to keep her under my sights while trying to figure it out.

However, it never left my mind that I had to find a way to understand what was happening to her. One might compare the situation to an alcoholic taking a drink even though the doctor has warned that their liver is under duress. Just as Vincent pointed out, it seems that my need to fix her overpowered my common sense.

Rain begins to drizzle, barely more than a mist, but by the time I reach my car, it's a full downpour. The sound of it hitting the metal roof is deafening, as if nature itself is pounding on me to do something right for a change.

I lean forward and rest my forehead against the steering wheel. As much as I want to blame the medication for everything that has happened, I can't ignore the nagging truth: I let this happen.

The broken record continues to toy with my sanity.

My role wasn't passive. It wasn't entirely protective. But it was selfish.

The realization settles like a crushing weight on my chest and guilt is the heaviest part of it.

I've spent my life's work analyzing people, understanding what drives them to do the things they do. But I've never turned that lens on myself—not until now.

I take a shaky breath, my fingers tightening around the steering wheel. I actually whisper the question aloud. "Why did I let her stay?"

Vanessa was never just a symptom to me. She was... a break from reality. A version of Paige that was untethered, uninhibited. She challenged me, tested me, made me feel something I hadn't felt in years.

Alive.

My chest tightens as guilt continues to grow heavier in my chest, leaving me struggling to take a normal breath. What kind of husband allows that? What kind of psychiatrist indulges in a fantasy when his wife is unraveling? I tell myself it was for her, that I needed to understand Vanessa to help Paige. But deep down, I know it wasn't just about her.

It was also about me.

I wallow in my guilt and self-torture and attempt to come to terms with what I've done, then tell myself I'm ready to do the right thing. I'm ready to make this right, and I can't let my guilt shame me into becoming a coward now.

As I'm pulling away from campus, my phone begins to ring over the car's speakers, jolting me from my downward spiral of what-ifs.

It's the hospital. Reluctantly, I answer it.

"Hello."

The woman on the other end says, "Michael. He's demanding to see you."

She doesn't have to say his name—I know who she's talking about. "I'm not sure I can get there right now—"

She interrupts. "He's more agitated than I've ever seen him. Sam can't even calm him."

Sam is the night nurse and is one of the few that can reason with Vincent when he becomes extremely agitated. His shift ended hours ago, which means Vincent has been more than difficult this morning.

As far as anyone knows, I'm in Canada at a conference. I start to keep up with the lie, but the nurse says, "I was told that you came back early from your conference, otherwise I wouldn't have bothered you. Do you think you can come?"

For a moment, I'm stunned. The only people who know that I'm back are Jack and Trish. I feel a twinge of frustration. Trish has always been a little loose with her tongue.

I huff. "I'll be there in less than an hour."

On my drive, I attempt again to rehearse what I'm going to say to Paige, but no matter how I word it, it all sounds monstrous. I have to shove it down for now.

I approach the nurse's station of Vincent's hallway and Edna, the nurse who phoned me, moves around the counter to greet me. "He calmed down as soon as I let him know you were coming."

"What set him off?"

"Sam said he had someone visit him early this morning—someone from Behavioral Management Services. Supposedly here to question patients about their care. Something about the visit set him off, because shortly after, Vincent began storming around his room like a wild animal. When he checked on him all he would say over and over was get Michael. I have to talk to Michael."

"But he never said what set him off?" I ask.

"He wouldn't say anything other than those words. More like shouted them."

"Sam still there?"

"No. He went home after Vincent calmed down."

"Okay. Thanks, Edna." I hesitate for just a moment, not really in the mood for Vincent's riddles. I'm sure whatever he wants to tell me is only going to escalate the downward spiral of my own current state of mind.

Some of Vincent's words come back to me and for the first time they're all beginning to piece themselves together. I don't want to believe it, but it's as if he's known all along what's been happening in my life. Paige, Vanessa—me.

But how?

I pause and listen outside Vincent's door before I quietly twist the knob and ease the door open. His room feels and smells stale, the air unmoving. There's a faint scent of antiseptic, urine, and unwashed hair.

Vincent sits on the bed in the same position I always find him in —back against the wall, forearms propped on his knees. The only difference is, he isn't wearing the usual long-sleeved shirt under his scrubs, exposing his bare forearms.

"Hello, Vincent," I say as I sit in the same chair, waiting for my eyes to adjust to the dark room. The only light comes from the hallway, spilling through the small window in the door. "I hear you wanted to see me."

Vincent reaches over and switches on the reading light clipped to the headboard of his bed. When he brings his bare arm back to rest on his knee, I notice a strange-looking tattoo on the inside of his forearm. It looks homemade—I can't make out what it is.

He doesn't greet me, just jumps straight into his usual quandaries. "You've come to a revelation, haven't you, Michael?" Vincent's voice is barely above a whisper, but it's unnerving.

I catch my frown just as it's forming and bite my lip. "What would that be, Vincent?"

"I think it's time now to dive deeper into the fact that someone wishes you harm—well, not necessarily you, but your wife. They're going to use you to get to her. In fact, they already have and you don't even know it."

I feel my emotions bypass confusion and jump straight to frustration, so I refrain from saying anything just yet.

"Someone is playing mind games with you, but a completely different kind with Paige."

The air seems to become even more suffocating in the room and I try to maintain an even rhythm with my breath. I'm almost certain I've never said Paige's name out loud to Vincent before, but I can't be sure. "What makes you think this?"

"Because people who do bad things always get what's coming to them."

His words immediately anger me and I have to get myself in

check before I open my mouth. Who is he talking about? Me? My wife? I teeter on the edge of snapping at him, but he doesn't give me the chance to speak. He continues.

"Karma delivers itself in all shapes and sizes and it knows no boundaries. Sometimes it's God that presents it in a neat little package—signed, sealed, and delivered. Others, it's man that distributes it, packaged up inside a tidy box of revenge and often sealed with the kiss of death. That's the worst kind of karma—it's messy, and its consequences linger. Do you know why?"

I shake my head while I continue to allow my breath to keep my emotions under control.

"Guilt becomes the deliverer's punishment and it can last a lifetime. This is often the case when someone acts like God and chooses to take the act of karma into their own hands for the sake of ridding the world of something evil. They play God and then their lifetime of punishment begins."

I try to see the correlation of what he's saying to what is going on in my life right now. Just because I've taken the wrong route to helping my wife doesn't mean I'm trying to play God. I use caution as I say, "I'm not following you, Vincent."

Vincent leans forward, aims his face in my direction, and it feels as though his eyes are piercing my soul even with the blindfold on. His voice shifts into an unnerving tone. "Three can keep a secret, if two of them are dead."

My blood turns cold and I snap before I can catch myself. "What did you just say?"

"Three are carrying a secret and in order for it to remain that way, two must die. But Michael," Vincent pauses and pulls down his blindfold. "I'm not talking about the secrets you carry."

I squint my eyes at him in confusion.

"It's someone your wife has come to trust of late. And this person holds the secret to it all."

# 34

D<sup>arlene</sup>

**Now**

As soon as I look into the devil's eyes, it's as if the picture burns me, and I drop it again.

I don't even realize I've been holding my breath until I feel as though I'm going to pass out. I'm not sure if it's actually from the lack of breathing or if it's because I fear that yesterday's choices are now demanding their dues.

This piece of my history is one that I've never told anyone—not even Paige. It's probably one of the reasons I've always prevented myself from getting too shitfaced on alcohol around others, for fear that my drunken tongue might betray me. For many, alcohol often works like a truth serum. Once they've swallowed copious amounts of it, their mouths detour into long, unobstructed ramblings of all sorts of dirty little secrets.

There have been a few times I've been stupid and allowed myself to go over my limit, and when I did, I said things to Paige that should have never come out of my mouth. I'll regret it until the day I die.

But this secret—it's the kind that could end the peaceful sanctuary I've created for myself.

The long trek back to my trailer doesn't seem like a long one at all. At least, I barely remember any of it. We make it back to the porch, and Ginger finds his usual spot, rotates three repetitive circles, then flops down to rest. I hang the canvas bags over one of the old wicker chairs and plop down in the opposite one—it crackles under my weight. I dig into my coat pocket, fish out a cigarette and lighter, and light up with a trembling hand. The long drag steadies my nerves, if only for a moment, then I release a slow exhale, letting the smoke swirl around me.

I pick up the photograph again and stare at the man who is cuddled up next to me—lock eyes with the emerald gaze that once made me feel alive and carefree. At one time they had the power to melt my defenses into following them wherever they wanted to take me. At least, in the beginning they did.

By all accounts, I shouldn't be seeing them now. This man is long gone.

Gone or not, it's a pair of eyes that will haunt me forever. He was the one and only person I ever allowed myself to call *baby*—the love of my life. Or so I thought.

The photo was taken twenty-five years ago. In fact, there were several photos taken on this particular roll of film. Most were snapshots of long drives and scenic landmarks where we stopped to admire the view. Others captured goofy moments when one of us would catch the other off guard and snap a picture without warning. We discovered them all when we picked up the developed film from the local pharmacy—pieces of our history trapped on a piece of paper, forever.

A forbidden history that I thought I'd buried all traces of long ago. Which is why I'm wondering how this picture even exists. Back then, I kept the photos in my possession, but I burned them not long after to erase any signs that I even knew Christian. The only other way someone could get their hands on these photos is if they found the negatives or had hidden this one away.

I look at the cryptic message again. *Three can keep a secret if two of them are dead.*

I run the quote over and over in my mind as I smoke the cigarette down to the filter. The only other person in this photograph wasn't much bigger than the size of a grape, although I didn't know it at the time this photograph was taken. No one else knew about her either.

Paige only asked me who her father was once. I told her he died in an accident before she was born—which is only a partial lie. I didn't want her to go searching for him someday.

I stuff the photo and paper into my coat pocket and stand. "Come on, boy, let's take one more walk."

Ginger groans as he stands stiffly, stretches into a down-dog position, and yawns. For a moment, he's all tongue and ears.

I haven't taken this particular walk in years. In fact, this memory trail isn't one I like to travel. My first initial hike of this path is the kind horror stories are adapted from. It's treacherous, but not in the physical sense—more for the buried trauma that I fear could unearth itself to cause me mental harm if I allow myself to go there very often —it's why I don't.

Even though I've only ventured to this part of the woods a couple of times over the last few years, I know exactly how to get there and the exact spot I'm looking for. It's marked by a tree that I planted shortly after the photo was taken.

The northern red oak towers above the grove of trees that surround it—its color and size unlike its companions. This time of year it boasts its red leaves and provides an ample supply of acorns for wildlife.

When I chose to plant it, I wanted to see something good come out of something that nightmares are made from. It's not that it allowed me to get over it—it just allowed me to twist it into a better story. At least, in my head anyway.

I thought that planting it and watching it grow into a beautiful, magnificent creature might somehow make up for what I'd done. Maybe God wouldn't punish me too harshly in the end if I gave life back after taking another.

The leaves on the ground crackle faintly under the morning dew as Ginger hangs close, allowing me to lead the way this time. It's as if he knows this is more of a secret hike rather than our usual perusing of the woods. He's even quieter than usual.

The bright red foliage is like a beacon among the spotty canopy of leaves around it. Most of the other trees are losing their leaves, yet the oak still looks ablaze. I feel my heart pound as I approach it, much like it used to behave when I would approach the man that is buried under it.

# 35

# Michael

Vincent's last words feel like a noose strangling my ability to remain calm or rational.

It's the thing he said about Paige trusting someone she shouldn't —at least, that's how I took it—that has me questioning who she may have interacted with as Vanessa.

Or maybe he's talking about me.

But how would he even know this—any of it?

Like all of my recent conversations with him, I'm left more confused than ever. I'm even questioning why I'd bothered talking to him in the first place. He'd insisted on seeing me this time, as if what he had to tell me was a matter of life and death. Yet he ended our visit the same way he always does—by rolling over and refusing to say anything else. He threw his little hissy fit, insisted on seeing me, then fed me more riddles. From where I stand, I've just wasted time I can't afford to lose.

I hurry out of the hospital to my car and attempt to call Paige. She doesn't answer. Typically, this wouldn't cause alarm, but right now it feels as though I'm stuck in a waiting game, and the prize at the end won't be a celebratory win.

I drive toward home, stopping at every insistent red light this small town has. I attempt to hold back my frustration as I grip the steering wheel and try to use the moment to figure out how I'm going to start my conversation with Paige. It's probably best to jump straight into it. Maybe she already knows about the episodes and hasn't told me.

If that's the case, she must be terrified. The thought makes me sick.

That's impossible—I'm sure she doesn't know. This reassuring thought attempts to calm all the negative ones, but it's like trying to plug a hole in a dam with a single finger.

As I consider telling Paige the truth, my mind scrolls through every possible outcome like a Google search. Each bold headline of possibilities feels useless—just clickbait for my thoughts. They frustrate me, pulling me back and forth in an endless loop of what-ifs, like I'm trapped in a search engine with no answers.

As I pull into the driveway, I don't see Paige's Rover. I shut off the engine but sit in the front seat while I stare at the house, clueless what to do now. The house seems to swell before me, and the thought occurs to me for the first time that my actions could cause me to lose everything. That my secrecy could be the knife that cuts me out of Paige's life.

One thing I've learned being a psychiatrist, and through my own therapy, is that secrets have a way of building walls where bridges should have been, isolating us until there's no way back. This secret I've been keeping from Paige will surely build a tight wall of distrust that'll take years to tear down—that's if I'm lucky enough to have the chance.

I put my key into the lock, the click seeming to echo against the quiet on the other side of the door. As I step inside, the faint smell of lavender floats in the air from the candle warmer that has grown cold. The air in the house feels the same—or maybe it's just me.

I set my things on the foyer table and step into the open living space. Even though her car isn't in the drive, I call for her anyway. "Paige?"

The only sound I hear is the hum from the large ceiling fan above and the air escaping the heat vents around the room.

This time I announce myself louder as I head up the stairs. "Paige?"

Nothing still.

A sick feeling begins to swell in my stomach as I cross the landing and enter our bedroom. I find both closet doors ajar, and nausea spreads into my chest and throat, making it hard to breathe.

My gut is screaming that something is wrong.

I swing Paige's closet door wider and look inside. Other than her robe lying on the floor instead of hanging in the bathroom, it looks the same as far as I can tell.

Panic follows me into my own closet when I see the drawer at the back open, the contents seeming to ooze out of it. The clothes that Laura hid back there when she'd make sure Paige made it home safely.

Paige must have found them. The fear of what must have gone through her mind at the time sends me into a deeper panic. I can't imagine what she must have thought upon discovering them.

What made her go looking in the first place? The question crosses my mind as I continue mentally scolding myself for keeping all of this a secret. I should have talked to her from the very beginning. But I chose the path of denial—something I seem to be good at. And denial can be much like gripping a fistful of sand. No matter how hard you cling to it, eventually reality slips through.

I pull my cell phone from my pocket and attempt to call hers again. It rings—downstairs.

Worry takes its turn as I race back down the stairs and find her phone lying on the kitchen counter.

In a grasping attempt, I dial Vanessa's number—the phone I'd provided her. At the fifth ring, when I had given up hope, someone answers. Instead of relief, terror jumps to the front of the line.

It isn't a woman's voice.

"Looking for someone?" The voice isn't feminine.

"Who the hell is this?" My voice comes out shakier than I want it to, but I push the words out more aggressively toward the end.

"Aw, Michael. Where's that calm therapist's tone? Vanessa isn't here right now, but I'll be sure to let her know you called when I see her. And I *will* see her—"

The line goes dead.

# 36

anessa

I don't know what scares me more—the thought that I'm someone else or the realization that Michael might have always known I wasn't just me.

I've never been one to run from a situation before, but then again, I'm not sure if this is true either—I don't remember anything about myself, and I suddenly have no idea who I am.

As I drive through the familiar, yet strange streets of this neighborhood, I try to remember even getting a driver's license, or learning to drive in the first place. I attempt to send my mind even further back than that—dig up any sort of memory of who I am. No recollection of a childhood, parents, friends—not even a first kiss. Doesn't everyone remember that?

There's something about being behind the wheel that makes it hard to breathe, as if a heavy weight is pressing on my chest. The urge to pull over and get as far away from the car as possible is over-whelming. I don't like this feeling—it's almost crippling. I don't even realize it, but my hands grip the steering wheel tight enough to turn my knuckles white as I stare out ahead of me. It feels like the vehicle itself is alive, humming with an energy that is feeding on my anxiety yet daring me to keep going. But stopping feels just as dangerous right now, as though some unwanted past might catch up with me if I linger too long. My mind begins to unravel as though it's trying to untangle something I'd rather not remember.

Images begin to flash in my mind like the erratic bursts of a strobe light—only slower, as if moving frame by frame, in and out of focus. I struggle to process them; there are so many, and they keep coming. My palms grow slick on the steering wheel as muted sounds and scattered images begin to speed up, each one sharper, clearer, and more vivid. My heart pounds harder with every flash, slamming against my chest like it's trying to break free.

I turn my head to the left and realize I'm reliving something that happened to me.

I flinch as I see a blinding flash of headlights cutting through the fog. Then comes the crunch of metal, the echo of shattering glass, and extreme pain down the left side of my body.

Just before impact, I see *him*. The man in the other vehicle, his face illuminated in the glare of his own headlights. Dark hair, a deep grin, dimples, and those eyes.

They're green, vivid and familiar, like I've stared into them before. Recognition threatens to seep through, but before I can remember, the memory pulls me back into the wreckage.

The screeching of brakes. The world spinning. And then—nothing.

My vision blurs and I blink back to reality. I realize I've slowed my car to a crawl and have veered dangerously close to the row of parked cars, so I swerve back into the street. A burst of breath escapes me as I realize I've been holding it, and it makes me dizzy.

What just happened to me?

A memory?

If that's what this was, I'm not sure I want to remember anymore.

The toot of a horn sounds behind me, and I see the driver in my rearview mirror as he throws his hands in the air in a displeasing manner. I force myself to push the gas and continue driving, determined to put as much distance as possible between me and the ritzy neighborhood I just left.

I continue to drive as anxiety knots itself tighter inside my chest, so I attempt to focus on my surroundings—the streets, the buildings, and the pungent, briny scent of the salty sea air. Clapboard buildings painted in soft coastal hues—blues, whites, and grays—line each side of the street. Everything about the scene screams seaside town. The streets are dotted with numerous shops, cozy cafes, and ice cream parlors. Windows are overflowing with nautical trinkets— whales and dolphins in every form.

Something about all of it feels like home, yet like a dream. As though I've only visited this place in my sleep. I make several turns and find myself in more familiar territory. Ahead, I recognize the oval wooden sign hanging above the weathered shingle roof—**The Thirsty Lobster**. It's the bar that is more like home than anywhere else.

I pull over into a vacant spot and shut off the engine, and the weight on my chest calms slightly. I'm not sure if it's because I'm in a familiar place, or if it's because I can already taste the shot of whiskey I'm about to take to calm it.

The walk to the bar counter isn't taken with my usual confidence. I don't even feel like myself—whoever that is anymore—and I doubt I look like myself either. Sliding onto a tall chair, I glance up as the familiar bartender approaches, a towel in hand, wiping the bar in front of me.

"Hey. You're back," he says, his tone casual but probing. "Remember anything else about being in here yesterday?"

I frown, caught off guard, and my words sound unsure. "I... remember... everything."

"Good," he replies, raising an eyebrow. "You sure were confused about it earlier."

"Earli—" I cut myself off from finishing the question. I don't even remember earlier, which means *she* was here. The darling little housewife.

I take off the girlie pink cap and run my fingers through my hair, flipping it around to bring back volume and softness. The bartender doesn't even ask; he just sets a shot glass down on the bar and fills it full.

"Looks like you could use this." He slides it toward me and I give him a forced smile.

When I raise it to my lips, instead of my mouth watering in response, I feel a wave of nausea swell in my throat.

I **despise whiskey.**

The three words parade through my mind, catching me off guard, and confusion marches in. A multitude of thoughts fall into procession behind this one. *My mother made me hate this stuff. Michael wouldn't want me drinking this. I'm trying to have a baby.*

More thoughts skip the line, marching forward, backward, and in random patterns. *Who cares what Michael thinks—he's always going back to her. No one's going to tell me what to do. I just want to have fun.*

As each arises, it's as if they form opposing factions, battling one another until it feels like an all-out war is coming. The outcome, I fear, will only deepen my confusion about who I truly am.

"You going to drink it or fondle it?"

The sexy, familiar voice sends a chill through me, laced with both excitement and fear. The identity crisis going on inside my head wavers to the side of throwing caution to the wind. My heart pounds and I lift the glass to my lips as I hold my breath and take a sip. It's all I can manage, but it's a start.

I turn to look at the man who has perched himself on the stool next to me, and an involuntary shiver runs down my spine. It's the same green eyes. An image flashes through my mind of him pushing me up against the wall, erotically pressing his body into mine. The image is both exciting and terrifying. A memory I don't recollect before now.

What is happening to me?

My mind shifts from the erotic memory to the words said to me in the tattoo shop.

*I came here to brand you.*

As if he's reading my mind, he says, "How's the tattoo healing?"

I force myself to take another sip of whiskey and barely hold back a gag.

"Is this what you do? Brand women?"

"Just those that need to be."

Another image invades my train of thought, making it difficult to focus.

*I'm waking—cold—pulling at my robe—frantic—I inspect the tattoo on my arm, as if I've never seen it before—as though I don't remember getting it.*

But I do remember getting it.

Other fleeting images begin to surface like pages of an open book flipping wildly in a gust of wind, giving me only a glimpse before disappearing again.

*I'm submerged in a bathtub—Michael's panicky grip pulling me from the water.*

*Michael's arms wrapped around me, the sound of the ocean in the distance.*

*I rub my fingertips over the slick surface of a brown, droopy dog as I avoid inhaling a puff of cigarette smoke blown toward me by a cool breeze.*

*The woman pulls the sleeve of her robe up to reveal a tattoo on the inside of her arm.*

I begin to feel as though my mind and my body have been split in half, and it's making me dizzy.

Then the horrific images from earlier reemerge.

Shattering glass, twisted metal, excruciating pain, and... green eyes.

I lock eyes with his and a voice inside my head begins to scream.

**"It's him."**

I don't know what that means, but instinct is telling me to get as far away from him as possible.

My heart feels like multiple fists pounding against my chest, and I struggle to form words. I make a slow search of the room for a way out, careful not to let my face or actions betray what I'm thinking.

*Go to Darlene. He can't find you there.*

I almost flinch as the words race through my mind, and it's immediately followed up with:

*Who the hell is Darlene?*

It takes everything in me not to scream as the chaos of two separate paths of thought collide, competing for control. My eyes scan the pub and find the bartender at the other end of the bar, polishing glasses and stacking them on a shelf. When he turns to fill a tall thin glass with beer, he finds me looking at him. I'm not sure what sort of face I'm wearing, but his eyebrows frown at me.

I clear my throat and give the man sitting next to me the best version I can of a confident smile.

"Excuse me," I say, keeping my tone light and casual. "I need to step away for a moment—too much coffee earlier." I force a small laugh, hoping it sounds natural, and begin to stand, making sure my movements are steady, not rushed.

But for some reason, all I want to do right now... is run.

# 37

## Darlene

**Twenty-five years ago**

As I lie here, spooned in Christian's arms, my mind is caught in a tug-of-war between the pull of sleep and the relentless chatter of my racing thoughts. Right now, my noisy inner monologue is winning.

Spending the evening with Christian, Donavon, and my dog Ginger turned out to be surprisingly pleasant. Ginger even seemed to welcome the change as she curled up on the couch with a tiny human—probably the first she's ever seen. I almost let myself sink into a quiet comfort—an unfamiliar feeling that terrifies me. Comfort is something I usually only find within the walls of my own home. But I'm not sure it's a feeling I've ever had completely.

We spent the evening snuggled in our blankets on the couch,

eating popcorn, and watching an animated movie about cute monsters and a big-eyed girl who isn't afraid of them—except for one. But don't we all have a monster of some sort that we're afraid of?

For me, the monsters that scare me can change. Today my monster comes in the form of self-doubt and mistrust. It has tormented me all day, even during moments of contentment. Even when I attempt to fully engross myself in all the events of the day, my mind keeps coming back to the same thing: the feeling that Christian is hiding something that could break us. But once again, I am battling with whether I should turn over a rock to see what's under it.

If there's one thing I learned growing up in the environment that I did, it's that you have to be ready for anything. That includes never completely trusting anyone no matter how much you care for them. Even though I've found myself crazy in love with Christian, there's still a small, nagging part of me that refuses to let my guard down, reminding me that love can be just as dangerous as any betrayal. At least, it is in my world.

The sound of Ginger's nails tapping on the hardwood floor as she paces around the bed tells me that she's anxious, or she needs to go outside. Being in a strange place, it's probably both. Once again, I'm sliding out from Christian's arm, trying not to wake him. I grab a long-sleeved flannel draped over the footboard of the bed and slip it on over Christian's t-shirt, then tiptoe out of the room. As always, Ginger moves as quietly as I do.

We ease down the squeaky steps and I pause every time one of them protests. Ginger manages to avoid all of the creaks and pops and waits at the bottom of the stairs for me. I make it through the living room and to the back door of the kitchen when I finally admit to myself that I'm not really here to take Ginger outside to relieve herself. Not really. I'm here to feed my curiosity.

What is it about being told something is off-limits that makes a need develop inside you to break the rules? I'm not sure it would have bothered me as much had it only been Christian claiming it's forbidden territory—but Donavon's insinuation that someone is in there forces me to do something I'm told not to do. I'm ninety-nine percent sure his little story is just the makings of an overactive imagination, but that one percent is beckoning me to find out. Half of that percent comes from seeing a ghost the first time I came here, and the other half is due to Donavon's secret drawings.

As I turn the wobbly doorknob and pull, nothing happens. Several inches above it, hidden under the faded curtain, is a deadbolt. I half expect alarms to go off when I turn it and open the door, but there's only a slight protest from the hinges.

The night air has a bite to it even though it's technically summer. I step out onto the back porch, the wooden boards showing their age even in the moonlight. There aren't any outdoor lights, but the moon is almost full and illuminates the backyard as if there's a spotlight highlighting it. The small porch has a metal roof above, the surface cluttered with toys and cheap plastic chairs you might find at a dollar store. There's even a child-sized one.

Crickets and other night insects perform their nightly ritual of sounds, while in the distance two different types of owls compete with one another. The Great Horned owl to my left emits a deep *hoo-hoo-hoo*, while the Barred owl on my right attempts to bellow his usual phrase that we Mainers hear as *who cooks for you, who cooks for you*. But in the distance, a Whip-poor-will wins my attention with his lonely calling of his own name, as if he's beckoning anything to notice him.

I've always been able to relate to the Whip-poor-will—calling out into the darkness, not expecting an answer—content to remain unnoticed. Until I met Christian. Now, I find myself torn between the comfort of solitude and the unfamiliar ache of wanting to be truly seen—wanted by him.

My mother dragged in all kinds of riffraff who called themselves men into our lives after my father died. One in particular was as mean as he was handsome. He emotionally and often physically abused her, but she would proclaim, *the heart can't help who it loves*, and kept allowing him to do it. I think he would have eventually ended up killing her had he not wrapped his car around a tree, preventing him from abusing her anymore. He survived; he just wasn't physically or mentally able to dominate her like he once did. Men like that only calm down due to age or something catastrophic changing them. She ended up staying with him until her death and claimed that the accident was the best thing to ever happen to him. *It humbled him*, she would say.

We often tell ourselves lies when it comes to what we think is love. But often, it is nothing more than our insecurities running—or ruling—our choices.

I suppose in some ways, I'm more like my mother than I want to admit.

Ginger plants her nose to the ground and follows a crooked line straight to the shed sitting under the trees. She pauses at the door, sniffing in quick succession along the crack, as if she smells something in there. I walk slowly toward it, and once I'm there, my heart feels more like fists pounding on my chest. I'm not sure why.

I reach out and grab the chain and padlock and, for some reason, my mind jumps straight to the tattoo Christian chose for me. A flood of unease washes over me as a thought manifests itself into a question.

*They're the same—aren't they?*

A marker. A symbol of control.

My mind attempts to spiral and I have to shake off the thought. It's then physically shaken from me when I hear movement inside the shack. Ginger must hear it too, as her sniffs grow more aggressive.

"He'll be very angry if he catches you."

The sudden jolt of Donavon behind me nearly makes me leap off the ground, my hand slapping my chest as though it's trying to keep my heart from doing the same. A slight yelp escapes me, but I catch it and pull it back inside, though my heart is pounding so hard it can be heard outside my body.

My voice escapes me and I have to locate it before I'm able to speak.

"You scared the shi— I mean, the crap out of me."

"If Daddy catches you around this building, he'll scare you away."

My forehead frowns in the moonlight as I question his wording. "Scare me away?"

"He doesn't want anyone to know about him."

"Him? Him who?"

"The boy in there."

# 38

# Darlene

**Now**

A breeze rustles the leaves above and sends a blanket of red fluttering around me.

I sit down on a bed of dried foliage, which crackles loudly with each shift of my weight, then prop my forearms onto my knees. Still gripping the photograph in one hand, I glance at it again, then let my eyes fall to the ground where the man in the image now lies. The memory of his stare forms behind my eyeballs, as vivid in my mind as if I had looked into them only yesterday.

I squeeze my eyes shut for a moment in an attempt to clear them away, then take a deep breath as I look around the forest, the silence around me heavy. My thoughts scream loudly inside my head, preventing me from being able to focus on the quiet sounds of the woods.

That's the thing about these woods—it's more than just trees and wildlife. It's dense, thick, and massive. If someone wanted to hide something—anything—this is the place. The floor of the forest is soft and pliable from years of rain and decay, giving it the ability to swallow a secret whole—my secret—and it's buried beneath layers of earth, time, and this tree.

There's no way anyone would ever think to look here, and even if they did, the forest has a way of erasing its scars, closing over disturbances as if nothing has ever happened. Acadia isn't just a forest; it's the keeper of my secret—the real reason I never left.

As I try to calm my racing thoughts, the pounding of my heart fills my ears, drowning out the sounds of life that surround me. Forgotten images flash through my mind, one after another, relentless and sharp. No matter how hard I fight to keep them at bay, the memories surge forward, refusing to stay buried—just like the secret beneath this tree.

Scenes from that awful night emerge like short movie clips, choppy yet vivid enough that each scene grows clearer, louder—merging together to make me relive that awful night. My hands begin to shake as my breath comes faster and more ragged. I stand and stomp a few feet away, turning my back toward the tree. Ginger pads up next to me and presses his body against my leg. I squat down and wrap my arms around his warm body as if to draw strength from him.

Ginger is my fifth bloodhound and he's the most affectionate of them all. He is far better at showing love than any human I've ever encountered, and he gives it freely, without conditions. In my experience, people rarely ever give true, unconditional love. They claim to love you, but the moment you choose not to conform to their beliefs or respond disagreeably, conditions often emerge, and more often than not, the result is being written off. Or, unless you change your ways or change your beliefs, you're no longer welcome. Close family members are often the worst.

I'm fine with the end result—those kinds of people are toxic and I'm better off without them.

I've tried my best not to look back. When I allow myself to do it, I only end up feeling lost and the future seems bleak. To remember the past often only hurts and casts a shadow on the here and now. And right now, my mind insists on taking me back to a memory that I thought was buried forever.

Someone else has dug it up.

Both my hands clutch the piece of paper and the photo—pieces of history that have been unearthed, and now I need to figure out who did it. Everything that happened that night felt like the sort of thing that only happens in a movie—the kind of thing that makes you hide your eyes, only to peek between your fingers as if it will soften the blow of what you know you're about to see.

Everything in me, leading up to that awful moment, screamed that something bad was going to happen, but I didn't listen. I didn't leave when my gut told me I should.

I read the quote again and again. *Three can keep a secret if two of them are dead.*

But two of them are not dead.

# 39

## M ichael

Fear has been a constant companion of mine since the day I found my mother in a bathtub, but I've always been able to bury it beneath logic—until now. At the moment, I'm powerless, and it's spreading through me like a rapidly growing disease.

I stand in the center of the kitchen, frozen, with my phone in hand, and stare helplessly across the vast ocean outside. The man who answered the phone I had given to my wife—or Vanessa—now has her phone. I immediately suspect he's the one behind the emails as well, and it almost sends me into panic mode.

I try to switch off my overactive imagination and prevent my mind from steering down the path of what-ifs, but it's no use. It goes there anyway—full speed ahead.

What if Vincent was right? What if Paige trusted someone as

Vanessa and now they want to hurt her? What if this person has Paige right now?

But the man on the phone said he *will* see her, which means maybe he doesn't have her. It also means he's looking for her.

I need to find her first.

As if I've thought of the devil himself, my phone pings with an email notification. The sender—*dirtylittlesecrets*.

I open the email to find a large photo of Paige posed as if she's kissing the camera, the backs of her fingertips touching her face, giving a full view of her forearm. A fresh tattoo is prominently displayed on her pale skin. I zoom in to look at it—it's definitely not something she would choose to scar her body with. In fact, it looks as though she found someone on the side of the street to do it.

I scroll down to find a short message that sends a shiver crawling through me:

*You've been enjoying your new wife... but now it's my turn.*

Terror grabs me by the throat, making it hard to breathe. I don't stare at the email any longer; instead, I call Laura. She answers after two rings.

"Michael, I think I found something."

"Laura, Paige's car is gone, and I just got another email. I think the person sending these emails might have her." I know I might sound overly dramatic, but at the moment panic has taken the driver's seat and has already reached peak speeds. "He answered the cell phone that I gave Paige—or Vanessa when all these blackouts started."

"When?"

"Just now."

"Let's not try to speculate. I patrolled by your house this morning and her car was still there, so she couldn't have been gone all that long. I took the cell phone back into the apartment just like always after I brought Paige home from the bar. So he had to have broken into the apartment sometime after that." Laura pauses while I wait impatiently. "I did figure out where some of the emails are being sent from. He used a VPN, but the one he used is cheap and isn't secure, so I was able to trace one of the IP addresses back to the Westside Café."

"That's just a five-minute walk from the apartment."

"And the bar where I found Paige," Laura says. "I'm headed over there now. Michael, keep in mind, he may not have her, and it's possible he's using you to find her. So sit tight. I'll go and let you know what I find out and what our next move is."

"Why is he targeting my wife?"

"I have no idea, but I promise you, I will find out."

"I think I should come with you."

"No. Just sit tight. I'll call you as soon as I know something. Who knows? Maybe Paige is just out somewhere and will show up any minute."

I know Laura's right, but I can't just sit back and do nothing.

I hang up but continue to grip my phone in hand as I pace circles around the first floor of my house, my thoughts pacing with me. I pause every so often to gaze out across the angry ocean. Today, the waves build in chaotic peaks, each one attempting to outdo the one before it, much like my escalating thoughts. A storm is brewing on the horizon, and just like the events of my life right now, nothing can stop it.

The memory of my conversation with Vincent resurfaces in my mind. Maybe I'm just desperate, but for some reason I have a gnawing suspicion that he knows more about my situation than what he's telling me. Even though everything he says seems to be nothing more than riddles, they make as much sense as anything else right now. If there's even a sliver of truth in his cryptic words, it might be worth digging deeper. After all, I feel as though I'm running out of options—and time. Before I know it, I'm heading back toward the hospital, determined to press him for answers.

The hallway of Vincent's floor is a bustle of activity as food-service aides collect trays and housekeeping staff tend to emptying garbage cans. I slip down the hallway unnoticed and quietly enter Vincent's room.

The same small light clipped to the headboard is aimed at the spot on the bed where Vincent usually sits, but Vincent isn't sitting in it. I look toward the bathroom door; it's standing open and the room is dark. Confusion twists my face into a questioning frown.

I consider asking someone where I might find him, but attempt to be patient and wait for his return instead. I take a seat in my usual uncomfortable chair across from his bed.

Next to Vincent's bed is a small, cluttered table, its surface buried under a mix of books, scattered papers, and an assortment of cups, each with its own bendy straw jutting out at odd angles. The space under the table is crowded with similar items as well, minus the cups. Wedged between the table's legs and the bed is a thick binder, pages protruding messily from it. In the dim light, it's hard to make out any details, but it piques my curiosity.

I slide it free and lay it on the bed, then adjust the gooseneck arm of the reading light to shine directly onto the binder. The outside covers are made of hard leather, and the yellowed, aged pages give it an antique feel under the dim lighting. It's almost as though I'm looking at something straight out of a *Harry Potter* movie.

I ease the front cover open, and the crackling of the leather even sounds antique. The first page that comes into view feels as though it's just grabbed me by the throat, cutting off my oxygen.

# 40

D arlene

**Twenty-five years ago**

"There's a boy in there?"

My voice squeaks—more like escapes me as a high-pitched squeal—but I keep it quiet. I don't want to get the boy in trouble for being out of bed.

I grab the lock and begin to yank on it.

"Don't!" Donavon grips my forearm with surprising strength. His wide eyes dart to the house, then back to me. "You can't," he hisses. "Daddy will know. He always knows."

I take his hand in mine, then gently grab his other hand and lean closer to his face. The moonlight casts a soft glow over his tiny body, making him seem even smaller. My eyes catch on his forearm—

something there drawing my attention. Earlier, I thought it was just a press-on tattoo, but now it's clearer.

I stare at it, rubbing my thumb over the design—it's smooth.

This isn't a fake tattoo.

"Is this... a real tattoo?" I whisper, the idea of a small boy having a permanent tattoo completely derailing my thoughts. But what consumes me even more is the image itself.

It's a crude-looking lock with a chain messily attached to it. Definitely not the work of a professional.

He looks up at me with wide eyes. "Daddy did it with his tattoo gun. He's got a tattoo too, but someone else gave him his—a key. He says it means I can never get away."

A sick feeling balls in the pit of my stomach, and even though I'm not inside, it feels as though walls are closing in on me.

I have to force myself to bring my focus back to his earlier words.

"Donavon," I whisper, "if there's a boy in there, we can't just leave him. What if he's hurt? What if—"

"He's not hurt," Donavon interrupts, his voice trembling. "It's where he lives."

I frown in confusion. "What? Who is he? Why is he in there?"

"Daddy says he did a bad thing and he doesn't deserve to be out in the world."

"How long has he been in there?"

The boy shrugs.

"Who is he, Donavon?"

He looks down at the ground and says, "He told me if anyone ever found him I wasn't supposed to ever say who he is."

"Is he family? Or did your father kidnap him or something?" Now my voice is getting louder, and Donavon shushes me.

Ginger makes a whining noise and jumps back, poised to bark, and I place a hand on her back to stop her. My eyes follow her stare down to the bottom of the door, and I see tiny, dirty fingers just before they dart back out of sight. Ginger eases back closer, sniffing, then the fingers appear again, touching the dog on the nose.

"Does your daddy punish you like this?"

"I just have to stay in the closet sometimes."

"How long?"

The boy shrugs. "Sometimes all day. If I do something really bad he makes me sleep in there."

Horrified, I press more. "What's something really bad?"

"Like leaving my toys on the bed or jumping on it. That makes him super angry. He says that beds are made for two things—I'm not old enough for one of them, and the other is sleep. He says if I can't appreciate it, then I don't deserve to sleep in it."

I'm sure my face has a horrified expression, so I try to smooth it out.

I point to the shed. "So what did he do that was so bad?"

"Daddy says he killed my mommy."

"What? When?" Frustration begins to build as a tidal wave of questions continues to rise in my mind.

He shrugs. "A long time ago. One day she was here and then she was gone. Then he was here."

"What do you mean then he was here?"

"He was in my mommy's belly. Then he was here and she was gone."

*Died giving birth.* Christian's explanation as to what happened to his wife. My earlier thoughts were right, but I couldn't fathom something like this. I try to make sense of what Donavon is saying, and the only conclusion I can come to is that Christian blamed this little boy for the death of his wife and is punishing him for it.

"How old is your brother?"

Donavon's voice becomes unsure, scared. "I didn't say he was my brother. You can't know that. No one knows about him."

"What do you mean no one knows about him?"

"Dad says he killed Mommy and he doesn't deserve to have a life."

"He killed your Mommy by being born? That's why he has to be locked in a shed?" I realize I'm asking a boy to answer an adult question—a sick question. One that makes my skin crawl at the thought of it.

An image of the baby growing inside me flashes across my mind, and my breath catches mid-inhale. I'm carrying the child of a man who has another child locked in a shack. Punishing him for doing something that was out of his control. Punishing him for being born.

I attempt to speak, and my words shake from me—choppy and barely audible. "How long has he been in there?"

The boy shrugs again. When he starts to speak, it's like someone opened the floodgates on his memories. He rambles out bits and pieces, his words tumbling over each other.

"He didn't cry when he was a baby, so Daddy left him in the crib a lot. The only time he cried was if he went too long without a bottle. I learned how to make it and fed him a lot. Daddy didn't like changing his diaper, so he only did it when it started smelling really bad."

Donavon pauses, glances back at the house, and lowers his voice. "You can't tell anyone this. You promise? I love my Daddy, and I don't want anything bad to happen to him."

I listen, and it strikes me that Donavon knows enough to understand what his father is doing is wrong—but not how truly cruel it is. The innocence of a child.

I soften the tone of my voice as I ask, "Do you remember how old he was when your father started locking him in here?"

Donavon shakes his head. "I don't know. I just remember he wasn't supposed to come downstairs, but he did, and Daddy caught him. He got real mad and locked him in there. It wasn't all the time, just for a while. Then... then he went outside the house. He really wasn't supposed to do that." He hesitates, his voice dropping even lower. "That's when Daddy locked him in for good. He's been there ever since."

Donavon looks back at the house again. After a long pause, he leans in close, whispering, "Sometimes I sneak and let him out at night."

My mind flashes back to the first night I was here. The dirty boy crouched by the stairs wasn't a ghost.

"Donavon, I know you don't want your dad to get into trouble, but this isn't right. He needs to be let out. No one should have to be locked in a shack." I choose my words carefully as I try to make a little boy understand that this isn't a way of life. "It might be different if there wasn't a lock on it and he could get out whenever he wanted to. Do you like it when your dad makes you stay in the closet?"

He shakes his head no.

Earlier, my mind was torn between loving this man and not wanting to lose him, and feeling as though he's hiding something, making me unable to trust him. Now I know why. Right now, that feeling has changed—I want to get as far away from him as possible.

I squat down in front of Donavon and grip his upper arms. "Donavon, I have to get him out of there, but I don't want you to get into trouble for me finding out about it. So I need you to sneak back into the house and go back to bed. Can you do that?"

Donavon starts to cry. "I don't want Daddy to find out that I told you. I don't want to get in trouble. I don't want my daddy to get in trouble."

"Don't worry about your Dad. He's a big boy. And I promise, he will never know you told me. Okay?"

He hesitates.

"I promise," I say again.

He nods and wipes his face with the back of his hand.

"Now, go back inside and sneak back to bed. Do your best to go back to sleep. I promise, I will find a way to get your brother out, and your father will never know you told me. I want to make sure he gets out of this shack for good." I intentionally lie with my next declaration because I know—or maybe I hope—that it won't end well for Christian. "And I promise, your dad won't get in trouble."

I don't even realize it when I cross two fingers on my left hand as I say the words.

Donavon takes one more look at the shack, then scurries back to the house. I turn back to the shed and ease closer to the door, then press my ear against it and listen for a moment.

I speak softly. "I'm going to get you out. Okay?"

I hear nothing.

"Show me your fingers if you can hear me."

Nothing. I wait a moment longer.

Tiny fingers wiggle under the door, barely visible in the faint moonlight. My heart pounds so hard I can feel it in my throat.

I whisper again, "Don't worry, I'm going to get you out of there. Just hang on."

I glance back toward the house, making sure Donavon is out of sight. Then I grab the padlock hooked through a chain on the door, inspecting it for any weakness. Ginger jumps up and stands on her back two legs, pressing her front paws against the door as if she's trying to help.

There's no way I can break the lock with my hands, so I look around for something on the ground. I find an L-shaped rod, and when I pick up its weight, I realize it's a tire iron. I first attempt to slide the straight end into one of the loops of the chain, but it's too big. I slide it through the shackle of the lock and yank downward on the iron, hoping to pry the lock open.

It won't budge.

I make several attempts, engrossed in what I'm doing, when a chilling voice behind me raises the hair on my arms—this time there's nothing warm or even sexy about it. It's terrifying.

"What do you think you're doing?"

# 41

# D arlene

**Now**

For the longest time Christian wasn't what he seemed—he was a storm disguised as my shelter. What I thought was refuge only turned out to be the eye of the storm that was waiting to consume me.

In the beginning, Christian was the sweetest of honey, and over time that honey became laced with poison in the form of manipulation followed by what I thought was a need for him. I had fallen so hard that I feared losing him and blamed myself when things between us became tense or unsettling.

I can close my eyes and still picture every detail of his face—those boyish dimples and that smile. The kind that reached his eyes, making them either devilish or innocent, depending on the situation. In the beginning, I didn't fear the devil in them—in fact, I loved it. Danger meant intriguing in my young, stupid mind.

I can close my eyes and still feel the shape of his body against mine, as if we were somehow formed together by the same mold. Laughter and conversation would so easily manifest between us, untainted and carefree.

At least, in the beginning.

Until an unnoticed, subtle shift began to occur, and I didn't even see it happening.

As time went on, I began to question my own actions every time he gaslit me into seeing things his way. Every time he made me feel small and then held me close as though he was the only one who could put me back together. He made me believe I was weak and needed him to be strong.

Those last few weeks—the events leading up to that awful night —forced me to prove that I was strong.

I did what I had to do.

During my early pregnancy I didn't want to carry a piece of him with me for the rest of my life. I buried him and tried my best to destroy everything else that reminded me of him—including trying to lose his baby. Paige. I couldn't afford an abortion, so I attempted to make it happen naturally—more like inhumanely and unnaturally. It was morbid, and another regret I will have to carry with me until I die.

For several years after Paige was born, I functioned like a robot. I went through the motions of motherhood, but never really felt it. I struggled not to look at her and see Christian. The only saving grace was that she hadn't inherited his eyes—hers stayed blue, like mine.

No matter how hard I tried, I couldn't erase the images of that night. For years, I continued to spiral out of control and lost myself in self-sabotage and delusions. I allowed my drinking to become out of control. Even though I kept writing down how much I drank, the number I gave myself permission to consume just kept growing.

It was a feeble attempt to drown the haunting memories.

What's worse is that in one of my drunken stupors, I think I even told Paige about how I tried to get rid of her, thinking it would deter her from ever allowing a man into her life.

It was stupid, and I was wrong.

Our minds during a drunken binge can often tell us stories that are untrue, far-fetched, or even terrifying. We wrongly believe what our brains are telling us, and during intoxication our judgment shifts into that of an unruly child, and we act out accordingly.

At that time I saw myself in the mirror, the state I was in, and my mind said, you have to protect Paige. Keep her from ever becoming you. Keep her from making the same mistakes.

I forced her to take birth control and ran boys off that she really liked. I used fear to instill fear in her. All I managed to do was cause deep scars that will carry with her through the rest of her life.

Despite all that I put her through, I'm surprised by the woman she's become.

All these years later, I'm glad I didn't succeed at losing the only good accomplishment I've ever made in my life.

But now, I fear that the whispers of this forest are ready to tell my tale. My secrets. Because I'm holding part of that in my hand—proof that the green-eyed devil is coming back to haunt me.

Someone has opened my book of memories of that night, and now my mind is flipping through the pages, landing on the horror sections of that story—a horror story with a terrifying ending.

# 42

P aige/Vanessa

My mind is like a house divided, my thoughts fighting for control, my emotions tearing at the foundations of who I thought I was—or think I am.

This is the battle going on inside me as I attempt to casually walk to the ladies' room. I can feel his green eyes fixated on me, and for some reason it feels as though they might physically hurt me.

The bartender walks in my direction, and our eyes lock onto one another. I'm not sure what my face communicates to him, but his eyes narrow as if trying to translate it. I try to send him an SOS message by pressing my lips into a firm line, my eyes large and pleading. I think the desperation in my expression sends the message—I need to get away from this man. The bartender seems to understand because he creates a distraction, letting the glass of beer he just filled slip from his hand. It shatters on the floor, sending shards and splashes of beer flying behind the bar. I use the opportunity to dart left instead of right into the cramped kitchen.

The odor of greasy, cooked food rushes toward me and so do all of the eyes in the hazy room. I struggle to form words.

"Please. Is there a way out?"

A grandmotherly-looking woman, her hair pinned into a tight bun, says, "Are you all right, dear?"

I struggle to form words. "No. I mean, yes, but is there a way out through here?"

She points across the kitchen to the back corner. "Back through there, but—"

I don't wait for her to finish. I rush around the tall, lanky man standing at the hot grill, steam skewing his features. The woman calls behind me.

"The gate has a padlock on the outside. Back corner, behind the dumpsters. There's a hole in the fence—if you can fit."

I glance over my shoulder only briefly but don't stop. Instinct is screaming inside my head to get out.

A man's voice surfaces in my mind, echoing unfamiliar words of warning. *I don't think a pretty lady such as yourself should be running around with the likes of him. If you ask me, he's trouble and not just the kind you find in a bar.*

The bartender? When did he say this to me?

I burst through the heavy door, which sticks on the first try. A rancid combination of rotting food and sewage assaults my nostrils, and I press my forearm over my nose. The air feels sharper and colder than before, and it bites at my exposed skin. The small rectangular space is enclosed by a tall, weathered fence. At the end facing the street, a pair of plank doors—likely meant for garbage truck access—stand shut, secured with a padlock from the outside. My chest tightens as I round the dumpster, ducking down, my heart pounding while I scan for the hole in the fence.

Grandma was right—I'm not sure I can fit. What makes it even more difficult is the fact that the hole is next to the ground and on the backside the ground rises slightly. In order to get through, I'll have to lie on my stomach and slide through like a cobra.

I slither through the tiny hole, my progress halting when my hips catch. Gritting my teeth, I wiggle and twist until I finally break free. The cold scrape of concrete gives way to damp earth on the other side, muddy and slick from recent rains. By the time I'm through, my black sweatshirt is caked with mud, the "E" and "A" of the word *READ* smeared and almost unrecognizable. I don't bother wiping it off; instead, I decide to let it dry before dealing with the mess.

Behind the fence is a narrow alleyway, hemmed in by uneven asphalt and flickering bulbs mounted on the backs of the buildings. I'm completely blocked in by another weathered wooden fence, its planks warped and discolored by years of exposure to salt air and rain. The fence stretches a great distance in both directions, the buildings as well, each cluttered with leaning stacks of crates and other discarded items. I pause, scanning the alley in both directions and try to determine which direction will lead me back to my car.

Pleasant and not-so-pleasant odors hover around me as I think about where I was sitting in the bar and the direction of my car from there. I decide to turn right and hope there's a gap in between the buildings at some point. If I remember correctly, my car is only two or three buildings down from the pub—but on the same side of the street. Thankfully, I fear if I have to cross the street, he might spot me. I still don't know why the idea of that scares me so much.

I pass one, two, three buildings and find no gaps that will allow access to the street. I spot a man in the distance with his back leaned against the concrete block wall, smoking a cigarette. He appears to be in his late thirties, early forties, eyes bloodshot. He has a thin, wiry frame and peppered hair and beard. As I approach him, I see his bloodshot eyes and realize he isn't smoking a cigarette. He snaps to attention, seeming slightly nervous.

"You lost?"

I fake a laugh. "I think I am."

He scans me up and down, taking in my muddy sweatshirt and jeans. "What happened to you?"

My laugh shifts to a nervous cackle. "Long story. Is there access to the street from back here?"

"Why don't you go back from the way you came?"

I wave my hand in front of my body. "Do I look like I would want to go back that way?"

A lazy laugh escapes him. He seems to relax a little and props his shoulder against the wall, his posture becoming casual. "You running from someone?"

His nosy questions aren't only slowing me down, but starting to piss me off. I just want to get out of here. "Is there access this way or not?"

His eyebrows shift to a suspicious frown. "Yeah, three more buildings down that way. But—"

I cut him off and walk past him. "Thanks."

My pace quickens in case he insists on saying something else. He doesn't—or if he does, I can't hear him. I find a narrow alleyway three buildings down, barely wide enough for me to walk through without having to turn sideways. As I reach the end, I pause at the edge of the sidewalk, glancing quickly in both directions. My eyes land on my SUV parked several spots down to the right. There are only a handful of people moving on the sidewalk, but traffic is starting to pick up with evening commutes.

I fish the key fob from my purse and hit the unlock button. I don't see the man I'm trying to avoid, so I dart quickly down the sidewalk to my car and rush into the driver's seat. A different kind of anxiety washes over me. I glance back toward the entrance of the bar, and anxiety turns to dread as I spot him stepping out, his green eyes scanning the street as though he's a predator looking for his prey.

The sound of screeching tires. Broken glass glittering on asphalt. His eyes—those same green eyes—staring at me through the windshield—now and then. My head throbs, and the memory slips away before I can grasp it.

*Get to Darlene.* My mind urges again just as his eyes find mine.

# 43

## Michael

The drawings aren't just ink, they're haunting windows into Vincent's nightmares.

I flip through the pages, one by one, and each image merges with the next to form what could be the makings of a horror story. Pages filled with dark, sinister tones and shades, each sketch growing more raw and visceral, amplifying what I assume are the horrors of Vincent's childhood.

Every page contains the same underlying themes, but as I flip through them, they grow greater in detail. It's as if Vincent is writing, or drawing, his own story and just as details emerge in an author's mind, he refines them on the page, each stroke of ink carving deeper into the darkness of his memories. The sketches become more intricate, more deliberate, as if he's piecing together a puzzle for the viewer to solve.

Bold, jagged lines form the outline of a crumbling shack with warped wooden planks that run vertically, nails shaded in displeasing patterns. I catch myself focusing on them with each page flip and have to start again to take in the rest of the disturbing images. The shack seems to sag under the weight of the dark shadows and jagged tree branches. The walls are shaded lightly as though one can see inside the shack. In the foreground are a pair of small hands etched in excruciating detail as if they're pushing against the wall—behind them crouches a small boy.

Just beyond the shack, the faint shadow of a man looms, his form drawn in monstrous details—broad shoulders, his face obscured but marked by hollow eyes—the only color on the page are the green orbs drawn in the center of them. He appears as though he's just stepped out of a horror graphic novel.

An involuntary shudder courses through me as each page reveals imagery alive with melancholy and despair. On every page, the shack is the center of focus and it seems to be swallowing the child inside —the child I assume is Vincent. He told me he had spent the first seven years of his life in the dark, and that's why he now chooses to live in the dark.

I knew his childhood was unimaginable, but these images are a clear indicator of that. I flip through the pages faster as though the images might permanently etch themselves on my brain if I look at them too long. I don't think it's going to matter—they will anyway. No one should ever have to live like this.

I freeze when the backdrop on the next page suddenly changes.

I move it closer to my face and tilt it toward the dim light. I recognize my wife's face immediately. Her eyes are closed, lipstick smeared across her cheek, while dark makeup is shaded unevenly around her closed eyelids. She's lying in a coffin and the outline of a man stands over her, trees and tombstones loom in the background. I assume the outline of the man is me.

It's the dream he told me about.

How has he drawn such an accurate description of her, having never met her?

I stare at the dark wall as I contemplate it. Vincent does read a lot. It's possible he's read one of her books—he could have seen one of her author photos. But how would he even know who to look for? She uses a pen name.

Maybe it's just by chance.

Seeing this only furthers my reasoning for coming to see him. He must know something. He has to. There's no room for coincidence in this—Vincent understands more than he's letting on, and I need to find out what.

Could he be tied to all of this somehow? At this point, I'm not sure I trust anyone anymore.

A distinct voice sounds from just down the hall—it's deep and lacking in emotional tone. There's no mistaking it's Vincent. I stuff the drawings back into the notebook and wedge it back into place, then sit back into my usual chair. The door swings open, flooding the room with light. It forces me to squint my eyes. Vincent doesn't even turn his head toward me, he just speaks.

"Twice in one day, Michael. Now I know I need to start charging you."

"Hello, Vincent."

He takes a seat on his bed and assumes his usual position, then turns his blindfolded face toward me as he says, "Would you like to look through the rest of my stuff?"

"Ho—" I don't get to finish the question.

"I explained this to you before, Michael. I'm not like other people. You've uncovered a lot about me when you looked through my things. But it was my drawings that unsettled you—the ones from my childhood, and especially the one of my dream about your wife."

I swallow hard, and I think he hears it—or maybe he just somehow knows.

"Did you see the ones I drew after that? Because new events have unfolded in your life since I made that one. Sometimes, the course of events can shift depending on the choices you make. They have, haven't they?"

I decide to just be blunt with Vincent—I don't have time to tiptoe around things anymore.

I clear my throat and go for it. "You were right, Vincent. Someone is toying with my wife. I'm not sure if they're doing it to get to me or if it's her they wish to harm. They somehow altered her medication, which altered her." I hesitate, struggling to admit my guilt in all of this.

"And you're battling with your role in the escalation of the situation?"

I nod, my admission coming out more as a grunt. "Uh-huh."

Vincent leans over and removes the wedged binder and hands it to me. "Finish looking."

I take the book from him with an unsteady hand and place it on my lap. Vincent unclips the reading light from his bed and hands it to me as well.

I open the cover, then pick up several of the pages at once and flip them over, not wishing to see the same drawings again or any like them. I flip past them with the intention of moving past the drawing of Paige lying in a coffin.

"You skipped past the important ones."

My eyebrows furrow.

"You were right in your understanding of the earlier years of my life, but I think you missed important key details. There's more to that story. As Ivan Pavlov would say, don't become a mere recorder of facts, but try to penetrate the mystery of their origin. You should understand more than anyone the value of attention to detail in understanding complex behaviors. There's a story you need to understand in the details of my drawings. A story that will give you the answers you're looking for."

# 44

D arlene

**Twenty-five years ago**

Ginger drops to all fours, growling low in her throat, her body tense. At first, I don't dare turn around.

"So, I tell you that shed is off limits and the first thing you want to do is sneak out in the middle of the night to see what's in it. I'm starting to realize you don't like rules, do you, Darlene?"

I grip the tire iron a little tighter in my hand as I attempt to speak.

"If you're going to have the privilege of being with me, then there are certain rules you're going to follow whether you like it or not. Disobedience is something I won't tolerate." He says the words as if dumping me is the thing I'm fearing right now. It's not.

My mind spins into a chaos of questions—do I try to explain that it's just curiosity, or do I reveal what I know? My throat feels paralyzed, trapped between fight and flight. Ginger's growl grows louder, breaking the stillness, and it's her fierce loyalty that shakes me from my frozen state.

I turn slowly and manage to keep my voice steady. "Who is locked in this shed?"

"What the hell are you talking about, Darlene?"

My voice threatens to break, but I push it out with false certainty. I attempt to conjure a believable lie to avoid pointing a finger at Donavon. "I brought Ginger outside to pee and she ran straight to this shack. I came to see what she was so frantic about and saw little fingers sticking out from under the door. There's someone in there."

Christian leans over, his arm crossed over his chest, and peers around me, his eyes searching the bottom of the door. "And you think someone is locked in there? A boy?"

I realize I've made the mistake of identifying him as a boy. "He told me he was," I lie.

He lets out a dry laugh, but there's no humor behind it—only malice. Then he just stares at me for a moment, his eyes slightly squinted. Something about the way the moonlight highlights one side of his face makes him look more like a predator studying its prey. Or maybe it's my mind playing tricks on me.

"Darlene." His voice softens as he takes a step toward me, and Ginger's growl deepens. "You've been listening to Donavon's ghost stories, and it's messing with your head. Stop and think about it. Doesn't this all sound a little crazy to you?"

"I'm not crazy, Christian. I know what I saw." My voice falters, and my heart feels as though it's transformed into multiple fists pounding against my chest.

He sighs through a loud exhale as though the conversation is exhausting him. "You're letting your imagination run wild. There's no one in that shed. It's empty—just some old tools and junk I haven't gotten rid of yet. You're turning this into something it's not.

But if you must know, I also have all of Donavon's mother's things in there. I didn't think I should get rid of them because of Donavon."

My resolve falters, but only for a moment. "If that's all it is, then open it and let me see."

His lips spread into a faint, condescending smile. "Why should I have to prove anything? You don't trust me?" He shakes his head slowly, appearing as if he's disappointed. "This isn't like you, Darlene. You used to be rational, grounded. This pregnancy thing is messing with your head."

I give him a defiant look. "Then ease my mind... open it. If there's no one in there, show me."

His stare hardens, his jaw tightening. When he speaks, his voice is low and menacing. "No."

Defiance takes hold of my actions and I whisk my body back around as I say, "Then I will." I stick the tire iron back through the shackle of the lock and begin to yank even harder than before, no longer worried about making noise.

A sharp, searing pain shoots down the back of my head and neck as Christian grabs a fistful of my hair and yanks me backward. I cry out as the tire iron slips from my grasp and clatters to the ground.

# 45

M ichael

The pages feel heavier this time. As if the weight of the past is seeping into the paper.

I steady the reading light, then clip it onto the edge of the binder. It shines over the pages like an interrogation lamp.

With a reluctant breath, I flip back to the drawings, carefully slowing my pace.

As I flip each page, the static images spring to life, like a flipbook animating a series of events. Each page shifts seamlessly into the next, the jagged lines of Vincent's sketches creating a haunting sense of motion—actions unfolding frame by frame. The drawings evolve with every turn, like scenes from an old silent film, each page more vivid than the last, dragging me deeper into the nightmare.

The shack reappears, but the details seem sharper now—almost as if the image is alive, shifting under the light. Or maybe my focus is clearer. The warped wooden planks, the jagged nails, the sagging roof... but now there's a figure standing just outside.

A woman.

Her image and features are blurred, shaded in frantic strokes that make her look like a blob, but now I realize it's portraying movement. Before, I was so fixated on the patterns of the shack, I didn't see it.

I continue to flip pages, focusing on her. With each one, her image becomes clearer. I land on the drawing of my wife in a coffin, and Vincent says, "Move past that one—its story has changed. We'll discuss that one later."

I look at him, perplexed at how he even knows which one I'm looking at. A chill seems to sweep through the room as the thought that he's reading my mind crosses mine. I shake it off and continue.

In the next image—one that I hadn't seen before—the woman is clear, and in her hands she clutches at the edges of the warped doorframe, fingers half-curled as though she's about to open it.

My eyes stop and fix on the woman's face, and I feel my own pale.

She looks just like Paige.

I try to swallow, but I can't make it happen. I open my mouth to speak, and the word barely escapes my lips. "Why—?"

Vincent interrupts me. "Keep going."

I stare at him, then back down at the page, dumfounded. I turn to the next one.

# 46

D arlene

**Twenty-five years ago**

Christian doesn't just yank me backward—he drags me across the yard as I scramble to keep my feet on the ground.

Ginger reacts to my startled yelp with a fury that seems almost instinctual. She charges at him, sinking her teeth into his arm with precision, as if she knows exactly where to strike. Christian howls in pain, releasing me as he flings her off. I stagger to my feet, but the sight of his crazed expression—half rage, half something darker— makes my stomach churn.

He draws his leg back, ready to kick her, and the sight ignites a surge of adrenaline. Without thinking, I shove him hard before he can make contact. He hits the ground, and the moonlight catches the fresh blood oozing down his arm, making it glisten.

I lock eyes with his, and I realize I truly am looking at the devil. The scariest of them all. And the look I see in them says he's going to kill me.

I don't question the thought; my instincts scream it's true.

I run.

I burst through the back door of the house, locking the deadbolt behind me. The seconds feel like ticks on a time bomb as I race through to the front, throwing the door open and whistling a high-pitched call I perfected years ago, back when I first got Ginger. Bloodhounds are notorious for wandering too far when on a scent, but they never forget the sound of their master's whistle. It's like a lifeline they can hear from miles away.

By the time I reach my truck, she's right on my heels. I yank the driver's door open, and without hesitation, she leaps in beside me with the kind of instinct you'd expect from a person.

Slamming the door shut, I fumble to lock it, my hands trembling so badly it takes three tries to get the key into the ignition. Ginger presses against me, and I can feel her low growl vibrating my arm as if she can sense the danger just as much as I can. My breath comes in quick gasps, and every sound outside seems amplified—the screams of night creatures, the faint rustle of leaves in the gust of wind that's suddenly joined the race.

The engine roars to life, and I don't wait to see if Christian is following. I throw the truck into reverse, tires spinning against the dirt before they gain traction. The headlights sweep across the house and trees, everything illuminated with an eerie stillness. Then, a shadow moves as a flicker of him steps into view. His face is illuminated just long enough for me to see it contorted in rage.

I slam the gear into drive and floor it. The truck jolts forward as the wheels bounce over uneven ground—I grip the wheel tighter, trying to focus. Ginger lets out a sharp bark and twists her body to look out the back window. Against my better judgment, I glance into the rearview mirror.

He's running after us.

Panic floods me, but I press the gas harder. I can't think about how far he might chase us or what he'll do if he catches up. All that matters now is putting as much distance as possible between him and me—and hoping that distance will be enough.

# 47

## Paige/Vanessa

I struggle to even push the button on the dash to start the car.

The man doesn't move, just stares at me with a half-cocked grin as I shakily put the car in gear, glance over my shoulder, and pull out onto the street. I fix my eyes on the road ahead and don't dare look back in his direction. As I pass him, I can feel the weight of his stare, and it threatens to make me push the gas pedal harder.

A patrol car heading in my direction prompts a mixture of apprehension and relief inside me. I'm not sure why. As it gets closer, the female officer comes into view, and I recognize her face—the same officer who took me home.

Home?

The word doesn't feel right, yet it does.

She seems to recognize me as well, because as our paths intersect, she turns to look at me. I can't quite read the look on her face, but her stare in my direction seems to linger, as if she's trying to piece something together. A flicker of concern—or maybe suspicion —passes over her expression before she looks back toward the road. My stomach twists. Does she remember something I don't?

Maybe she can help me? But help me with what? I don't even know what is happening.

I glance in the rearview mirror as the patrol car continues past, her brake lights flickering for a brief moment before disappearing into the traffic behind me. The word home echoes in my mind, unsettling and foreign, like I don't even have a home. I grip the wheel tighter, my knuckles white, as greater uncertainty spreads through my chest.

I glance over at the passenger seat to the unfamiliar purse. I pick it up, turn it over, and shake out the contents, which splatter all over the seat. Now regretting my stubborn decision to leave the cell phone behind, I spot the little blue book. I grab it and bring it to the steering wheel, gripping it tightly between both hands as I flip through the tiny pages.

My eyes bouncing from it to the road, only a few pages have notes jotted on them, but it appears to be documenting dates, locations, and times. Apparently Paige felt the need to keep up with her comings and goings. The places that have been written in here aren't places I remember going. Of course, my list of memories and locations is a very short one. A bar, tattoo parlor, and Michael's apartment. This list is things like a mall, post office, and a café. I find one entry of the bar, but I think I remember writing it. I'm not sure.

Why the hell would I write it down to begin with?

I flip the page and see another list of times and locations. I stop when I see the name that keeps going through my mind. Darlene. Apparently, I was there—or Paige was—yesterday.

Instinctively, though I have no idea how I know to do it, I turn to the GPS on the dash and press a series of buttons to access the "route replay" of trips made from this vehicle. I made a trip yesterday toward Acadia National Forest.

I'm not for sure, but something tells me this is where I will find this Darlene.

As soon as the name vocalizes inside my head, an image follows of a woman sitting in a rickety old chair, beer in one hand and a cigarette in the other. The sun casts a streak of light across her dishwater blonde hair, frayed edges sticking out everywhere. I immediately know it's Darlene and somehow know that I'm heading in the right direction. As I'm leaving the outskirts of town, I begin to recognize the road. Landmarks shift from strange to familiar. It feels like a veil is lifting from the edges of my mind, and the lines between what's real and what I thought was a nightmare become clearer. The terrifying part is this: what's real also feels like a fading nightmare I'm waking up from.

I press pause on my thoughts, trying to get a better grasp on which of the memories are mine and which of them seem like someone else's. It feels like waking up from a dream. The details are there, just out of reach—hazy shapes and sounds fading as I grasp for them. The harder I try to pull them into focus, the quicker they slip away, like debris in a storm. The green-eyed man lingers the longest, his presence vivid yet unplaceable.

For some reason, instinct is telling me to pull over and write down these immediate thoughts and memories before they fade completely. Before they become nothing more than events during a blackout—the kind that are lost to me forever. I find a wide spot in the road and hastily write down as much as I can remember.

I write down where I've just left as my mind tugs at trying to figure out why I just left there. At the same time, I can remember a man with green eyes. I write in all caps: *THE MAN WITH GREEN EYES. I THINK HE CAUSED MY ACCIDENT. HE SCARES ME.*

I pause and try to remember more about my day, and just like waking up from a dream, they drift farther away from me and out of reach. Now, I'm searching for something that doesn't exist.

I look out the windows of the car and try to remember where I was headed. Darlene's? Again?

My eyes bounce around as everything before this point is a blank. Like an Etch A Sketch, it's as if my mind has just shaken my memory and erased itself—erased everything that's happened today. I see the screen on the GPS and recognize the route as the one to Darlene's house and realize that is where I was headed.

Why?

I look back down at the tiny notebook in my hand and read the words on the page. Fear makes a crash landing as I read: *HE CAUSED MY WRECK.*

It must be why I'm going to Darlene's. I must have been—because she's not scared of anything.

# 48

## Darlene

**Now**

I'm terrified that my worst fears are becoming a reality.

History tends to repeat itself, even if people think they've chosen the right paths to avoid it. Especially when karma is choosing its course. But what I fear is that karma is coming in the form of revenge, and I need to be ready for it.

I've always known that even this forest wouldn't be able to stop it—that eventually someone would come looking for me after what I've done.

I attempt to collect myself and set my mind to preparing for revenge's visit. With a trembling hand, I fold the threatening letter and tuck it into my jacket pocket, my eyes lingering on the photo for a moment longer before slipping it away as well. I take in a deep, shaky breath and force my feet to move, the sound of my boots crunching dried leaves almost deafening. The air feels even heavier, and the canopy of trees casts mottled shadows across the ground.

I move around the tombstone tree and kneel by the first trap, a simple snare hidden beneath a bed of pine needles. The loop is still taut, undisturbed.

I follow a strategic path to the next one, my gaze scanning every inch of the dense underbrush. Near an old cedar, a tripwire has gone slack, its line tangled in the low branches. I crouch and reset it with practiced hands.

As I make my way back toward the trailer, I check other traps. These aren't meant for animals—though the occasional raccoon or deer might set one off. No, these are for something—or someone—far more dangerous. These are for what I've always feared might one day come for me.

The first one is a snare designed to catch a leg and pull tight, its heavy cord camouflaged beneath a tangle of leaves. I crouch low, checking the tension. The mechanism is intact, the trigger hidden perfectly beneath the forest debris. Satisfied, I reset the branch it's tied to and move on.

Ginger instinctually avoids it, and all I've had to do to make sure he steers clear is scold him if he gets close while I'm checking it. He's very observant and sees that I walk around it any other time—and so does he. So have all the other Ginger's before him.

I continue down toward the base of the ridge and pause at a more menacing trap: a series of sharpened stakes, a couple of inches in height, wedged in the ground at the bottom of a shallow ditch. The covering of twigs and moss over the top remains undisturbed, but I lean closer, inspecting for signs of tampering. It's crude but effective—one false step, and whoever stumbles into it won't be walking out the way they stepped in. It'll definitely slow them down, and they'll most likely walk with a permanent limp.

Following my memory and the path I've paced out thirty feet

above my trailer, I stop at the base of the gnarled oak and scan the forest floor for the thin tripwire hidden beneath the fallen leaves. I squat, brushing the debris aside to check the tension. The wire is taut, still threaded securely through the tiny notch in the hollow tree's trigger mechanism. Inside the hollow, the spring is compressed, its rusty spikes ready to snap forward with brutal force. I inspect the alignment of the spikes and adjust the latch to ensure it holds. The sight of the jagged metal makes my chest tighten—a grim reminder of how far I've gone to protect myself from karma's revenge.

I stand and survey the quiet woods, my hand resting on the rough bark.

"I hope to God this never has to be used," I mutter, my voice barely audible over the whisper of the wind. But as I step away, a chill consumes me, and it's as if the forest is whispering that it won't stay idle much longer.

As I step onto my front porch, an echoing clatter fills the air. My head snaps toward the road as my heart hammers in my chest.

Someone is coming.

# 49

## D arlene

**Twenty-five years ago**

My insides feel like the aftermath of a horrific car crash—mutilated emotions twisted, bent, and unrecognizable.

I beat myself up as I drive away, no longer seeing him in the rearview mirror. How could I have been so stupid and blind? Why did I let myself believe that he was different? That he was the one who could give me the life I felt I deserved?

I allowed him to morph my mistrust in people into a false sense of security. Allowed insecurity to steer my decisions, even though the cautioning engine light of my gut screamed at me to face the truth. Like so many women, I pushed gut feelings aside and fell into the comforting lull of his promises, ignoring the warning signs flashing in my mind like a highway full of detours. I let myself believe in the fantasy he wove—a life of safety, love, and belonging—even as the cracks in his façade began to show.

Now, I have to face the cold, hard truth—no one can take better care of me than me. And it is me who will have to protect me.

The road seems to stretch endlessly ahead, a blur of asphalt and guilt. I grip the steering wheel so tightly that my knuckles tingle, and the tremble in them betrays my resolve. I glance at the rearview mirror, half-expecting to see him there, but there's nothing except the empty road behind me. It feels symbolic—an empty, hollow feeling moving with me the more distance I put between us.

I search for a place that might have a discreet payphone, and somewhere I can pull my truck out of sight. I know what I have to do, even though my insides are torn between what I thought was love, denial, and regret. I need to alert the police that Christian has a child locked in a shack who has been there for God knows how long. Hell, he didn't even tell me the child existed, and we've been seeing each other for more than six months.

I have to wonder what his plans were. He had to have known it wasn't something that could stay a secret for long. Did he think I would accept it and be okay with it? That one day we would get married and I would tote meals out to the poor child as if it were something normal to do? As I repeat it all back to myself, I realize how crazy it all seems. I struggle to believe that any of this has happened.

My thoughts attempt to veer down another path: I'm going to lose him for good after this. Images of small moments between us flash like a camera's shutter—each one opening and closing, leaving behind haunting snapshots of what I may never have. I shake my head, desperate to cap off the lens of my thoughts, to shut out the pain before it consumes me.

As I search for a phone, there's still a small part of my opposing brain that is challenging what I know I saw—questioning everything that just happened. Christian insisted that being pregnant is just playing tricks on me. I've heard other women talk about how the pregnancy brain can be confusing—like an unreliable narrator, sending your thoughts in the wrong directions. I rerun the events of the evening back through my mind—Donavon's story, the tiny fingers reaching under the door hoping to pet Ginger on the nose, and Christian's violent reaction to me trying to open the lock.

As I replay everything once more, it temporarily shuts down the opposing side of my thoughts.

I spot a gas station that appears to be open and pull my truck to the right side of the building, which is mostly in the dark. There's a dimly lit payphone in the darkest corner of the lot, perfect for making a discreet call to the police. It's barely visible from the road.

I shut off the engine as scenarios attempt to run through my head as to what the outcome might be if I do this. I push it aside and force myself from the truck before the what-ifs consume me. I grip the coins in my hand as if they're my lifeline, their edges digging into flesh. Each step toward the payphone feels heavy, weighed down by the possible outcomes if I follow through. What if I'm wrong? What if Christian is right, and my pregnancy is clouding my judgment? My stomach feels as though it's relocated to my throat. I pause a few steps from the payphone and hesitate. The image of Donavon's face and small fingers under a door drive me to take the last few steps.

The night air feels colder, chilling me to the bone, and I begin to shake. What if he finds out I called? The image of his face as my headlights flashed across it becomes very vivid. I take another step as I look over my shoulder toward the truck. It isn't too late to abandon this and run back to it. I'm not sure if I'm more afraid of Christian finding out or of the guilt I'll carry if I don't do this. It drives me to take another step.

I pick up the receiver and press it to my ear, and the dial tone seems to scream. I hover a trembling finger over the buttons. This isn't just about the boy locked in the shack—it's about me. If I call, I'm severing every last tie to Christian and the illusion of the life I thought we could have. I'm choosing to burn the bridge, to walk away for good, no matter what fallout comes next.

I take a deep breath and hold it as I press the buttons.

9-1-1.

As the line connects and a calm voice answers, I clear my throat, forcing my voice to steady. "There's a child," I say, my words trembling but sure. "He's locked in a shack. Please, you have to help him."

# 50

## Michael

Vincent's hospital room feels colder than before, though I assume the thermostat hasn't changed. The chill isn't physical—I can feel it in my bones, a creeping unease radiating from the pages in my hands.

The perspective in the drawings has shifted. Before, it was as if I was on the outside of the shack, looking at it. Now, as I look at it, I feel trapped inside the claustrophobic space, looking out. Just the sight of it constricts my chest. I'm only viewing a sketch—a vivid and extraordinarily detailed one—but I can't breathe.

In the foreground, a dog's face looms, as though it's sniffing me out. Behind it, a woman stands, her gaze piercing the darkness like she's searching for something—or someone—unseen. Her features are drawn in sharp detail. She resembles Paige, but there are subtle differences: her frame is more petite, her hair slightly darker and longer. Still, her expression—the determined look Paige gets when she's set on doing something—is unmistakable. Only here, it's tinged with anguish and fear.

My mind drifts, unbidden. I picture Paige finding the drawer in the back of my closet—the one where I've hidden things I swore I'd tell her about when the time was right. I imagine the look on her face when she discovered it: shock, confusion, anger. What must she have thought?

As my mind spirals into guilt, Vincent's voice cuts through my inner chatter. "You have to stop beating yourself up, Michael. It's counterproductive and it accomplishes nothing."

I swallow hard and glance at him. How does he keep doing that? I drop my gaze back to the sketch in my lap, unsure if I should be unnerved or impressed.

The next drawing forces me to linger. The monstrous man is behind her now, his eyes pinning mine in place. They aren't just terrifying—they're familiar. My heart pounds, my breath quickens, and I fight the urge to close the binder. I glance at Vincent, his blind-fold in place, as usual. Maybe this man seems familiar because of him. A flash of memory flickers: Vincent pulling down his blindfold, revealing his eyes—mostly black with a tint of green. My mind tries to connect the dots, but it's like trying to grip a fist full of air in my hands.

"Are you the one in the shack?" I ask, even though I pretty much know the answer.

"Yes."

"Is this your father?"

"Yes."

"Is this your mother?"

"No."

I hesitate, then ask even though I know the timing wouldn't add up. "Is this my wife?"

Vincent's expression remains calm, unreadable. "No. But she knows her."

The air in the room seems to grow thinner. "Knows her? How? I don't understand."

"I never knew the woman's name. I just know that your wife is connected to her. I learned this through you."

"Through me?"

"Through your thoughts. Your wife's connection to the woman was buried deep in your thoughts. It wasn't until recently, when I pieced together your memories, that I understood her identity."

A shiver makes its way up my spine. The pieces of this puzzle, the one Vincent has helped me piece together for weeks, the one I dismissed as nonsense, begin to click into place. I look back down at the drawing. The determined expression, the slight curve of her shoulders—it all clicks. This woman isn't just connected to Paige. She is Paige's mother, Darlene.

"Is this a particular incident that happened to you?" I ask, unable to project my voice above a whisper.

Vincent nods. "This is the night she freed me."

"She?" I echo. "You mean... Darlene?"

"Yes." His voice softens.

It was Darlene that freed Vincent from his prison. I can't believe this. What a small fucking world.

The thought of Darlene stepping into Vincent's nightmare to free him feels too large to grasp.

Vincent continues. "I now know why I've been having the nightmares I'm having. Why they're about you—well, not just you, but your wife and this... Darlene. But I'm not the only one who has discovered their identity and your connection to them. Someone else has uncovered the truth, and they're not happy about what Darlene did. They want revenge—for what she took that night."

# 51

D arlene

**Twenty-five years ago**

The deed is done, and I can't take it back.

It's like that when it comes to our actions—and especially our words. Once they leave your body, they have the power to help or damage. In this case, I'm not sure which I've done. All I know is, the repercussion is going to hurt someone in the end. I'm just not sure who will feel it the most.

I drive around aimlessly until the darkest hours of the morning. I know I should go home and try to salvage a few hours of sleep, but I don't even want to go there. I recount my phone call to the police, even though it isn't going to change anything now.

After giving the dispatcher Christian's address—the one he had given me when I first visited his house—they asked how I came to know about the boy locked in the shack. I told them I couldn't say and insisted on remaining anonymous. I explained that Christian had two small children who were being abused. I described how one of them was locked in a dark shed behind the house, hidden partially by the trees. I added that the shed had no electricity and likely no heat. I urged them to hurry, emphasizing how dangerous Christian was and how I didn't know what might happen if he found out I had reported him.

A sick feeling takes up residence inside my stomach, and my mind shifts to what else is growing inside there. Something I now know for sure I don't want. Something I know I need to get rid of. I can't stand the idea of giving birth to a child with the same genes as someone who would do something so horrifying. It all still seems like a nightmare I should be waking up from.

Ginger whines in the seat next to me, and I realize she must be ready to get out of this truck.

"Okay, girl, we'll go home now," I say as I rub her slick, saggy ear. We bounce down the one-lane road to my hidden oasis from the rest of the world as a sudden bone-tiredness hits me, and I'm now eager to crawl into my bed. As we pass the old green truck, I can see in the full moonlight that it now has a small tree growing up through the bed. It and everything around it are eerily visible. The surrounding branches appear as crooked fingers reaching outward, giving them an almost human appearance. Everything around me seems hauntingly quiet this time of morning. Too quiet.

I pull my truck into its usual spot next to the trailer, the partially finished roof and porch casting a shadow over most of it. I spot a quick movement to my left, which makes my pulse soar. Ginger sees it too, but only lets out one low bark. It's just one of the many deer that show up here, and she quickly disregards it.

I crawl out of the truck with stiff legs, and the dog does the same. She stretches, yawns, and then her nose hits the ground, following a scent toward the trailer. This isn't unusual, but this time she pauses, lets out a low growl, and sniffs the air. Suddenly, she darts behind the trailer and out of sight. Her behavior doesn't seem too unusual at first, but then it turns more aggressive, so I take it seriously. I creep after her to the small backyard behind the trailer. There's only a small patch of grass back here; the rest of the yard fades into trees and forest.

As soon as I round the corner, I see it—the back door is wide open, the glass in the window shattered.

Ginger's growl deepens and becomes more vicious. She stands at the top of the three steps staring toward the open door, and I cautiously climb behind her. The small back porch isn't much bigger than the area it takes to swing the door. As I climb the steps, my heart does the same, pounding harder and faster.

The dog doesn't move, just stands there as if she's either staring at whatever is responsible for breaking the window, or she's afraid to go in. So am I.

My heart begins to thud in my ears to a deafening level as I ease around the dog, wishing I had something in my hands to defend myself. The thought of it being Christian was only a brief flicker in the back of my mind—until now.

He sits at my kitchen table, his tattooed forearm resting on it. I see the key—the one that claims he owns me, and his kid too. He doesn't smile, just stares at me with a cold, demonic glare. He's surpassed devil, because the devil at least had a soul once—the look in his eyes resembles someone without a soul altogether. I read it in those same piercing green eyes, only now they're frightening.

I don't step fully into the trailer; instead, I keep one foot inside and the other out, my body poised to bolt at the slightest movement. I finally summon the courage to speak.

"What are you doing here, Christian?"

Again, he just stares at me.

I tilt my head in the direction of the door and ask, "Is this your handiwork?"

"You shouldn't have done it, Darlene."

His tone sends chills crawling up my spine. I try to hide the hard swallow my body needs to take before I speak. "I don't know what you're—"

He interrupts. "If I'm going to go to prison, then it's going to be for something far worse than punishing my child."

Instinct screams RUN. I listen to it.

I jump down the three steps and hit the ground, my feet landing unevenly. I stumble, taking several steps to steady myself. Ginger's growl shifts to a vicious bark, followed by a thud and a sharp yelp. Fury courses through me, but I know I have to get away from him or what he does to me is going to be far worse.

I force myself to keep moving, even as rage courses through me at the sound of Ginger's wail. My legs pump harder, and I veer toward the narrow path leading into the woods. I know these trails like the back of my hand, and I know exactly where I need to go.

Branches that earlier looked like arms and fingers now scrape and claw at me as I dart through them. My breath comes in short, frantic bursts. Behind me, I hear his heavy footsteps crashing through the brush, closing the distance faster than I can manage.

Up ahead, I spot the area I'm aiming for and pray it's him who finds it, not me. It's a snare trap designed to deter mountain lions and bear. One my stepfather set years ago, back when he thought teaching me to trap and hunt would somehow make up for every-thing else. He left that behind when he wrapped his car around a tree, but the trap remains—a small, bitter advantage to his presence in my life.

It's been a while since I last checked it. On one of my hikes, I decided to see if it still worked—it did, so I reset it. I'm not sure why I kept it active, but being out here alone, it seemed like a good idea at the time. Now, I can only hope it works. It won't kill him, but it might buy me enough time to get away.

I spot the gnarly-looking tree I'm searching for and dart around its right side. The trap should be to the left, so I double back, hoping he'll take the path of least resistance—straight into the direction of the trap.

I hear a snap, then a guttural yell as the trap catches him. I don't stop to look back, but I can imagine what happened—the snare yanking tight around his leg, the rope pulling him off balance and sending him crashing to the ground.

His curses echo through the woods, sending even more adrenaline through me. His voice is raw and furious, and my heart hammers in my chest as I push forward, weaving through the trees. I know it won't hold him for long, but it might be just enough to put more distance between us.

As I run, I stick my middle finger and thumb in my mouth and let out a sharp whistle, signaling to Ginger where I am. It doesn't take long before I hear the rustle of leaves behind me, her four paws pounding the ground as she catches up.

Ginger's panting grows louder as she reaches me, her presence giving me a fleeting sense of relief. But it doesn't last long—behind us, I hear the faint sound of snapping twigs and the unmistakable thud of boots again. He's free.

The terrain grows increasingly steep on either side, slowing me down. My breath comes in ragged gasps, my vision blurring as a sharp pain pierces my right side. But I can't stop. Behind me, Ginger struggles to keep up, evident in her sharp coughs as she climbs beside me.

The sound of Christian's footsteps grows closer—dangerously close. The incline becomes so steep now that I'm forced onto all fours to climb, just as Ginger is. We both lose our footing repeatedly, sliding backward and scrambling to try again. On one attempt, my foot slips on a root. I lose my balance and slide several feet down, slick mud and leaves speeding my descent.

When I finally stop, I try to climb again—but Christian's hand clamps around my ankle, yanking me farther down. Panic surges through me as I flip onto my back, kicking at his face, but my foot misses. Desperation fuels me, and I try again, but he's already on top of me, his hands wrapping around my throat.

We slide down the mountainside together, dirt and leaves tearing past us. My fingers claw at the ground, searching for anything to grab hold of—anything to stop the fall or defend myself.

My frantic fingers scrape against a jagged rock, and I grab it, the sharp edges biting into my palm. With all the strength I can muster, I swing my arm, the rock making solid contact with the side of Christian's skull. He lets go of me instantly, his grip loosening as he recoils.

Before I can fully react, Ginger is there. She lunges at him, her teeth sinking into the same arm she bit earlier, a low growl rumbling deep in her throat. He releases me, and I seize the chance to scoot a few feet away. Frantically, I kick out with both legs, and one foot connects with his face, giving me the opportunity to put more distance between us. He grabs one of Ginger's floppy ears and yanks her head back. She yelps and lets go, but she doesn't back down— her barking and growling are relentless, unlike the true nature of a bloodhound.

He turns his head back to me, the look in his eyes pure evil. Blood oozes down the side of his face, which looks almost black in the moonlight. A new round of fear and adrenaline pumps through me as I read in his eyes what he's getting ready to do. My own gaze darts to my dog trapped in his grip, and I don't even think—I just react. I dive toward him, and I believe it throws him off guard. He lets go of Ginger and lunges to grab me, but my position above him gives me the advantage. I throw my weight into him, knocking him off balance, and we both tumble down the ravine. His grip slips, and the extra hundred pounds of his body propels him farther and faster as gravity takes hold. I dig my fingers into the soil, sharp rocks, and twisted roots, each biting into my palms. I manage to stop myself several feet above him. My chest heaves, my breath shallow and ragged. His groan echoes through the trees.

I don't wait—I react. Adrenaline propels me to my feet as I scan the forest floor, the moonlight blocked by the trees making it hard to see. My eyes catch on a jagged rock, bigger than the one before. My hand trembles as I wrap my fingers around it, feel its weight.

He's climbing back toward me now, blood streaked across his face, and it looks as though he's wearing war paint. Ginger's whimper pulls my focus for just a moment, but it's enough to remind me why I have to end this. If not, he'll kill us both. My breath steadies as I tighten my fingers around the rock.

He lunges, his movements unyielding, but I'm ready. I feel my own scream rip from the deepest part of me and swing the rock with all the strength I have left. It connects with a sickening crunch, and he staggers, blood now pouring freely down his face.

He collapses, and for a moment, the forest is silent except for my own ragged breathing and Ginger's soft whines. The rock slips from my hand, landing with a dull thud beside his motionless body.

The night seems to stretch around me, eerily still. My knees buckle, and I collapse to the ground, pulling Ginger into my arms. Her warm body against mine is the only proof I need that it's over.

He's gone.

The forest is quiet, even if it's only for now.

# 52

# Michael

I try to grasp what Vincent just said—*she took that night.*

It shifts to a question in my head. *What does he mean took that night?* I give him a questioning frown, daring myself to ask—*what did someone take that night?*

As though he's still reading my mind, he says, "I never saw my father again after that—only in my nightmares. Of course, my home has been in and out of places like this my whole life. No one has ever told me anything other than the fact that my father disappeared and hasn't been seen since."

I flip through several more sketches, the pages filled from edge to edge, and the story of the night Vincent was freed unfolds before me. A man and a woman; she's on the ground as he towers over her, a fistful of her hair in his hand while a dog grips the man's other arm. I flip the pages one after another. The woman is running, the dog after her as the man appears to be getting up from the ground. In the next sketch, the view widens with the house seemingly farther away. The man is to the right of the house, and in front of him is a truck, tires blurred as though they're spinning, dust and debris flying through the air.

The next page reveals police cars and officers scattered across the scene, flashlights and guns in hand. The images are smeared, distorted by a layer of charcoal, as though seen through a haze of memory. In the following drawing, the perspective shifts to the front of the shack—this too is distorted, the details blurred. The clearest detail is the crouching boy with his hands pressed over his eyes.

On the next page, another boy appears, clutching a tiny bear, surrounded by officers. As I study the chaotic scene, a realization sinks in—there are *two* boys this time. I lean closer to the drawings, unable to pull my eyes away.

Vincent's voice barely registers. "The past never leaves us, Michael. It's like ink—it stains everything it touches. Sometimes, you can't see what's really in the picture until the stains begin to fade."

The pounding of my heart makes itself known as realization settles like a heavy weight in my chest. Is this Vincent's way of warning me? Or is it something else entirely? His words pull me deeper into the images. I turn to the next sketch and feel a chill crawl up my spine.

The drawings loop back on themselves, as though the same nightmare is being replayed in a darker, more twisted form. This time, the man drags the woman through the murky surroundings, similar to the other one. The details remain smeared and unrecognizable, except for three things: the man's menacing figure, the woman's terror-stricken face, and in the background, a large tree with its sprawling branches stretching toward them like clawing fingers.

Something about this terrifies me, because the woman in this one is different. My breath holds in my chest as the realization hits me. *It's her.* The shape of her body, face, and the look on her face—the kind she makes when she watches a jump-scare horror film—it's Paige. My mind races, trying to make sense of how she ended up in Vincent's nightmare. Or worse, how it might not be a nightmare at all. The woman in this one is my wife.

Words escape me, so Vincent fills the silence. "Sydney J. Harris once said, 'History repeats itself, but in such cunning disguise that we never detect the resemblance until the damage is done.'"

His voice drops lower, carrying the weight of something far darker. "The damage is always done before we see it, Michael. History doesn't just repeat itself—it mutates, taking on a new form, a new face. The disguise changes, but the destruction is always the same." He tilts his head, his blindfolded face aimed directly at me, as if he can see my fear. "Sometimes, Michael, it's not the past chasing you. Sometimes, it's the damage itself that finds you. And it's never forgiving."

"What are you trying to tell me, Vincent?" I mutter the question even though I'm not sure I want to know the answer.

"Like blood soaked deeply into a fabric. It may hide the past, but it's never truly gone."

Frustration barks through my words. "Stop quoting riddles and just tell me what you know!"

Vincent pulls his blindfold down and leans forward. The hollowness of his eyes—their shape, their emptiness—makes my stomach churn. His voice is low, deliberate. "Look at the next one."

I'm growing tired of circling around Vincent's quotes and puzzles. Frustration builds, rising from my stomach to the top of my head, and I feel an almost unbearable urge to scream at him. Instead, I steady myself, forcing just enough tolerance to look at one more.

I turn the page and freeze.

It's a sketch of this room—this chair where I sit, and his bed where he sits.

The man on the bed is Vincent. But the man in the chair isn't me, but I know who he is.

I flip back to the drawing of the man dragging the woman, the massive tree lurking in the background. Then back to the man in the chair.

They are the same.

I send my mind backward to sessions I've had with Vincent— he's never talked about a brother, and anytime I asked about family, he would deter the conversation elsewhere. I didn't push. I encourage patients but never push when there's resistance to talk about certain people. It usually comes when they are ready.

Now I wish I had.

When Vincent speaks again, he confirms what I now already know. "He's the one that's been coming for your wife. My brother— Dr. D. J. Eirkson. Donovan Jack Erikson."

# 53

P aige

Relief washes over me as I catch sight of the disheveled woman standing on the rickety, old porch. It's a strange feeling, foreign compared to the unease I usually feel when I come here. For the first time in my life, seeing my mother feels like coming home.

My head is clearer now, except for the black hole of hours that vanished before I found myself bouncing down this makeshift road. Once again, I've lost a lengthy period of time, and I have no idea where it went. But the sick feeling deep in the pit of my stomach tells me that some of it is coming to find me.

I'm still clutching the tiny book in my hand as though letting go of it might erase what last bit of clarity I have left. The scrawled notes inside feel like breadcrumbs leading me blindly into a story that hasn't been written yet—or has, and I have no idea the course it's taking. I can't explain it, but I fear it's the bestselling thriller I've been trying to write, only it's starting to feel less like fiction and more like a thriller I'm about to live through.

I step out of the Rover, the sharp scent of pine needles mingling with acrid woodsmoke. The sun has long since disappeared behind the mountains, the edges of the towering trees melting into shadows. Something about them seems menacing, as if they could close in on me. Darlene's expression doesn't help—it mirrors the unease knotting in my chest. When she speaks, her tone is the same old Darlene, but it's missing its usual sharpness, replaced by an edge of nervousness.

"I like seeing you and all, but this is starting to become a habit."

I'm not sure if she's joking, but it prompts a nervous laugh from me. "I think someone wants to hurt me. Or maybe I'm just losing my mind."

Darlene's face shifts, her confusion blending into worry. "What's happened?"

"You remember you told me that I should write everything down?"

Darlene nods but doesn't speak. She pulls a pack of cigarettes from her pocket, lights one, and sits in her usual broken-down chair.

I sit on the edge of the other worn-out chair and jump straight in, my words spilling out like rambling. "Well, I've been doing it, and up until today—I think it was today—hell, I don't know anymore. I don't remember making the last entry, and I'm pretty sure I wrote it on my way here. I came out of one of my blackouts while driving, scared as hell and confused. The only thing I could seem to remember was that I had to get somewhere safe."

I hand Darlene the tiny booklet, open to the page I want her to see. She takes it and brings it close to her face, squinting as she struggles to read it in the dim light. I watch the shift in her face as it moves from curiosity to deep concern. Her lips part as if she's about to speak, but no words come out. She just continues flipping through the pages.

"Describe this man to me," she says finally, her voice low and careful.

"I'm not sure I can, but I think he was someone I saw in a café the other day during a meeting with my agent. Or at least, looked like him. But I think I may have encountered him again—today. I found the tattoo shop and talked to the man who did this." I lift my arm, pointing to the tattoo. "He said I came in with this man, who had apparently instructed him days before on the type of tattoo he wanted him to do. He also said that the man had one just like it, only his was distorted slightly as if he'd had it most of his life—maybe even as a child."

Darlene's tone lowers further, cautious now, as though afraid of the answer. "Did he... know this man?"

"No. Just that the man had a tattoo on his arm very similar to this one, and that he wanted me to have the same tattoo. All he could really tell me was the man's name."

Darlene's eyebrows lift, her face tightening with an emotion I can only read as fear.

"He said his name was Christian."

# 54

D arlene

**Now**

Hearing Christian's name come from his daughter's lips sends an icy chill racing down my spine. This can't be right. Christian is dead.

"You're sure he said Christian?"

"Yes. But that's pretty much all he knew. Apparently, I was playing a game of truth or dare with him, and that is how this tattoo came about. But I don't remember any of it."

I suck on the cigarette so long and hard that the filter feels hot against my lips. There's no way for Paige to know that name unless someone who knows it told her. And if this person had a similar tattoo on his arm, then it could only be one of two other people. Both of them would be just a few years older than Paige. Both of them would have the same tattoo.

This means... they've tied Paige to Christian. And to me.

After that horrible night, I remember reading about two boys in the news—abandoned. The headline read: *Two Boys Found Abandoned: One Locked in a Shack, the Other Left to Wander Alone.* The article didn't show their faces but listed their ages and mentioned matching tattoos. It went on to state that there was no immediate family and that the boys had been separated. One of them, described as quiet and withdrawn, was placed into foster care. The other, a boy who was said to be highly sensitive to light and prone to erratic behavior, was sent to a psychiatric facility for treatment.

The details had stuck with me, though I tried to push them aside. But now, hearing Christian's name and thinking about those tattoos, I can't ignore it anymore. Those boys... they weren't just any abandoned children. They were connected to Christian. And now, somehow, someone has made the connection to Paige.

Beneath that same article was another headline: *Missing Man; Wanted for Neglect and Abuse.* The news followed it daily in the beginning, but soon it all slowly faded behind other breaking news. The last thing I heard was a year or so later; one of the boys had been adopted.

I realize I've smoked the cigarette down to the filter. The bitter taste of nicotine-soaked cotton taints my tongue, and it snaps me back to the present. Paige is staring at me with wide eyes, and for a moment, I'm transported back to when she was ten—wide-eyed and scared one night when I came home late. She'd been alone, had heard a noise outside, and snuck that year's Ginger into the house. I remember feeling guilty and couldn't bring myself to scold her for breaking the rules. After that, I started letting her bring the dog in anytime I left her alone.

Now, guilt for my past decisions threatens to creep in, but I shove it aside before it takes hold.

I have to tell Paige the truth—at least part of it.

I don't know how it all connects to her blackouts, but it can't be a coincidence that they started now. Someone has made the connection. Someone has found her.

I exhale slowly, pulling a folded letter from my pocket. My voice is steady, but inside, my pulse pounds. "Have you received any kind of threatening letters?" I ask. "Anything like this?"

Paige takes the paper from my hand and unfolds it. Her face drains of color. She doesn't speak right away, and that silence—that hesitation—tells me everything. My worst fear is coming true.

My past hasn't just come back to haunt me. It's found my daughter.

Her hands shake as she grips the letter, and when she finally speaks, her words tumble over each other in a rush. "I—I received the same message," she stammers, her breath uneven. "Along with pictures and videos of me doing things I don't remember doing."

An ice-cold dread moves up my spine. My throat goes dry. Someone has been watching her. Documenting her blackouts. This isn't just paranoia—this is calculated. Deliberate.

Paige looks down at the letter again, her fingers tightening around the paper as though it might slip from her hands.

I glance at the small notebook she's been scribbling in, my mind racing. There's someone out there with green eyes, connected to Christian, and they're not only fucking with me—they're fucking with my daughter.

I reach into my coat and pull out the faded photograph—a piece of my past I never thought I'd need to look at again, much less show to my daughter. I shakily turn the photo toward Paige.

"Do you recognize the eyes in this picture?"

# 55

P aige

I pull the photo close to my face, and my mind spins into a chaotic storm of images, sounds, and blaring lights. My eyes lock onto the green ones in the photograph.

I don't know who this man is, but his eyes stir something inside me. A strange sense of déjà vu sparks as I stare into them, and suddenly, I'm dragged into a memory I didn't even know I had. It unfolds like the flickerings of a faulty neon light—frame by frame, light and dark. Then—

A blinding flash of headlights cuts through the fog.

The crunch of metal.

The echo of shattering glass.

Searing pain seems to shoot down the left side of my body.

In the split second before impact, the man's face comes into view, lit by the glare of his own headlights—dark hair, dimples, and those same piercing green eyes.

The eyes in this photograph.

My breath lodges as I try to speak, preventing my voice from rising barely above a whisper. "This is the man who hit me."

The memory rushes back in full force, no longer flickering in pieces but playing out in sharp, unbearable clarity. I couldn't remember anything before—not the car, not the crash, not him. But now, it's all crashing down on me, and even if I wanted to stop it, I couldn't.

My body trembles from the inside out. My hands won't stop shaking.

Darlene watches me, her expression unreadable. Then, with a slow inhale, she gestures toward the photo. "That man there—" she taps the face with one calloused finger, "that's Christian. But he's not the one who hit you."

I blink at her. "How do you know?"

Darlene doesn't answer right away. Instead, she lights another cigarette and takes a long drag, then exhales a slow, curling breath. The smoke swirls around her, then shifts in the breeze, drifting toward me.

"Because he's dead." Her voice is flat. Matter-of-fact.

I stare at her.

Darlene makes the cigarette look calming. And in this moment, I almost wish I smoked. I need something to steady myself. I don't have any anxiety meds with me.

"But the tattoo guy—" I start.

"He probably did say that was his name. But if I had to guess, it isn't his name. That was his father's name—the man in the photo." She exhales another slow cloud of smoke, her eyes turning upward, locked on the treetops. "I'm guessing he used it hoping it would get back to me."

"Why?"

Darlene takes another slow drag, then mutters under her breath, almost like she doesn't mean for me to hear, "Because I did him a favor."

I frown. "What favor?"

She doesn't answer. She continues to look up at the sky as if searching for something in the branches above us. I follow her gaze. The moon is higher now, peeking through the twisted limbs of the trees. Somewhere in the distance, a low, mournful howl rises into the air. Dusk is quickly fading. I shiver.

A coyote calls to its pack from the edge of the forest. The sound lingers, stretching into the dark edges of the trees around us, blending with the faint chirps of crickets. The woods feel too still, as if the whole forest is waiting along with me.

She finally looks at me. "Have you talked to anyone about me?"

My first instinct is to say, "Hell no. Why would I?" But I don't. I force myself to think about the question. And then the only person I can think of is Michael.

For some reason, I say it reluctantly. "Michael."

Darlene gives me a puzzled look as I scan my memory. Another name—the only other person I have talked to about my mother—pops into my mind. I hesitate before I say it because I know she might either laugh or comment about how it's a waste of money.

"My therapist." As soon as I say it, I feel the need to add, "But he's also a friend of Michael's."

"What's his name?"

"Jack. I mean, Dr. Eirkson. He—"

She interrupts. "Eirkson?"

I pause, and my face shifts into a questioning look. Before she responds, a sharp metallic clatter jolts both of our attention toward the makeshift doorbell. My stomach clenches.

Darlene's homemade alarm system—the one she rigged up with aluminum cans—clatters loudly. Her eyes snap to mine, wide and alert, and in them I see fear—an urgency.

She crushes the cigarette butt into the bucket of wood ash. "It's him. We don't have much time," she says, her tone dropping into something darker.

"Him who?"

"Your doctor friend."

"What?"

"I don't have time to explain."

I suddenly feel the weight of whatever she isn't telling me pressing down on us.

Darlene moves quickly, standing and reaching out a hand—something she rarely did when I was a child. "Come on," she says, her voice urgent. "I don't think we're safe here."

My heart reacts by slamming against my ribs. I don't hesitate. I take her hand.

She pulls me along with her, guiding me around the trailer toward the narrow path leading into the woods. The scent of damp earth and pine hits me first, grounding me for a brief second—before the urgency in Darlene's grip yanks me back into reality. We move fast, our footsteps crunching against the underbrush.

A branch snaps beneath my foot. I flinch—but before I can react, headlights sweep across the path.

Shards of light move through the trees, spotty but piercing.

My pulse surges—at first frantic, light, like the quick taps of a bongo drum. Then the headlights sweep over the path a second time. My heart's rhythm changes—heavier, harder, like the deep, resounding thud of a bass drum.

I fear it's already too late to run—whatever or whoever it is we're running from.

# 56

**M**ichael

I don't think I've taken a full breath since Vincent's revelation—Jack is Vincent's brother.

Vincent believes his brother became a psychiatrist to better understand his own demons—or maybe to fix what their father had broken in Vincent. He said that he and Jack rarely saw eye to eye. Jack never got over their father's disappearance, while Vincent's feelings about him were the complete opposite—though he wouldn't elaborate on that. He did say one thing clearly: Jack never stopped searching.

It was purely coincidental that Paige began seeing Jack for therapy. Jack was considered one of the best in this area. She stayed on a waiting list forever to get a spot. But once Paige started seeing Jack as her psychiatrist, confided in him about her difficult mother, her childhood, and how her father disappeared before she was born, Jack must have put it together. He must have dug and researched until he tied Paige to Darlene.

Then after her car accident, it only put Jack in greater control over the situation. Opened the door to tampering with her drugs. All of it to get to Darlene. What better way to punish her than to go after her only daughter.

As I'm running it over in my mind, especially the timing of Paige's accident, another question arises. Did Jack have something to do with it? Did he see Darlene at the hospital one of the few times she came to see Paige, which only drove his need more? Did he recognize her?

All of these thoughts and questions flood my mind, and it drives my guilt in all of this deeper—guilt that's been holding an arrow aimed straight at my gut. How could I have not seen it? There is a resemblance between Vincent and Jack, but it's hard to tell with the constant lack of lighting and the blindfold.

Can Vincent read minds, or is it that he knew about Jack's intentions all along? Or both? I don't think Vincent has bad intentions, but right now I'm not sure who I can trust. I don't even know if I can trust myself when I think about the role I had to play in it reaching this point.

I find Edna seated at her computer, scrolling through something on her phone. She's so engrossed that she doesn't look up until I clear my throat rather noisily. Her eyes dart up over her glasses, but her head remains in place. When she does this, I instinctively push my own glasses higher on my nose.

"Hey, Michael. I'm seeing you here a lot lately. Everything okay with Vincent?"

I force my voice to stay calm, though my words nearly stumble over themselves. "Yeah. You know Vincent. Never a dull moment." I pull out my phone, bringing up a picture of Jack. "I need to ask you something."

I watch her expression carefully as I hold the screen out. "I'm sure you've seen him before, but he doesn't usually treat in-hospital patients—only those in crisis or outpatient. He'd rarely be on this floor. But has this man visited Vincent?"

Edna pushes her glasses up and leans in toward the phone. "Yeah. Not real often, but more lately than usual."

My stomach tightens. I'm not sure why I felt the need to ask her this—maybe I just didn't want to believe Vincent. Maybe it was one last attempt to convince myself that none of this is real.

"I'm pretty sure he's a doctor here," Edna continues, frowning slightly, "but when he visits Vincent, he never wears a name badge."

"Thanks, Edna," I blurt, and go.

Her confirmation sends a jolt of urgency through me. As I descend the stairs and push through the door into the parking lot, my mind races.

Jack has the knowledge and the means to mess with Paige's medication. I trusted him. Then I came to him for advice about my "so-called patient" with personality shifts, followed by telling him it was Paige. Of course, he already knew who I was talking about. I replay that conversation over in my head, trying to determine if there were any signs of menace or deception—anything I should have picked up on but didn't.

My gut twists with the realization that I handed him the perfect opportunity on a silver platter. I all but confirmed Paige's vulnerabilities, unknowingly giving him more control over her.

I shove my phone into my pocket and break into a jog across the lot, my breath fogging in the cool air. Why would Jack target my wife? According to Vincent's drawings, his father had a connection to Darlene—one that possibly didn't end well.

If Jack believes Darlene is responsible for his father's disappearance, that could mean only one thing: Paige is collateral damage. He's using her to punish Darlene.

It's the only thing that makes sense.

My car feels miles away. The cold bites at my face, but it's nothing compared to the icy fear that courses through me. Thoughts pound inside my head in rapid succession.

Jack has been seeing Vincent.

Jack has access to Paige's medication.

Jack knew exactly what I was asking when I went to him for advice.

Jack was never trying to help—he was orchestrating the entire thing.

The weight of it all lands on me as I slam the car door shut and grip the wheel.

If Jack has been manipulating Paige, Vincent... even me, then what's his endgame?

More importantly, I have to find Paige before he does.

My phone rings over the car's speakers, the sudden sound making me flinch. It's Laura. I answer without greeting her.

"Laura, I—"

She cuts me off. "Michael, you're not going to want to believe this, but I'm pretty sure I know who's been sending the emails... messing with Paige's meds."

I go still. "I—." A thick silence settles in the car, and I'm unable to speak as I wait for her to either confirm what I already know or possibly prove that I'm wrong.

"I've been digging into restraining orders, harassment filings— old cases that never went anywhere. There's a woman who filed a complaint over a year ago against an ex-boyfriend—a doctor. No charges were filed, but she swore he was drugging her. She'd wake up disoriented, feeling sick. He convinced her she was just stressed, gave her medication, said it would help her anxiety." Laura pauses. "And then, one morning, she woke up with a tattoo she didn't remember getting. Sound familiar?"

A sickening weight drops into my stomach, heavy enough to drag me under.

Laura exhales sharply. "I tracked her down. At first, she didn't want to talk to me. Said she had buried all of that shit and didn't want to dredge it back up. But eventually, I got the name out of her." She hesitates, then drops the final blow.

"Michael... it's Jack. It took me a minute to piece it together—Dr. Donavon Jack Eirkson."

Now it's confirmed. This isn't just a wild theory or coincidence.

"Also," Laura continues, "I saw Paige—she was heading out of town. I'm guessing to her mother's?"

I drag the words out of myself almost kicking and screaming, but I force myself to remain calm. "I know. That means Paige must have figured something out. Maybe she's trying to warn Darlene." I tighten my grip on the wheel. "It's hard to explain how, but I think all of this ties back to Darlene. Right now, I just need to make sure Paige is okay."

"How is Jack tied to Darlene?"

"It's too much to explain now. All I can tell you is, she knew Jack's father."

Laura goes silent for a moment, and all I can hear is the crackling of her police radio. "If Jack has done this before, then he's left a trail somewhere. Proof. I have to find it if we have any chance of filing charges or arresting him."

I hesitate. "How are you going to do that without a search warrant? If you tip him off—"

"Sometimes you have to bend the law a little," she says. "And by bend, I mean maybe do a little breaking and entering."

"Laura—"

"I'm assuming he isn't in his office at this hour?"

"He shouldn't be. But you never know with Jack."

"You let me worry about that. You go find Paige. I'll call you if I find anything."

"Same."

I end the call and press the gas pedal hard, tearing down the road toward Paige. I attempt to remain calm and try to prevent my thoughts from following the same chaotic pattern they've pursued all day. But guilt has taken the reins and steers the course.

That's the thing about guilt—it's designed with the strongest of glues. It sticks to a person, and it's impossible to remove all the remnants of it no matter how many good deeds you think you've done. I'll never be able to forgive myself for this—for allowing any of this to happen.

I helped create this nightmare, and now I fear I may have to deal with devastating repercussions.

Or, I'll have to find a way to fix it—whatever that may be.

# 57

## D arlene

**Now**

"Why do you think it's him?" Paige blurts as I pull her along.

"Trust me. It has to be him. I don't get visitors, and I don't believe someone showing up at this exact moment is a coincidence."

I squeeze Paige's hand and lead her in the direction I want her to go. A strange sense of déjà vu sweeps through me. I've been here before—only then I was alone with only myself to protect. Now, I have a whole new kind of fear. One that only a mother could feel. It doesn't matter how old your children are; you'll do anything to protect them, even die if you have to.

I may not have been mother of the year, but loving my only daughter was never something that was lacking in me—I just didn't know how to show it. Affection was in short supply when I was a child, so I guess I was never taught how to use it—or give it.

The cool, misty air clings to my skin as we push deeper into the trees. Every step seems so loud as the brittle leaves and twigs beneath our feet betray our movements. Ginger hangs close to us, light-footed as always.

Paige's question lingers in my mind—what if I overreacted? What if—?

A twig snaps behind us.

I freeze, but my heart barrels forward, hammering against my ribcage. I'm wishing I would have run inside and gotten my gun.

Paige stiffens, her fingers tightening around mine. We stand there, breathless, listening. The forest is too still, like it's afraid to breathe. I strain to hear past the pounding in my ears. Was it just an animal? The wind?

Then—another sound. A shift in the leaves. Slow. Measured. Deliberate.

Someone is there.

My grip tightens on Paige's hand, and I inch forward, careful to step quietly, but my head screams at my body to run. I can't—not yet. Not until I'm sure how close they are.

The stillness breaks when a voice, smooth yet chilling, echoes through the trees.

"Why are you running? Don't you want to introduce me to my sister?"

A chill invades my spine and neck. My stomach tightens and twists into a ball of nausea as my mind seems to unravel. The past isn't just catching up to me—it's here. There's no doubt now about who he is, and no doubt his trip here isn't to visit memory lane.

Paige's eyes shoot toward me, wide and questioning. She starts to say something, and I press my finger over my lips and shake my head no.

His words send my thoughts soaring.

Paige must have told him all about me in their sessions—enough for him to wonder. Enough to make him dig until he was sure. I should have changed my name back then. Living off the grid wasn't enough.

I hold my breath, willing all of this to be nothing more than a bad dream. But it's a lost cause.

His footsteps crunch at a slow, steady pace, and I strain to pinpoint his location in relation to ours. Every instinct in me screams to keep moving, to put as much distance as possible between us— but not blindly. I need an advantage.

I release my grip on Paige's hand and point toward higher ground. As I move, she and Ginger follow, stepping as lightly as they can. If there's one thing I've learned, it's that the hunted always has a better chance when they hold the high ground. And right now, we need every advantage we can get.

"I know what you fucking did. The moments before you peeled away in your truck, out of my life for good. The fact that I trusted you with a secret—and instead of fixing it, you took everything from me."

A chill spreads through me.

"I may have only been eight, but even eight-year-olds can do basic math. And what happened after I told you that secret? It was calculated." A pause. His tone turns icy. "Christian didn't just disappear, did he, Darlene?"

I keep moving, but his next words stop me cold.

"I think you made sure he was never seen again."

Silence hangs thick in the air for a moment.

Then—his voice, lower now. "And now that I look at this place, I'm willing to bet he's here. However many feet underground you decided to bury him."

Paige's footsteps stop. I look at her as my breath catches. I see the confusion twisting into a questioning expression, and it sends a surge of anger through me.

The truth is out now.

# 58

P aige

I look into my mother's eyes, and the horror there tells me he isn't just throwing out accusations—he's telling the truth. And the only truth I can decipher? Darlene killed his father. And now, he wants revenge.

The emails. The twisted game of truth or dare that branded my skin with a tattoo. The blackouts that swallowed whole pieces of my life. Could this all really be Jack?

I struggle to believe it even though his voice sounds like Jack's. He's been so good to me. Good to Michael. I search my mind trying to recall my sessions with him. He was always so professional—helpful. Even when I talked about my mother, he never let on. Never probed too deeply about her. At least, not enough to make me wonder about his interest in her.

How on earth can Jack be behind all of this? How did I not recognize him even during my blackouts? All of it's making my head hurt.

I thought keeping the emails and other details to myself would protect Darlene and Michael. I told myself the less anyone knew, the better everyone else would be. I would figure it out myself. But I was wrong.

Even so, we're in this together now.

I realize now where Darlene is directing us to go. An unspoken understanding passes through us as we begin to move faster, no longer caring about noise—a need to put as much distance between us and Jack as possible. Even the dog understands it.

As our pace quickens, so does his. Darlene darts around the right side of a gnarled, dying tree, and I follow close behind. I know she has traps hidden all around here—I just don't know exactly where. She knows every inch of this forest better than I do—better than anyone.

Up ahead, the terrain becomes steeper, leading to another ridge. If I remember correctly, there are two traps up there—both are far more dangerous than the others. This is a place where my mother would take me hiking—show me where they were—but would never allow me to hike this way on my own. I've never seen them in action, but I know what it takes to set them off. And I'm guessing that's exactly where we're headed.

Since my accident, my left side still lacks the strength and flexibility of my right. I don't know if I can do it—but I have no choice.

I hear him gaining on us—his footsteps pounding closer. Then, suddenly, they stop.

*Snap.*

A sharp yelp follows as the first trap sends him crashing to the ground. Only then do we realize he has a gun—because the moment he lands, it fires.

The shot cracks through the trees, echoing in all directions. We freeze for just a second, glancing over our shoulders. Then, as if jolted awake, we scramble forward, frantically climbing. My pulse hammers in my chest, racing to match my panic.

Darlene is surprisingly agile and strong for her age and I struggle to keep up. We don't gain much ground before we hear him moving again.

"You're gonna have to do better than that, Darlene," he barks, his voice sounding furious. Then, his attention shifts to me.

"I don't know why you're running, Paige. We're family—I made sure of it—you have the brand, just like our father would've wanted." His tone turns almost mocking. "My quarrel isn't with you, dear sister. It's with your mother. You know—the one who never even gave you the chance to meet your father."

The terrain becomes steeper, and we use all fours to climb. The smell of dirt fills my nostrils, thick and suffocating, and mud cakes beneath my fingernails. We manage to make it to the next ridge, the ground leveling. Darlene takes my hand and leads me to the right, behind a large tree. She squats down, pulling me with her and speaks in a low, strained tone.

"You remember that tree?" She points.

I follow her gaze to the hollowed-out trunk. Jagged branches stretch toward the sky, casting crooked shadows in the moonlight. It reminds me of The Tree of the Dead from *Sleepy Hollow*. It gapes open like a hungry mouth.

I nod.

"You remember what it does, right?"

Another nod. But my pulse begins to pound in my ears and suddenly, I'm not sure.

"There's a second one up there," I say, my voice barely a whisper. "Right?"

"Yes," Darlene breathes. "It's farther up—just past those boulders." She motions toward a cluster of massive rocks, their outlines barely visible in the dim light. "It's a deadfall trap. There's a tripwire under the leaves—thin, almost invisible."

I swallow hard. "How do I—?"

"You have to get above him and trigger it yourself."

Nausea churns in my gut. "But I don't—"

"You just have to step on the right spot," she cuts in. "Hard. It's a pressure trigger.

"I'm going to go that way—get him to follow me." She points to my left along the ridge.

For the first time in a long time, I feel like a child again and I find myself wanting to cling to my mother—something I rarely ever did.

"Wait," I say, not sure what it is I want to say. I can't come up with anything.

She waits for a moment, then stands and takes off running. Despite being a smoker and her age, I think Darlene is in better shape than I am. These woods have always been her home and she knows them like the back of her hand.

Darlene disappears into the darkness—it's as if the moon's light can't reach the direction she's going. I feel like the only light it provides in this moment is on me, like a beacon showing where I am. I press my back tighter against the rough bark—I'm sure fear is placing the worst in my head.

I can hear Darlene's footsteps crunching swiftly but consciously through the leaves. Ginger sprints right behind her and I'm completely alone. I squint in her direction and catch glimpses of her through the shifting moonlight—sporadic beams breaking through the trees, making her seem as if she's flickering in and out of existence, like a film missing frames.

A shot fires. The second it reaches my ears, everything stops—my heart, my breath. Even the forest stands still. I no longer hear Darlene running. In fact, after the shot rang out, I thought I heard a crash, as though someone were falling. I tell myself it is only my brain preparing me for the worst. *Darlene is okay.*

I finally hear movement, but it's slightly below me, going the direction Darlene went. I still don't hear movement from her and panic threatens to paralyze me. Every instinct screams at me to run to her. To make sure she's okay. But what if he's there? What if he's waiting? I battle with myself—paralyzed.

*Move, Paige.* The words scream at me inside my head and it prompts me to run toward Darlene.

I crouch low, my steps light, the earth soft and cluttered with protruding roots and jagged rocks. My foot catches, causing my body to lurch, but I stagger three steps and keep going.

Then, I see her.

Darlene is crouched behind a tree, just past the gaping hollow one. She sits perfectly still, her form barely a shadow against the moonlit bark. I veer wide, careful, unsure where the tripwire is buried. I'm out of breath when I reach her and I struggle to keep it quiet.

We wait.

His footsteps stomp closer and I can see him now in the moonlight. His outline, his form, then his face aims in our direction. The light of the moon strikes across his face and my stomach moves up into my throat. It's the same face I saw in the headlights just before he crashed into me. That's when I realize, Jack is the one who hit me. The link of the chain that set all of these events in motion. And then more images flash across my mind. I saw him earlier today. Inside the bar, then in front of the bar after I ran out the back.

Memories keep rushing back as images flash through my mind— like a camera quickly snapping photos. Memories I didn't even know I had.

Click. Headlights exploding. Snap. Red lipstick gliding across my lips. Click. Music pulsing, my body swaying. Snap. Whiskey burning down my throat. Click. Thigh-high stockings sliding up. Snap. Hands peeling them off. Click. Wrists bound. Snap. His weight pressing down. Click. Hunger in his eyes. Snap. Michael's face.

They come one after another—attempting to crowd out everything else and I squeeze my eyes shut to force them away. *They can't be real*, I attempt to convince myself.

The footsteps are on us now. My mind snaps back—back to now.

Another step forward. He stops. The faint snick of a latch releasing—then his body jerks. He tries to leap back, but it's too late.

The tree groans. Spring-loaded spikes burst outward, jagged tips flashing in the moonlight. A sickening thud. One spike slams into his shoulder; the other barely misses his side. He crashes to the ground.

Darlene whips toward me. "Run!"

She's already moving, pushing off from behind the tree. A gunshot rips through the air just as I break from the cover of the trees, my eyes locked on Darlene in front of me. She stumbles—just for a breath—but keeps going, driving us forward toward the next ridge. Toward the second trap. I crouch low as I move in closer to Darlene, then I see it. A darkness creeping across her shirt, spreading like ink blotted on a page.

She's been hit. Panic threatens to slow me down, but I push myself harder, closing the space between us. The moon catches her face which is consumed with a strained expression.

"Mom?" The word slips out more like a plea, and in my head I sound like a small child again.

She doesn't look at me, she only says, "We have to keep going."

I hook my arm around her and she shifts her weight against me. She begins to slow down and now I'm almost dragging her. There's no way we're going to outrun him now.

Up ahead, a massive boulder leans against the trees, held in place by years of stillness. I grip her tighter and pull her toward it, dragging her around to the other side. I lower her down, pressing her back against the cold stone. My pulse seems to hammer inside my ears as I try to catch my breath. Ginger nudges in close, sniffing at Darlene, a low whine escaping him.

"I'll keep going—make him follow me," I say through gasps.

She nods. "You remember the rock that's shaped like a penis?"

A quick chuckle escapes me. I nod. The first time she pointed that out, I had no clue what she was talking about. I'd never seen one before—not in person, anyway. Curiosity got the best of me after that.

"You need to get there," she says through gritted teeth.

I glance down at Darlene's shirt—it's soaked in blood—her blood. Only then do I realize my arm is too. Fear makes a crash landing between us and threatens to immobilize me. She's worse off than she's letting on. I tighten my grip on her hand, and for a moment, she just looks at me. Then she exhales—a half-laugh, half-growl.

"Don't get all warm and fuzzy now," she mutters, her voice rough. "It's gonna take more than this shit to take me out. You have to go—now."

I hesitate. Just for a second. Then I run.

I make it to the base of the ridge and the incline is sudden and steep. I drop to all fours, climbing as fast as I can. For the first time since he went down, I hear his footsteps moving again behind me. It worked—he's following me.

My lungs burn while my right side feels as though it has a knife stuck in it, but I push through it. At last, I reach a plateau where the ground levels out again. For a brief, disorienting moment, I struggle to get my bearings. I whip my head around, scanning for the penis-shaped rock. The moon's glow catches its edge, and there it is, standing about waist-high. I sprint toward it.

Dropping to my knees, I force myself to breathe quietly, straining to listen. There's only silence. My gut clenches. Did he realize Darlene isn't with me? My heart pounds so violently I'm sure he can hear it.

Just as I start to debate running back for her, I hear him. Frantically, I pat the ground, sweeping my hands over the leaves in search of the buried wire. My fingers graze the thin, steel line—the tripwire that'll release the trap. I brace myself on my hands and knees and glance up to look for the log. It's nearly invisible—just a dark outline nestled high in the branches, like a shadow lurking in the canopy. From this angle, the log doesn't even look that big, but it's the height, the weight, and the countless strands of barbed wire wrapped around it that make it lethal.

Now I can see him several feet below me, and the sight of him sends my heart back into overdrive. I glance up, then back down, trying to gauge the right moment to release it. If I mistime it—then what? This is my only weapon. Our only chance.

"Darlene?" He draws out her name in a long, mocking tone. "Is this what you did to my father? Lured him out here and killed him? That's why he was never seen again, isn't it?" He huffs. "Makes sense now. Truth is, I don't think the world missed him all that much. And I don't think they'll miss you, either."

He climbs a few more steps, then pauses to say, "Fitting, really. I'm sure you buried him out here somewhere. I could just bury you with him. Wouldn't that be karma at its finest? The two of you not happily ever after."

I watch him move closer, and my whole body begins to tremble. I look at the man I once thought was a saint—the one I believed was helping me. But now I see him for what he truly is: a man who almost killed me once. And I have no doubt, he'd try again. I take a deep breath and hold it, then yank the wire as hard as I can, the thin metal tearing the flesh of my hand before it even registers. For a heartbeat there's silence, then it snaps. The log wrenches free from the branches, followed by a whooshing roar as it swings through the air like a wrecking ball. Branches snap and break as debris falls like heavy raindrops.

When he hears the rush of movement above him, he looks up but it's too late—his only reaction is to throw his hands out in front of him. The log connects. The sound is worse than the sight of it. A deep, stomach-turning thud as wood meets flesh and bone. The impact drives him backward, the force so brutal that his body bends around it before snapping away. Moonlight catches him as he crashes against a tree. A sharp crack splits through the air, then nothing. I hold my breath, staring into the dark. I can't see much— just a motionless shape slumped at the base of the tree.

I release a breath and attempt to slow my heart one more time. I inch forward still on my hands and knees and wait a bit longer. He still doesn't move.

I ease down the rough terrain, turning my feet sideways as I step and slide my way down. I approach his body slowly, there's still no movement. I stand and look down at him and catch sight of my stained hands, covered in blood, and follow it to his blood-stained body sprawled on the forest floor. His green eyes are open, face frozen in a scream that never left his body. His hair, face, and shoulder are coated with sticky, red blood—jagged edges of leaves cling to it. It forces me to swallow hard, a coppery taste coating the inside of my mouth. I hold back the urge to throw up.

This was something I had to do in order to survive, I tell myself.

That's the thing about survival. Our minds instinctively develop instruction manuals throughout childhood for all sorts of horrors we'll face in life. We're just not aware of the process and have no idea they even exist until something triggers one of them to become visible—readable. Step-by-step instructions on how to endure pain, adapt to los...escape danger. These invisible blueprints remain hidden deep in our minds, waiting for the right moment, or the wrong one, to surface. Sometimes, they guide us flawlessly, like an autopilot kicking in during a storm. Other times, they're incomplete —like a map with missing or inaccurate roads, leaving us to figure it out ourselves. These manuals aren't always written solely by us, they're pieced together by trauma, molded by fear, and often written from someone else's story of survival. And when they're made to appear, they don't just offer instructions, they teach us who we really are.

My mind threatens to rewind and replay the events that led to this moment. Images jump chaotically from hours ago to just minutes before. I try to hit pause, to freeze them in place, but my mind keeps pressing play at random, forcing me to relive each horrific scene of what I've just done.

It was my mother that prompted my mind to write the instructions for what happened tonight. Simply by her upbringing, she equipped me to do the unimaginable. Prepared me with the ability to kill in order to survive. "Sometimes good people have to do bad things," she'd said once. "Sometimes bad things are right for good people."

I snap out of it, remembering my mother. I run to the rock where I left her and freeze when I see her slumped body. Ginger whimpers and nudges her with his nose, and I fall to my knees next to her.

———

*I sit frozen, the cool, damp earth soaking through my jeans. My heart pounds out a rhythm against the silence of the forest. A rhythm that I'll never forget.*

My fingers hover above the keyboard. I take one breath, steadying myself, then type the words I've been circling around for months:

THE END

— *Paige Thomas*

# 59

P aige

I lift my fingers from the keyboard, exhaling as I lean back inside the small corner booth. The café hums around me—the low murmur of voices and the occasional clang of coffee cups. Outside, the rain has picked up, droplets streaking the fogged-up windows. I look up at the stained sky streaked with what looks like watered-down ink—pale smudges of light tangled with dark, splotchy clouds.

I rub my temples, then pick up my cooling, untouched latte. I *should* feel relief at typing the last words of my story—I *should* feel more satisfied. Something other than this dull, aching hollowness that lingers like an unfinished sentence.

My eyes drop back to the screen. *Is that really how it happened?* An involuntary shiver courses through me, though I'm not sure if it's from the draft slipping in through the café door or the thought itself.

I flex my fingers, hovering over the keyboard and think, *I could change it—soften the details, shift the ending. Make him beg. Make him fight harder. Make him win.*

My pulse stutters at the thought. No. That would be a lie. Or maybe the lie had already started, somewhere between memory and the page. I exhale, force myself to keep going.

In the end, Donavon got what he deserved. Or at least, that's what I made happen. Because it's my story. My version. And in my version, the monster doesn't get to win.

The cursor blinks.

Outside, a car speeds past, its tires hissing over the wet blacktop. The café door swings open, sending a rush of cool air through the space. I barely register it.

I could end it here. But endings are never that simple.

I could debate it forever and never finish the damn thing. But instead, I go back and forth a while longer, then make my final decision. I zip the file, attach it to the email, and hit send. Now it's in the hands of my agent.

I pack up my computer and dart out of the café into the rain. Sliding into the front seat of my old Land Rover, I sit there for a moment, gripping the steering wheel, my emotions torn. Excited that I've finished my first fiction novel, yet sad that I can't share it with Darlene.

My gaze drifts to the street ahead as an idea occurs to me. I guess I can. Not the way I want, but I can still tell her.

I drive out of town toward Acadia National Forest, toward my mother's home place. The rain slows to a drizzle, and in the distance, the sun peeks through the clouds in long, narrow streaks. By the time I reach the rough, narrow road leading to Darlene's, the rain has given way to full sunlight.

I roll down my window and inhale the scent of rain-soaked cedar and pine—I can almost taste its resinous tang. A hint of wild herbs—maybe rosemary or mint—stirs in the breeze. The mint reminds me of Darlene, of the way she would chew on a wild leaf to cover her cigarette breath.

I bounce past the rusted truck that is as much tree now as it is metal. As I drive over a certain spot, I imagine the clanging of Darlene's old homemade alarm, the one she rigged outside her trailer. But the trailer is gone now. Torn down. The land is smooth, the wildness cleared away. Michael and I had a dozer come in and clean it up last spring.

I get out of my Rover, pull on a thin sweatshirt, and head down the path into the woods.

Not too far in, there's another cleared space, this one quiet, manicured, and covered in fresh grass. At the center stands a single headstone. My heart swells, heavy and aching, as I step toward it. Then, slowly, I sit down beside it.

Darlene has been gone for almost a year. It happened too fast— one day, she was told she didn't have long to live, and then, almost as soon as I could process it, she was gone. I never really had time to say goodbye. I never got to have the relationship with her that I know we could have had.

We always think there will be more time. But there never is. We wait for the perfect moment, for the right conditions—for life to align. And then it's too late. Because ideal moments don't exist. And when they're gone, you realize—you shouldn't have waited.

I look at her headstone as I speak. "I did it. I finished my first thriller. I think you would have liked it. You would have said, *it's better than all that other sissy, new age shit you write.* I can hear you now."

I ramble on for several minutes, then I fall silent and listen to the forest around me. The faint calls of creatures large and small fade in and out. If you listen close enough, long enough, even they all have stories they want to tell.

Everyone and everything has a story. Sometimes they're sweet and sometimes they're tragic. Some stories are long and full of detail. Others are short and vivid, or choppy and lacking in depth, like pieces of a forgotten dream. Some unfold in neat, predictable arcs, while others twist and unravel, sometimes leaving one with more questions than answers. Some stories are meant to be shared, passed down like well-worn books, while others remain locked away, unfinished, known only to the ones who've lived them.

Pieces of my life since the car accident feel like clips of a dream—there, but always just out of reach. Michael has been helping me since the day I woke up in the hospital. Through hypnotherapy, medications, and his guidance, I've slowly pieced together memories.

The most heart-wrenching is my mother's rapid battle with cancer and my struggle to cope with her death. We weren't that close, yet somehow, losing her felt bigger than I expected—like a grief I didn't fully understand until it consumed me.

But what seems to be more puzzling than anything is the way my mind twisted that grief into fiction.

That's what Michael says, anyway—that my novel is how I processed everything. That the missing pieces, the gaps in my memory, are just my brain protecting me. But sometimes, I wonder. I wonder why certain details feel sharper than they should, or why my memories of my mother's illness seem like scenes written by someone else. Michael tells me it's normal, that trauma distorts time, that the mind bends reality to make pain easier to bear. And I believe him. I do. At least, I think I do.

I close my eyes and breathe in the damp, earthy scent of the forest. The scent of pine and moss overpowers everything, and it gives me a sense of grounding. But as I sit here, something gnaws at the edges of my thoughts—a question I never quite dare to ask.

If my mother was sick with a debilitating illness, why don't I remember more? I *should* remember the smell of antiseptic and hospital sheets, the sound of her voice growing weaker, the way she looked at me in those last days. The funeral is more like a dream than a memory. All of those memories are faint and hazy.

I press my palms into the damp ground, steadying myself.

Michael says that's normal, too. That I was too overwhelmed, too deep in my own struggles from the accident to fully process it at the time. That's why therapy helps. That's why the medication works.

But if the medication works, why do I still feel like something is missing?

I think about my book, about the way the story poured out of me as if I were remembering instead of creating. Michael calls it *catharsis*. He said my mind wove my pain into fiction, that I needed a way to make sense of the things I couldn't face. It was my mind's way of protecting itself. That when pain becomes too much, the brain finds ways to rewrite it, reshape it—turn it into something easier to understand.

*"That's what your novel is,"* he told me once. *"You took the chaos and turned it into a story. A beginning, a middle, and an end."* He said it like it was a good thing. Like it was healing. And maybe it was.

I remember nodding, letting his words settle into place, allowing them to explain the empty spaces in my memory. But sometimes, I still wonder. Why does it feel like I'm forgetting something, instead of making sense of it?

It's all making my head hurt, and now I want to leave. I push myself to my feet, brushing dirt from my jeans, and start back toward my car. As I walk, the pieces shift again, like a sliding puzzle, and as each piece attempts to move into place, I realize one absolute truth. Michael is the one who helped me. Michael is the one who put me back together. Michael is the one who told me what was real.

I rub my eyes and shake my head, exhaling a deep breath. I'm so tired of trying to piece together an unsolvable puzzle. Maybe it's time to let it go.

I stop mid-stride and say aloud, "That's right. Michael loves me. He's the only thing sure in my life. I have to trust him."

The words sit heavy in the air. For a second, I wait—like I expect something to argue back. A crack in the logic. A memory I shouldn't have. Nothing comes.

I climb back into my Rover and check the time. He'll be home soon.

I start the engine and bounce down the bumpy road, gripping the wheel a little tighter. I can't wait to get home. To cuddle with Murray, Ginger... and my husband.

# 60

## Michael

**Six months later**

I watch Paige curled on her side, blanket drawn up to her chin as I lean down and kiss her cheek. She stirs faintly, but deep sleep has finally found her—the pills on the nightstand saw to that. She hasn't slept much lately, and when she does, her body twitches from nightmares. But I tell her that's all they are—just nightmares.

Her grief now has an arc—an explanation, a boundary. There's no need for her to ever know the full story—what I've kept from her. She doesn't need to know.

I'm helping her to overcome all of this the way a husband should. That's what husbands are supposed to do—protect their wives at all costs.

Grief can be malleable—so can memory. If it is shaped carefully, it can take the edge off pain. Soften it. Make it manageable. And what does it matter if the edges aren't real? The truth isn't always the most merciful version of a story. Sometimes it must be bent for the sake of love. For the sake of sanity.

I've simply helped her to read from a different script now—one I've gently rewritten with care, repetition, and time. A safer story. One that won't break her.

I dread leaving her alone, but I have to see some patients today—particularly Vincent. He's expecting me. I've been avoiding him, but I can't do it any longer. I committed myself to him, and I need to fulfill that promise. After all, sometimes I think I still need him as much as he needs me.

Vincent's room has moved to the other end of the corridor. He's making significant progress in his ability to interact within the walls of the hospital. It's leaps and bounds from where he used to be. His next steps will be to make short trips to the outside world—get him acclimated to a different space, then possibly a part-time job.

When I reach his door, I pause. He always knows when I'm coming because I hear his voice before I even open it.

"You're late, Michael."

"I know. Sorry, Vincent."

He doesn't even give me time to settle into the room before his ramblings begin. "You've been rewriting pages, haven't you?"

I close the door behind me. This room is different—the lights are off, but it has a small window, letting in just enough pale light to give the room a dull, washed-out glow. Still, it's a far cry from the dungeon-like space he used to live in. He's sitting cross-legged on the bed, blindfold in place, head tilted slightly.

"Pages?" I ask, setting down my clipboard on the adjustable bedside table that's been shoved up against the wall.

He shrugs slightly. "Stories. You've been writing some of your own."

I frown as my eyebrows greet one another, but I decide not to speak, to see where Vincent is going with this.

"Some stories are truer when you change them. Easier to carry. That's what you believe—isn't it?"

I cross the room and take a seat in the chair by the window. "I'm not sure what you're talking about, Vincent."

"Mm," he hums. "And yet, they always have a way of dragging behind us. Even the ones we've buried."

His fingers twitch in his lap.

A wave of apprehension washes over me. I fear that what he's hinting at is the very thing I'm battling with. I don't want to confirm his quandaries, so I stay silent.

"Do you know what Jung once said?" he asks suddenly.

I lift both eyebrows and attempt to be passive. "Jung said a lot of things."

"'The most terrifying thing is to accept oneself completely.'"

He tilts his head again, listening—to something in the air, or maybe in himself. Or me.

"But the mind has tricks, doesn't it? Especially when we don't want to accept something. It invents shadows. Swaps endings. Maybe even tells bedtime stories to the parts of us that still flinch in the dark."

My throat tightens slightly, but I don't respond.

Vincent shifts, then leans just slightly in my direction.

"But even shadows cast footprints, Michael. Even the stories we think we've buried leave trails."

He turns his head toward me, though his eyes are covered.

"You're very good at helping people—keeping them safe—sometimes from themselves. Just be careful you don't lead them too far from themselves in the process. Altering perceptions can be construed as playing God, and it can have unpleasant consequences. Just because one claims to do it all for the sake of love doesn't mean the person you're trying to save won't feel what's missing. It also doesn't mean it will have a happy ending."

He lets the silence stretch a beat longer before adding, "Jung also said, 'You are what you do, not what you say you'll do.'"

He lifts his chin slightly, as if studying my silence. "Some of us like to think of ourselves as protectors, healers... even saviors, sometimes. But identity isn't in the intention—it's in the action. And sometimes, even love can disguise control if you dress it in the right words."

I swallow hard, unsure of whether I should respond. I don't.

"I'm not judging you, Michael, just simply... reminding you that even the most carefully crafted illusions eventually demand a reckoning."

I tell myself that Vincent doesn't know what he's talking about. He doesn't know the whole story—only pieces of it. I shift the conversation back to him.

"I don't think we're here to talk about me. Let's talk about you and all the progress you've made."

"Mm," Vincent hums again. I wait for him to respond, but he doesn't. Then he finally says, "I think we're done for today, Michael. I think it's *you* who should take this time for reflection."

I frown, but don't argue. I just stand and simply say, "Okay, Vincent. I guess I'll see you Thursday."

He nods.

I step into the hallway and assist the door to hush quietly shut behind me.

Each step echoes a little too loudly against the scuffed tiles, my reflection rippling in the smudged glass as I exit the hospital doors.

*Even shadows cast footprints.*

*Even the stories we think we've buried leave trails.*

Vincent's words follow me. I tell myself I've done what's best.

Paige remembers that Darlene died—the hospital visits—a quiet goodbye. She doesn't remember anything else. Not exactly.

As Paige was writing her first fiction novel, she asked me not to read it. Not yet. I agreed that I wouldn't—not until it was done. She even made me promise.

But one night, she left it open on her laptop—her first fiction story—the temptation was too great. The cursor blinked like it was daring me to look.

I had to.

I told myself it was loving curiosity, concern. Love. But I read every word.

I'm glad I did. Some scenes were almost exact. Some were worse.

I didn't touch the draft itself. But I had to make sure what she believed was reshaped into something else. I finally admitted that I'd read it, and at first she was a little upset, but then I was able to suggest ideas that might deepen the plot, or blur the lines of what was real and what was fiction. Nudges. Small corrections. Careful redirections. I helped her keep the worst parts locked in the pages, called them imagination. Helped her believe it hadn't happened that way—couldn't have.

"It's fiction," I reminded her. "Just a story."

And now, when she laughs and says, "Honestly, the line between fact and fiction is so blurred, who even knows who the real Vincent is? Or the real *you*?"

I just smile, kiss her temple, and whisper, "Yeah. Who knows?"

I've rewritten the story for love.

# EPILOGUE

P aige

I never thought I'd be here.

Standing behind a microphone, in front of a crowd of readers who know my name. Fans waiting to hear me speak as if I have something wise or clever to offer. The bookstore hums with quiet anticipation—buzzing with bodies and paper and coffee. Rows of chairs have been squeezed between shelves of thrillers and memoirs, and a soft glow spills from the overhead track lighting like a set of stage lights. It all feels so warm and inviting. Almost *too* inviting.

"My name is Paige Thomas," I begin, my voice steady as my pulse thrums a little too fast, "and I'm the author of *I Saw You.*"

There's polite applause as cameras click. Somewhere in the crowd I hear someone whisper my name as though it means something.

"This book began as a way to make sense of something I couldn't explain. After my accident... I started experiencing intense anxiety, and writing seemed to be the only thing that really helped. It gave me a place to pour all of this pent-up nervousness."

I pause, searching for the right words. "And my husband, Michael, encouraged me to keep going. He believed in me when I didn't believe in myself. Without him, none of this would be possible."

The crowd smiles—they love what I'm saying. But the moment my words land, I look at my husband, Laura sitting next to him, and something inside me feels... wrong. Like I've just told a beautiful lie, but everyone claps, pleased at my words.

I brush it off quickly.

I finish speaking, and now I sit behind a table, a line of eager faces and smiles stretched before me. They trail down the aisles, winding past shelves filled with someone else's stories. But they aren't here for those. They're all here for *me*. In this bookstore—not too big, yet not too small. The kind of place that makes you want to sit and stay awhile.

Behind me, a glossy poster shimmers under the soft glow of the overhead lights, my name in bold, iridescent colors. On the table before me, a neatly stacked tower of books waits, the title catching in the light—*I Saw You*.

The letters are bold, raised, and textured beneath my fingertips. They're real. Just like all of this. At least, that's what I tell myself.

Everything feels surreal. Like it's all just a dream. Much like my whole life has felt lately.

My debut thriller quickly became a *New York Times* bestseller. Critics call it "darkly evocative," "psychologically harrowing," and "utterly addictive." Readers dissect it, pulling apart every line, convinced the story is more than fiction.

I tell them it isn't, although I sometimes wonder myself when I wake from a dream that seems so vivid with details. I tell myself that it's because I've been so engrossed in writing the story that I'm bound to dream about it.

Another fan steps forward, a woman clutching the book to her chest, her eyes bright with excitement. "I read it in one night. I just couldn't put it down. It felt so real," she beams.

I force a smile. "That's the goal."

Her voice lowers. "Was it inspired by anything? Like... something that really happened?"

The pen in my hand stills. A hint of something cold washes over me, but I push it aside.

I give her the answer I've rehearsed. "Writers pull from all kinds of places. We let the story play out in our heads, so it does become something we've lived through. We fall in love with our characters, and sometimes, we loathe them."

She giggles and nods, satisfied. I sign her book, then watch her disappear into the sea of faces before me. The line moves, bringing more smiles. More thank-you's. More people telling me how my words kept them up at night. How they couldn't look away.

I sign book after book until it starts to become almost robotic, yet with each signature, I feel a surge of euphoria. A smile is plastered across my face and I don't think anything could wipe it away. I reach for another book as an unnerving voice cuts through the chatter in the room.

"How do you write something so morbid and make it seem so real?"

I look up.

A man stands at the front of the line, tall and thin, large, dark sunglasses covering his face. He pulls them down just slightly—just enough to reveal dark hollow eyes. I think I see green, but the pupils swallow most of their color. A shudder moves through me. Something about them tugs at a buried memory.

I swallow the unease creeping up to lodge in my throat and manage a polite smile. "That's the job of a writer. To make you believe."

The man lifts one side of his mouth into a smile, revealing a dimple. "Yes. To make us believe."

He doesn't reach for the book I've just signed, rather places one in front of me. Not mine.

I hesitate before glancing down.

*The Conditioned Mind: How Fear Shapes Reality.*

A quiver moves its way up my spine.

"You should read the inscription," the man says in an encouraging tone.

I feel my smile falter a little. I stare down at the book before flipping it open. Inside the cover, words are scribbled in slanted handwriting:

*"Give me a dozen healthy infants, and I'll guarantee to train any one of them to become any type of specialist I might select—a doctor, a lawyer, an artist, even a beggar or a thief." — Dr. John B. Watson*

My stomach suddenly joins the unease wedged in my throat and I find it hard to even blink.

He tilts his head slightly and looks deep into my eyes. "This doctor had all sorts of morbid beliefs. He once said, 'A child is not afraid of a rat—until you make them afraid.' He believed that anyone could be programmed to believe anything. He also believed that humans can be trained just like animals. I thought you might enjoy this book."

The man taps the book once, then turns and walks away. No signature. No picture. Just... gone.

Another quiver travels through my body as I frown and open my mouth to speak, but can't form any words. I exhale and try to shake it off quickly.

I try to pass it off as just another fan. A strange one, but still.

I notice a small slip of paper sticking out of the edge of the book. I slide it free and my breath catches as I unfold it, the inked words staring back at me.

*Three can keep a secret if two of them are dead.*

My stomach clenches. I flip the note over, fingers shaking. At the bottom, a single initial...

V.

# REDACTED DOCUMENT

**[REDACTED DOCUMENT – INTERNAL USE ONLY]**
   **Patient File 314**
   **Subject:** Thomas, Paige
   **Date:** [REDACTED]
   **Referred by:** M. Thomas, DO (spouse)
   **Clinician:** Dr. L. Boucher
   **Case Overview:**
   Subject was referred by spouse for trauma-related dissociation and episodic memory blackouts following a car accident. Subject demonstrates fixed false beliefs rooted in fabricated memories, consistent with delusional ideation.

   **Clinician Notes:**
   Upon evaluation and treatment, patient was provided with a memory-redirection protocol intended to "relieve her suffering" and "stabilize her reality."

   **Pharmacological Response:**
   Experimental treatments administered under controlled condi-

tions. Subject demonstrated high susceptibility to narrative restructuring, particularly in post-hypnotic states. Implanted memory framework (i.e., maternal death via illness) has held across three verification sessions. Subject reports no recollection of original trauma.

# ALSO BY CHERANN WRIGHT

Where Secrets Stay

Book 1 of The Secrets Trilogy

**Some houses don't just hold memories.**

**They awaken them.**

When artist Kevan returns home after her grandmother's death, she intends to close the door on a past she has spent years avoiding. What she doesn't expect is an inheritance—an abandoned house in the woods, untouched for years yet heavy with the weight of something unfinished.

As Kevan visits her hometown, she crosses paths with a stranger, Nathan, who is searching for answers to his sister's disappearance more than two decades ago—an unsolved mystery that may be tied to the same house in the woods.

Kevan's art begins to take a darker turn, pulling her toward images she doesn't remember creating. The deeper she digs, the more unsettling her memories become—especially those of her childhood best friend, Beth. But as Kevan begins to uncover the truth, she realizes that some bonds run deeper than reason, and some memories are buried for a reason.

As past and present collide, Kevan must untangle a decades-old mystery of betrayal, buried bodies, and the twisted bonds of friendship and family. And when the final pieces fall into place, she'll learn that not all hauntings come from the dead—some are just echoes of sins still waiting to be reckoned with.

*Where Secrets Stay* was inspired by actual events.

**\* This book explores dark themes, including trauma, abuse, and violence. Proceed with care.**

# ALSO BY CHERANN WRIGHT

Where Secrets Sleep

Book 2 of The Secrets Trilogy

**When a little girl hums a twisted ballad no child should know, the past awakens.**

Kevan watches her daughter, Frannie, skip in from the woods of the Ivymond estate, pockets full of treasures she's found—a small carved bird she claims was hidden inside a hollow tree, left there by *"Grace, the girl that lives here."* Soon, Frannie's drawings and Kevan's dreams begin to reveal the same dark-haired girl, one who claims to live in an abandoned stone cottage—the place where secrets go to sleep.

But Grace isn't just any teenager. She lived on the Ivymond plantation decades ago, before someone erased her story. She's always believed that boys wear their horns well-hidden and holy men hide rot. Yet caught between innocence and awakening, she fell for the preacher's son and uncovered something his father would do anything to keep buried.

As Kevan and her husband, Nathan, investigate the mystery behind their daughter's strange new friend, they uncover traces of a history steeped in buried sins and holy men with hidden horns.

As past and present bleed together, one family's search for truth will awaken what was meant to stay buried...

**and reveal that not everything laid to rest is meant to sleep.**

**Book 3 - Where Secrets End - Coming December 2026**

# ALSO BY CHERANN WRIGHT

The Truth is a Lie

**A childhood lie. A deadly truth. And a name that was never supposed to exist.**

Abby has spent her life running from a childhood tragedy—one she's convinced she caused: the death of her twin sister. As a child, Abby blamed an imaginary friend named Tina. But no one believed her. And over time, even she has begun to doubt herself.

Now, years later, she's a mother trying to leave the past behind. But when her young daughter begins whispering to an invisible friend—one with a familiar name—her carefully rebuilt life starts to unravel. Desperate for answers, Abby uncovers eerie childhood drawings in the basement—along with a name scrawled in childish handwriting: Tina.

Tina was never real. That's what they told her. But they were wrong.

For generations, Abby's family has been cursed—one 'good' twin, one 'bad' twin—a legacy steeped in jealousy, betrayal, and tragedy. Determined to break the cycle and prove her innocence, she turns to the last person she ever wanted to trust—her ex-husband. But the deeper she digs, the more she realizes: Some imaginary friends were never imaginary at all. And the truth is more dangerous than the lies Abby has told herself.

# ABOUT THE AUTHOR

 CherAnn is a member of the International Thriller Writer's Organization. Her books have sold worldwide and are soon to be translated into other languages. She is a teacher by day and an author by night. Her love for writing began early, penning dark poetry as a teenager as a way to escape the world. Though her passion for storytelling never faded, it was put on hold for many years. After raising two amazing daughters and sending them off to college, CherAnn finally embraced her dream and wrote her debut novel, Where Secrets Stay.

When she isn't writing, she spends her time curled up with a good book, or lounging on the sofa with her husband, two dogs, and a noisy rescue cat.

# ACKNOWLEDGMENTS

To *Caroline Leavitt*, best-selling author and editor. Thank you for seeing the heart of this story and guiding me to write this spectacular book. Your guidance, encouragement, and razor-sharp insight pushed this story to become what it was meant to be. I'm endlessly grateful for the care you poured into *I Saw You* and for believing in me.

Special thanks to audiobook narrators *C.J. Locks and Gabriel Gage* for their exceptional performances. Their skill, emotional depth, and attention to nuance brought *I Saw You* to life in ways I could never have imagined. I'm deeply grateful for the care and artistry they gave to this story.

To my husband, *Paul*. Thank you for loving me through the long writing sessions, the rewrites, the self-doubt, and the chaos that comes with being married to a writer. Your steady support, humor, and faith in me are the quiet backbone behind every page I write.

To my daughters, *Brooklin and Ashley*. You two are my greatest joys. Thank you for cheering me on, for celebrating every milestone with me, and for reminding me why I chase big dreams in the first place. I'm proud of you every day, and I hope you always make space for your own stories.

To my *fans and followers*. Thank you for reading my work, sharing it, reviewing it, talking about it, and showing up again and again. Your messages, excitement, and passion for psychological suspense keep me writing. This book exists because you're out there waiting for the next twist.

To *Jackie and Sherry*. Thank you for always being my first readers, my early encouragers, and my trusted sounding boards. You see the raw pages before they're ready for anyone else, and you still cheer like it's magic. I'm lucky to have you in my corner.

To my *students*. Thank you for asking about my books, for wanting updates, for being curious, and for making me feel like the coolest teacher in the hallway. Your enthusiasm fuels me more than you know. Keep chasing your own dreams.

Contact Info: www.cherannwright.com

ISBN: 9798988655794 (Ebook), 979-8-9940363-0-3 (Paperback), 979-8-9940363-1-0 (Hardback), 979-8-9940363-2-7 (Audiobook)

First Edition 2025

10 9 8 7 6 5 4 3 2 1

Final Edits and production by:

Sleuthing Sloth Press

*Sleuthing Sloth Press*

www.ingramcontent.com/pod-product-compliance
Lightning Source LLC
Chambersburg PA
CBHW030238120726
47903CB00005B/1530